MAROONED ON TRAN-KY-KY

It was absolutely too bloody much.

First he had bumbled into an absurd hijack attempt by a pair of ridiculously inept kidnappers. As it turned out, they had somehow managed to snatch an unwanted intruder (himself) and, to make matters worse, a gargantuan drunk who kept getting in the way. And, as if that weren't bad enough, the whole mismanaged operation crashlanded on a totally uninhabitable deep-freeze world.

Ethan Fortune wanted out . . . and fast.

But first he would have to contend with the starved local fauna, happily drooling over the prospect of fresh meat. And the total lack of life-support for humans. And the 60° below zero temperature.

And that was only the beginning . . .

". . . A SCIENCE-FICTION *ADVENTURE* STORY RANKING WITH THE BEST OF HAL CLEMENT . . . ALL IN ALL THIS IS A *FUN* BOOK, AND ONE WELL WORTH READING FOR ANYONE WHO REMEMBERS WHEN SCIENCE FICTION WAS FUN!"
　　　　　　　　　　　　　　　　—*Vertex*

ICERIGGER

ALAN DEAN FOSTER

A Del Rey Book

BALLANTINE BOOKS • NEW YORK

A Del Rey Book
Published by Ballantine Books

ISBN 0-345-27799-6

Manufactured in the United States of America

First Edition: March 1974
Fifth Printing: December 1978

Cover painting by Tim White

For
Carol Fran
Here's proof of insanity in the family

I

The man in the *Antares* bar-lounge didn't quite bang his head on the curved star-ceiling on this, his fourth attempt. Or maybe it was his fifth. This failure came as a disappointment to a number of the luxurious lounge's more vocal occupants.

When standing erect—a rare happenstance, of late—the fellow stood just under two meters tall. A haberdasher worth his salt would have estimated his mass at about two hundred kilos. This not counting the booze he'd been putting away at a prodigious rate. That he'd even managed to come close to the roof of the lounge and its simulacrum Terran sky was due in part to his considerable stature.

Starting from the far end of the lounge he'd make a mad elephant sprint toward the bar, leap onto the polished maple-wood counter, and soar ceilingward from that deep-grained launch pad. A reach, stretch, grab, and down he'd come in a spectacular displacement of plastic bottles, glasses, and swizzle sticks. Whereupon he'd fight off the angry flailings of the robot bartender, now on the verge of electron psychosis, stagger between the tables, and try again.

Now he struggled to his feet, downed another slug of whatever it was he was currently drinking, and stumbled toward his launch point. His elegantly clad, youngish cheering section spurred him along. Among this group, the sporting blood was up. Bets continued to be exchanged. Would he finally kill himself by falling on his swozzled skull this fifth (or sixth) time? Or would he simply knock himself out by successfully cracking it against the roof?

Three-dimensional cumulus clouds, fat and fleecy, drifted across the dome. For all their apparent reality they were only clever projections on treated duralloy. Still, while this kanga-

1

roo-brother's head was clearly solid bone, in any conjunction of the two the gentle clouds would surely win out.

There was a stir at the back of the room. Bobbing like emerald corks among the laughing, applauding gamblers and the outraged but intrigued patrons were the first mate and two sub-engineers of the *Antares*. For the last fifteen minutes their prime objective in life had been to bring down this galloping, great, aged simian with as little damage to self and company property as possible. So far their efforts had come to zilch. And they were beginning to draw a few laughs themselves.

Now the first mate, who was an educated man and spent most of his work time planning overdrive maneuvers and juggling the grav field of a small artificial sun-mass, didn't think it was even a tiny bit funny. Matter of fact, he was just about fed up.

There was no point in re-checking the book, though. Company regs specifically forbade shooting a paying passenger, no matter how obnoxious. Other methods had so far met with abject failure. One of the sub-engineers had already taken a steel-like straight-arming from the hurtling acrobat. He wiped his lower lip and considered braining the anthropoid sot with a chair. He could always plead temporary insanity. Pension or no pension.

"Spread out, boys, here he comes again."

Waving a half-filled bottle of Uriah's Heep and howling at the top of his astonishing lungs, the incipient Icarus started at the bar again, picking up speed with each step. With agility amazing for one so old and so soused, the man soared high and gained the top of the bar in a single bound.

Up he went, up, up, an arm outstretched for the ceiling. Barely he missed one of the floating pseudo-clouds. There followed a satisfying and by now familiar crash from the other side of the bar. Plasticine jugs and unbreakable glass joined in a rainbow-colored fountain and bounced to the floor. Money changed hands in the crowd.

After a lingering pause, the first mate decided on a new course. He would try reason. Besides, the fellow hadn't gotten up yet. Perhaps he'd gone and croaked himself. That would save everyone a lot of trouble.

Gesturing to the sub-engineers, he tiptoed up to the badly uffed maplewood and peered cautiously over the top.

No such luck.

True, the fellow was momentarily incapacitated, having tangled himself in the now completely inoperable mechbar. at he was snorting and mumbling with dismaying energy.

"Sir, I appeal to your moral sense. Public drunkenness is d enough. Eliminating our evening bar business, not to ention the bar, is worse. But your refusal to heed the admotions of a ship's crew in free space is insulting. What have e done to offend you?"

After a short search in the region of the floor, the man emed to find his feet. Staggering more or less upright, he ut two huge fists on the bar and leaned forward.

"Offend me? OFFEND ME!"

The mate shrank from that spiritual effluvia and tactfully rned his head to one side. It was pure self-defense. Surely ey could put the man away! He was obviously flammable nd constituted a real danger to the ship.

The eyes waggled until they came to rest on the bottle ipped tightly in one paw. He drained half the remainder.

"Offend me!" he blurted again. "Listen, you unmentionable azard to navigation, that piddle-pot swine over there," and e jabbed a great knobby finger in the direction of an espeally smug-looking young gambler, "that piece of plith-seed id claim to a greater knowledge of posigravity than *I*. Than e. ME! Can you fancy that?"

"I'm not sure," the mate replied. He was experiencing some ifficulty in following the other's train of thought. Maybe the cal change in the atmosphere had something to do with it. he two sub-engineers were edging around to one side of the ar. If he could keep this creature talking . . .

"Sexactusly," the man said, then belched. "So we are enged in a scientific experiment to settle the matter once and r all. You ain't one of them anti-empiricists, is you, bub?"

"Good lord, no," the mate admitted truthfully enough.

"Yeh. Well, we calculated a bit of the ship's field, see? An' ccording to my calculations, I ought to be able to touch the of, there."

"That one over our heads?"

"Yeh, that's the one. You ain't so stupid as you lo
matey. Now you unnerstand what I'm doing, eh?"

"Of course." The sub-engineers were not quite in posit
yet. "Still, while I'm sure you know your computations, t
young chap you pointed out *is* the son of a well-kno
yachtsman and something of an interplanetary sprinter h
self. He just might know what he's talking about."

He stared across at the exploding shock of white hai
virgin corona; at the great hooked beak of a nose, chin lik
hatchet-head, oil-black eyes under break-wave brows, and
gold ring in the right ear. The hair on the man's bare ar
though, was blond. And there were fewer wrinkles in t
tanned face than you would suppose at first glance. The o
that were there, though, were really canyon wrinkles, genu
gully-gapers. No question but that the nose had come fi
like Bergerac's, and the face had been constructed around
bits and scraps sewn on here and there. The wrinkles
neatly in place, like seams in leather.

"I'm not sure, however," continued the mate, "who y
are." And the court will want to know, too, he thought.

For a moment he thought the other might be having
attack. Still clenching the bottle in one hand, the man shc
his fist at the first mate and at the whole lounge in gene

"By the Heavenly Hosts and the whole Horse's Head,
Skua September, be who! In the manner of men and all ot
beings I can out-drink, out-fight, out-fly, out-sleep, out-
out-whore, out-run, out-talk, out-shout and out-love any n
in this end of the Spiral Arm!"

September seemed more than willing to continue this ca
logue of dubious attributes till the millennium. The tira
however, was interrupted by a belch of such brontosaur
proportions that it momentarily rattled everyone in the loun

At that point the two lesser ratings both hit him from
hind and the resultant ménage à trois crashed to the floor
front of the bar. One of them snatched up a bottle full
mould-gold something or other and hefted it over his he
But the first mate extended a restraining arm.

"No need, Evers. He's out cold."

There was silence for the first time in quite a while. It v

broken by a single pair of hands, clapping politely. The mate turned to the yachtsman's son, who was applauding them all . . . whether respectfully or sardonically, he couldn't tell.

"Bravo," trilled the playboy.

Not a creature was stirring, not even a *mus musculus*.

The sentiment was proper but the subject inappropriate, thought Ethan Frome Fortune as he moseyed toward the rear of the passenger's blister. Mice and rats had not been able to handle the exigencies of interstellar flight. Oh, they could get on board shuttles and from there to a ship, and they'd been a problem at first.

Then someone got the bright idea of turning off the posigrav field for half an hour in the passenger sections. One man with a net swam around collecting the badly befuddled vermin and that was sufficient for pest control till next port of call.

It was just as well, Ethan mused wryly. If said rodentia had been able to make the adaptation, the company might have stuck him with mousetraps to peddle.

As a moderately successful luxury goods salesman for the House of Malaika, his stock ran more to jeweled knickknacks, perfumes, and intricately wrought, expensively priced mechanical gadgetry. Jeweled mousetraps would not be a prime seller.

He passed a small observation port, paused to look at the planet pirouetting heavily below. Such ports were less frequent at this rearmost end of the passenger's compartment, but then, so were passengers. He was tired of idiot small talk and there were no bulk sales to be made with this bunch.

Most of Tran-ky-ky still swam in darkness. Probably coincidence that nightside happened to fall on the ship as it orbited in sleep period. Ethan seemed to be the only non-crew member up and about.

Tomorrow, slim as chances for business seemed from the apes, he'd take the shuttle down. That would mean enduring the usual gaggle of tourists. Oh well, shoving was all a part of existence, no matter which law you indexed it under.

Tran-ky-ky was a figurative whistle-stop on the *Antares'* run. The giant interstellar transport would remain a day or two in the planet's vicinity. Most of that time would be spent

transferring down cargo for the single humanx outpost on th
forbidding surface.

The fact that the outpost was Terranglo-named didn't nec
essarily mean the world had been discovered by humans. I
could have been a mixed crew or all thranx. The forme
seemed more likely, though. No tidy-minded thranx would b
likely to name a Commonwealth outpost "Brass Monkey." Be
sides, the heat-loving insects would consider the globe beneat
a choice slice of icy hell.

What little of the planet sat in sunlight formed a brigh
almost painfully white crescent at its edge. Mestaped infor
mation on the dark sphere floated to the surface of his mind

Tran-ky-ky lay on the fringes of humanx settlement an
was a recently discovered world. Among other more signif
icant things, that made it fresh territory for eager types lik
himself. However, it was not classified as a potential colony.

While humans could live on it, as they did after a fashion ii
Brass Monkey, it was far from hospitable. No New Riviera
this! Besides, it was classed 4-B. That meant it was inhabite
by a native race of fair intellectual potential living at a pre
steam level of technology and probably lower.

Topographically, the planet boasted a few small continents
large islands, really, and thousands of small ones. Some wer
reasonably level, like Brass Monkey's Arsudun, others precipi
tous and tectonic in origin. All lay scattered about the planet'
shallow seas, which were permanently frozen to depths a
great as three kilometers in some places and barely ten meter
in others.

Gravity .92 T-standard, day about twenty ts hours, distanc
from sun—too much. This charming resort world, he though
sardonically, reached a positively balmy three degrees centi
grade at the equator. A heat wave in Brass Monkey. Tem
averaged around minus fifteen and dropped to an absur
minus ninety some nights.

Moving away from the equator, things began to get chilly

Oh yes, a charming stopover on our tour of the frayed
flayed edges of civilization, yes! Other salesmen were assigne
tours of territories like the twin pleasure worlds of Balthazza
and Beersheba, or even Terra itself. Ethan Fortune? Alway

his back to the warm inner worlds of the Commonwealth, always his profit margin poking hesitantly, narrowly, thinly, among empty places in strange spaces. Nuts!

Oh, there were some minor compensations. For example, he made a very good living.

And he was still the insane side of thirty. Doubtless any day now someone in the home office would take note of his incredible, astonishing record under impossible conditions. Then maybe he'd be handed something better suited to his exceptional talents. Like marketing jewelust lingerie to the famed ecdysiasts of Loser's World, or to freshly-minted debutantes on New Paris.

He blinked, turned from the almost hypnotic white sickle, and tried to concentrate on more prosaic considerations. Like how he was going to explain the workings of an Asandus portable deluxe catalytic heater to the locals. Mestape gave him a working knowledge of the language—he always prepared for each new world as thoroughly as possible—but offered little in the way of crucial tidbits like local customs and trading nuances. Tran-ky-ky was too new for tapes to be available on anything but basic facts. Anthropological studies would have to come later. So his range would be limited.

At least he had one item he should be able to unload completely on the natives. The Asandus line was made on Amropolous and was a marvel of power and miniaturization. One of the pocket-sized heaters could maintain a fair-sized room at sunbathing temperature even in trannish climate. Since the natives were adapted to extreme cold, an Asandus ought to last almost indefinitely. Just keep the heat up to zero and let grandpaw and the kiddies luxuriate.

Without some such device, and with winds up to 300k producing a really ridiculous chill factor, a human caught unprotected on the surface of Tran-ky-ky for even a few minutes would be good for nothing but snow sculpture afterward.

Come to think of it, there'd probably be a few humans in the settlement who'd be glad of a little luxury heater they could pack along in their scooters. They couldn't see his class of merchandise too often out here. Now if he could only keep his hands from shaking while he set the burner up . . .

His mind was already well into a sales pitch of heroic proportions when he turned the corner to the personal baggage
area and came upon a tableau that was all very wrong.

Five humans were clustered around a lifeboat port. Said
port was open. Very, very wrong. Had a lifeboat drill begun
while he'd had a lapse of deafness? He could hear his heart
beating. Well, ears fine, but message from eyes still wrong.

Ah yes, it was definitely the eyes. Two of the men were
waving lasers about with drunken nonchalance.

One of the gun-wielders, a short ferret-faced chap with a
bad case of the digifits, kept his laser more or less focused on
an older man attempting to put up a bold front. That worthy
was clad in an exquisitely cut suit of snappy emeraldine laid
over a ruffled shirt of deep azure. To the left of this nattily
attired sexagenarian, a mousey-looking little guy was eyeing
the gun almost as if he was considering tackling its owner.

The other gunman was a huge chunk of brown with flat
face, rainbow-hued teeth, and formidable biceps. Right now
he was trying to control his laser and subdue a package of
squalling, scratching femininity that was apparently human.
Apparently, because it seemed to have eight legs and twelve
arms, all pinwheeling at once. The curses that issued from somewhere within the bundle, though, were undeniably Terranglo.

Ethan caught a few and blushed. Her handler was cursing
also, a basso profundo—or profano—counterpoint to the girl.
Ethan wondered what she looked like. She was moving so
much he couldn't tell.

His attention was drawn back to weasel-face, who was
talking to the older man.

"I'm not going to tell you again, du Kane! You want us to
knock you out?" The hand holding the beamer was shaking
slightly. "Get in that boat, now!" A nervous glance at one
wrist. Both gunmen ignored their other prisoner.

"Well, now, I don't know . . . I'd like to oblige you, but
it's so hard to remember what the right thing to do is, any
more. Maybe I'd better wait . . ."

Weasel-face threw up his hands and looked to heaven for
help—not caring that its position in the universe was only
relevant to the temporary set of the ship.

The big man said "Ow!", in no uncertain terms. He

promptly dumped the girl to the floor. She rolled over from the ungentle landing and sat up slowly. Her curses diminished in volume but not originality. Ethan slumped a little. She weighed at least two hundred pounds and she was not especially tall.

"Bit me," said the big man unnecessarily. He sucked at the injured member. "Listen now, du Kane. We're running out of time. It's out of our hands, see? First this shrimp shows up," he indicated mousey, still watching attentively, "and now you've got to be obstinate. Won't do you any good."

"Well, I don't know . . ." du Kane said hesitantly. His eyes moved to the girl.

"You stay put, father." She looked up at the big man and Ethan noticed that that plump face had two startlingly green eyes peering out of it. "If you hit my father, you'll likely kill him . . . he's an old man. Give this idiocy up. I'll see to it that you're not shot out of hand, at least. And father won't press charges. He's too busy to bother with your variety of scum."

Du Kane! Well, that placed him and the girl . . . mighty calculating type, her . . . gambling on her father's frailty like that. Hellespont du Kane was chairman of the Board of Kurita-Kinoshita Ltd. Among other things, they made the drives for interstellar ships. To say he was wealthy was to say the planet below tended away from the tropic. No doubt here was a man of whom it could be said, he really *was* made of money.

A good salesman, Ethan rapidly summarized the situation by categorizing the players. Two kidnappers, two kidnappees, and one trapped innocent bystander. He wondered why they didn't shoot the little fellow.

The question was now of more than academic concern because the big man with the sore thumb was staring right at him. It occurred to Ethan as he stared down the muzzle of the beamer that he'd spent a little too much time gaping and far too little in disappearing. He took a step backward.

"Just on my way to luggage bay three . . . sorry to interr—"

"Hold it right there, flotsam." The big man turned to his partner. "What now, Walther?"

"Rama, not another one! Is everyone on this ship nocturnal?" Another glance wristward. "We've got to get out of here! Take him along, for now. Whitting expressly said not to leave any scraps, Kotabit."

Ethan didn't like being referred to as a "scrap." It sounded downright threatening. Right now, however, he was stuck.

"Get over there, you," ordered Walther, gesturing toward the other captives with his beamer.

"Listen, really, I can't join you. I've got a very important sales conference in half an hour and . . ."

Walther melted a small hole in the deck between Ethan's feet. Ethan promptly walked fast, stood next to the little man on du Kane's left. The man seemed to be adjusting a contact lens.

"Is this really a kidnapping?" he whispered as the two gun men conferred among themselves.

"I'm afraid so, friend." His accent was soft, the words precise. "We are now technically accessories to a capital crime." He sounded very like a schoolteacher instructing his students.

"I'm afraid you've got things confused," Ethan corrected. "An accessory is someone who aids or abets the crime. You and I are victims, not accessories."

"It's all a matter of viewpoint, you know."

"Everyone, get in the boat!" Walther bawled, not caring anymore if anyone heard.

"Why not just knock 'em all out?" queried Kotabit.

"You heard, fatso . . . dangerous. Especially goin' down."

Colette du Kane was staring at Ethan. Maybe that name fitted her as a child, but now . . . well, something like "Hilda" might have been more apropos. Those remarkable eyes chilled him. She didn't smile.

"Why didn't you go for help, whoever you are?"

"I just walked in and I wasn't sure right away what . . ."

"You weren't sure? Oh, never mind." She sighed and looked resigned. "I suppose I shouldn't have expected otherwise."

He would have given her an argument except for the awkward fact that she was absolutely right. He'd really overdone his watch.

"Why aren't you beautiful?" he said idiotically. "Damsels in distress are always beautiful." He smiled, intending it as a joke, but she saw it otherwise. Those eyes came around sharply, then the whole body sagged, quivering, bloated.

"Now you listen," growled Kotabit. His voice was steadier, more self-assured than that of his companion, even though the smaller man seemed to be in charge.

"If I were to cut off your daughter's legs, say, starting at the big toe and working slowly upward, I don't think it would inconvenience our plans. Does that convince you?"

"Ignore him, father," said Colette. "He's bluffing."

"Dear me . . . !" The old man, for all his billions, was a pitiful aged sack of indecision. Then something seemed to rise out of his mind and into his tone. He stood straighter and spat once at Kotabit. The big man dodged it easily, his watchfulness undiminished. Du Kane seemed pleased with himself. He turned and entered the tiny flexible lock leading into the lifeboat.

Ethan thought of taking a swipe at Walther's gun, but Kotabit showed no signs of the other's jerkiness. While his death might complicate their scheme, Ethan entertained no illusions about what the other would do if he charged either of them. He followed the small man with the contacts into the boat.

"My name's Williams, by the way . . . Milliken Williams," offered the latter conversationally, as he entered the lock ahead of Ethan. "I teach school. Upper matriculation."

"Ethan Fortune. I'm a salesman." He glanced back at the girl. She was followed too closely by the two gunmen. Thoughts of shutting the lifeboat door in their faces had occurred to him, but they pressed too close.

It was dark in the lifeboat. The only light came from the fore instrument panel, which was always kept on. Neither of the two gunmen made any effort to turn on the boat lights. Obviously they were afraid of triggering a telltale in the control bubble. He considered hitting the switch regardless of consequences, but was balked by one fact. He'd never been on a lifeboat except during drill and wouldn't know the interior light toggle from the self-destruct switch.

So they stumbled around in near-night, strapping themselves into the couches at threatening words from the gunmen. There were twenty seats, in addition to the two pilots' couches forward. Walther was already in one, doing unseen things to the main console. Kotabit was lazily strapping himself into the other. He'd swiveled his couch around to watch the rest of them. Ethan didn't feel like testing the other's night vision.

There was no warning siren when the boat door snapped shut. That, at least, had been cut in advance to prevent warning the ship's computer. It seemed certain they'd be noticed as soon as the boat left the ship's hull, but Ethan was no engineer and couldn't be certain.

Walther was muttering something that sounded like, ". . . set enough apart . . . hope . . . "

"Better strap in tight, everybody," Ethan advised the others. "I don't think we'll be setting down at the regular port."

"Brilliant!" Colette du Kane's voice was as easily defined as her shape.

"And it will probably be rough," he concluded lamely.

"Two Einsteinian deductions in a row. Father, I don't think we've a thing to worry about. Not with a genius of this peasant's caliber along. Next he'll astound us with the knowledge that these two megalocephalic proteinoids mean us no good."

"Listen," Ethan began, trying to locate her in the dark. His eyes were growing accustomed to the dim light. How Walther could manipulate the controls in it he couldn't imagine. They must have rehearsed this a hundred times.

"I'm still not entirely sure what's going on here. Along I come intending to inspect my samples, minding my own business, and your little family problem has to intrude."

"I hypothesize a ransom attempt," said the elder du Kane. "As these thersitical traducers are no doubt aware, I am not without resources."

"Watch your mouth," blurted the hulking Kotabit, not quite sure what to make of the manufacturer's charge.

"I am sorry you and Mr. Williams had to be drawn into this. Clearly those two did not expect to be interrupted at this hour."

"I'm sorry too," said Ethan feelingly. A low vibration passed through the little vessel, then another. Soon there was a continuous, steady thrumming at their backs.

"They'll find us once we're down," he continued, trying to encourage the other. "It shouldn't be hard to plot our descent."

"I would concur, young man, except the thoroughness which our vile companions have displayed thus far . . ."

There was a lurch and Ethan found himself rapidly becoming lighter. They'd detached from the ship and were moving out of its passenger field.

"We've left the ship," he began. A familiar tone interrupted him.

"Oh god, I am amazed once again!" Colette said with mock piety.

"Well, you go ahead and interpret everything for yourself, then!" Ethan replied peevishly. "Nothing's likely to happen until we're ready for setdown."

He was wrong, of course.

In fact, several unlikely things happened right away.

Something hit the boat a giant hammerblow on its side, set it tumbling crazily. Ethan got a fast glimpse of the planet running all around the circumference of a port, much too fast. Colette started screaming. Forward, Walther was cursing and groaning as he worked the controls, yelling about the time he no longer had and the time he'd wasted.

Another sickening lunge brought the sunlit *Antares* into view. It was far off and receding rapidly. But not so rapidly that Ethan couldn't make out the gaping hole in its near side.

He turned back to the interior of the boat. All of a sudden there seemed to be a fifth figure in the passenger section. It was not strapped in and lurched about drunkenly back near the storage section. For a moment Ethan thought his eyes hadn't become properly adapted.

The boat rolled insanely and Walther yelled helplessly. Williams shouted "Oh my!" And this strange rearward apparition bellowed in slurred Terranglo, "A joke is a joke, but by all the Black Holes and Purpling Prominences, enough is *enough!*"

At that point Ethan's eyes unadjusted to the darkness and everything else.

II

He was indisputably dead, frozen alive. He shivered.

Wait a minute. If he was dead he shouldn't have been able to shiver. To make sure, he shivered again. His body jerked, once, twice. It occurred to him that there was an external source behind the jerks. Blinking, he turned his head. The ebony face of Milliken Williams stared down at him.

"How are you feeling, my dear Fortune?" he inquired solicitously. Ethan noticed that the schoolteacher was wearing a thick coat of some heavy brown material. It had orange patching and was puffed in spots, but looked warm.

He rolled over and sat up. The effort made him dizzy and it took another minute for his eyes to focus. Immediately he noticed that he was clad in a similar garment, that it extended well below his knees, and that it was at least two sizes too large for him.

Williams offered him a cup of black coffee. It steamed ferociously. Ethan took it in the coat-gloves and downed half the boiling liquid in two gulps. At the moment he didn't care if he vulcanized his esophagus. Something at his back seemed willing to support his weight, so he leaned back, sighed deeply, and inspected his surroundings.

The du Kanes sat across from him. They wore the same brown-orange overcoats, only theirs fit. The elder du Kane poked thoughtfully at a tin of something in front of him. A wisp of steam floated from it. Selecting from the contents, he popped something into his mouth, frowned, swallowed, and resumed his poking. His daughter sat to one side, leaning on one arm and glaring at nothing in particular.

They were sitting in a small room of some sort. The floor was covered here and there with a thin coating of white. Even to his dazed mind it was obviously snow or some other frozen

15

liquid. He knew they were on the surface. The temperature told him that. A questioning glance at Williams.

"We're in the rear storage compartment of the lifeboat. It stayed fairly airtight."

Fairly was right, for air was clearly coming from around the edges of the single door. The metal walls were badly dented, especially the rearmost section leading to the engines. He finished the coffee and crawled to the access door. Door and wall leaned inward at the top. There was a single small window three-quarters of the way up.

Standing, he peered out the glassite, not caring that he was cutting off most of the light to the little compartment. Colette offered a suitably cutting comment of this lack of consideration, but Ethan was too engrossed in the view from the little port to pay any attention to her.

He was staring down the center aisle of what had been the shuttle's passenger compartment. Huge gaping holes showed sky where the roof had been. A waterfall of brilliant, blindingly clear sunlight filtered into the hull. He became aware of the goggles and face shield built into the hood of the coat he was wearing. More than half of the acceleration couches had been torn or twisted off their mounts.

Turning his head and craning his neck, he could see that the right side of the vessel had been badly pitted. The left side was ripped open along half its length, a single metal-shredding gouge. He was no mechanic, but even a mechanical idiot could see they'd be flying a new ship before they'd be repairing this one. Right now, his expense account was the worthier vehicle.

A light dusting of snow covered the floor of the cabin and many of the tumbled seats, especially on the torn left side. The airbrushed whiteness muted the rented duralloy and convulsed floor. Here and there amidst the snow, shards of fractured glassite threw crippled rainbows about the interior. If a single viewport had survived intact, it was out of his line of sight.

Maybe he overdid the straining and turning. In any case, the dizziness returned. Bracing his back against the door, he sat down carefully, put his head in his hands until it cleared.

"Are you all right, Mr. Fortune?" Williams inquired again. His face showed concern.

"Yes . . . just a little queasy there for a moment." He blinked. "It's okay now, I think." Pause. "Although all of a sudden it seems I can't see too well."

"You were staring out the port too long without protection," surmised Williams. "I expect it will pass quickly enough. Don't worry. It has nothing to do with your head injury."

"That supposed to be encouraging news?" He could feel the lump at the back of his skull. At least it was intact. His skull, not the lump. By rights it ought to have as many holes in it as the boat's hull.

"You should use those." The teacher pointed at the goggles resting high on Ethan's forehead. "To prevent snow blindness," he added unnecessarily.

"Thought of everything, didn't they?" Ethan grunted. He shivered again. "Any idea what the temperature is?"

"I'd guess about twenty below zero, centigrade," Williams replied, as though it were the most natural thing in the world. "And I believe it's dropping a bit. But you can tell for yourself. There's a thermometer built into your left cuff." He grinned slightly.

Sure enough, a tiny circular thermometer was sewn into the fabric, just behind the end of the glove. At first he thought the teacher must be mistaken. The red line seemed almost all the way around the dial. Then he noticed that the *highest* reading on the meter was the freezing point of water. From there it went down, not up. This was impressive for what it implied, not what it read.

Something very funny occurred to him. He laughed. In fact, he roared. It did not seem amusing, nor particularly natural, to the others. They watched him a mite apprehensively, especially du Kane. Colette looked as though she'd been expecting something of the sort all along. He forced himself to stop when he found that the tears were freezing on his cheeks.

Then he noticed the way everyone was looking at him.

"No, I haven't gone crazy. It just struck me that among my trade goods on board the *Antares* I have an even four dozen

Asandus portable deluxe model catalytic heaters. For trading to the poor backward natives, you know. I'd trade my grandmother for one of 'em right now."

"If wishes were fishes we'd never want for food," said Williams philosophically. "Russell . . . twentieth-century English philosopher."

Ethan nodded, drew a snow spiral on the floor with one finger . . . real leather in those gloves, he noticed. A thought occurred to him as he surveyed the little group. His mind was running a few paces behind his eyes, still.

"Speaking of the *Antares,* there was something very wrong with it when we blasted free. Yes, a hole, back of the passenger blister! I saw it as we tumbled."

"Very wrong and much too blasted," echoed a nervous, vaguely familiar voice from a dark back corner. A small, morose figure edged out into the dim light. Its right arm was crooked up in a makeshift sling and there was an ugly scar healing slowly on one cheek.

"You sure got a way with words, chum," it finished.

"Hey, I remember you, all right," said Ethan with certainty. "Your name is . . . let's see . . . the other guy called you 'Walther.' The big guy." He tried to see behind the other into the furthest recesses of the compartment. "Speaking of the big guy . . ."

"The bigger guy . . . September . . . did him in," informed Colette du Kane. "Console lighting went out, but I'm sure it was him. It sure wasn't y—" She checked herself. "I wonder where *he* came from?"

Ethan thought back, recalled the ghostly, cursing apparition that had risen in the cabin behind him just before he lost consciousness.

"I think I know who you mean. Scared me half out of the wits I had left . . . his popping up in the middle of everything like that."

"It certainly was interesting," began du Kane. "I remember a time when—"

"Be quiet and eat your food, father," said Colette. Ethan looked more closely at the girl, who looked like a pink Buddha in her survival suit. Who was chairman of what, here?

She returned her gaze to Ethan. It was a frank, open, uncompromising stare. Sizing him up. No no . . . that was supposed to be *his* prerogative. He turned away and she must have sensed his nervousness.

"You got the hardest knock of us all, I think, Mr. Fortune," she said consolingly. Ethan knew she was deliberately trying to make him feel better. But the knot at the back of his head conceded the truth of her comment.

"He had a gun?" Ethan asked her. Her reply was coldly matter-of-fact.

"No, as a matter of fact, I think he broke his neck. Neat job."

"Oh," said Ethan. "Look, I want to apologize for calling you f . . . I mean, for what I said back there."

"Skip it," she muttered softly. "I'm used to it." And that, he reflected, was the first obvious untruth she'd uttered.

Du Kane seemed to sense the awkwardness. He cleared it away nicely. "You're wearing the dead chap's coat, I believe."

"Doesn't fit very well, does it?" Ethan murmured absently. He held up his arms. If he wasn't careful he could lose the gloves. But his funny looks didn't bother him. It was warm. Though not as warm as Colette du Kane probably was. He glanced around.

"Where is this guy . . . uh . . ."

"September. Skua September," supplied Williams.

"Yeah, him."

Colette gestured loosely in the direction of the door. "After we discovered that this compartment was still fairly intact . . . he carried you in, by the way . . . it seemed the natural place to take refuge. Conserve body heat, get out of this wind. The emergency boat rations are in this twisted locker behind me. I'm glad to say they survived, by and large. He had a bite to eat and disappeared outside. That was some time ago. He hasn't come back."

"Quiet sort," put in du Kane. Food dripped from his mouth and he suddenly mopped at it embarrassedly.

"I expect he'll be all right," put in Williams. "He took one of the two beamers with him. I," he continued, holding up the little weapon, "have the other. He suggested I use it to discourage any antisocial actions left in our nemesis, here." He indicated the sullen Walther.

The latter eyed the gun, a bit wistfully, Ethan thought. "Huh! Fat lot of good it'd do me, too!" He shivered. Apparently he was even colder than Ethan. Several bunched-up shirts, plus an emergency thermal poncho from the lifeboat's stores gave him a squat look, like a fat frog. But the poncho hadn't been designed with temperatures like this in mind and the little hood was having a hard time of it. Well, that was just too bad.

Ethan considered the clothes worn by du Kane and his daughter. They fitted almost perfectly, as if they'd been made to order in a thranx tailor-shop. Which they might have been. Clearly the kidnappers wouldn't want their charges to freeze to death. Williams, then, was probably wearing Walther's fur. He'd already noted the grisly origin of his own.

Well, if someone was destined to freeze to death, he had no compunctions about nominating the ugly little man with the busted wing. When he thought of the commissions this little detour was going to cost him . . .

Wait a minute. If he was wearing the dead Kotabit's jacket, and Williams was using Walther's, and the du Kanes had their own—then that meant the odd Mr. September was prowling around *outside* somewhere without a coat. Unless the kidnappers had carried extras, and that didn't seem likely. Well, that was September's problem. Just now there were other items uppermost in his mind.

"Any idea," he asked Williams, "where we are?" It was Walther who replied, however.

"We were supposed to land," he began bitterly, "about 200 kilometers southeast of Brass Monkey. The rendezvous was all arranged. Thanks to several damn delays though, and some bad fusing, we got caught in the explosion we set in the *Antares*. Chewed hell out of our navigational capacity. I can't be sure, the way all those instruments were whining, with a busted 'puter, but I'll bet we're halfway around the planet. And if you want to buy my chances of getting out of this, you can have 'em for a 'Sime."

"Set explosion?" prodded Ethan. But Walther had obviously said all he intended to for now. He lapsed into glum silence and slid further back into his corner.

"Probably a fair-sized bomb, set to go off after we'd left

the *Antares*," commented Colette professionally. "Since no alarms went off when we entered the lifeboat or sealed from the ship, I assume they took care of that earlier. Obviously the bomb was a cover maneuver, designed to convince rescuers that anyone in that section of the ship had been vaporized—especially father and myself."

"I see," nodded Ethan. "That way everyone would assume you two were dead . . . until these two were safely away and ready to put their demands. And no pursuit. Very clever. Of course, anyone walking that section of the ship when the bomb happened to go off would just be plain out of luck." He glared at Walther, who ignored him.

"That's about it," continued Colette. "But with all the hemming and hawing, they blew their timetable and didn't quite get away in time. Wouldn't have gotten away at all if Father hadn't . . ." She shrugged.

"You ought to thank him for saving your life," Ethan said reprovingly.

She gave him another withering stare. "What life? Got any idea what it's like to be rich, Mr. Fortune? It's great. But to be rich and laughed at . . ."

"Why don't you re—?" He bit his tongue. But she noticed.

"Reduce? Can't. Glandular—irreversible, the docs say." She turned away irritably. "Oh, go freeze yourself!"

"Listen," put in Walther, sticking his head out into the light. "Regardless of what you think, we planned it so nobody would get caught in that blowup. That's the only reason I didn't shoot you, and you, the minute you stuck your faces into that lifeboat bay. If a search team found your body, or his, or bits and pieces, then they'd start wondering just maybe why there was no sign of theirs," he indicated the du Kanes. "A small chance, but Kotabit and the others wanted to be sure. Yeah, good and sure! And now," he concluded with acidic finality, "we'll all freeze good and surely dead."

"I'm not thrilled about dying in your company, chum," said Ethan with as much toughness as he could muster, which wasn't much. "And I sure don't plan to. Anybody think of checking the boat tridee?" He didn't have to ask if it was in working order.

Colette du Kane was shaking her head slowly. "Just scrap.

That's what September told us, anyhow. I wouldn't know about such things myself, but I'm inclined to believe him."

"It certainly seems that we have nothing capable of even rudimentary communication," agreed Williams heavily. "Let alone something that can transmit a continental distance."

Briefly, then, they were stuck.

Less briefly, they were stranded on a barely known world, thousands of kilometers from its only humanx settlement, in weather that would make a corpulent walrus dive for his winter woolies. And the only people they could inform of their predicament were each other.

Worse, unless by a very long, long chance someone had seen the boat tumbling toward the surface, no one would come looking for them, no one would believe they were alive. Including Walther's partners, who'd be expecting him a few kilometers from the town.

Ethan didn't mind frozen food—but he wasn't ready to become some!

Thinking it over, he had to confess that his prospects for the immediate future were anything but heartwarming. Or anything warming. On the other hand, he never made a sale by sitting on his duff and waiting for the customer to come to him. At least moving around would keep his blood from getting any funny ideas about going on strike.

He scrambled to his feet. The hood fit loosely over his head but the goggles and shield were adjustable and snugged down tight.

"Where do you think you're going?" asked Colette.

"Outside, to have a look at the neighborhood. And to see if there's a store around that sells electric beds."

He snapped the top snap on the coat, tried to tighten the floppy hood and failed. Flip went the goggles. Things immediately grew darker. He had to fumble twice before he got a hand on the door latch. Turn and push—so.

It didn't budge—so.

He shoved again. "Stuck."

"Oh deity!" she began, "save us from such awesome, overwhelming, analytic . . . !"

That was another good reason for getting outside. The door received a good swift kick and a couple of choice curses.

Either the kick knocked it free, or maybe the curses had a warming effect on the frozen joints. In any case, it popped open a few centimeters. From there it moved, reluctantly, on its bearings.

He shut the door carefully behind him and turned. Making sure of his footing—the snow could have covered all kinds of holes—he started down the center aisle of the ship. Cold flakes crunched under his feet. It sounded as though he was walking on glass. The wind moaned and howled through the torn metal. His breath formed a tiny cumulus cloud, a small shadow of life that stayed just ahead of him.

He could feel his lungs expanding and contracting. They seemed pitifully tiny in the frozen air. Each breath was painful, full of bee-stings and wire-wool.

The center aisle was tilted downward. Nose down, the shuttle had come to an abrupt halt.

Then he did what might have been considered by some a foolish thing. But he was a purveyor of cultured gee-gaws, not a planetary scout. And his taped information said nothing against it. So he knelt and scooped up a small ball of snow. It certainly looked like regular, old-fashioned, smack-in-the-face type snow. It caught the light like snow.

He brought it to his mouth, felt a sudden momentary chill greater than the air. It dissolved in the oral furnace, went down, stayed down. Plain old usual terran-type H_2O snow. He knew from the tapes that Tran-ky-ky's atmosphere was practically Terra-normal. What he did not consider was the possibility that the snow might contain acquired traces of toxic elements.

But it didn't, and nothing happened. The snow and his stomach got along just fine.

By way of experiment, he raised his goggles just a smidgin. It was a short experiment. He had to blink away a couple of freezing tears before sliding the dark glass back into place. The glare was fierce and unyielding. With the goggles, everything showed as clearly as before, but he could look at the snow without having his optic pathways turned to mush.

He reflected that a man caught here without goggles could go blind without even being aware the process was going on. It was far more deceptive than night blindness. Being caught in the light, it seemed, was worse than being caught in the dark.

A slick part of the floor and he slipped, had to catch himself with his gloved hands. For a minute he didn't move, just stood, caught his breath. Watch it, stupid! This was no place to twist an ankle.

He reached the end of the aisle. A fast glance back to the total destruction in the passenger compartment, and then he turned to look into the pilot's cubby. The door had been bent inward like the lip of a can. The shuttle's nose was buried. The lensless ports were filled with a mixture of loose earth and snow. It poured into the small forecabin, oozing over the panel and instrumentation.

What he could see of the mangled console and the precision switches made him wonder that the little kidnapper had been able to bring them down safely at all. As for the boat tridee, it was so battered he barely recognized it.

Turning to leave the cabin, he stumbled again. Once more he was lucky and didn't hurt himself. But he was beginning to get mad. He turned with the intention of visiting a few suitable gripes on the twisted hunk of metal that had so cleverly insinuated itself between his legs. The gripe got as far as his lips, fizzled there when he saw the obstacle wasn't metal.

It was twisted, however.

The body was nude, lightly dusted with snow, and had begun to turn a color that did not imply a state of advanced good health. The back was facing him. He'd apparently stumbled over the head.

Kneeling, he put a hand on the back of the motionless skull. It moved freely when he touched it. Too freely. Du Kane had been right.

He experienced a sudden, sickening urge to see if the eyes were open or closed, like in the tridee shows. He could close them gently if they were open, just like the fictional heroes. However, he opted for backing away carefully, without even checking.

Brushing the snow from his knees, he averted his eyes from the half-frozen corpse. Instead he tried to imagine how this September fellow could go rambling about outside the protection of the boat without one of the special coats. Then it occurred to him that he'd have a double set of clothing.

Nothing in the cabin looked operable, useful. However, if one took the extent of his engineering knowledge into account, this observation meant nothing. He left without touching anything. Slipping and sliding, he made his way to the gaping tear which dominated the left side of the boat. Torn insulation puffed out from the double walls. Bracing himself against it, he cautiously looked out.

The snow-dusted ground lay only a half-meter down. To the right he could see where the boat had burrowed its crumpled snout in what seemed to be a hill of good, solid earth. It didn't look like much of a hill. Probably you could walk around it. But it had been high enough and solid enough to arrest the forward slide of the boat.

From the hill, what looked like stunted evergreens stuck their bristly crowns sunward. They hardly bent at all in the stiff gale. By now he was so numb he hardly felt the wind anymore. Needles shifted their position relative to the sun. A few flakes of snow scudded lazily from one pebble to a little hollow. The trunks of the trees were thick and looked solid as duralloy.

Much of the ground to the west and north of the land was covered by a greenish down. It looked like short, very thick grass. Turning and raising his head, he looked out into the west, toward the horizon. That supplied another interesting discovery.

It looked as though it had been drawn with a pen. The line dividing earth and sky was straight, flat, and altogether too sharp to be real. Human eyes expected something slightly blurred or wavering on most inhabited planets. Not here. You could grab that line and pluck it.

Overhead, the sky was a deep cerulean blue, pure as old pewter dishes. The even oil color was unsullied, the dome of heaven smooth as a baby's bottom. It was utterly devoid of clouds, which was just as well. A cloud in that pit of ice-blue would immediately surrender its aspect of lightness and take on the character of solid white rock. A real cloud floating overhead would be upsetting.

With the exception of their tiny blot of dirt, there was

nothing else in any direction but flat, sparkling, virgin ice, lightly dusted now with snow. Another bit of taped knowledge drifted upward to the surface. Mostly shallow seas, frozen solid. They were adrift on an ocean of ice.

The glare of the unchallenged sun on that unwavering sea would have been intolerable without the goggles.

He jumped down to the ground. Mildly worried that the snow might make things awkward, he was relieved to discover it was barely a centimeter deep. Inside the boat it had piled a little, forming tiny drifts.

He walked a few paces away from the ship. Looking back toward the tail he could make out a pair of deep grooves in the ice. They ran straight toward the southern horizon. He couldn't see under the boat, but it had obviously skidded badly on setdown. The landing struts had probably been torn away or worn down to stubs. Then the boat itself slid who knew how many meters on its belly, until it had chanced to run up against this swept-together dustpile of dirt and rock.

A few steps brought him down to where the ground vanished. Brushing away the snow, he found that he could see for a few centimeters into the ice. There the ground sloped away beneath, to unknown frozen depths. The grass, he noticed, grew right out into the ice itself. It clustered thickly, but in a very orderly fashion. There was always a little space, however small, between each blade and its neighbor.

None of this told him how big the island—for such it had to be—was. The inside of his mouth was a frozen crust. Running his tongue along it was like caressing cardboard. With thoughts of circling the island, he took a step out onto the ice.

Another facet of Tran-ky-ky promptly introduced itself. Any man trying to walk normally without special equipment would soon find himself in closer contact with the surface.

Fortunately, he didn't slide very far on the freezing ice. But he had to crawl back on his hands and knees. By the time he'd regained solid ground his palms and knees were thoroughly numbed.

The boat's emergency supplies were designed mainly with median range humanx-type worlds in mind. Therefore, if anything they tended to lean more toward the upper register of the thermometer in supply execution.

He didn't believe ice skates had been included in the inventory.

As if to insure that he shouldn't get any more comfortable than was necessary, the wind picked up and was now proceeding to cool things down a bit. The planet was clearly determined to freeze him solid and then blow away the remnant.

Tonight, when it first grew cold—the very concept of cold was taking on new meaning in Ethan's mind—any real gust would add a chill factor that would make things very dangerous. They'd have to take care to prevent being thoroughly cubed—and not in the mathematical sense, either.

Without the relative shelter of the boat, of course, they'd probably freeze to death even with the special coats.

His vision was improving or the cold was starting to work its way into his brain. The horizon remained sharp as a paper cut on a fingertip. But now he thought he could make out what might be larger land masses far off in the distance. He couldn't be certain.

For a moment he thought they might be imperfections in the material of the goggles. But when he moved his head, the distant objects stayed in the same places.

He turned to his right and froze. Figuratively, this time. Something else was visible off in the distance, coming around the side of the island. When he moved his head this time, though, the figure not only didn't stay in the same place, it got larger.

As it came closer, it resolved into a fairly human figure. But there were discrepancies. The feet were bloated, distorted pads. It waved. Not having anything else to do, Ethan waved back. He stood up. If the thing weren't human, he'd be better off meeting it in a stance more suitable for absenting oneself rapidly.

It was human, all right, although the figure was huge. The double set of clothing it wore made it seem even larger. That made Ethan think again of the coat he was wearing, designed for a much bigger man. That size man. He felt a little bit guilty.

At least September had snow goggles with him. The goggles gave him a faintly amphibious appearance. Ethan wondered if he looked as silly. Probably more so. If the man minded the intense chill he didn't show it.

As he came closer the bloated feet explained themselves. Apparently September had ripped up one or two of the acceleration couches. The luron upholstery had been shaped into a pair of fat pads and strapped to his big dogs. It seemed the luron was sufficiently rough to give some purchase on the ice. Tough and long-lasting, the artificial material would not wear off no matter how rugged the surface. And the padding did more than just cushion his feet: it also put some crucial distance between them and the heat-sucking ice.

The improvised snow-shoes looked awkward, but as a method of temporary transportation it far exceeded sliding on one's fundament.

Ethan took a closer look at the personage who'd saved or condemned them. Not exactly a giant, but damned large, bigger even than the recently deceased Kotabit. A good two meters up, broad in proportion.

He tried to take the other's measure, failed, and was upset without immediately knowing why. After all, he wasn't going to try and sell this guy anything. He took in the white hair, predator beak of a nose, and the incongruous gold earring. There was a deal of the old English lord about him, with a lot of Terran-Arabic. Bedouin stock, maybe.

September stopped, his breath coming in short heaves. A miniature fog-bank swirled about that scimitar proboscis. He extended a hand and grinned down at Ethan. The hand was sandwiched in between layers of torn seat-foam. Ethan stared at it.

"Not as good as those survival gloves you've got on, maybe, but it keeps a body warm . . . after a fashion. It's hard to handle things, but then, I don't expect to be doing much watch-making for a while."

"That's for sure." Ethan grinned back and shook the hand. Or rather, allowed himself to be shaken by it. "You must be Skua September."

"Better be," the other replied, "or else someone badly

fooled Mrs. September. Although she preferred a climate more on the toasty side."

He stared over Ethan's head into the distance. Slapping both hands together a couple of times, he blew intently between the layers of foam. His eyes never left the horizon while he spoke.

"How are you getting on, young feller? That was quite a swack you took. Couple of minutes there, I was afraid you weren't going to come out of it. Be hard enough to rouse yourself here without piling a coma into the bargain."

"Perchance to dream? No, a prolonged sleep certainly wouldn't be a good idea, here," Ethan agreed. "You'd never know quite when you finally froze. And I don't want to miss that when it happens."

September nodded. "Ought to be interesting at that. Wonder how a body'd freeze here. From the top down or the inside out?" He crossed arms and slapped opposite shoulders. "What do you know about this refrigerated habitat? I only took the standard general tourist mestape—language, highlights, so forth. So did the little fellow—Williams. I think he'll be okay. Quiet. Not taciturn, just likes to keep to himself. And that unspeakable fermentation, Walther, can surely manage the local patois. Although I'd sooner remove his tongue before I'd let him do any translating. You?"

"Well I'm a salesman, and—"

September didn't let him continue. "And so you've stuffed yourself as full of verbs and prepositional phrases and epiglottal stops as a grilled pepper! Excellent, young feller."

Ethan shrugged. "It's no more than anyone else in my position would have done. I also had a few general planetary tapes on native conditions—cultural stuff, flora and fauna, the like. Just business."

"Or survival." He gave Ethan a friendly pat on the back that made him cough even with thick padding to insulate the blow. "Fine foresight, lad. Exemplary! As of now, you're in charge."

"Huh?" Somehow Ethan got the feeling he'd missed an important paragraph or two in amongst the praise. "In charge of what?"

"Why, in charge of seeing our little party return safely to civilization, of course. Expedition's got to have a leader. I hereby appoint myself your faithful deputy. When can we expect to come in sight of the nearest bar, commander?" Under the brows, there was a twinkle.

"Now wait a minute," put in Ethan hastily. "I think you've formed some wrong ideas about me. I'm not the leader type. Anyway, what about you? You seem plenty competent. The way you handled that chap Kotabit—"

"Yes, well, that's a nice ability to have certain times," September agreed, studying his clumsy mittens, "but rather limited. Besides, he's dead. That particular problem will not require further attention. Now, I have this tendency to get impatient with people and break heads when patting them would be more practical. Darned if I can figure out why, but they seem to feel threatened by me when I've but the kindest of intentions in mind.

"What is needed is a cool, reasonable hand experienced at working with people and changing quickly in unfamiliar situations without making folks feel threatened. Doesn't it take all that to change in mid-pitch from one sales talk to another? Presence of mind and quick thought, lad."

"Sure, but—"

"Persuasive without being overbearing. A diplomat."

Ethan finally succeeded in stalling the unending enumeration of his virtues.

"Look, I'm not sure selling Poupée-de-Oui Scent No. 7 exactly qualifies me as a combination of Metternich and Amundsen."

"But it's helped you convince people that white is black and good for 'em. Here all you have do to is convince 'em white is white. Duck soup."

"All right, all right. I accept."

"Thought you would."

"Only because you think it's necessary. And only temporarily, mind." He started fumbling with the catches on his jacket. "Now as leader of this expedition, my first order, effective now, is that you put this suit on. It's obviously built for someone constructed more along your lines. If there's anything I despise, it's waste, and I'm swimming in it."

"Sorry, lad." September put out a hand and halted the unsnapping. "You're in charge, agreed. But this is still a free society, not a dictatorship. That means any decision ought to be ratified by a majority vote. Since you and I are the only ones present, it's up to us. Well?"

"I vote for you to put this coat on."

"And I vote for you to keep it. How much do you weigh?"

"Huh?" That was Ethan's second use of that brilliant expletive in a few minutes. Ah, the dazzle of a rapier-sharp wit! He murmured a reply.

"I thought about that much," said September. "You lose."

"Look, you'll make better use of it," Ethan argued. "You're more the explorer type than I am. I can manage without it."

"No, you cannot manage without it," September said sharply, not grinning. "And if this wind gets much worse," he continued, turning into the rising breeze, "we're all going to wish for a damnsight more in the way of clothes."

"Besides, if I am more the 'explorer type,' as you claim, I should be able to stand the cold better than you."

"You're contradicting yourself," Ethan pointed out.

"Don't be obtuse when I'm being illogical. Anyhow, that Kotabit fella was wearing special thermal underwear. It's a mite snug in a few wrong places, but it keeps me fairly comfortable with this double layer of top gear. That Walther has it on also, no doubt. He's not as cold as he makes out to be.

"Maybe it's not as cozy as those special jackets, but I won't freeze, feller-me-lad. A glass of good brandy, now, but . . . " He licked chapped lips wistfully. "You worry about yourself and not old Skua."

"Just how old are you, anyway?" asked Ethan curiously, eyeing the long ropes of muscle that bulged the fabric. He hoped the other wouldn't be offended.

He wasn't. If the broad smile that creased his face was any indication, he was more tickled than anything else.

"I'm older than that pudgy pullet du Kane has for a daughter, and a bit younger than the moon. But about garments, again. All your survival suits are a dark brown. My own outer clothing is white. You stand out against this landscape like an old raisin in lemon cake frosting. Me, I'd just as soon be a little chillier and a mite less conspicuous. Old habit.

"Those tapes give you any way to judge how cold it's likely to get tonight?"

Ethan squinted up to where the sun hung like a failed flare in one corner of the sky.

"If we came down anywhere on a line with the settlement, meaning on the equatorial belt, it will probably only drop to minus 30 or 40 tonight. You can add to that a steady wind of anything from 80 to 100 kph. We seem to have come down in a positive calm."

"Absolutely sybaritic, hmmm?" September murmured. "Remind me to stay out of drafts." He kicked at the scruffy thin snow. "Wonder if the du Kanes know anything?"

"I dunno," replied Ethan. "They're a funny pair. The old man seems pretty shaky for someone holding the reins of empire. And the girl . . ." Ethan's expression wrinkled in confusion when he thought about Colette. "She seems competent enough . . . maybe even more than that. But she's so full of bitterness and bile . . ."

"About her looks?" prompted September. Ethan nodded. "Too bad . . . all that credit and built like a marshmallow. Sinful, positively sinful.

"But she won't be a burden on us, I don't think, and on this world I wouldn't mind a few extra kilos of insulation myself." His thought changed abruptly. "Might be an idea to mount a watch tonight."

He put both hands on either side of the hole and heaved himself up into the boat. Turning, he knelt and gave Ethan a hand up.

Ethan noticed a flash of dark brown forward as he was hauled aboard. He gestured toward the pilot's compartment.

"What exactly happened? As we were coming down, I mean."

"Ummm? Oh, that." September gave a shrug. "It was bloody peculiar. See, I'd been drinking a tinge . . . not that I was drunk, you understand!"

"Perish the thought," said Ethan placatingly.

"Yeah, well, I'd been sipping a little. And while it's difficult to believe, it's not entirely inconceivable that I might have gone just a teensy bit over my limit. Anyway, an assortment of misbegotten crewmen of indeterminate ancestry got it into their lighter-than-air skulls that I was acting in a manner not conducive to the general well-being of your usual milksop passenger. So they jumped me.

"Next thing I know, I'm thrown out of a sound sleep into near total darkness and zero-gee while a bunch of dwarf miners are using my skull for sinking an exploratory mine shaft. And to top it, I'm all tied up.

"Well, there were several possibilities. One, I was having the DT's, which I haven't run across in a long age, lad. Or maybe I was paddling through the great-grandfather of all hallucinatory hangovers. When it finally dawned on me that my misery had purely human causes, I was pretty upset."

"I see," said Ethan. "The crew tied you up and dumped you into the lifeboat to sleep it off."

"Sure!" agreed September. "If they'd taken me to the brig, or whatever they use for a brig on those big luxury ships, they'd have had to get formal about things. Swear out affidavits, make out forms in triplicate. Much easier to chuck me into an empty lifeboat.

"At first I thought all the tumbling and jolting was a gag. But knocking about in freefall back in those seats *hurt*, dammit! Wasn't a bit funny, no. Then it occurred to me that the boat had separated from the ship and was diving on an unscheduled jaunt dirtward. I don't like kidnapping on principle. It's worse when I'm the kidnapee.

"Pretty soon the boat is skipping through atmosphere like a rock on water. And none too gently, as you know. I wasn't sure what was going on, but I hadn't been consulted. So I broke loose and went forward to find out. Most of you had been slung around pretty bad. I don't remember who was conscious and who wasn't, but no one offered any advice.

"That fella in there," he jerked a thumb in the direction of the pilot's cubby, "was awful surprised to see me. First thing, he goes to pull a beamer on me. Now right away I know I'm not going to be able to reason with this bloke. So we had a bit of a tussle. Meanwhile that punk Walther can't make up his mind whether to stick by his controls for the landing or pull his own beamer and help his partner.

"He ended up trying to do both and did neither very well. He did get his beamer out and he did get us down. The ship got broke and so did his arm. As for the other chap, I didn't intend to kill him. It just happened. He was sure trying to kill me, though."

He dug into a pocket, showed Ethan the other beamer. "Want it?"

"No thanks. I'd probably shoot myself in the foot. You keep it."

"Okay." September shoved it back into a fold of clothing. "If it really gets rough tonight we can heat one of the walls. I'd rather not do that, however. I don't know how much of a charge is left in these things and we've no way of re-priming them."

Ethan had handled beamers before, despite his refusal of this one. Business occasionally made it necessary. There were planets where the natives would decide in a stroke of primitive brilliance that the best bargain was to do away with the trader and confiscate his goods, thus apparently proving the old adage about getting something for nothing.

This time, however, the gun would prove more useful for warming his own backside instead of some ignorant savage's. Better that September kept charge of it.

The latter broke into his reverie. "How about food?"

"You mean local? I don't know. Don't you think there's enough in the ship?"

"A shuttle of this size is built to hold about twenty people," informed September. "There are only six of us. But it's presumed by the powers that be in their infinite wisdom that such ships as these will only be used to get from an uninhabitable ship to an inhabitable planet. Whereas we seem to have gone vice versa, what? So I wouldn't count on finding more than a couple of weeks concentrated survival rations back in there, with plenty of vitamin pills.

"That ought to give us enough food for about four terran-length months. Longer, if we husband the stuff. That's assuming," he added, "that everything came through the landing in edible condition. At least we don't have to worry much about spoilage. Not in this climate."

There was a question Ethan had put off asking long enough. "What do you think of our chances?"

September looked thoughtful. "Two weeks plus concentrated food for twenty people will mass a fair amount. We've got to find a way to transport it. And also a better way to get around on this frozen cue-ball than this." He indicated the makeshift ice-shoes. "That would be a beginning.

"Then we'd have to find a way to keep warm during really cold nights, and to block off this damnable wind. We have to figure a method of determining where we are now, where Brass Monkey is, and how to draw a straight line between the two we can stay glued to.

"Assuming we can do all that, we might make it in four months. But I wouldn't lay a tenth-credit on it. Could take a year, too. That's why I'm curious about local foods."

"Well," Ethan tried to remember details from the tapes that were not pertinent to salesmanship, "there's that."

He hopped onto the ice and walked over to the island. There he stooped, plucked a few blades of the "grass" from the frozen surface. He had to pull hard, several times. Even then it came up with the greatest reluctance.

The thick stem, or leaf, or whatever it was, grew no longer than ten centimeters. The further out onto the ice it grew, the shorter the stems. It wasn't a sharp-edged blade, like terran grass, but thick, fat, and substantial. Rather a bit like a pointy triangular sausage. Even the coloring was different.

There was a large proportion of red mixed into the green. Other stalks varied in color from a bright emerald to a deep rust. In form it probably came closest to resembling terran iceplant, another incongruity. It was taller, straighter, and did not form clumps nearly as thick as the familiar *Mesembryanthemum crystallinum*.

"If I remember the tape correctly, this stuff grows wild all over the planet," Ethan said. "It's called pika-pina and is edible, although nutritional value is still uncertain. But it's high in mineral content and bulks a fair amount of raw protein. It's not a true grass, but lies somewhere midway between them and the mushrooms. Even grows on bare ice. Very complex root system.

"Needless to say, it's not a flowering plant."

"I can believe that," asserted September. "No self-respecting bee would be caught dead on this world." He took one of the thick sprigs awkwardly in one mittened hand, stared at it with interest.

"High in protein, you say? That's good. We're going to need all the rough fuel we can manage if and when we run out of supplies." He bit off the stalk halfway down, chewed reflectively.

"Not as bad as some," he said after a moment. "Long way from spinach salad, but better than dandelions."

"Dandelions?"

"Never mind, feller-me-lad. We're not likely to run across any." He swallowed, popped the remaining half in his mouth and finished that also.

"Tough skinned, and it's got a consistency like old shoe. But the taste is kind of interesting. Sweetish, but bland. Parsley and not celery. If we had the fixings, a good dressing might make this stuff almost civilized. I don't suppose we've got any vinegar?"

"No, unless you count du Kane's daughter." Ethan snorted. "I think some of those other plants on the island are supposed to be edible too, but I don't recall for sure. It's hard to trust mestaped information on only a single sitting. I was more concerned with the local monetary system and rules of barter, I'm afraid. But pika-pina, I remember that."

"How about animals? I'd be willing to try a steak."

"I can't seem to remember the section on fauna at all." Ethan's forehead wrinkled as he poked at his memory. "There are animals, though. And fish, of a sort. I do remember that the fish are edible. Supposed to be extremely tasty, too. They've evolved a low-oxygen metabolism that enables them to survive beneath the surface."

"Fish, hummm? I'd even prefer that to a steak."

"There is the problem," Ethan reminded him, "of getting at them through eight or nine meters of ice, at the minimum."

"Oh," said September, the great beak dipping a little. He looked crestfallen. "I'd forgotten that little detail."

"What do you suggest we do now?" asked Ethan. It was all very well and good to be able to dish out interesting facts about the planet, quite another to propose immediate application.

"First thing, we've got to start preparing for the night as best we can. I'm not afraid of getting to sleep here. But I want to do it with some assurance I'm going to wake up. If we can get through the night without too much trouble, maybe tomorrow we can see about rigging up some sort of sled and improvising navigational gear.

"Our friendly kidnappers might have had local charts, though I doubt it. Depends where we came down. I got a look at the beacon lock just before we hit and we were so far off it barely registered. No, the settlement's definitely not around the corner. But charts are a possibility. Remember to ask our surviving poorslip about 'em."

"Think he'll cooperate?"

"Why not, young feller-me-lad? He's a candidate for the big deep-freeze, too. Meanwhile, dig into that mestaped knowledge of yours and see if you can position Arsudun with respect to any major landmarks or outstanding surface features.

"Me, I'm going to think about keeping warm tonight. I'd rather not build a fire inside our compartment. Close quarters. But I don't see a way around it. I suppose we should be thankful we ran up against a wood supply, of sorts. If we'd come to rest in the middle of this," he indicated the endless ice-ocean, "we'd really be in trouble."

It occurred to Ethan that nothing on the shuttle was burnable. Naturally not. Nor was the packaging for the self-heating meals, nor the padding in the acceleration couches. Patrick O'Morion himself couldn't have made a fire with the materials available on the shuttle. You might start a fire with the heater from some of the emergency rations, but you still had to have something to burn.

A man would be better off back on old Terra, in the days when transportation was made of organic wood and burned organic residue for fuel, too.

September gestured at the island. "We can cut trees with the beamer. I hope they're not too full of sap or we'll never get 'em to burn. Wonder what they use to keep it from freezing?"

The mention of freezing made Ethan take another look at the sun. He was alarmed to see how far it had dropped. With it went a good deal of the day-heat—no, you couldn't rightly call it heat—of the more manageable cold. He recalled that the day here was about two hours shorter than Terra's, or ship-time.

The door to the storage compartment opened with a squeaky protest. Colette du Kane stuck her head out into the wind. A big badger or woodchuck checking out of hiberna-tion, Ethan thought. He was angry at himself—what had she done to him? But he couldn't keep thinking along those lines.

I can't help myself!, he thought in silent apology. She wasn't psychic, and didn't look over at him. Instead, her gaze seemed intent on the drowsing sky.

"Find anything?" she asked. The question was directed past Ethan's right ear. He shouldn't have resented it, but he did.

"Some trees. But it'd be rough cutting 'em now."

"Come on, Skua," blurted Ethan unthinkingly. "Let's take a whack at those trees. Give me the beamer."

"Thought you didn't want to bother with it," said the big man, surprised.

"I changed my mind. I'll cut and you carry . . . and don't do that!" September's hand paused in mid-air. "Another friendly pat on the back from you and I won't even be in condition to lift *this*." He took the beamer and held it tightly in one gloved hand.

"All right, Ethan. I'd like to get a decent cord cut soon as possible. Before it gets much darker, anyway. Or windier," he concluded, hiking multiple collars higher on his neck.

They turned to leave the ruined boat. Colette watched them thoughtfully until they disappeared. Then she shook her head and smiled ever so slightly before closing the door be-hind her.

The sun had vanished into a frozen grave and exchanged itself for a baleful icy eye of a moon by the time they pushed into the small metal room. Ethan was concentrating com-pletely on not shaking himself to pieces. He was shivering so violently he could visualize bits and pieces of himself flying off and bouncing across the duralloy floor. A finger here, an eyeball there. At least they were out of that infernal wind. Only the protective face heaters set in the hood of his survival suit had kept his skin from freezing. How September had stood it he couldn't imagine.

And it was going to get worse. Much worse.

Something bumped from behind and he managed to stumble out of the way as September staggered in behind him. The big man was buried under a huge load of wood, cut cleaner than the finest axe could manage.

Ethan shifted to one side, away from the door, and sank slowly to the floor. If he got out of this with all his component parts intact, he was going to take a nice, peaceful, *warm* desk job somewhere within the bureaucratic bowels of the organization and toast his tootsies in peace. The beamer he slung into a far corner.

Walther, who by now bore some resemblance to a trapdoor spider, pounced on the weapon in much that fashion. Immediately he whirled and made stabbing motions with it in September's direction. That worthy was unconcernedly stacking the cut wood next to several empty food crates—all nonflammable plastic, of course.

"That wasn't very bright of you, buddy," the kidnapper said to Ethan, not taking his eyes off September. "Don't you try anything either, sourpuss!" he warned Williams. The schoolteacher, however, hadn't budged. Nor had Colette, nor her father.

Ethan edged back into the cartons, trying to find a warm spot and failing miserably. September had arranged some of the wood and smaller twigs on a pile of greenish-brown needles in the center of the floor. There were also a few clumps of what looked like dried lichen but probably weren't.

Colette sat up thoughtfully, turned to her father.

"Father . . . your lighter."

"Eh?" The old man looked confused, then brightened. "Why, of course!"

He reached into a pocket inside his jacket and tossed something small and shiny to September.

"That should help, Mr. September. It's not full, I'm afraid. No point in hoarding it. I can do without a smoke for awhile." He smiled hopefully.

September flipped on the tiny, solid-fuel lighter—solid iridium filigree plating, Ethan noted.

"Thanks, du Kane." The old man looked pleased. "This is better than using the heater from one of the food parcels, and easier."

The small needles caught almost instantly, and Ethan reflected that there would be little need for much fire-proofing on this world. The wood spat and crackled like a Chinese holiday at first, but it was going to catch.

It would have been easier to gather pika-pina than cut trees, but that tough ground cover held far too much moisture to burn very well. It would have been like trying to light a wet sponge.

"You!" Walther began, having had about enough of this byplay. He was supposed to be in control of the situation, but no one was acting like it. It made him nervous. At first he listened to them all with puzzlement. Now he was mad.

"I'm going to blow your head off," he grinned at September. "Drill a nice little hole right through your skull."

September prodded the fire a little more, making sparks jump. He looked over at the door, shifted the blaze with his foot so that it drew on the breeze seeping in past the bent edges. Then he looked idly over at Walther.

"Not with that, you aren't."

"If you think you can bluff me . . ." the kidnapper quavered.

"Dry up, runt. Crawl back in your hole. Can't you see I'm busy trying to keep you alive?"

Walther shook. His eyes widened and he clenched his teeth. His finger tensed on the hooked trigger.

"He's going to shoot you," said Colette calmly, "the poor sap."

There was a tiny flicker of green at the tip of the beamer. Then nothing.

Walther glanced at it in disbelief, pulled the trigger again. This time the glow was hardly visible. On the third attempt, not even a hint of light came from the barrel.

With a little gasp that might have been fear or anguish, he dropped the useless weapon and scuttled back into the shadows, favoring his bad arm. The wide, now frightened eyes never left September.

It was quiet for a few minutes. Then September stirred the fire again.

"Calm down, Walther. While I'd cheerfully wring your chicken-neck and toss you next to your rigid compadre up forward, I've no intention of doing it just now. I'm tired and cold. I might feel differently tomorrow, or the next day. Fact is, I'd've done it earlier, but you're such a pitiable excuse for a man it hardly seemed worth the exertion. So I only broke your arm. Now don't bother me anymore."

He settled himself next to the door and concentrated on stuffing several narrow strips of shredded seat-padding into the crack on the hinged side. The other crack he left unblocked, to circulate air both for them and the fire.

"Maybe we can keep a little of the wind out, anyhow," he muttered half to himself.

Colette was rummaging among the other food cartons. She pulled one out and looked down at the label.

"Escalloped chicken." She grunted. "Nice for us, but damned unprofitable. Give the condemned a hearty last meal. Somebody on this shipping line has a sense of humor."

Ethan looked up in surprise. It was the closest thing she'd said to a joke since this'd happened to them. If it had a deeper meaning, it escaped him.

She started passing out the self-heating rations and he was so hungry he finished the first before he thought to look at the label.

September grunted as he continued to jam and press the recalcitrant material into the fissure. He looked over at Williams, huddled quietly to one side of the fire.

"You handled yourself very well there, schoolmaster. I was kind of interested to see what you'd do."

Williams acknowledged the compliment with a barely perceptible nod.

"I did not expect that Mr. Fortune would be so tired or foolish as to throw a useable weapon in the direction of that person. Therefore I assumed it must have burnt out or otherwise been rendered useless. This is a very nice fire you've made here."

"Enjoy it and welcome, while it lasts," September answered. "I think we've got enough wood to last the night, anyway. You did say the nights were shorter, young feller-me-lad?" Ethan nodded.

Ethan rolled over, trying to set himself as close to the flames as possible barring sudden immolation. He hadn't found that warm spot. And if there was a soft piece of duralloy, that had escaped his notice as well.

Trouble was, there were six of them to crowd around the energetic but tiny fire. That meant you couldn't get too much of you next to it. It was impossible to remain both polite and warm. So when one end of you was partly defrosted, the other was still in the figurative freezer. It was most disconcerting.

III

They disposed of the packages by stacking them in the empty shipping carton and shoving it into a far corner. September was for taking all the garbage outside and tossing it to the winds. He wanted to keep their hideaway neat, as long as they were stuck in it.

By now, though, the gale outside had risen to brobdingnagian proportions. That wind carried quick, freezing death, despite the protection of their suits and face heaters. Outvoted four to one, the big man assented.

"Wish I knew more about these natives," he muttered. Another log was sacrificed to the greedy flames. Huddled in their survival suits around the orange-red kinetic sculpture, they looked like so many frozen carcasses awaiting the butcher's saw. But the wood continued to burn comfortingly, although sometimes the fire took on an eerie purple halo. A nice little pile of coals was growing beneath. Even the supporting duralloy seemed to be taking on a reddish tinge under the steady throb of flame.

"It's not surprising we haven't encountered any yet," said Ethan. "For all we know, we might have come down in the middle of the biggest desert on the planet."

"It's all right, father," Colette was murmuring to her sire. "Your flowers are being well taken care of . . . and International Lubricants of Goldin IV was up six points, last I looked."

"You'd think they would have noticed the boat coming down," September grunted. "As clear as this air is, we ought to have been visible for hundreds of kilometers."

"We might have been seen," Ethan conceded. "Even so, it might take days or weeks for the locals to organize an expedition to reach us. Assuming they are so inclined."

"Still, we should post a watch," said the big man.

"I haven't taken anything but the basic mestapes," Williams began, "but it seems to me that your natives, no matter what their makeup, wouldn't be abroad on a night like this." Another gust rattled the door, as though in support of the schoolmaster's theory.

"This could be a tropical evening to them," Ethan countered. "But if we're as far away from the settlement as we seem to be, then the locals couldn't be familiar with flying craft. We can't tell how they might react. We might have come in over the local metropolis, too, and scared the populace half out of their wits. In which case they might declare this section of ice forever taboo, or the local equivalent. I've seen it happen before."

"Let's hope not," said September fervently. "I'm beginning to think we're going to need outside aid if we're ever going to see the inside of a brandy snifter again. But that's not why I think we should stand watch.

"And it has nothing to do with *him*." He gestured at Walther. A thin whine from the kidnapper's location was the only reply, a mouse of a snore. Already sound asleep.

"Although, as long as he entertains thoughts of attack, and as long as we still have one operational beamer"—he patted his vest pocket—"it would be a good idea if everyone didn't drift off to slumberland all at once.

"No, my main concern is keeping that fire going. If that goes, it's liable to get downright chilly in here. And we might never wake up."

"Quite so," agreed Colette promptly.

"I usually remain awake late at night," Williams informed them. "If no one objects, I would be pleased to take the first, uh, watch."

"Very well . . . and I shall take the second," volunteered Colette. "But you will have to excuse my father from such duties . . . he's not up to it, I'm afraid."

"But my dear . . ." the elder du Kane began. Colette kissed him perfunctorily on the forehead.

"Hush, old man. Lean on me."

"But your mother would think—"

Colette's eyes grew suddenly so wild that Ethan missed a

breath. She looked about to scream, but instead her voice came out under airtight control—barely.

"Don't mention that woman to me now," she snapped out. "But—"

"Don't!" There was more than just a hint of warning in that voice. Ethan thought about putting a subtle question to her, took another look at those penetrating green orbs, and decided against butting in. Mind your own business, stupid! He rolled over twice, facing the fire.

It seemed he'd only just put his head down after concluding his two-hour watch when he was suddenly awakened. He was facing the fire a half-meter away. For a moment something very primitive deep inside him was badly startled. It did wake him quickly, though. He rolled over and found himself almost nose to nose with Williams.

The schoolteacher held fingers to lips. Ethan sat up slowly and stifled his questions. Across the glow of the fire he could see Colette du Kane. Her expression chased the rest of the sleep from his eyes. She was chewing on one set of knuckles. Her father was kneeling tensely next to her, an arm around her shoulders.

The Hephaestean form of Skua September, outlined by the fire, stood to one side. He was staring intently at the door. The remaining beamer was clutched tightly in his right fist. It hadn't grown much colder inside, thanks to the fire, but you could feel the alien darkness pressing close on all sides.

Ethan was aware of something new and unpleasant in the tiny cabin. Humans are not as adept as their dogs at smelling fear, but they can recognize it in each other.

"It was during Mr. du Kane's shift," the teacher whispered softly. "He woke Mr. September, who thought it best to rouse the rest of us." Ethan turned just enough to see Walther sitting alertly in his corner, hands twitching uncontrollably.

"It seems Mr. du Kane thought he heard something moving around outside," Williams continued. "And while he confesses to a lack of knowledge of the local life, he doesn't believe it's one of your natives. He cannot be certain, of course."

At that point, as abrupt as ship ignition, there was a ringing bong as of something heavy striking metal. It came from outside. September dropped into a crouch. Back in his corner, Walther giggled unnervingly. September hissed for him to shut up or he'd get his neck broken.

Ethan could make out a distant scuffling and rattling. It sounded a thousand miles off. Unfortunately, that was not likely. In addition, above the wind, he distinctly heard a low moaning sound. It was like the noise people make when waking suddenly from a bad dream. It went off and on, off and on, like an idling engine. Very deep it was. Occasionally it was broken by a bass cough.

There was a loud thunk. Then uninterrupted silence. The big man hadn't moved, hadn't shifted. Ethan watched him.

September stayed in his crouch, straining for sounds of the unimaginable.

The wind continued to carry its load of lonesome song— a lowing, an unceasing monophony that drew a cold white chalk line down Ethan's spine. Already he was half believing there was nothing outside but wind whistling through torn metal. It might be a loose couch bouncing around in the ruined hull.

He crawled slowly over to the door. Putting an ear near the open crack, he ignored the wind that bit at him. He was careful not to touch the metal, though. By now even the inside of the door was quartz-cold. Skin would stick to it.

He looked back at September and shook his head to indicate he couldn't hear anything new. September nodded once. The hand holding the beamer remained steady.

Ethan thought he could hear a thudding sound outside, realized it was his own heart. He felt very out of place here. This was all silly, of course. If there had been anything out there it had gotten tired of snuffling around and wandered off. Though it was not pleasant to consider what could be moving around in this midnight Ragnarok.

He started to stand, straightening his half-frozen knees and wondering if the joints would stiffen solid before he made it. He desperately wanted to get back close to the fire. Slowly, easily, he came up to the level of the window. He peered out.

The porous hull admitted enough of the light from the

planet's single moon to bathe the ruined interior in ghost-light. A little more new snow had seeped in, burying a few other human symbols and gestures under virgin white. The wind had apparently carried off more of the left side of the boat's wall and roof. That was no surprise. It was amazing that the rest of it had held together at all in this gale.

He turned to the others, let out an unconscious sigh.

"It's okay. If there was anything out there, it's gone now." Tension melted, slipped out of the cabin. It wouldn't be hard getting back to sleep, no. He turned back to the glassite port for a last glance outside.

He found himself staring into an unmoving blood-red eye not quite the size of a dinner plate. A vicious little inkblot of a pupil swam in its center.

He was too shocked to faint. But he was frozen speechless to the spot. Cold had nothing to do with it.

The horrible moaning came again, faster now, excited. The eye moved. Something hit the door like a two-ton truck. The hinges bent in alarmingly and he stumbled backward a few steps. A triangular pattern appeared in the tough glassite.

Dimly he heard someone screaming. It might have been Colette, it might have been Walther. Or maybe both. He was hit from the side and shoved out of the way. September. The big man had a look through the bent door at whatever was outside and it made even him flinch away. He shoved the beamer through the gap, pulled the trigger.

Nothing happened.

The door was struck again and September was jolted back, cursing at the startling rate of three curses per step. They'd been carefully hoarding a dead beamer.

A loud, nervous rasping came from both sides of the dangerously bent door, a monstrous scratching and pawing. The door took another blow. This time the top hinge snapped off like plastic and the upper half of the metal was folded inward. Ethan was lying on his back and had a fine view through the new opening.

What he saw was a big rectangular head. Two horrible red eyes, like wild lanterns, stared straight at him. A mouth not quite as big as an earth-mover filled with what looked like a couple of thousand long, needle-like teeth gaped open. The teeth grew in all directions, like a jumble of jackstraws.

It either saw him or scented him. The huge skull plunged downward. It pushed, and jammed halfway into the fresh opening. He could have reached up and touched one of those gnarled fangs. It was close enough for him to smell its breath —cloves and old lemon.

Metal groaned in protest as the thing twisted and pushed against the doubled door like a starving dog, moaning wantonly. Off to one side he saw September edging right up next to the door. He jumped across, threw something in the monster's searchlight eyes, and ducked just as the steam-shovel head snapped at him. The teeth clashed like a gong just above flying white hair.

It blinked, and there was the most awful bellowing scream imaginable. The head disappeared with astounding speed. As it thrashed about in the ruined hull it shook the entire boat. Ethan was hard-pressed to keep from being tumbled into the fire.

Then, all at once, it was quiet again.

September was trying to force the strained door back into place. The weakened bracing gave a little, but a gaping hole remained. He picked up a large chunk of torn couch padding and stuffed it into the gap, jamming it down into the cracks on either side. It stayed.

"Somebody open some coffee. None of us are going back to sleep right away anyhow, I think." September shoved a great fist down into the padding. "I could use a mug. Woe that it's but the juice of the brown bean and not something stronger."

"Lord!" panted Williams. It was the first time Ethan had seen the schoolteacher excited about anything. But only a robot could sit through what they'd just experienced without missing a heartbeat or two. "What was it?"

Surprisingly, Ethan found himself answering, after the first choke on his coffee.

"The section on fauna comes back to me now. That was a nocturnal carnivore. The natives consider it quite dangerous . . ."

"Do tell," commented September. He was still wrestling with the padding and the door. "No single critter has a right to that many teeth . . . Damn this wind!"

"It's called a Droom," Ethan added, turning. Then he noticed that Colette was still sitting close to her father . . . and damned if she wasn't shivering a little. She looked frightened, too. Of course she would be—anyone would be—but it was so unlike her.

She noticed his gaze. Defiantly, she sat straight and let the old man's arms slip away. He didn't protest. She tried to turn that overwhelming glare on him but it wasn't there this time, and she looked away awkwardly.

"I suppose you think I was frightened of that thing."

"Well, that's okay," began Ethan. "Nothing to be ash—"

"Well I wasn't!" she shouted. Then she grew quiet again. "It's just . . . I'm not afraid of anything real, anything tangible. But since I was small, I've . . . I've always been afraid of the dark."

"It's her mother, you see—" du Kane started to explain, but she cut him off.

"Be quiet, father . . . and get some sleep. I've got thinking to do."

Ethan rolled over and stared at a place on the floor that sent the firelight back into his eyes. He thought, too.

The wind had dropped some but still blew steadily from the west. The sun had been up for a couple of hours already, though Ethan thought anything that put out so little decent heat unworthy of the name. He took his own good time getting up. After all, there was no great hurry. His first appointment wasn't for half a day, yet.

In an attempt to conserve their rapidly dwindling supply of wood, the fire had been allowed to pass on to wherever it is dead fires go. Williams was industriously arranging twigs, needles, and dried lichen-substitute for the evening blaze. The du Kanes were devouring a breakfast of hot cereal without either making a demand for eggs Benedict. Colette, he noticed, was apparently on her third helping. He sighed for lost dreams.

He got off his elbows, sat up, and trapped knees to chest.

"Morning, schoolteacher. Where's our beastmaster?"

"Gone outside again. His tolerance for this weather is absolutely amazing, don't you think?" He reached across the ready pyre, tossed a cylindrical package back at Ethan. "He told me he doesn't sleep much. Wastes time."

"Huh." Ethan grunted, started to tear at the top of the package. At the last moment he noticed that the red arrow on its side was pointing down. Hastily he reversed the container. Sighing at his own clumsiness, he gripped the tab again and tugged.

Off came the top, activating the tiny heating element in the packaging. Sixty seconds later he was sipping the hot soup he'd almost dumped into his lap.

After finishing most of the pack, he stood up. Either he was adapting to the temperature or his nerve endings had become so numb that he was divorced now from such mundane concerns as knowing when he was frozen.

Why, it was a perfectly lovely day! Couldn't be more than, oh, fourteen or fifteen below.

He downed another swallow of the soup, which was already barely lukewarm.

"I'm going out," he announced to no one in particular, "for a breath of fresh air. It's getting positively tropic in here."

"If that's an attempt at humor," Colette began, pausing with spoon in mid-flight, "I never . . ."

But Ethan was already dogging the crumpled door shut behind him.

He flipped down his snow goggles and peered along the center aisle of the boat. He found September examining the edges of the big gap on the port side of the vessel. It was indeed larger than it had been yesterday.

Wishing he could shrink himself and go swimming in the cup of soup, he strolled over. The self-heating liquid was struggling manfully. But it was badly overmatched in this super-arctic climate. He gulped down the last.

"Good morn, Skua." He had to move closer and repeat himself before the other looked over at him.

"Hmmm? Oh, I suppose it is, since we're all still about to

see it, young feller-me-lad. What do you think of that, eh?"
He stepped away from the wall and pointed.

Ethan didn't have to look closely, nor ask for explanation,
to see what his companion was studying. The wind hadn't
made those deep, curved gouges in the duralloy. There were
six of them, spaced in groups of three. Others were visible
high up on the plating.

"At first I thought it was the wind done it," Skua said
academically. He shook his maned head. "You think we could
expect a return visit from that . . . what did you call the
thing?"

"A Droom," Ethan replied. He ran a gloved thumb along
one of the grooves in the metal. It fit snugly.

"The tapes didn't go into detail on animal life. I don't
know anything about its habits." He paused, staring at the
rough surface of the stripped wiring running through the hull
wall.

"Look, I know I wasn't much help last night. That screaming and tearing, I—" A big hand came down on his shoulder,
comfortingly.

"Now don't you waste another thought on it, me lad. Why,
that monster would've chilled the guts of many a dozen pro-
fessional soldiers I've known."

Ethan turned to face the other. "You didn't freeze, though.
Are you a soldier? Or what? We don't know much about you,
do we? We know the du Kanes, and Williams and certainly
Walther, and I've talked about myself. What *about* you?"

September shrugged, turned away and stared out across
the bleak landscape. The wind had blown away most of the
light snow. None had fallen last night, since early evening.
The endless icefield sparkled from a billion flaws, except
where red-green patches of the hearty pika-pina grew. They
were marooned on a diamond.

"Let's just say I've seen worse than that thing," he muttered
softly. "I might also tell you, though I don't know why I
should, that I'm a wanted man. On at least four planets my
head, not necessarily delivered in conjunction with the rest
of my corpus, could bring you upward of a hundred thousand
times ten credits." He turned and stared down at Ethan with
shining eyes, the thick frosted brows crashing together.

"What do you think of that?"

"Very interesting," replied Ethan levelly. "What did you do?"

"That's enough for you to know, me lad . . . for now. Maybe sometime I'll tell you more."

Ethan was a good salesman. He knew when to press for a commitment and when to change the subject. He ajudged correctly this was the right time for a change.

"What did you throw at the thing, anyway. The scream it let out was enough to chill your blood . . . if it wasn't frozen already."

"Salt," replied September, as though they'd been talking of nothing else. "From my dinner pack. There wasn't much of it left. But then I don't expect the creatures on this world have much contact with it anyway, especially in the raw state and powdered."

"I suppose they can get all they need from licking the ice," mused Ethan, "since it's frozen sea water. But try *your* tongue on it and it might never come loose. I'd have tried a brand from the fire."

"That would have come next. The salt seemed as good a bet, and safer."

"Safer?"

"Sure. Listen, me lad. There are worlds where fire is a lot rarer than it is on humanx-type planets. This would seem to be one. It's only a guess, but on similar worlds I've seen beasties charge straight for a flame and attack it. They think it's some new kind of enemy. A living creature. Saw one roll over and over with a burning log in its mouth. Clawing and chewing at it. The fire, not the log. If your Droom—"

"It's not *my* Droom," Ethan protested.

"—had reacted likewise, it might have charged even harder instead of backing off from that busted door. We won't know, because the salt worked. The fire might even have attracted it. On a world like this I'll bet plenty of animals can sense heat at a fair distance. Our fire might have put out as much as another Droom, say. Are they territorial?"

"I don't know that, either," confessed Ethan.

"Hard to leave much of a spoor on naked ice." September

pulled a now familiar red-green stem from a jacket pocket, started munching on it. Ethan could hear it crunch.

"Does taste rather like parsley. How does it grow so far out onto the ice?"

Ethan reached under the hood of his coat, rubbed his scalp. "As I remember the tape, the root system extends out to a certain distance, putting out branch roots and surface stems all the way. When it reaches that point, growth halts and the end of the main root begins to swell. Nutrients are delivered from whatever central land mass the plant is based on. In that way it builds up a good sized food-rich node at its far end.

"The plant puts out just enough heat to slowly melt its way through the ice. The new nodule acts as a springboard, or advance base, putting out new roots in several directions. If the roots from one node encounter another they grow together, whether they're from the same parent plant or not. This broadens and strengthens the network, insuring survival of the whole if a central branch is knocked out.

"There's a giant variety called pika-pedan that grows up to three and four meters high. Its nodes can grow to be several meters in diameter."

"I see." September hummed to himself a moment. "Then if we follow an outcropping of this weed, we'll eventually come to land?"

Ethan smiled. "Good thought. Trouble is, there are reports from the single Commonwealth survey of green patches growing fifteen hundred kilometers and more from the nearest body of land."

"Oh," said the other simply. He looked disappointed. "Look, I haven't had my breakfast. You?"

"Just some soup. I could do with something solid." He tossed the empty cylinder out of the boat, watched it bounce and roll across the pale surface.

"Okay, after breakfast, what do you think we ought to do, leader?"

"Well," Ethan considered, "I definitely think we shouldn't remain here." He looked at the other for confirmation, but the big man just stared back. He continued.

"We're not making any progress toward Brass Monkey by sitting here. A really first-class blow could send this whole boat spinning. I think the first thing we should do is look for some more substantial shelter. Maybe a cave on a big island. You circled this one the other day?" September nodded.

"As I said then, it's not very big. Certainly saw nothing we could use as shelter, unless we dig our own. Given the likely consistency of this frozen earth, I wouldn't care to try."

"Swell. After you eat, then, I think if you'd climb—"

"Climb? Uh-uh, not me."

"All right. *One* of us ought to climb the tallest tree on the island and get a good look around. Maybe we'll see something."

"Like an ice-cream stand?"

September guffawed, slapped Ethan on the back. "A good thought, young feller-me-lad. But first I'd better get about putting something substantial in my belly. Otherwise I won't have the strength to watch you fall."

"Even if we should spot another body of land," asked Colette du Kane, "how do you propose reaching it?" September worked on his oatmeal while he considered her question.

"You said yourself that walking on this ice is damned tough even with makeshift aids," she continued doggedly. "Since there's nothing within easy walking distance, any trek we try will measure in the kilometers. This may be swell for you, but I'm not built for cross-country hiking. And father would never make it."

Du Kane started to protest, but she raised a hand and smiled.

"No, father. I know you're willing, but corporate directorship doesn't inure one to much physical hardship."

"Something more corporate directors should note," said September, putting down the empty container.

"Despite what you may think, young lady, I don't relish trying such a hike myself. We'll have to try and rig up some kind of sled. Maybe we can break loose a torn section of hull. If we could sharpen some long branches to a good point, maybe tip 'em with metal, we might kind of pole our way along. Be slow and ugly, but better than walking. Not exactly the Intercity Central on Hivehom, but we ought to be able to take along most of our supplies."

"The weather would have to hold," said Colette thoughtfully. "I don't know if I could take another night like the last, and out on the bare ice."

September looked troubled. "I've no way of knowing that myself, Miss du Kane. It's not a pretty thought. And if another of those snaggle-toothed nightmares happened onto us, why, we'd be just so many cold hors d'oeuvres.

"One thing's for sure, though. We wouldn't be any worse off than we are in sitting here. And at least we'll be making some sort of progress toward the settlement."

"But what if someone should send over a rescue shuttle?" put in du Kane plaintively.

Ethan surprised himself by answering.

"It's most unlikely anyone would think to search the surface for survivors, sir. If they did, they'd have the whole planet to choose from. Not much chance of picking us out against this ice, us with no power, nothing casting. But if by some wild chance someone did come looking for us and did find the wreck, they'll assume we've started off toward Brass Monkey. They'll trace us back along the most likely routes. We can leave signs. At least we know it's somewhere to the west."

Well, he said to himself, a bit startled, you've just articulated your own probable demise, Mr. Fortune. Rather a sad end for the fair-haired young sales genius of Malaika Enterprises, hmmm? That's right, go ahead and shiver. Tell yourself it's the cold.

"Like it or not, we're on our own, as the young fella says," September added.

Ethan heard himself speaking again. "There is one other possibility, of course." Even September looked startled.

"His people might decide to come looking for us." From his corner Walther glared back at him.

"Not a chance," the little kidnapper spat. "They're not that imaginative. We're as good as dead right now. All thanks to *him*." He looked at September with bitter hatred.

"There's enough rough metal around," the big man replied easily. "You can cut your throat any time you want to."

"Or yours, maybe?"

September just smiled slightly. "You're welcome to try, any hour of any day you choose. One way or the other, it would be a solution of sorts for you, wouldn't it?

"Right now, though," he said briskly to them all, "I think we should all take a little stroll around the chunk of dirt we've run up against. It's not very big, but it's home. For another day, at least. Besides, most of you haven't been outside. It's time you started getting used to the kind of country you'll be spending a long, long time with."

There were no arguments, not even from Colette. It was Ethan who noticed the obvious problem.

"Wait a minute. We only have four sets of ice goggles."

It was true. Both Williams and the kidnapper were without the vital pair of protective lenses.

The teacher, however, had his own solution.

"I don't need them, Mr. Fortune. That's why I gave mine to you." He dug under his coat, showed Ethan a tiny black case. Carefully shielding it from the steady breeze that blew in past the bent door, he crouched over. When he stood again, he was squinting.

"I wear protoid optical contacts." He put the case away. "The ones I'm wearing now are high-glare configuration. They're supposed to be used for intensity sunbathing. I don't expect to be doing much of that, but they should do for outside, if not as well as the goggles. I'll manage. They're more comfortable, anyhow."

Despite his small stature and soft look, Ethan had to admit that the little teacher certainly sounded competent. He expected they'd have to count on him as a third man if the going got really tough.

Just as he would be depending more and more on September. On a wanted man. Very wanted, by his own description.

Well, time enough for that later, if there was a later. He put a hand on the door latch.

A voice piped nervously from the back.

"Hey, what about me?"

"You're coming too," September growled. "I don't trust you by yourself with the food or the wood. Not til I'm a lot surer of your mental balance."

"But I haven't got any goggles or special glasses," Walther pointed out pleadingly. Clearly he knew what would happen to his eyes under outside conditions.

"A couple of days unprotected and I'll be blind as a cave cricket! A week or two and it becomes permanent." Despite the cold, he was sweating.

"Tear some cloth from your shirt or underwear," September suggested, "and tie it around your head. Use thin dark stuff to cover your eyes. And keep 'em closed as much as possible. You won't see much, but you won't go blind, either. Damn sure you won't try anything."

"I'll freeze, too," Walther persisted. "I haven't got a survival coat or double set of clothing like you."

"Too bad. When we get the sled put together, we'll do what we can to keep you out of the wind. I wouldn't expect you to do any honest work anyway. Personally, you can stay with the boat and freeze to death, if you prefer. But if you're coming with the rest of us, you're coming outside, now."

The kidnapper gave a little moan and unbuttoned his jacket. Shivering, he began fumbling with the material of a shirt sleeve.

Ethan found himself feeling sorry for the man. It was not reasonable, considering what the fellow had done to them, or planned for them. Nonetheless, it was soothing to his own conscience.

"Wait a minute. Before you start ripping up your clothes, look around in the cabin for a large piece or two of loose padding from the couches. There seems to be plenty lying around. Also loose hull insulation. Try stuffing it between your jacket and shirt. It'll be clumsy, but it might keep you warm."

"Thanks. Really, thanks," Walther beamed, closing his jacket. "It might at that."

"Why bother with him?" asked September casually. "Why not let him freeze?"

"Have you ever listened to a man slowly freezing to death?" countered Ethan.

September started to say something, halted, looked strangely at him and turned away. If pressed, Ethan would have had to confess that he'd never seen a man freeze, either.

"Have it your way, me lad. Williams, keep an eye on him and make sure torn padding is the only thing he picks up. The rest of us will hike."

If anything, the little island proved to be even smaller than September had implied. Mostly rocks and frozen soil, it didn't look rich enough to support a bachelor toadstool. Not to mention ground cover, bushes, and fair-sized trees. But they were there. A couple of the scruffy bushes even supported an iron-red fruit that resembled a cross between raspberries and stringbeans.

Ethan considered the fruit, but the parent plant was a blank in his stored memory. He pulled one fruit loose and shoved it in a loose pocket for later consideration. It looked edible, which meant absolutely nothing. It might contain concentrated nitric acid for all he could tell.

There was also animal life on the island, the first they'd seen besides the Droom. Especially little balls of dark fur with bright pink eyes and short, stubby legs. They popped in and out of gopher-sized holes with startling speed.

And once while September was inspecting a particular tree, a pair of creatures like bats wearing mink coats swooped and darted at him. It was all bluff but he moved away. Whatever they were, they probably had a nest somewhere in the upper branches. They continued to insult him from a safe distance.

Ethan tried to imagine what kind of nest arboreals could build that would withstand a good blow on this world. Say, a 200 kph gale straight off the ice. He failed, turned to examine a blanket of thick red moss that grew in the shelter of a rock clump.

Hellespont du Kane was studying the same growth. "You know," Ethan said to him, "there's a lot of red in the pikapina . . . and now this stuff, it's almost crimson."

"Beautiful, isn't it?" said du Kane. The old man was obviously enraptured. To Ethan it was only an alien fungus. The old man leaned close. "You know, I raise flowers. Oh yes! Considered quite an expert in some circles." Then something seemed to go *click* again behind those eyes and the voice turned mercenary. "It might mean there's a lot of iron or manganese on this world."

"I don't know," Ethan replied, trying to separate flowers

from ore. "The tapes didn't say much about internal geology."

"Ah well, an interesting supposition," said du Kane. He stooped to examine the greasy-looking plant more closely. "I wonder if it's as soft as it looks. Many plants concentrate interesting minerals in their substance in commercial quantities."

He stuck a finger into the middle of one patch, pushed . . . and jumped away with such surprising speed that Ethan jumped himself.

September and Colette must have heard the little screech du Kane gave, because they were there seconds later.

"Father . . . what happened? Are you all right?"

Since du Kane was sitting on the ground, gritting his teeth in obvious pain and holding his wrist, Ethan was tempted to offer some suitable comments on female semantic brilliance. At the moment, though, he was too concerned with the older man's welfare.

"He stuck his finger in that bed of moss . . . or whatever it is," Ethan replied.

"Felt like acid," said the industrialist tightly. "It hurts rather intensely." *Click.* "Colette?"

"I'm here, father," she said evenly.

"Can you make it back to the boat?" September asked. Du Kane stood, still holding his wrist, and began edging the glove down.

"Boat? Yes, I believe so. I'm not dizzy or anything. It just pains."

"It was a foolish thing to do, father," scolded Colette.

"Now, look," said Ethan, "it looks harmless enough, and your father had no idea it might be lethal."

"And you had no idea, period," she said, slipping an arm around the old man. Ethan started to object. After all, it wasn't described on any of his tapes. Might even be an unknown species. But she wasn't interested.

"Let's just hope it isn't toxic," she said quietly.

Du Kane was controlling himself with an effort. Ethan wondered about the oldster's on-again-off-again moments. One second he was a tower of power, steel-haired duralloy-spined master of a hundred industries. The next, he was a half-senile old man desperately hungering for approval and protection. Which was real, which was sham? Probably only Colette knew the answer to that one—and she wasn't volunteering any information.

"No way to tell," said September, jarring Ethan's thoughts back to the problem at hand. "It might be no worse than a bad bee sting. On the other hand, you could keel over for good in the next minute. But I doubt it. Rich folk only die from overworking or overeating." Colette threw him a furious look, but du Kane came close to smiling.

"Animals and plants that live in cold climates rarely carry poison. When they do it's usually nowhere near as powerful as that toted by their tropical counterparts. And this is a completely alien ecosystem. It might be instantly fatal to other plants and animals and harmless to us. Or vice-versa. That's enough talk, now. Get back to the boat and put something on it. To kill the pain, at least."

Father and daughter started slowly back toward the wreck. Ethan watched them go.

"You really think he'll be okay?"

"Yep. It does look a little like a mild acid burn. Can't be certain. Know better tomorrow. But it's a damned good thing he had that glove *on*.

"And now I think it's about time you climbed that tree."

"I'll try," sighed Ethan. "I'm not much for this kind of athletics. Now, tennis or poef or golf—"

"Do you good, young feller-me-lad. Besides, if the branches get dense near the top, you can slip through them a lot easier than I could. And you can go higher, as well."

Ethan refrained from pointing out that September could snap off the branches that Ethan would have to dodge.

They found the highest spot on the island by the simple expedient of walking uphill until they were going down. From there they circled a couple of meters to a likely-looking tree. One leg went to the trunk's right side and Ethan prepared to scramble to the lowest branch. He needn't have bothered. The shove September gave him sent him flying into the lower branches.

After catching his breath and soothing a slightly scraped left hand, he started up. The branches grew very close together and made for easy climbing. The tree topped out at perhaps twenty meters. Trunk and stubby branches alike were thick and covered with a dense bark, to conserve heat and withstand the hurricane-force winds that swept the tiny islet.

Ethan was able to scramble within a meter of the crown, which swayed slightly in the steady wind. In fact, the wind had not ceased howling since their initial setdown.

From the top he was a good thirty meters above the ice, perhaps more. He looked down to his left. From this vantage point he had an excellent view of the crumpled lifeboat and the arrow-straight skid marks in the ice that extended unbroken to the horizon.

Off to his right, he thought he could make out in the distance a greenish tinge to the ice. More pika-pina, or maybe its giant relative, pika-pedan. Further off, there were one or two bumps on the horizon that might be large islands. Unfortunately, they lay due east. Not that they wouldn't head for them if they proved to be the only land in sight, but he'd prefer to move in the direction of civilization.

He turned, keeping a firm grip, and was gratified to see what looked like similar bulges off to the west. They appeared to be just as large—if indeed there was actually something there besides a mirage or a figment of his wind-chilled sight. It was harder to see on this side because he was looking directly into the wind. While the tree remained thankfully solid, the ice goggles expressed a perverse tendency to shift position under the shield on his face. He reached around and fumbled with the strap, managed to tighten them a little.

He squinted harder.

On the ice between their island and those distant humps, he thought he could see a dozen or so dark spots on the ice. They weren't pika-pina, because they seemed to be moving.

September's voice floated up to him. "See anything, lad?" The wind made it sound farther away than it was. He turned out of the breeze and yelled downward.

"I'm not sure! Maybe a pack of animals. Then again, we might be due for an invitation to a feast."

"Okay!" A wide grin split the shrunken upturned face. "Let's hope we're offered a menu and not put on one."

Ethan had another look at the distant dots. He assured himself that they were really moving toward the island before beginning to pick his way down the ice-hard trunk.

Little clouds of frozen breath, the two men jogged their way down to the boat. Williams and the others were waiting for them. The schoolmaster helped September close the compartment door behind them.

Ethan saw that Walther's jacket and pants were full of awkward bulges. It gave him a falsely gnomish appearance. His head was swathed in torn cloth and black eyes peered out through a small slit. It wasn't pretty and couldn't have been very comfortable, but maybe it was warm. And the kidnapper was in no position to quibble about fashion.

"How's that finger?" September asked Colette about her father's injury.

"We put some anesthetic cream on it," she told them. "It seems to have brought the swelling down. The pain is still there, but it's not as severe."

"Beautiful creature," breathed du Kane. "Fascinating defense mechanism. Or it might be offensive. We pulled several dozen tiny stingers out of the tip of the glove. I'd very much dislike to step on it barefoot."

"A lot like the terran jellyfish," added Williams.

"Speaking of stingers," offered Ethan as casually as he could, "I think we're due for a visit from the local welcoming committee." Would *that* shake her up?

"About time," she grumbled. "Damned inefficient."

"Might be a hunting party," September added cheerfully.

"Natives!" blurted Williams excitedly. "How marvelous! I must try to note as much as possible. My students will be fascinated." He seemed utterly oblivious to the fact that he might be some other student's main course before the day was out.

"Do you think they'll be friendly?" asked du Kane hesitantly.

"Not much we can do if they're not," said Colette coldly.

"Might even be cannibals," added September, apparently determined to lighten the atmosphere. "Lad, you've had the tapes, you do the talkin'. I'll stand to your right and try to look friendly. Williams, you take his left, since you had a tape too."

"If the dialect isn't too thick, I should be able to understand them pretty good, too," piped Walther.

"I assumed that," September replied. "You stay in the back and keep your mouth shut."

"I couldn't try anything," said the little man, hurt. "You all understand as much as I."

"It's not your language that worries me, it's your ravishing appearance. It's sufficiently distorted to frighten even a well-balanced primitive. I'd rather show a little surface symmetry until we know them better. They might be skittish. We can't take a chance on frightening away potential help."

Walther grumbled but couldn't find an argument to counter with.

September turned to the du Kanes. "With all due respect, neither of you understands the language. So you stay behind us, too." That seemed to suit the two cosmopolitan travelers quite well.

"Everyone knows his or her place, then? Good!" He turned to Ethan. "All right, young feller-me-lad, it's yours."

Ethan put a hand on the door latch, spoke to September.

"Know any good opening lines for interspecies contact? They've probably never seen a human being before."

"No but hum a few bars and I'll wing it." He chuckled, shoved. "Now get going."

Fortunately Ethan had already opened the door. The shove might have sent him through it.

IV

Sir Hunnar Redbeard squinted hard, but they were still too far away to make out the number of figures standing next to the mass of odd shaping. It truly seemed to be made of metal.

When Eer-Meesach had come running into the Great Hall babbling his hysterical tale of a fiery thing of metal falling from the sky, Hunnar had been one of the skeptical ones.

The wizard had insisted that his telescope told him the outside of the thing was at least coated with solid metal that shone like a dancer's tiara. And on top of that, he'd insisted he'd seen two creatures emerge from the metal and walk onto the island.

Now he could see it for himself and he momentarily forgot about the creatures. So much metal! If it were as good as steel it would be a valuable prize indeed. They would need every scrap they could gather if the Longax's plan to contest the Horde were to pass in Council.

It would be crucial to deal correctly with the strange beings. It would also be nice merely to chivan up and lop off a few heads. But not necessarily practical. For one thing, Eer-Meesach would never forgive him. Hunnar made a Sign. He didn't want his bed turned into a rollicking Gutorrbyn in the midst of a mating.

Also, any beings who could make that much metal stay up in the sky might be able to do unpleasant things to a person. No doubt they knew the value of their metal.

One thought had troubled him all the way out from Wannome. Could they be gods? Gray-maned, omnipotent, immortal gods? It could not yet be ruled out.

However, the wizard's description of the way in which their craft had descended implied lack of control by infallible immortals. Rather it sounded more like cubs caught on a runaway sled.

But he would reserve his final judgment until after viewing. That would please his teachers.

But so much metal!

He stared at the fallen thing. One fact seemed certain. Whatever they were, their eyesight seemed as good as his own. A group of them appeared to be assembling just outside the ship—he'd reluctantly come to consider it a vessel of sorts. They were standing on the edge of the island. This in itself was an odd thing to do. But by voluntarily restricting themselves to land, they might be making a friendly gesture. Hunnar had the right idea but the wrong reason.

He grinned ferociously. It might mean that these strangers were afraid to do battle with him. Otherwise they would have come out to meet him.

There were five . . . no, six of the beings. It looked like only one was built along warrior lines. Better and better.

"Suaxus!" he shouted to his first lieutenant, "break left! Vasen, Smjör, with him!" He turned, eating air. "Budjir, break right with Avyeh and Hivell!"

The nine tran immediately split into three groups. They would make a three-pronged approach. Not only was it a sensible precaution, it should also impress their visitors. He'd given Suaxus the left and slightly less wind. The squire was impatient and something of a problem, but basically one of the soundest in training.

And you, Hunnar? Whose grandfather are you, eh? Maturity, he reminded himself, was not necessarily a function of age.

He signaled. On one side of the arrowhead formation, three tran abruptly dropped their left arms. The tough membrane that stretched from wrist to hip folded and the three soldiers leaned slightly to the left. The wind pushed hard and steady into the right wing as three sets of claw-blades dug hard into the ice. The squire and two soldiers made a neat sixty-degree turn to port. Budjir and his men duplicated the maneuver to starboard.

They were getting close already and Hunnar wondered if he'd delayed too long.

"Hafel down!" he ordered his companions. They all lowered their arms and cut speed. It wouldn't do for them to reach their objective in advance of their flanking companions. Certainly Eer-Meesach and possibly the Landgrave himself were watching from the wizard's tower. This was no time for sloppiness.

"And be careful when you brake!" he added. Greeting their visitors with a shower of sharp ice-chips would not be facile diplomacy either.

His lance felt light in his right paw. They were almost on top of the strangers, who'd made nothing resembling a hostile move. They were pink-faced and seemed a surprisingly light color, except for one who was a dark brown. While their color varied from individual to individual, by and large it was like that of a fresh-born cub.

He saw Suaxus approaching rapidly from the left and let out his own wings a little more. Budjir would notice the speed-up and match pace perfectly. Looking ahead to the strangers, Hunnar could not make out a single sword, axe, lance, even a knife. Of course, he reminded himself, there could be fifty others armed to the teeth hiding within the metal bottle.

Still, if they wanted to fight they'd have to move from land to ice, and Hunnar had both wind and sun behind him. Let them try something! These first six, at least, would go down like a herd of mewing hoppers.

Be careful, idiot! You're not thinking diplomatically again. Then the time for daydreaming was past.

"Up lances!" he commanded loudly, "and brake in!"

Suaxus and Budjir arrived almost simultaneously. Neatly done, he complimented himself. Anyone in the castle observing the maneuver couldn't be anything but pleased.

Hunnar and his men raised their weapons to the perpendicular, turned slightly left, and dug in. Torn free by the sharp claws of the tran soldiers, a shower of ice fragments flew in a glittering cascade to the left. They missed the aliens completely. A couple of them flinched, but the ones in front held proper ground.

One in the rear, however, did utter a short, high-pitched sound. It sounded a little like a yip of uncertainty to Hunnar.

But for all he knew of these odd folk it could have been laughter. The same being had immediately clutched tight to another. Mates, he decided. Another good sign. As yet it was difficult to tell male from female.

It might be impossible to tell without a dissection. There you go again, he cautioned himself. If only this had happened a year ago, his mind would move more easily.

Well, if there were more of the odd creatures concealed in the metal ship, then these were excellent bluffers. Not a one had thrown a look in that direction. With one exception, these all appeared badly undernourished. None of them were children, either. No, they were not that short, but they *were* dreadfully thin. And much of that seemed to be clothing.

For their part the little knot of humans was suitably impressed by Sir Hunnar himself. But then, the knight was an impressive specimen even among his own people. He stood as tall as September and was nearly twice as broad. Great thick arms ended in hands with three fingers and thumb. These supported folded membranous wings between wrist and hip.

The feet were short, with thick, elongated toes. Each of the three toes held a greatly stretched single claw that narrowed to a sharp blade at the base, forming a kind of triple skate on each foot. The fourth toe was short and had shifted around to the back of the heel. It sported a squat, stubby point that served as a brake when dug into the ice.

While traveling toward the lifeboat, the tran had presented a shorter appearance. This because they moved in a crouch, offering less surface in proportion to wing area. It also helped to maintain balance in the tricky winds.

The barrel-chested torso was covered with short, soft fur. Each soldier wore a thick coat of rich, umber fur from the hessavar. This was cinched at the waist by a belt of hammered gold disks and tooled leather. A short, double-bladed sword was strapped securely to Hunnar's left leg. An evil-looking dirk rode on his right hip.

A necklace of ugly saw-edged teeth from the krokim fell from the thick neck onto the coat. The hood closely resembled the hoods of their own survival parkas, with the exception of twin slits made to admit the furry, triangular ears. A strap ran around the front edge of the hood and tied beneath the chin to keep the wind from pulling it off the wearer's head.

The face that stared down at them was uncompromisingly feline, with slitted eyes of bright yellow. The pupils were a startling deep-space black. A broad flat nose, high brow, and wide mouth filled with flat and pointed teeth completed the portrait. The tran were omnivorous.

Body fur was steel-gray, a couple of the soldiers sporting patches of black over the muzzle and at the tips of the ears. One other besides Hunnar possessed a short beard. Hunnar's beard and facial fur were distinctive in their rust-tinge, almost ochre.

"Say something to 'em, young feller," whispered September out of the side of his mouth.

Ethan hurriedly tried to assemble a proper opening sentence, dropping verbs into place, shoring up uncertainties with the right pronouns.

"We are a . . . uh . . . caravan that has lost its sails," he began. "The wind blew us false and we travel now on the breath of mercy." He took two careful steps onto the ice—this was no time for a pratfall—and stood on tiptoe. Then he took a deep breath and exhaled right into the native's face, praying all the while that none of the germs in his body could effect this mountain of fur in front of him.

Everyone remained motionless for a moment. Then the ferocious-looking primitive relaxed his mouth into a wide grin —without showing his teeth. He leaned over and breathed a fog of frozen air back into Ethan's face.

"My breath is your warmth," he said, not with a little relief himself. At least these strangers were civilized. Tactical advantage or no, he was gratified that a fight didn't seem in the offing.

"Put up your lances," he instructed the others. "They appear to be friendly." The last wasn't really necessary. They'd all heard Ethan's little speech and observed the greeting.

"We are very trusting today," Suaxus grumbled, but mostly to himself. He did not relax.

The tran eased, retracting their blades almost entirely. At that point Ethan almost made a fatal mistake.

"Would you like to go inside our ship," he offered smoothly, "and get out of this infernal wind?"

Hunnar jerked back and two of his men reached for their swords. He wished he could read the alien's expression.

"Why?" Hunnar asked tightly, his palm itching for his own weapon. "Why would we want to get out of the wind?" he prompted, since the other seemed dumbstruck by their reaction.

"I think I understand," said Ethan finally. "Where we come from, up there," and he pointed skyward, "our world is much warmer than this. Your unending hurricane is hard on us. I didn't think you'd regard it otherwise. Honest, that's all I thought." The soldiers relaxed again. Hunnar didn't bother to correct the alien's reasoning. Leaving ice and wind would take away their small tactical advantage. But it seemed the other was truly ignorant of this.

"I accept your words," he said, "but find some of them hard to believe. This is a very pleasant summer day. One could even travel comfortably coatless. But in truth, I would like to see the inside of your vessel."

He'd put that awfully crudely, after his initial reaction. But that was one of their prime objectives. He was a knight and not a herald, dammit.

"It would make things easier for us," Ethan replied. "Of course you may."

September clambered into the windswept boat, leaned out and gave Ethan a hand up.

"I caught most of that," he said softly. "Why did that line about 'getting out of the wind' put them on guard at first?"

"I don't know," Ethan answered, struggling for a foothold. He got in, turned to help Williams.

"No, wait, I think I do know. Obviously this is a bunch of local troops, or militia, or whatever. Once out of the wind they must sacrifice a great deal of maneuverability. The way they can move on that ice! Did you notice that none of them came up onto the island?"

"That's true," September agreed. "A large scale battle on

this world must combine the actions of infantry with old-time sailing ships. Fascinating!"

"I've no desire to see even two of them angry," Ethan countered. "Look at their size. Better not to provoke them."

"Might be different than you think, lad." The humans were aboard and now the tran were making their cautious way up. "I noticed something a mite intriguing myself."

"Do tell," asked Ethan, watching Hunnar. Watching the way his eyes tried to drink in every detail of the ruined boat.

"Well, their weight should have driven those claws of theirs a lot deeper into the ice than it does. They may be the greatest muscular specimens since the Pitar, but I'll wager a platinum doubloon that their bones are light. Maybe even partly hollow, like birds. I'm sure they're much lighter than they look.

"You, young feller-me-lad, may be only half as big as one of those blokes. But you might come out ahead in a shoving match."

"I've no desire to test that theory," Ethan replied feelingly, "not even by friendly arm-wrestling."

While Hunnar wasn't in the wizard's class when it came to rapid cogitation, even a ten-year cub could tell that this amazing vessel was in no condition to fly anyplace. The great open holes in roof and sides, the shredded acceleration couches and twisted fixture mountings; everything indicated the vessel had not set down as its designers had intended.

He also noticed the instantly recognizable scratch marks on one wall and the roof of the boat and looked at the aliens with new respect.

"You had an encounter with a Droom."

"I'm afraid we did," said Ethan. "Scared the crap out of us."

Candid, too, Hunnar filed away mentally.

Of course, no true warrior would confess to fright in a battle situation—even when confronted by a Droom. If they'd been attacked by a rampaging stavanzer, now! But that was a special case. Why, even he might . . .

"Your vehicle," he began innocently, "seems to have incurred some damage. I myself, since I did not witness your arrival, find it hard to believe that this much metal (keep the envy from your tones, knight!) truly descended from the sky." Then he couldn't keep the awe out of his voice. "Is it really a flying machine?"

"It is," answered Ethan. "We came from a ship many hundreds of times larger than this one." Hunnar couldn't repress a little start at that.

"It was bringing us to this world from another, where live some of our number, and thence to others. We paused in the . . . above the air of your world, when a small disaster overtook us. We were forced to flee our ship in this tiny lifeboat. A second misfortune befell us and we were unable to land properly. One of our number," he added by way of afterthought, "was killed in the landing."

"My sorrowings," said Hunnar politely. Of course, he didn't believe this creature's fantastic story. Other worlds, indeed! Every child who'd studied with a Knowledgable One knew that Tran-ky-ky was the only world in this star system that could harbor life. No, they must be a stunted, nearly hairless variety of tran from the far side of the globe. Ethan's next words tended to support this assumption.

"There is a small settlement of our people many . . . many satch to the west of here. That is where we were trying to land when our craft went out of control. If you could aid us in getting there, our ancestors would dance your praises through eternity."

"How many satch?" inquired Hunnar, not impressed by the flattery.

Ethan did some furious figuring in his head, utilizing their last beacon reading and September's guesswork.

"Eight or nine thousand, I think."

One of the soldiers made a muffled whining sound. Hunnar glared at him. But he was hard put to keep from smiling himself. Eight or nine thousand satch. Just a quick chivan around the province and back.

"Such matters are best discussed with the Landgrave," he replied smoothly.

"The Landgrave?"

"Yes. At the great castle of Wannome. You will meet him —and the Council—when we arrive."

"That suits us," September said, speaking for the first time. "And I think, laddie, it's time we all introduced ourselves."

"Agreed," said Hunnar. "I hight Sir Hunnar Redbeard, son of Stömsbruk Redbeard's Son, grand-grandson of Dugai the Wild. My squires, Suaxus-dal-Jagger"—a tall, slimmer soldier stepped forward stiffly—"and Budjir Hotahg. His Landgrave's men-at-arms and truemen," and he proceeded to name the soldiers in turn, "Vasen Tersund, Smjör Tol, Avyeh-let-Otkamo, and Hivell Vuonislathi."

"I hight Ethan Fortune. This hight Skua September, Milliken Williams . . . " and he went down their little group.

"Only one calling?" Hunnar said, indicating Walther.

"A criminal, uh . . . consigned to our care," Ethan improvised hastily. "As such, he is entitled to but one."

As to the du Kanes, Hunnar was mildly discouraged to learn they were father and daughter. He'd badly misjudged ages and relationship. A small point, but it piqued him. Sire and cub, then, and not mates. That was interesting.

"Despite your greeting, friend Ethan, I must be certain you are of the true warm blood and not deviants like the hoppers. Before we can think of aiding you freely, this vital thing must be settled."

Budjir chivaned over and whispered to his leader. "What needs this, sir? They would clearly seem to be—"

"Be silent, squire. The stjorva appears as a bush, but it bites." Taken aback, Budjir growled to himself and stepped away.

"What now?" September was asking Ethan.

"I think they want to be sure we're of the same basic stock as they are. We're not, of course, but I think he's hunting for comforting similarity." He turned to the knight. "How can we prove this small thing to you, Sir Hunnar?"

The huge tran walked past Ethan and confronted Colette. She held her ground well but stared up at the carnivorous face apprehensively.

"What does this thing want?" she stuttered in Terranglo.

Ethan conversed briefly with Hunnar. September smiled.

"Our very lives are at stake," the big man rasped. "You'd better cooperate." In Trannish, he addressed Hunnar. "Be careful, the She's a mite skittish."

The knight nodded. Ethan noticed that the native's coat fastened at the shoulders with leather ties. He spoke in Terranglo to Colette.

"I think you'll have to open your parka, Colette. You'll only be cold for a minute."

"Open my . . . are you out of your *mind?* You think for one minute I'm going to let this elephantine pussycat leer at me?"

"He just wants to make certain that we're faintly mammalian," said Ethan easily. "You're our best and only convincing proof. Would you rather be barbecued?"

"Now Colette," began du Kane, "I'm not sure—"

"Very well," said Colette evenly. She began working at the snaps on her parka. Ethan noticed that the other tran soldiers were observing the operation with something more than clinical interest.

She shook a little when Hunnar put those great clawed paws on her, but otherwise she bore the brief inspection stolidly.

"Satisfied?" September asked him the moment he'd finished. Colette had turned away and was resnapping her jacket.

"Eminently." Privately he felt this only added validity to his theory that these people were merely thinner variants of his own stock with a much more advanced technology.

"You okay, Colette?" Ethan inquired in solicitous Terranglo.

"Yes, I think so." She was shaking a little and didn't even insist that he call her Miss du Kane. "I just hope these aborigines don't carry lice or fleas."

"What did the She say?" Hunnar asked.

"That she was flattered by your attention," Ethan replied smoothly.

"Umph. Well, friend Ethan, it is for the Landgrave and the Council to decide if anything can be done about your request for help in reaching your home."

"It's not our home," said Ethan, unconsciously avoiding the other's neat trap. "Just a single settlement our folk have established on your world."

"To be sure," Hunnar murmured. "In any case, the full Council should debate it." Actually, with the Horde only a malet or two away, any request for so much as a sword blade or scrap of spare sail was apt to be treated with kindly indifference at best. He didn't say that, of course. Possibly these people could be of some help. There was no point in discouraging them early.

Now, if they voluntarily agreed to contribute the wreck of their boat, that would surely be a point in their favor. A point he ought to bring up about now.

"Is your vessel truly no longer capable of flight?"

"That is so," said Ethan sadly.

"Can it not be repaired?"

"I fear not," September put in. "It would take the facilities of a full O-G dock. The nearest is parsecs away."

Hunnar looked across at him. He already felt at ease with Ethan. Less certain was he with this stranger who was nearly as big as himself and whose accent was even more abominable than Ethan's.

The big human seemed only amused by the intent scrutiny the knight was giving him.

"Then," he continued casually, "would you object to our making some use of it?" He waited tensely. He didn't wish to spill blood here, but for so much worked metal . . .

He did not bother to point out that they were in no position to deny it. Even so, Ethan's ready answer surprised him.

"Sure. Help yourselves." Even Suaxus looked startled.

"One thing you ought to know, though," added September. "I don't think your people will be able to work it."

"Our smiths," replied Suaxus, drawing himself up to his full height, "can work bronze, brass, silver, gold, copper, junite, iron, visiron, and good steel."

"Very impressive. Believe me, I wish them only the best of luck. If they can mold duralloy in your local version of a manual forge, I'll be the first to applaud. Now, if you could train a Droom to manhandle the stuff . . ."

That was one several of the soldiers could not keep from laughing at. It lightened the atmosphere, lessened the tension born of acquisition.

"If we could do *that*," smiled Hunnar, "we wouldn't need the metal."

"There are some bits and scraps already torn free that you

might be able to make some use of," September continued. "Like the acceleration-couch frames, heating units, and such. I'd like to offer you a couple of miles of wire, but I'm afraid there just isn't much in the boat." He wasn't about to try and explain solid- and fluid-state mechanics. A frustrated warrior could become an angry warrior, apt to relieve his frustration by making short choppy motions with sharp objects.

"We shall see," said Hunnar. He looked at Ethan. "You surely have no objections then, friend Ethan?"

"No, the boat's all yours, uh, friend Hunnar."

"Fine. Now I think it be time to go meet his Lordship." He was exhilarated. Not a drop of blood shed to win such a prize! And mayhap some allies as well. Tiny allies, 'twas true.

"We're ready as you," said Ethan. He took a step forward, then stopped. A look of consternation came over his features.

"Um . . . how do you propose to get to this castle of yours?"

Hunnar reconsidered. Perhaps he'd been wrong. Maybe these really were children, or at least adolescents.

"We will simply chivan over," he said patiently. "It is only a short 'lide. Fifteen minutes out, perhaps three times that back, against the wind."

"By 'chivan' I guess you mean to skate?" Hunnar said nothing, confused. "I'm afraid we can't do that."

"Why not?" blurted Suaxus, hand moving slowly toward his sword-hilt again.

"Because," Ethan continued, opening his coat and raising his arms, "we don't have any wings and," resnapping the coat and lifting a foot, removing the boot, "we haven't any claws, or skates." He replaced the boot hastily as the cold bit at his heel.

Hunnar stared at the now-covered foot and rapidly made some astonished reappraisals. Firstly, his pet theory that these people were but slimmer varieties of his own vanished like a sweetclub down a cub's gullet. And then the full alien-ness of them—the way they moved, talked, their impossible sky-ship —all came down on him at once with a solid mental crunch.

Invincible knight of Sofold though he be, he was still shaken.

"If . . . if you have neither dan nor chiv," he asked helplessly, "how do you move about? Surely you do not *walk* all the time?"

"We do a lot of that," Ethan admitted. "Also, we have small vehicles that move from place to place." He demonstrated a walk, feeling ridiculous. "We also run." He forbore demonstrating this other human activity.

"We too 'walk,' with our chiv retracted," muttered Hunnar a little dazedly. "But to *have* to walk to cover any distance . . . how terrible!"

"There are plenty of humans who feel exactly the same way. They do as little of it as possible," confessed Ethan. "On our world there are few places to chivan, anyway. Our oceans are not solid, like this, but liquid."

"You mean, like the inside of the world?" Hunnar gaped.

"That's interesting." Williams spoke for the first time. "Clearly they have seen or have memory of occasional breaks in the ice. Since it's as much a part of their surface as these islands, it's easy to see how their wise men would conclude that the world was hollow and filled with water."

"What a sad place your home must be," commiserated Hunnar, honestly sympathetic. "I do not think I should like to visit it."

"Oh, there are places on many of our worlds, including Terra, where you'd feel right at home," Ethan assured him.

"Can you not chivan at *all?*" pressed the knight. It was hard to accede to such a monstrous abnormality.

"Not at all. If I were to try and chivan . . . We do have artificial chiv of metal on some worlds, but brought none with us. It's not standard survival gear on our lifeboats. And I wouldn't know how to use them, anyway. I think I could make a few meters from here into the wind before falling flat on my face."

"Couldn't hurt," said Colette. He ignored her.

"I will call for a sled," Hunnar said decisively. "Budjir, you and Hivell see to it!" The squire indicated acknowledgment and headed for the ice, the soldier following.

The humans watched their departure with fascinated stares. Williams in particular was utterly enraptured.

Once on the ice, the squire dug into the soldier's backpack and drew out a highly polished mirror about a third as big as his torso. It was set in a dark wooden frame and had what looked like a large metal screw set in the base of the wood.

While the squire aligned it with the sun and balanced it, the soldier jammed it into the ice and began twisting until it was screwed in tightly. It was facing those same western islands Ethan had spotted from his treetop vantage.

There was a simple baffle-shutter arrangment that slipped over the mirror. While the soldier steadied it against the wind, Budjir began opening and closing the baffles in a distinct pattern. Almost immediately there was an answering series of bright flashes somewhere along the horizon, at which the squire began fluttering his shutters more rapidly and for some time.

"Clearly, any kind of aural communication," September mused, "like drums or horns, are out of the question here. This wind would swallow up a good drum inside a half-kilometer or less."

Williams asked Hunnar, "What do you do at night?"

"Torchlight reflected by mirror serves well enough," the knight replied. "For long distances we have developed a system of relay stations with bigger mirrors. Except, of course, where they have been destroyed."

"Destroyed?" said Ethan. It was the inflection in Hunnar's voice and not the word itself that prompted his curiosity.

"Yes. The Horde burns them so that no word can be given of their passage. Indeed, it forbids their construction. But many feign ignorance and rebuild them."

"Horde?" probed September disinterestedly. "What Horde?"

"I fear you will have chance to discover," replied Hunnar. "We have a while to wait. I should like to learn more about you, and your amazing sky-raft, in that time."

"There isn't a great deal you would under . . . find interesting, Sir Hunnar," said Ethan. "But I'll be happy to show you around. Now, if I had my damned sample case with me . . . "

In the discussion that preceded the arrival of the sled-raft, Hunnar revealed a fair knowledge of basic astronomy. Tranky-ky rarely had cloudy weather for any length of time, Ethan reflected thoughtfully.

After Williams had answered several pointed questions about his home world and the ship, Hunnar asked if the little schoolteacher was a wizard. When informed that he was a teacher, the knight shrugged off the difference. No doubt, he reflected, Williams and Malmeevyn Eer-Meesach, wizard to the Landgrave himself, would have things to say to one another. Certainly Williams did not try to hide his own enthusiasm at the prospect of such a meeting.

Williams tried to explain a full-sized KK-drive ship to the knight. Hunnar would have none of it. Nothing that big could be made out of metal.

"Why does it not land to pick you up?" he asked.

"Little reasons aside," answered Williams, "it can't. No KK-drive ship could. It would make an awful mess of this part of your world."

"Ha!" grunted Hunnar. A ship of metal that large. Did they take him for a complete fool?

Likewise he could not grasp the concept of weightlessness. But gravity he understood. When you cut a man's head off, it fell *down*. Colette looked a little ill when September helpfully translated this for her. Also, he knew of the gutorrbyn and krokim and other flying things that were odd but clearly not weightless. He'd killed enough of them to know that.

The tran examined the inert body of the dead Kotabit with interest. In the icebox climate it hadn't decayed at all, for which Ethan was grateful. An experienced warrior might have been able to tell that the human's broken neck had not come from, say, being thrown against the console. But corpses, even alien ones, were not the items of prime interest. The control board, with its now frosted knobs and dials, drew longer stares. At the same time, Ethan and September were learning about Tran-ky-ky from Hunnar.

Wannome, it developed, was the capital and only near-city of a large island named Sofold. Sofold lay oh-so-many kijat to the west. It also claimed sovereignty over a number of smaller nearby islands. This tiny islet they'd smashed up against was one. A few, larger than this, were garrisoned and settled.

Wannome Sound was an excellent natural harbor and supported a flourishing commerce. There were active hot springs on the island crest. These provided a natural location for the small but vital foundry and the smithies. The island was also rich in deposits of certain metals but had to trade for others.

Cultivation was widespread. Like most inhabited islands, Sofold was virtually self-sufficient foodwise. Gathering of wild pika-pina, which grew back as fast as it could be harvested, was also a major industry.

When Ethan asked if they also harvested the much larger pika-pedan, Sir Hunnar threw him an odd stare. Suaxus whined mirthfully.

Only the foolishly brave or the ignorant tried to make a living gathering the pika-pedan, he explained. It was on the pika-pedan that the stavanzer grazed.

"Stavanzer? What's a stavanzer?" asked September interestedly.

Again Ethan's mestaped memory came up with a blank on fauna. "I don't remember. I get the feeling I should, but there's nothing . . . It's all on the edge . . . must be a mental block. Won't come. Why? You planning on starting a ranch?"

September smiled. "Farming isn't one of my multitude of talents," he said.

"Oh, wait a sec. I do remember what the name means."

"Yeah?" prompted the big man.

"Thunder-eater."

September pursed his lips. "Sounds harmless enough. Okay, so we don't volunteer for any pika-pedan pruning expeditions, what? Ask him about the local thieves . . . government."

The much-mentioned Council, it seemed, was composed of local dignitaries and nobles who served as administrators, mayors, and justices-of-the-peace of the countryside. The Council was presided over by the hereditary Landgrave, whose word was final but could be challenged in Council.

The Landgrave's hereditary power was rooted in his ancestry. A great portion of his personal wealth and treasury was derived from customs fees and commerce taxes.

"What sort of bird is your Landgrave?" asked September.

"Fearless, brilliant, a genius at administration and a true wizard of decision," replied Hunnar. He leaned over and whispered to the two humans. "He's as tough as a year-old piece of vol jerky, but if you talk true with him from the first, you'll do well enough."

"He sounds most imposing . . . a true leader," replied Ethan loudly. Then he lowered his voice in return.

"I understand. We've one like that ourselves . . . sometimes."

Hunnar nodded, then looked uncertain. "Sometimes?"

"I do not fully understand myself, Sir Hunnar. Some day soon, perhaps . . . He has a disease of age . . . and something more, I think." He looked up, smiled, stopped when he noticed Hunnar draw away.

"Sorry. I forgot that showing one's teeth is not a sign of friendship among meat-eaters."

"Truly a strange custom of yours," agreed the knight.

"That's something else we've got to attend to." He looked evenly at Hunnar. "While I'm sure your chefs are the noblest practitioners of their art on the planet, we do have a certain amount of our own foodstuffs we'd like to bring along."

"If the quantity is not great, there should be plenty of space on the raft."

"And it's about time we set to moving it outside," said September.

"I was afraid you might bring that up," Ethan sighed.

The sled-raft was awkward-looking but solid. Twenty meters long by ten wide, a bluff, no-nonsense triangular shape in hard wood, it was built from heavy timbers. There was a matted floor of some vegetable material and a wooden rail running around it at waist level. Tran waist level.

There was a crew of four. The owner, a merchant named Ta-hoding, stared at the ruined lifeboat with an open and unabashed greed that Ethan found positively homey.

A single mast was set about a third of the way back from the pointed bow. This supported a single large square sail held between two sturdy crossbeams top and bottom. The raft rested on three sharpened runners of gray stone, two at the rear corners and a slightly smaller one at the front. The two at the stern were connected to a double wheel that took two sailors to handle.

"A handsome ship," Ethan said to the captain.

"My ancestors are forever honored to have you on board my pitiful craft, great visitors from the stars! My sire is forever in your honor. My family shall bask in the glow of your radiances forever. My cubs and mate . . ."

Ta-hoding continued to heap suffocating praise on his passengers until September whispered something to Hunnar that Ethan missed.

"No, it wasn't supposed to be made known to the general public," replied the knight. "Actually, the Landgrave desired it be kept as quiet as possible. However, where money is concerned . . ." He shrugged, a very human gesture. Ethan was beginning to get an inkling of just how much wealth their ruined lifeboat represented hereabouts.

"I see," said September. He caught another crate of survival rations the soldiers were passing up and stacked it on the wooden deck. It took two soldiers considerable effort to lift the box up to him. Hunnar watched the operation silently. September wasn't sure whether or not the knight had caught the ease with which he'd handled the first crate. Damn! The big man strained almost theatrically on the next ones.

"A beacon that will shine . . ." Ta-hoding was following the other humans around, still spouting hosannas.

"Pardon me," began Williams, and Ethan gratefully slipped away as the schoolteacher rescued him from the seemingly endless assault of frozen platitudes.

"Why are your vessel's runners made of stone?" Williams asked.

"Alas," said the captain, "wood wears away too quickly and metal is beyond the reach of even wealthy men, which I assuredly am not . . . There is a great raft, owned in whole by the people of Vad Ozero, six times the size of my poor craft. Its sails would cover a large inn and it has runners made from solid stavanzer backbone." He shook his head mournfully. "The ease with which it turns, yea, even into the wind. The maneuverability, the sensuous 'lide of it under full sail, the speed, the profits . . . ah, the profits!"

Yes, alien though he may be, here was a being that was one with him in spirit, Ethan reflected. A race of philosophers with long beards who scorned material wealth might exist in the galaxy—somewhere. Thus far they remained undiscovered.

"I think that's it," said September with satisfaction, and it was. Ethan found himself looking forward to the sight of Hunnar's home.

Hunnar watched the last of the humans clamber aboard. "We are ready then?" He turned to the captain.

"Let out, Ta-hoding! We are aboarded!"

"As your boldness commands," effused the skipper. "I bask in the light of—"

"I'm not one of your customers, Hoding," Hunnar barked in reply. "The Landgrave is paying you, so don't waste any of your flattery on me." He turned to his first squire.

"Suaxus, take Smjör and report in for us. If the wind blows true, we should follow you by ten tuvits. Make also a report to the Longax and see that the wizard is aroused. If he awaits you not already with slavering tongue. Straight this time, with none of your bloodthirsty embellishments, mind."

"Done, sir," acknowledged Suaxus, a trifle coldly, Ethan thought. "Thou canst depend on me."

Hunnar replied with another of those tight-lipped smiles. He exchanged breath with the other. Although there was no obvious difference in their age, Hunnar seemed to Ethan years the eldest.

"I know I can, Suaxus. Wind with you."

Suaxus clapped his knight on one shoulder. Then he yelled for Smjör and disappeared over the side of the raft. Leaning over the rail, Ethan could see them streaking off at an angle to the southwest. Soon they'd probably begin tacking back against the wind, eating up the distance to their home.

It was no surprise that a single native could move faster than the bulky raft. He turned away from the wind and rubbed at the ice crystals that had formed on his upper lip.

The raft boasted a single wooden cabin. It rested squat against the back of the single thick mast. A summer day to the locals it might be, but he was just plain cold. Inside, the du Kanes were huddled up against a residual pile of trading goods, well away from the tiny windows.

The purpose of some of the objects in the pile was obvious.

And what looked like a small stove had a pipe leading into the flat roof. It wasn't lit.

Williams was sitting by the door. As usual, Walther had crammed himself into the furthest, darkest corner.

"Well, it's a long way from first class," Ethan essayed in a feeble attempt at humor, "but on such short notice . . . "

Colette just glared back at him. Williams said nothing either. He was totally absorbed in examining the interior of the cabin.

"See?" he said, pointing to a joint in one wall. "They use notched logs and wooden pegs, reinforced in the difficult places with iron and bronze nails. Most of the implements on that stove are bronze, but a few are beaten copper and the stove itself is iron. There are one or two steel-tipped spears in that locker, back there. The handles have the most beautiful scroll-work."

"Must be Ta-hoding's pride and joy," Ethan commented, mentally guessing at the artifact's curio value.

"I should not be at all surprised," the schoolmaster agreed. "I found nothing like pottery. Water would freeze on the potter's wheel."

The raft gave a sudden lurch. Colette squeaked.

"*Now* what's happening?" she moaned.

"I," said Ethan with commendable enterprise, "will go and see."

"I think the captain has turned his vessel slightly into the wind," informed Williams. "Shortly we should . . . "

His voice faded as Ethan left the sheltering cabin. He rounded the side and stepped into the wind. He wasn't used to it but it was no longer unique enough to warrant a curse. September was up near the pointed bow, in conversation with Hunnar.

The sail cracked. They were following the course taken by Suaxus and Smjör, who by now were well out of sight. The two turned as he came up to them.

"Be your companions well?" inquired the knight solicitously.

"As well as can be expected, Hunnar." He glanced up at September. "Walther sits in his corner and glares at nothing in particular. Colette is alternately brazen and scared, her father says nothing until he has to, and Williams is too busy taking mental notes to notice much of anything."

"And you, young feller-me-lad?" The wind whipped a single loose strand of white hair across his forehead.

"Me? Well, I'm . . . " Come to think of it, he'd been so busy he hadn't had time to consider his own feelings. "I'm cold."

"A pithy summation, lad." He moved to clap Ethan on the back again. This time Ethan avoided it, grinning. The wind clawed at his face.

"We're really picking up speed." The sail fluttered and rattled between the bracing spars.

One sailor was positioned at either end of the lower spar while Ta-hoding and the other manhandled the double wheel. The captain was carefully trying to match wind speed with desired direction. His eye moved continually from sky to sail to ice.

"Stand ready!" he bellowed above the howling atmosphere. Then, "Hard over!" and he was straining furiously at the wheel, forcing it to the right.

The raft slowly began to move to starboard. There was a split second when it was facing directly into the wind and the mainsail snapped back against the mast with a crack like shattered planking. The two spar men pushed and pulled as one, the sail snapped into a new configuration, and they were traveling at high speed to the northwest.

"Nicely done!" yelled September admiringly. He pulled himself sternward, bracing against the railing. Ethan followed curiously. He wanted to have a closer look at the sail. Anything that could take the kind of continuous pounding it was being subjected to might have commercial value.

It was thicker than sailcloth, a material Ethan had no formal knowledge of. Despite this it seemed flimsy for taming the high winds it had to take on this world. It was a bright yellow—surely not the natural color. Hunnar came up behind him and confirmed it.

"The inside of the pika-pina is soft, but the exterior is tough and thin. When dried, treated, and drawn out through looms, it makes a very strong fiber. Sails, ropes, a dozen useful things."

"You don't say?" commented September, who'd returned from his brief examination of the raft's steering mechanism. Then he did something that almost gave Ethan impetus to scream.

Gripping the lower edge of the sail in two powerful hands, he wrenched suddenly in opposite directions. At any moment Ethan expected to see the big man go down under a swarm of four angry sailors.

No one paid him the least heed. Ta-hoding didn't even glance up from his post at the wheel. Neither did the other sailors. Budjir and the other soldiers continued their story-swapping.

Eventually September let out a deep breath and let go. As near as Ethan could tell, he hadn't made so much as a tiny rip in the material.

"Strong is the word," September wheezed. "I'd think that several layers of this stuff, tightly woven and laid over each other, would make a very respectable shield, what?" Hunnar looked at him with new respect.

"You are a military man, then, friend September?"

"Let's say I've had occasion to do some scrapping."

"It might," admitted the knight, "except that treated hes-savar hides laid to wood or bronze or iron are better. For one thing, they're harder to burn."

"Um. I didn't think of that."

"Would you like to try my sword?" Hunnar offered, leaning into a particularly violent gust.

September looked tempted. But rather than risk exciting attention, or give away any hidden abilities, or lack of same, he politely declined.

"Not today, friend Hunnar. In the future, in less awkward surroundings, should there be another opportunity—"

"When the Horde comes you'll have plenty of opportunities," said the knight grimly. He walked between them and stalked off to chat with the captain.

"What's this 'Horde' he keeps referring to?" September asked Ethan.

"I don't know." He stared after the knight. "I've got this feeling, though, that we're not going to get much nearer Arsudun until we find out."

V

Actually they made slightly better time than Hunnar had estimated. The wind rose to a steady 60 kph, but under the skillful paws of Ta-hoding and his tiny crew, the ungainly raft fairly flew across the ice. The merchant might be comically effusive, but he was a master seaman—or iceman, rather.

It was an exhilarating experience just to stand in the sharp prow of the raft and let the wind shriek past your face. It battered at the snow goggles and whipped the too-large hood which now enveloped Ethan's entire head and face. The angry air had all the softness of a newly minted scalpel. Exhilarating, yes. But how much more exhilarating it would have been to be warm again . . . would he ever be warm again?

He grew aware that Hunnar was standing next to him. "Wannome," the knight murmured, "and Sofold Island. My home. Yours, too, for a while, friend Ethan."

For another moment there was nothing but a blur on the horizon. But as the little raft flew closer, the scene seemed to leap across the ice at him. Before he knew it, they were cruising beneath towering stone walls amidst a swarm of similar craft. All were built along the triangle design. Most were about the same size as their own ship.

There were a few two and three times as long, and one great raft that must have gone at least ninety meters. It had a two-story central cabin with smaller cabins fore and aft.

Decks were piled high with crates and boxes, all securely lashed down against the wind. Many were protected with material made from the same stuff as the sails. The big raft's fittings were brighter, with here and there decorative flashes of metal and bone. Sails were splashes of rainbow against the ice. Ethan realized that any color other than white or green could be easily spotted many kilometers off.

Moving with the westwind behind them, several ships shot past them at tremendous speed. All were moving from or to the same spot, an opening in the walls. The entrance was flanked by two massive towers of gray stone. Great walls stretched off to right and left, curving into the distance.

Ethan staggered over to the cabin entrance, yelled inside. "Mr. du Kane, Colette, Milliken, you can come and look. We're here."

"Wherever that is," grumbled Colette.

A moment later they were all clustered along the bow of the raft. With delicate handling and elaborate curses, Ta-hoding was maneuvering them skillfully through the swarm of shipping.

Along the tops of the flanking towers patrolling tran were visible. The raft slid between the walls, edging near an exiting merchantman with orange sails and ornately carved handrailing. Once, the merchantman's low spar, riding higher than their own, almost clipped the raft's sail. Ta-hoding hurled a stream of invective at the other, of which Ethan managed to understand perhaps half.

Bow in hand, the first mate of the other vessel came to the rail. It was the first indication they'd had that archery was known to the natives. He made threatening gestures with it in their direction until Hunnar walked over and spoke quietly —as quietly as one could above the wind—to the other. That worthy shut up fast and disappeared.

"How do you close off the harbor?" Ethan inquired. "I don't see anything resembling a gate."

"With nets of woven pika rope," replied the knight. "A gate would have to rest on the ice."

"What's wrong with that?"

"A good fire on the ice would easily undermine such. The walls themselves are built deep into the ice but a gate, naturally, could not be so. Also, there is the Great Chain. It is passed from one gate tower to the other and can keep out all but the tiniest ships. The nets serve to keep out men on foot."

The walls, Ethan observed, were several meters thick, with plenty of room on top for maneuvering troops. They stood about twelve meters high, with battle towers slightly higher.

Once inside the gate he could see that the walls completely encircled the harbor. It was a very respectable feat of basic engineering.

Wannome was ideally suited for an iceport. The island itself lay on the east-west axis, with harbor and city at the eastern tip. Once within the harbor, ice-sailors would have the island to shield them from the constant westwind. On leaving the harbor they would pick up the prevailing gale immediately. Travelers coming from the east would have a more difficult time of it, but would still find the same quiet landing and protective wall.

Ethan took another survey of that impressive construct. He wondered what threat could make an individual like Hunnar worry despite it.

Dozens of rafts, including small pleasure craft, plied the broad harbor. The merchantmen tied up at long, narrow piers which were built directly out onto the ice. Since the ice-ships had no draft and did not bob up and down on non-existent waves, the piers were barely above the "water." Wooden cranes and pulley hoists added to the confusion in the harbor.

At the eternally unchanging tide-line where ice met land, a farrago of small buildings began. Tran of all sizes and shapes moved about the ice-front.

The humans were by now turning quite a few heads on passing rafts, but Ethan was too engrossed in the approaching scene to notice. The ground sloped sharply upward from the piers. It disappeared in a crazy-quilt jumble of two- and three-storied stone buildings and houses.

Near the houses, narrow streets paved with smooth flat stones were visible. Each had a broad swath of smooth ice running stripelike down its middle. All of the buildings seemed to sport chimneys of stone or black metal and high gambrel roofs. If Ethan had spent more time thumbing through history tapes instead of sales catalogues, he might have been struck by the town's resemblance to medieval European cities.

The ice median strips were artificial, having been made by melting ice and then allowing it to refreeze in the desired place and pattern. Even at a distance Ethan could see furry dots dropping harborward at high speed. It was equally clear that the ice ramps were for descent only. It would take a mighty powerful eastwind to permit upward chivaning.

Rapid transit in Wannome, then, was no problem—as long as you were going downhill.

Above the town, steep crags rose to right and left. There was a low saddle between them. Clinging to the rocks on the left and seemingly a part of the mountain itself was the great castle of Wannome. It descended in stone levels to merge with the harbor-girdling wall.

The castle, Sir Hunnar informed them, had been founded by a wandering knight, one Krigsvird-ty-Kalstund, in the year 3262 SNC. Ethan's knowledge of the trannish dating system was nil, but the castle looked awfully old.

The island was built like a doorstop, with the harbor and town of Wannome at the high end. From the town the ground rose abruptly to the island's high point. From there it dropped in a long, gentle sweep to the ice and a great field of pika-pina. A steady stream of black smoke rose from the mountains.

"The pika-pina," Hunnar had explained, "protects us from attack from the west, out of the wind. The great wall and castle does likewise for the town and the eastern island."

"What about your north and south?" asked September.

"There is wall around much of the island, but far lower and weaker than this. But the granaries, ships, and foundry are all at this high end of Sofold, protected by the wall and by steep cliffs. An attacker could come from north or south and make a successful landfall. Then he could devastate the fields and herds, the country downs. This would gain him naught but pleasure. Fields can be replanted, houses rebuilt, especially with the wealth of the province intact.

"Wannome can support and shelter the entire population of Sofold should it prove necessary."

"What about an attack on the city from the landward side," continued September.

Hunnar gave him a patronizing look. "I see you do not understand us. No tran will fight on land when he can maneuver four times as effectively on the ice. It must be different with you, since you have no chiv or dan. That is why ships and caravans are at their greatest danger when out at ice. Few can move faster than a fighting man with a good west-wind behind him. To try and take a high position from land . . . no, such an attack could never succeed.

"A landing might be made as part of a siege-plan, to prevent the townsfolk from getting supplies from the rest of the island. But never with the thought of taking the city from that side. No one could move fast enough. For one thing, there are ice paths running all around the island. They give us the ability to move rapidly on land. These would be destroyed before any invader could make use of them. We would still retain those in the heights and the town. Thus we would have great mobility while an invader would struggle clumsily about in the dirt." He pointed at the encircling harbor wall as they pulled up to an empty pier.

A large gray pennant fluttered at the end of the pier. It was divided into four squares. A large tusk occupied the upper right-hand corner, crossed by a sword. An anvil and hammer decorated the lower left, while the opposing squares were a solid red and yellow, respectively. An exquisitely carved and appointed raft with an unusually tall mast was tied up at the pier nearby.

"The Landgrave's yacht," Hunnar explained.

"About the wall," prompted Ethan.

"Yes. An ice path also runs along its top. So the men above have equal mobility with those on the ice below. And except on unusual days, an enemy has the wind in his face and side at best, and the sun in his eyes in the evening. Not the best conditions under which to pursue an assault."

The two spar men reefed in the single sail. One side of the triangular raft struck the pier with the slightest of jars. Immediately young tran appeared beneath the raft. They placed large stones in front of and behind the triple stone runners.

Suaxus was there to greet them.

"I have given your messages and my report to the Protector," he intoned, after he and Hunnar had exchanged breath and shoulder-claps. "You are to bring them to his presence immediately."

"Has the Council been informed?" Hunnar asked. Ethan

thought he detected more than mere curiosity in the knight's voice. It was hard to tell. Mestaped language was hard on inflection. Still, there was something going on here that was being kept from them.

Suaxus grinned tightly. "The Landgrave in his wisdom felt that a private audience might better serve the present needs of the province . . . at the first. No point is there in shocking the other nobles with the sight of these strange ones."

"Come along, my friends," said Hunnar. "It is a substantial walk, although perhaps not for you."

The harborfront had an easy familiarity to Ethan. He'd worked in dozens of such on half a hundred worlds. Some had been more, some less, civilized. All were concerned with the task of acquiring material wealth.

Business proceeded all about them. Trading, bargaining, loading of rafts, unloading, fighting, pickpocketing, with everywhere masses of children somehow finding space to play. A seething mob of sentient greed. Oh well. The universe was not physically perfect, either. Hundreds of furry tran filled the harborfront with a warm, musky smell. It was not unpleasant, but in hot or humid air it could have been overpowering.

Many of the locals paused in their business and chatter to eye the alien procession. But no one ventured to stare very long, or to pose comment that might be overheard. This was probably due, Ethan considered, to the presence of Hunnar and his soldiers.

The children, however, were not so shy. Miniatures of the adults, many clad in just jackets or short coats in the gentle breeze, stopped and stared at them with wide cat eyes, compact fluffs of light gray fur. He had to forcibly resist an urge to cuddle them, contenting himself with an occasional pat on an adolescent head.

"The townsfolk don't seem overly friendly," September finally commented.

"Being in my care," Hunnar replied, "it is apparent to all that you are royal guests. It would not be seemly for you to mingle with the common folk."

"Well, I'm afraid I'm going to have to mingle for a minute, tradition notwithstanding." And before Hunnar or anyone else could make a move to stop him, he'd broken away from the tight little group and sauntered over to halt before a small open shop.

Stal Pommer, the elderly proprietor, looked across at the smooth-skinned alien, then helplessly to right and left. His normally loquacious neighbors studiously ignored him.

"How much?" asked September, pointing.

"I . . . uh, that is . . . noble sir, lord, I don't know that—"

"You don't know?" September interrupted, aghast with mock outrage. "A shopkeeper who doesn't know the price of his own merchandise? How do you stay in business?" He tugged at his doubled-up shirtfront. "I, as you can clearly see, desperately require a good warm coat. I'd like to purchase that one."

"Yes, lord," Pommer stammered, regaining a little of his composure. He looked in vain for September's wings, then gave up in disbelief when he finally realized there was nothing between the big strange one's wrist and waist but empty air.

"Don't just stand there gaping," urged September impatiently. "Take it off the rack and let me try it on."

"Surely, lord, surely!" Pommer went over to the revolving wooden rack, drew off the indicated coat. He handed it to September. The latter stepped into it and drew the back half up over his shoulders. Then he bent and brought up the front. Holding it closed with a hand at the shoulder, he tied first the right and then the left side with the leather ties. The length was all right but it was a mite too broad. Ethan would have swum in it.

"A little loose at the sides. As I have no need of a wing-slit, why don't you just sew them shut? That should bring it in enough. Leave me just enough room to get my arms through, eh? The leg holes are fine."

"Ye . . . yes, lord."

Under the watchful eyes of the soldiers, the rest of the humans, and half the children in Wannome, Stal Pommer set up the unnatural task of sewing closed the sides of the hessavar coat.

"You will not be able to open these now, lord, even to don the garment."

"That's the idea, tailor. It'll be like slipping into a turtle shell, but I'd use rivets if I had to. Clover, it's the first time I've been halfway comfortable since we came down."

Pommer ignored the itching temptation to inquire into the nature of turtles and rivets and concentrated on his sewing. The needle he used could have doubled as a small sword.

Pommer stepped back. September swung his arms, did a few deep knee bends.

"Not bad a'tall. Wish it had sleeves, though. How much?"

"Um . . . eighty foss," suggested Pommer, hesitantly peeking around the alien bulk.

Sir Hunnar growled softly and put his hand to sword hilt.

"But for you noble lord," he squeaked hurriedly, "only sixty, only sixty!" Hunnar grunted and went back to studying the pavement.

"Well, I haven't any of the local lucre," mused the big man, rubbing at the ice mat on his chin. That woke the old tailor up. For a minute there the human took on the appearance of a shifty type that transcended race, Landgrave's men-at-arms or no. "But maybe this will do." He removed something from his shirt, blocking it from Hunnar's view with his body. "This," he explained, "is combination knife and fork. Very simple instrument. Made of duralloy. Standard survival kit issue. We've others."

"What knife?" asked the oldster, intrigued. "I see only a little square of metal."

"Press this depression, here, in the center of the square." Pommer did so, hesitantly. He jumped a little when knife and fork sprang from opposite ends of the square.

"I can't for the life of me imagine what you'll do with the fork," said September conversationally. "But that blade ought to be useful in your work. It's a damnsight better than your best steel. And it'll never lose its edge, nor break. Should last you and your kids a long time, what? That survival stuff is built to take it."

The tailor didn't understand this odd creature completely. But he could tell the bargain of the age when he saw it.

"Uh . . . it surely seems an equitable exchange, lord." He was so excited and nervous he missed the square in his first grab at it. He pulled it out of sight quickly, before Hunnar or any of the other soldiers could see what it was. "Thank you, lord, thank you!" he muttered, bowing obsequiously. "Please visit my humble shop again."

Hunnar was fidgeting aimlessly. "Are you quite finished?"

"Yes, thanks," replied September.

A familiar voice piped from the little knot of humanity.

"Hey, what about me?" said Walther.

"What about you?" replied September coldly. He turned back to Hunnar. "This is the first time since we landed on your world that I've been warm. I couldn't wait any longer. Sorry if I upset your protocol. Say," he finished innocently, "aren't we going to be late for that appointment?"

"I should not be surprised," Hunnar snapped, turning away. Ethan noticed that the big man kept the knight answering questions all the way up the hill. Probably to keep him from thinking about what September had paid the tailor with. It might occur to the knight later, but by then it would be a little late to invalidate the exchange.

The walls of Wannome castle were surrounded by a deep, narrow moat. Empty, of course. This was spanned by a short drawbridge. The walls themselves rose vertically for fifteen meters and more, solid gray and black rock and masonry. Wannome had its share of craftsmen, Ethan reflected, and not only smiths.

Two lancers flanked the sides of the bridge entrance. They wore coats of inscribed tooled leather with shields of leather and worked bronze. Each carried a slim, steel-tipped spear. The helmets had openings for the ears, and a nose-piece down the center. They swept out and down in a backside flare to protect the neck.

The young tran who met them just inside the high gate was garbed in similar fashion. Only his leather was inlaid with silver in sharp relief and he wore a sword much like Hunnar's strapped to one leg. Also, his helmet was made from silver-inlaid leather and had imitation silver flames worked along the crest. A four-square gray patch, a tiny double of the pennant at the pier, was sewn over his left breast.

He arrived panting for breath. "The Landgrave bids you to him quick."

Sir Hunnar frowned, made a half turn to Ethan. "Not good. I hope we haven't gotten you off on his Lordship's bad side." He glared over at September as though that worthy were personally responsible for any forthcoming dire consequence. September whistled cheerfully and smiled back.

"Now I must ponder on a fair excuse," Hunnar muttered.

"Why not tell him the truth?" queried September as they followed the garishly-clad herald across a courtyard. "That I stopped to buy myself a coat because I was freezing to death?"

"On a day like today, of pleasing warmth? No, even I still cannot realize that you are used to living in fire itself. But to confess that you stopped to converse with a tailor before the Landgrave himself . . . ?" Hunnar looked horrified. "No, no! He would have you all spitted out of hand."

"Easier said than done," replied September, unmoved. "Besides, if I'd frozen solid I wouldn't have presented much in the way of available conversation, would I?"

"There is that," admitted Hunnar seriously. "His Lordship does appreciate candor. We'll see. He may be so curious about you he will forget to be insulted."

They passed through another small open area. Ethan noticed a smith taking the dents out of a bronze shield in a glowing cubby off to their right. The attraction was in the fire. A few soldiers leaned idly at arms to the side of another door, a far cry from the ramrod-straight troops they'd encountered at the drawbridge entrance. Another bunch were seated in the shade playing what appeared to be a variant of the universal game—dice.

They entered the inner keep, walked through a long hall to a wide staircase.

Up they went, then a turn, then up another. They'd gone halfway up the second when there was a sudden squeal of surprise from behind. For a second Ethan thought they'd lost Colette. But she'd only strayed too far to the center and stepped onto the gleaming ice path. From there it was a short but fast slide back to the bottom step. Her dignity and one other part were bruised, but there was no lingering damage.

After remounting the stairs their guide made a hard left.

They passed another set of ubiquitous guards. Then a right turn down another hallway, and another, and they entered a long, vaulted hall. A group of three tran awaited them at its far end. To one side a great fire blazed in a huge fireplace. The temperature in here might even be slightly above freezing, Ethan reflected.

"No, I shall announce you," the herald cautioned. He strode off down the long, brightly dyed rug that covered the bare stone floor. There was a seemingly endless table to each side, with chairs and odd writhing candlesticks.

"Remember," Hunnar whispered to Ethan as they walked slowly behind the herald, "he's tough and stringy, but not vicious. Not intentionally so, anyway. I'm told we've had harder rulers. At least he's not an idiot, like his half-brother."

"Will we get to meet this half-brother?" asked Williams clinically.

"Not unless you've even stranger means of transport than your metal ship. When his fault became obvious, he was put to death."

"Dear me," replied the schoolmaster, taken aback. "That seems rather extreme."

"Our way," said Hunnar simply.

"This is an extreme world," added September. "You don't get supported by others here, what?" Then he spoke to Ethan. "Take your time, young feller, and say what you think best."

The herald had stopped ahead of them. Now he turned and boomed, "Sir Hunnar Redbeard, Squire Suaxus-dal-Jagger, and Squire Budjir Hotahg, with the party of outlanders!"

"Outlanders?" September looked askance at the knight.

"That is what they've been calling you," Hunnar replied. "For lack of a better term. Slowly now; watch me."

They followed the knight the last dozen meters. Ethan had a moment to scan those awaiting them. Then Sir Hunnar bowed low, crossing his arms over his head and covering himself with his wings. They all imitated the movement as best they could, not rising until the knight had done so.

"My lord," he began, "these folk crave mercy for intruding upon the province of the people. They seek protection and mayhap service. They are on a . . . " he hesitated for a

second, "a pilgrimage to far parts of the world. Their metal
sky-ship was disabled as though by the Father of Rifs and
they are cast upon us for deliverance."

An old, tall tran with solid gray fur put both hands on the
arms of his throne. The Landgrave stood erect. Ethan noticed
that the back of the throne was carved from what seemed to
be a single unbroken pillar of ivory that rose all the way to
the high roof. It was inscribed with symbols and etching as
far up as he could see. The thing was as big as a good-sized
tree.

The Landgrave was dressed in flowing leather and silks.
Hammered metal plate decorated with silver thread formed
a complex, flashing breastplate. A single leather band with
a bright metal rectangle of gold set in the forehead was all
that passed for a crown. He did, however, wield an elaborately carved wooden staff nearly two and a half meters tall.
It was thin, a polished mahogany-color, studded with cabo-
chons in red and bright blue. A few faceted gems adorned
the knob at the top.

"Sir Ethan Frome Fortune," declaimed Hunnar, pointing
Ethan out before he could protest the undeserved title, "I
present you to the right-true-and-just Torsk Kurdagh-Vlata,
Landgrave of Sofold, and True Protector of Wannome."

"We are honored in the presence of your father's father
and self, son-of-the-wind," Ethan intoned, giving the rehearsed speech his best sales pitch.

"You are welcome, outlanders," the Landgrave replied. His
voice was startlingly high for a tran, compared to those they'd
already encountered. The Landgrave gestured to his right at
an incredibly shriveled but bright-eyed old individual
dressed entirely in black silks. He wore a black headband.

"My personal adviser, Malmeevyn Eer-Meesach."

"The honor is mine, noble sirs," responded the wizard
smoothly. He was eyeing them with such obvious naked anticipation that he made Ethan a little nervous. That same
stare had been applied to laboratory rats with uncertain fu-
tures. As it developed, he was doing the old tran an injustice.

"And this," continued Kurdagh-Vlata, turning to his left,
"is my daughter and only cub, the Elfa Kurdagh-Vlata."

The gesture was directed at a surprisingly lissome and

nearly naked female tran. She gazed down at Ethan with a stare far more disconcerting than the wizard's. Considering the temperature in the great hall, her garb seemed an open invitation to pneumonia.

Something hit him a sharp rap in the shin and he spun. September smiled at him.

"Time enough later for sight-seeing, me lad," he murmured in Terranglo. "No wonder friend Hunnar was convinced of our similarity."

"What?" he said brilliantly. He returned his gaze to the throne, found the Landgrave watching him impatiently.

"Your companions," whispered Hunnar urgently.

"Oh, yes." He stepped to one side and made a grand sweeping gesture. "Um, Sir Skua September . . . "

September performed a bow full of intricate hand gestures. It confused Ethan but the Landgrave appeared delighted.

"Hellespont du Kane, a . . . ah . . . merchant of great renown on his world. His daughter, Colette du Kane . . . "

Du Kane executed a marvelously supple bow that surprised both Ethan and September. Colette hesitated, then followed with an awkward curtsey.

"And Walther, um . . . "

"You're still not going to learn my last name, buddy, until it's too late to do you any good," the kidnapper muttered in Terranglo.

"Yes?" prompted the Landgrave.

Ethan looked uncertainly to September.

"A criminal in our custody," said the big man easily. "One not to be trusted and to be watched every moment. He secreted himself aboard our ship and . . . "

"It's all a lie!" shouted Walther abruptly. "They're the criminals, not me! I was taking them all to justice, when—"

September turned on him. "Quiet, punk," he said in Terranglo. "I can break your head right now. The Landgrave and I can argue about who was telling the truth afterwards. I'll let your spirit know how it comes out."

The little kidnapper shut up.

"Sir Hunnar?" queried the Landgrave. "What means this outburst?"

"I believe what Sir Ethan and Sir Skua say to be the right

truth, your Lordship. The hysterical one is evil and clever."

"Well then, can we not do our new-welcomed guests a service? Order him dispatched out of hand!".

"Ah, that is not the way of our people, your Lordship," put in Ethan hastily. "He must present himself and his crimes before a special machine. The machine, being impartial and unemotional, will give justice fairly."

"Where is justice if your emotions are not involved?" the Landgrave countered. "Not to mind. We have but just met and here find I discussing the fine points of jurisprudence. Other matters attend. I welcome you as friends and allies. You shall be given rooms and whatever you need for personal comfort. Tonight dine with my knights and I. Your home is here now." Whereupon he sat down with great dignity and obvious satisfaction.

Ethan paused. "There is one matter we should discuss now, your Lordship. The question of aid for our continuing journey westward."

"Journey? Journey? What is this, Sir Hunnar?" said the Landgrave gruffly. "Squire Suaxus, you said nothing to me of a journey."

"I did not have time, my Lord, for——"

Sir Hunnar broke in "They do not understand, my Lord. Remember, they are truly from another world."

"Be that as it may," said Kurdagh-Vlata stiffly, "we know nothing of moving from one world to another."

"That is so, my Lord," continued Hunnar. "Yet they say their folk have a town aways from Wannome. Tis there they wish to travel. Some eight or nine thousand satch."

"An afternoon jaunt, yes."

"But if they could reach their friends, Lord, they might bring more metal and perhaps other——"

"Enough!" snorted the Landgrave. "They would no doubt require a raft for this journey, perhaps several?"

"Possibly more than one, Lord."

"With full crews, and provisions, and soldiers to protect from pirates?"

"True, my Lord, but——"

"Tis out of the question!"

"But your Lordship—" began Ethan.

"They are gifting us with their vessel, my Lord," said Hunnar. "A veritable mountain of metal. Without obligation. 'Twould pay for such a trip many, many times over."

"Yes it would. Tis generous of them, to give away what they can no longer use. Nor protect."

Ethan started to protest, but guessed rightly that was just what the Landgrave was hoping he'd do. He kept silent.

"Absolutely impossible—at the moment. Perhaps in a malet or so. After we have treated with the abominators."

"Yes, my Lord!" boomed a huge voice from the back of the hall. "How *are* we to deal with the abominators?"

Everyone turned to the source of those stentorian tones.

A tran they hadn't seen before was striding toward them. He was resplendent in azure and emerald silks, overlaid with fine leather bindings and straps. His beard was longer than Hunnar's and tinged with white over the steel-gray.

The eyes were sunken deep under hairy brows. As he drew closer another aspect of his person was made clear. Here was the first really fat tran they'd encountered.

"Darmuka Brownoak," announced the herald, rather after the question. "Prefect of Wannome!"

"What's all this mean?" September whispered to Hunnar.

"Darmuka is prefect of the city and a powerful member in Council besides," the knight replied. "A very forceful and stubborn individual. Also ambitious and greedy. And very wealthy, which in the long run tis more important than all the others. There are few richer than he. The Landgrave is one, of course. Of the others, some support him, some Darmuka."

"Hmm. Political conflict," murmured Ethan to no one in particular. "I thought the Landgrave had absolute power?"

"In all decisions the Landgrave has *final* power," said Hunnar. "This does not mean he imprudently acts against the wishes of a majority of influential citizens." The knight quieted as the prefect came within hearing distance.

Darmuka put one foot up on the dais and surveyed the gathering with interest and undisguised contempt.

"So these are the strange ones who come on a raft of flying

metal, eh?" he said almost challengingly. "They surely are strange strangers."

"You're no interstellar sex god yourself, fatso," countered September. Ethan winced, but the prefect merely grunted satisfaction.

"There will be no insulting of guests in my presence," declared Kurdagh-Vlata rather lamely.

"Insult?" The prefect put both paws delicately on his chest and drew himself erect. "I, insult a visitor to the Council Chamber? I?" He turned and looked intently around the room then, so hard that the herald and even the Landgrave couldn't resist doing the same. The prefect stared at the ceiling and even raised the corner of a throw fur to glance beneath it.

"By the by," he continued in mock surprise, "where *is* the Council? I do believe a quorum is not present. Here we have six alien creatures of unknown power and intentions. They bring with them a ship of more forged metal than Wannome has seen since the Great Sack. And not a member of the Council present . . . other than my poor, hastily arrived self, of course." He looked innocently at the Landgrave. "Is this in accordance with the Charter of Council? Perhaps the Council should be called into session, to discuss their absence. Since they are not here, it cannot be debated. Dear me, a paradox."

"I did not feel it necessary yet to trouble the full Council with such an odd matter," replied Kurdagh-Vlata. It sounded mighty feeble to Ethan.

"I see," said Brownoak. "As is well known, his Lordship's wisdom exceeds all of ours combined. I bow to his decision." Darmuka executed a sloppy half-bow. "However, as I entered, I think twas mentioned something about 'dealing with the Horde.' Would you say, milord, that anything which relates to that matter is of more than odd nature? Worthy perhaps even for discussion by Council, as it does affect every adult and cub in the great land of Sofold?"

"Yes, surely," Kurdagh-Vlata responded.

"Then might it not be prudent to postpone any discussion of matters relating to such until full Council has been gathered?" Kurdagh-Vlata said nothing and Darmuka prompted, "Is this agreed, milord?"

"I . . . oh, very well, Darmuka! Confound your impudence!" He stood abruptly and struck the floor twice with the base of the jeweled staff. Sir Hunnar and Darmuka both bowed. The humans copied them. The Landgrave then retired, taking his daughter and advisor with him.

"Tis good to see you returned safe and whole, Sir Hunnar," said Brownoak. "Did your expedition include any successful massacres?"

"We met no one, so we fought with no one, spineless messenger," replied the knight stiffly. He smiled slightly at the other. But this time a flash of white was visible between his lips. Clearly he was controlling himself with an effort.

"How very fortunate. I should be distressed to see one of our finest knights injured over such an odd matter. Especially with a crisis approaching. Good day to you, outlanders." He bowed toward Ethan. "We shall undoubtedly see more of each other."

With a fluttering of sea-colored silk and rich brown hides, the prefect stalked off down the hall.

"Well," said Hellespont, "I may not have the grasp of the local language that you gentlemen possess, but that chap is of a type I need no words to recognize."

"He's a character, all right," September commented in Trannish, nodding. He looked over at Hunnar and grinned. "You two aren't exactly blood-brothers, I take it."

"The Brownoak has less blood for battle than a jelly-moss," spat the knight, staring after the other. "That one so bereft of heart should wield so much power . . . Worse, he is an unconscionable butcher who would dress the whole province for rape, content in the rightness of his way!"

He sighed. "Come. I will take you to rooms. And there is something of great significance you should be informed of before we can discuss your journey any further. Or before you are put before the Council . . . I will see to the transfer of your food to your apartments. The Council, however, will expect you to dine with them. Can you eat our food?"

"It's a long way from the Honeybucket Room in the Grand Hotel on Hivehom, but I think we can manage," replied September.

"That one," said Ethan, reminding Hunnar of Walther's presence, "should dine alone in his room, with a guard in attendance. One who is not susceptible to bribery."

Walther shook his head but said nothing. "I'm even smaller than the lady du Kane and you're all frightened of me."

September just laughed.

"I will see to it," said Sir Hunnar.

VI

Ethan's room was neatly furnished. He suspected his accommodations were fancy by local standards. If Wannome was a typical province capital, then the trade prospects for the planet were far better than anyone had guessed. Why, in precious metalwork alone . . . and these marvelous coats . . .

Now, if he could only find a way to file a report! . . .

The big canopied bed had damask-like draperies and covers. He wondered how such material was made. All of the wealthy tran they'd encountered so far had been clad in similar material. Neatly worked, too. He doubted the material came from silkworms. If there were insects on this world they kept themselves scarce. Any self-respecting silkworm would turn to a small lump of frozen flesh in a short day. And they didn't seem advanced enough for artificial fabric. Another mystery to unravel.

The bed was probably intended for a single occupant, but it was three times the width of any single bed he'd ever slept on. The wooden chest at its foot was intricately carved. A huge mirror covered much of one wall, no doubt just the right size for an adult tran.

A real double bed must be an ocean of morphean comfort.

The door bolted solidly—from the inside only, he noted—although the bolt itself was made of hardwood and not metal. Wannome's designers had left nothing to chance in creating their guest suites. The door would hold well enough to keep out the casual thief, but not well enough to resist a concerted charge from a couple of well-muscled guardsmen.

He also noticed a small but elaborately set whetstone. It was placed near the foot of the bed and could be operated with one foot. Its purpose escaped him for a moment. It was too low to conveniently sharpen a knife, for example. Then he realized it was for putting an edge on one's own chiv.

That must be the normal routine on awakening, he mused. Rise early, wash, clean, and sharpen your feet.

Something else was troubling him more, until he chanced to open the heavy chest. It was filled with thick, wide furs. They weren't as smooth-looking as the odd diaper-like coats everyone wore, but they were heavy and warm. There was no fireplace in the room, and the single window was open to the sky. Without the furs there would be no way he could sleep through the temperature drop at night.

He walked over to the window, which was high and narrow. There was a complicated wooden shutter arrangement that would serve to keep out the wind if not the cold.

It wouldn't keep out a determined enemy, though. Then he looked out and down. He'd forgotten how many steps they'd mounted.

The south side of the island was precipitous here, and the castle of Wannome was built right to the edge. It was a killing fall to the ice below. With a little imagination he could almost see waves breaking against the cliff. Perhaps they had once, millions of years ago. This side of the castle, at least, was invulnerable.

Leaning out into the biting wind, he squinted and saw that the high cliff continued westward for a fair distance before dropping down to the ice. An occasional flash of green broke the whiteness.

A look at the sky. Let's see, he thought. The tran have their evening meal at sunset. That should leave him a couple of local-time hours before he'd be expected to put in an appearance. When he had time it might be a good idea to revisit that tailor. Maybe he could make underclothes as well as coats. The outfit he'd been wearing on the *Antares* when he'd been abducted—was that one or two thousand years ago?—was not conducive to strenuous living.

The special survival parka he was wearing was holding up beautifully. But below the surface, so to speak, things were beginning to get a bit raunchy. There was a knock at the door.

"It's open," he said without turning.

The voice that replied did make him turn. It said, "Good wind," and wasn't human.

The Elfa Kurdagh-Vlata, heiress to the throne of Wannome, closed the door gently behind her. Her caution was disconcerting. She bolted it. That was ominous.

"I apologize for these rooms." Her speech was husky. "They were the best father could do on such short notice. And we've little idea of your needs."

Ethan walked away from the window and not incidentally put the bed between them. If that was supposed to faze her she didn't show it. She walked over and sat on the end. The human contour analog was astounding. She drew swirls in the silken coverlet.

"Do you really come from another world?" she asked breathlessly. Her outfit was done up like holiday packaging—by a clumsy six-year-old. The fact that the skin beneath was covered with light gray fur made it appear no less naked. Excepting the feline head and broad feet, and those piercing vertical pupils, she might have passed for a tridee starlet clad in skin-tight mink.

"Yes, we do," he replied eventually, with some emphasis on the "we." If she was expecting him to prolong the conversation she was sorely mistaken. He couldn't for a moment forget that her father was not only a grouch with a reported short temper, but also had the power to remove head from shoulders with a wave of his hand. Until he knew a great deal more about local mores, he was going to be as quiet as a monk. This was no place to depend on mestaped information.

Besides, she was as tall as he was and much broader, which made for rather an intimidating personality.

"It's surprising. You're not so terribly different from us, it seems," she said, her flashing yellow eyes fixed on him.

Dammit, if only she weren't so farking attractive! Now watch that, he told himself. She isn't even of the same species. Of course, there were aberrant humans who had a thing for other species. He knew one chap who . . .

Quit that!

"I think this is all very exciting," she said finally into the growing silence. The finger paused in its silken whirlpool. "You don't even have any fur on your bodies, except on top."

"Actually," Ethan responded, trying to be scientific, "that's not entirely true. We do have some elsewhere." He was about to mention "chest" when she interrupted him.

"Really? Let me see." She made a spring that carried her halfway across the bed.

In dream-troubles most folk are the epitome of suaveness and sophistication. Ethan was no exception. Reality—cold reality, to say the least—had too many improvisations.

First of all, he couldn't quite decide whether she was trying to kill him or kiss him. Apparently loveplay on this world was as aggressive as its climate.

He'd have told her to stop it, but his mouth kept getting full of gray fur. It seemed certain she was trying to bite him. At least, those four major canines gave that impression. Now, if someone like that Darmuka fellow or her father were to stroll in, bolt or no bolt . . .

He redoubled his efforts. Putting both hands out to push her away, his palms encountered something soft and warm. Human or not, it wasn't a shoulder. She moved even faster. Shifting his hands, he shoved frantically.

The result was both gratifying and educational.

She seemed to fly off the bed, land on her feet, and slam into the far wall, where she crumpled slowly to the floor. For a horrible moment he thought she'd hit too hard. If he'd killed the Landgrave's only cub, that would remove all the uncertainties from their immediate future.

Fortunately, she was only shaken, and stayed conscious.

"M . . . my, you *are* strong!"

He was torn between offering her a hand up and refusing further body contact. "Are you okay?"

"Y . . . yes, I think so, good knight." She rose slowly and felt the back of her head and neck. Then she did some re-arranging on her clothing, which had become delightfully disheveled. With a shoulder against the wall for support, she looked at him oddly.

"I hadn't expected quite so . . . overwhelming a rejection," she murmured.

"I'm sorry," Ethan replied, unable to forgo some sort of apology. "Our situation is very serious and it's hard for me to take anything lightly right now. I'm afraid, I, uh, don't know my own strength."

"Well *I* certainly do." She blinked. "I shall retire and consider this further," she said cryptically. "I will see you again, Sir Ethan. Good day."

Putting hand to forehead to wipe away the freezing sweat, he became aware that it was shaking badly. He grabbed the offending member. That only made the whole arm shake. Its companion was none too steady either. He let out a long breath, then put both hands under his backside and sat on them. That stopped the shaking and kept them warm too boot, but now he couldn't do anything about the sweat.

Hopefully he'd handled the situation correctly. Now he'd worry about Elfa's reaction and future feelings toward them. It was a damnable thing to have happen.

He was still pondering and sitting when September walked in.

"Well, young feller-me-lad," he began, glancing back the way he'd come, "I just passed her highness in the hallway. Seems you've made something of a conquest, what?"

"Or a mortal enemy. I'm not sure. It was more on the order of an opening skirmish. Hey, how come you're sure she came from my room?"

"You've just confirmed it."

"It might have been a veiled murder attempt, too, you know."

"I understand the penalty for playing around with the off-spring of nobility is—"

"Dammit, Skua, I wasn't playing around!" he said indignantly. "She was playing around with me. That is—"

"—death by slow torture, with all sorts of intriguing local variants on time-honored themes. Hunnar's been filling me in on some blanks, since you were occupied."

"Oh God. Does he know too?"

"I don't think so. Someone was sent to fetch you, tried your door. Finding it bolted, they assumed you wanted privacy. Good thing, too."

"Phew! Say, I found out something interesting, too. We were right about body composition. Almost certainly their skeletal system is less solid than ours, or whatever the proper medical term is. I gave her what I thought was a sharp shove and ended up throwing her halfway across the room. Scared the hell out of me."

"Really?" grinned September, the gold ring in his ear flashing. "Tell me more. Are they covered with that fur all over? Or are there certain places where—"

"For Harmony's sake, Skua!" Ethan said disgustedly, "nothing happened."

"Then why'd you find it necessary to toss her across the room?" he pressed, leering.

"I didn't find it necessary," Ethan continued patiently. "That's what I'm trying to tell you. She was so much lighter than I expected."

"That ought to be interesting."

"Will you stop, already?"

"Okay, young feller. Relax. I'm just joshing you," September continued in a serious tone. "So despite their greater size, their actual body weight is less. Then a good-sized human like yourself is probably as strong as most of 'em."

"Not necessarily," said Ethan. "Just because they're lighter doesn't mean they're not stronger. There's an awful lot of muscle on those frames. I just took her by surprise."

"Still," considered September, "in any kind of wrestling match, you'd have a tremendous advantage. Useful."

"What did Hunnar tell you?" Ethan sat back on the bed and curled his hands behind his head. "By the way, did everyone get single rooms?"

"Yes. Except the du Kanes. Colette refused to be alone, so they arranged for her to have a bed in with her father. That mold Walther has equally sumptuous quarters—only his door bolts from the outside and there are bars on the windows. Not that he's going anywhere that way. Have you looked outside? I wouldn't care to try a descent without a good strong cable and crampons."

"In this wind?" said Ethan. "I wouldn't like to try it even then."

"Hmm. Now according to Hunnar, most of the people on his world, hereabouts anyway, are peaceful. Aside from fun things like swiping someone's daughter now and then or bashing in a few heads. Fine, upstanding folk."

"Me, I want a nice quiet bar or nullball course with my old clubs and shooting companions," said Ethan dreamily. A blast of frozen air cut his cheeks. "Okay, they're all charming fellows. So?"

"I said most," September continued, inspecting the wooden chest at the foot of the bed. "There are also, it appears, bands of nomadic barbarians. Usually these do no more than attack an occasional raft, sometimes successfully, sometimes not."

"There had to be a reason for the castle and the soldiers," said Ethan.

"Other than protecting everyone from his neighbor, you mean? Sure. Anyway, over many years a couple of these bands have grown large enough to acquire the status of nations in themselves. They migrate on a fairly predictable circuit, living off tribute from the peoples they encounter. Hunnar told me what it's like when they move in. It doesn't make for pleasant listening.

"In addition to the standard tribute of money and food and clothing and such, they take over the town or raft or whatever for about a week, local-time. They take what they like from the shops and aren't above broiling the occasional shopkeeper who might venture an objection. Raping or carrying off the local girls who haven't been safely hid, killing a few kids for fun . . . oh, they're your usual happy primitive innocents, free from the corrupting bane of civilization!

"If there's any hint of opposition or resistance, the town is put to the torch and the entire populace down to the youngest cub massacred. Excepting a few women, they don't even take slaves, so they've no compunction about killing. No wonder everyone elects to pay tribute."

Ethan grunted. "They sound almost human."

"Don't they? They move in long columns perpendicular to the wind and sometimes three and four ships deep. They've dozens of sleds, on which they spend their whole lives. Even carry livestock and feed for same . . . the males take turns running scouting patrols, but the rafts never stop, except when they've moved in someplace."

"Like army ants on Terra," said Ethan.

"Yes, or Turabisi Delphius from that new thranx world, Drax IV. Hunnar likens them to other elemental forces they have to endure, like the wind and lightning. The nomads are the same people physically. But culturally and maybe even mentally they're throwbacks to an earlier, less civilized age."

"How often do they have to undergo this?" Ethan asked, staring out the window. He could hear the full-bodied wind howling outside. The window framed an unmarred rectangle of glacier blue.

"About every couple of years, sometimes three."

Ethan looked away from the sky. "The Horde that everyone keeps mentioning."

"That's it," September nodded. "This group has been taking tribute from the people of Sofold for a hundred years or so. Also most of their neighboring provinces. Seems we arrived at an interesting time. Hunnar and a lot of the younger knights are sick of paying tribute. They want to fight."

"That sounds like something they've been through before," said Ethan. "Have they got any chance of getting permission?"

"Well, as you would figure, such a proposition has to be approved by this so-called Council. By themselves, Hunnar and his fellow bucks would just amuse the moneybags. But there's a chap named Balavere the Longax who's the number-one general-type in this dump and he's thrown in with 'em. Hunnar says he's convinced Wannome has a fifty-fifty chance of standing an attack and siege."

Ethan whistled. "Not very good odds with the survival of your entire people at stake."

"Maybe not. But this old boy has gone through something like twenty-odd tribute periods himself. He's good and fed up. As you might guess, the opposition to the fighters is composed of those who have the least to lose. Country mayors and growers, this prefect fella Darmuka, others. Balavere and Hunnar have the support of a lot of the local merchants and traders. During tribute time the country folk are spared much of the burning and rampaging that goes on, since the barbarians naturally concentrate where most of the people and goods are, meaning Wannome."

"I'm better at haggling prices," said Ethan. "How do our host's chances look?"

"Well," said the big man, sitting down on the edge of the bed, "as is typical in such cultures, most of the able-bodied males on the island have had some sort of combat training, however informal. Hunnar says they can put about eight thousand armed men in the field. Of these, maybe two thousand have had some form of advanced military training. There's a standing permanent garrison of about five hundred, under the direction of some fifty or so knights aided by about a hundred squires and another hundred squire-apprentices."

"Three thousand soldiers and five thousand militia," said Ethan. September nodded.

"And this Horde?"

"At least four times that."

Ethan said nothing.

"According to Hunnar," September continued, "this tribe is led by an especially nasty son-of-a-bitch with the charming moniker of Sagyanak the Death, Scourge of Vragan. Vragan was a small hunting community they razed about ten years ago. The Death has the interesting hobby of taking folk he doesn't care for and nailing them to the ice. They have these short lances mounted on tiny double stone runners, with little sails. The Death and other assorted uppers go upwind until they can barely see the stake-out. Then they set their lances and release them.

"By the time they reach the condemned, those sail-powered lances have built up enough speed to drive halfway up someone's body. The head of the victim is always propped up so he or she can see the lances coming. Isn't that cute?"

"I wish you could have saved that little anecdote till after dinner," Ethan mumbled. He believed he had a reasonably strong stomach, but this world . . . "Okay, you've convinced me he's not a nice fella. What does Hunnar want from us? He wants something, that's sure, or he wouldn't have spent all that time telling you about it. Nor describing what a bastard this Sagyanak is. Sales technique. And he said there was something important he wanted us to know about before dinner tonight."

"Good lad," said September approvingly. "Here it is, then: As you would expect, Hunnar and this general Balavere are being very careful about the whole idea. They'd much rather convince the Council that tribute isn't a paying proposition and it's more logical to fight. But if they can do it by creating so much emotion for fighting that no one will speak against them, then by the Black Hole, they'll do it that way."

"Which means?" asked Ethan, digging his toes into the warmth of a fur blanket.

"That when they put their proposition forward, it would be appreciated muchly if we spring up like good chappies and swear to fight to the last dribble of blood alongside 'em."

"Umm. Don't you mean that they want us to support their idea of fighting?"

"No," said September bluntly. "We are to agree to pick up swords and spears and make suitable hacking motions alongside our Sofoldian brethren."

Ethan sat up quickly. All thoughts of napping remained stuck to the blankets.

"They want *us* to fight? But why? We're not citizens of Sofold and we're surely not warriors . . . at least, I'm not."

"That will change," September replied placidly. "While the locals seem to have responded to our appearance with a great deal of calm, Hunnar assures me that we've created quite a sensation. Otherwise their attitude might lead one to think that strange aliens dropped in on them every day. Hunnar would like the opposition to believe we're some kind of omen, what? The signs for battle are auspicious and all that sort of thing . . . But if we cower in the castle while the real fighting is taking place, all potential psychological lift will go down the tubes. So we'll be expected to march happily into the action, spending the blood of the enemy left and right with mysterious alien devices. Eh, me lad?"

Ethan had gotten stuck in a mental cul-de-sac several sentences back.

"Fight?" he murmured wonderingly to himself. "I can handle a nullgee club or a tennis racket. And I'm not bad at ricochet golf, if I do say so. But as to standing up and exchanging ax blows with one of these super-muscled pussycats—"

"In return for this minor physical but major moral support," September continued smoothly, "Hunnar has promised us all the aid we need to reach Arsudun."

Ethan threw up his hands. "Oh great! Assuming that any of us are left alive to take advantage of his munificence. I suppose in that event he'll personally see to a splendid funeral cortege. We'll be deposited with much weeping and heaving of anguished breasts at the foot of a reluctant Landgrave. I know one thing. There'll be no smile on *my* corpse. Suppose we don't go along?"

He expected September to counter with something like "we can't refuse," or "they'll chop off our fingers until we agree." His reply was a surprise.

"Nothing." He shook his head slowly. "They'll just do the best they can to persuade the others, without our commitment. If we want, we can leave for Brass Monkey tomorrow and make our own way as best we can."

"Oh." He thought again of Hunnar's face when, at last, the chance to fight had been mentioned. "When are you going to ask the others?"

"I already have. Colette du Kane thought it over real hard. Then she said we had no alternative. I'm beginning to think that girl's got a mind as sharp as her torso is flabby . . . You know how the old man is. Odd fella. One minute he was trying to tell me about how he's got to take care of himself so's he can get back to his bloody flowers, the next it's 'down with the cowardly invaders, up Sofold!' He went along . . . Walther said no, not surpri—"

Ethan was surprised himself. "You asked him?"

"Sure I asked him. He started to say no, but changed his mind. Just wanted to make it unanimous." The big man smiled.

"And Williams?" Ethan was trying to visualize the schoolmaster in helmet and armor with battle-ax in hand. The picture served to cheer him.

"He's been holed up with that top-dog wizard . . . what's his name?' . . . Eer-Meesach. Barely looked up from their confab long enough to nod at me before diving back into a stream of chatter I couldn't follow. Don't know if he's even aware of what I asked. One of us seems to have made a real pal among the locals."

"It's hardly surprising," said Ethan thoughtfully. "Think of the things someone like this Eer-Meesach could learn from a Commonwealth plain citizen—let alone a teacher. We can use an open-minded native or two on our side. A man of science is helpless by himself, but two of them constitute an entity capable of ignoring starvation, freezing, and prospects of imminent death just by chatting about some item of mutual interest," he concluded.

"Really?" mocked September, caterpillar eyebrows arching. "Are you in that category too, young feller-me-lad?"

"Who, me?" He chuckled. "Right now my greatest scientific aspiration is to annihilate the biggest steak in this quadrant. With Hammoud's barbecue sauce, crisp-turned reshka, and a bottle of Lafitte Calm Nursery Blend '96, or maybe '97. Speaking of which," he continued, turning on his side, "what are we going to do for food tonight?"

"A question of real significance," agreed September, nodding. "I suggested to Hunnar that we use our own food from the boat. Looked positively shocked, he did. Wouldn't hear of it. Claimed our alien odors and smells might make some important councilman ill. I pointed out that if one of us threw our dinner all over said councilman it wouldn't do his contingent any good either. He wouldn't buy it. Said it would be a poor way of showing our solidarity if we refused to tear meat with them . . . at least, that's how I mangle the metaphor he used . . . So we're stuck with whatever the chef has in mind. I didn't have a chance to wangle a copy of the menu. You said we shouldn't have any trouble handling the food, right?"

"I hope not," Ethan replied thoughtfully. "I don't anticipate any, from what I remember. That doesn't rule out the possibility of there being one or two just bad goodies in the banquet. I'd advise sticking to one or two plain dishes and not trying to play the interstellar gourmet. Probably most of it will be hearty and bland. Did you happen to find out anything about local etiquette?"

September smiled. "You eat with your fingers. Beyond that you improvise. And armor is optional."

"I asked Hunnar about the local manners myself," Ethan mentioned to September. He was nervously trying to adjust the brilliant gold sash that swept diagonally across his brown spotted-fur dress jacket. The royal tailor had gone through a triple funk trying to fit them with clothing suitable to the occasion.

Since, with the exception of September, the humans were as tall as tran adults but not nearly as broad, any formal outfit was big enough to swim in.

Stitching and cutting at children's clothing with near lightspeed, the royal tailor had somehow managed to outfit them all.

September whispered back at Ethan. "Don't worry about it." He winked in a way Ethan didn't fancy. "Just watch our neighbors and do as they do. I'm told that fighting for a choice section of haunch is permissible, so long as no one spills blood on his neighbor or gravy on the Landgrave."

Du Kane plucked at his modified coat unsteadily, but Colette seemed to have him well under control. As to her own "gown," it at least served to minimize her bulkiness—though it would pass unnoticed among the broad-beamed tran. As to its composition, all she could say was that it itched.

Ahead, sounds of Trannish chatter mingled with rough bellows of good humor, defiance, anger, outrage, enjoyment. Occasionally a sonorous belch would rise above all.

There was also music from stringed instruments, drums, and something close to a profoundly sick oboe. Odors of broiled meat and boiled vegetables tweaked other senses. Admiration and uncertainty at the presence of strange visitors apparently did not extend to waiting dinner for them.

Hunnar met them outside the entrance to the Great Hall. He appeared more nervous than Ethan could recall.

"There you are! By the great wild Rifs, what took you all so long? I was starting to believe that perhaps after all you had decided to . . . to go your way by another path."

"Not a chance, Hunnar old man or whatever," said September, clapping the knight on the shoulders. It didn't faze the tran, Ethan noted with a twinge of envy.

Hunnar looked past the big man. "Where is the little quiet one?"

"Oh, Walther's here too," replied September, jerking a thumb to the rear.

Even in splendid silks and furs the kidnapper still managed a ratty appearance.

"I don't think Hunnar means him," added Ethan, looking over their little assemblage. "Where's Williams?"

September had a glance himself. "Yes, where *is*—"

"Rest at ease, gentlemen, here I am." The familiar voice came from the far end of the hall. The schoolteacher appeared with the wizard, Eer-Meesach. Williams smiled apologetically as he drew next to them.

"I'm sorry for my tardiness, friends. I hope I haven't upset anything."

"No, no," said September. "Confound it, man, must you apologize for everything?"

"I'm sorry," Williams replied automatically. "Malmeevyn has given me some information that could be of great import." The wizard bowed slightly.

"Ya, sure," grunted September, unimpressed.

"Tis time," interrupted Hunnar, before the teacher could continue. "Follow me and be at your ease. I don't believe many will stare at you anyway. In that respect your arriving late is beneficial. But those with interested eyes will note who you enter with."

Malmeevyn obviously had standards of his own, because he'd left them already. As they started in Ethan sidled over to Williams.

"What's your news?"

"What do you know of Rex Plutonicus?" whispered the schoolmaster.

"Rex Plutonicus?" Ethan's brow crinkled. He looked knowledgeably at the other. "That's the monster volcano they spotted on the first survey, isn't it? Active, about eleven kilometers high? I didn't know you'd taken a terrain tape."

"I didn't," Williams replied. "That was broadcast as part of a general passenger orientation—to sell shuttle-down tickets, I suppose. It's the most outstanding single topographical feature on the planet."

"I must have been asleep," Ethan answered. "I only remember it from the tapes."

"Do you recall its location?"

"No. Wait . . . yes. It's about four hundred kilometers due east of Brass Monkey."

"Correct. Sight-seeing trips are run from the settlement."

"I may be dense, but I don't see the import yet."

"The wind here blows almost continually from the west," said Williams with carefully controlled excitement. "Malmeevyn says that on very windy days great clouds of black smoke and ash descend on the earth. They darken the land and make the crops bitter. The smoke and ash come always from the same southwesterly direction. No one from Sofold has ever been there, but occasionally a trading ship will arrive that has passed near. Its a great burning mountain. The Trannish name means 'The-Place-Where-The-Earth's-Blood-Burns.' "

"Damn! I see what you mean. Reach the volcano and from there to Brass Monkey is easy. Southwest and then we're warm again!"

"There could be variations in the smoke pattern," cautioned Williams. "But the wizard was quite insistent about it always coming from the same direction. Most of the time the wind blows due east, so smoke and soot from many eruptions would pass far south of here."

Ethan was rubbing mental hands together. "At least we have a direction now for our raft . . . if we can get a raft." Suddenly he found himself beside a chair. September was whispering in his ear.

"For O'Morion's sake, young feller, sit down!" He tugged at Ethan's jacket. "Sit down! Want 'em all staring at you?"

Ethan sat. Then he became aware of the Boschian scene he'd been drawn into.

They were seated on the outside of a great table shaped like a long letter "U." Tran of all sizes and descriptions were seated both inside and outside the arms of the table. The Landgrave, his daughter, and Eer-Meesach were sitting at the base of the U, on the outside, facing three empty chairs.

"For the Landgrave's ancestors," explained September.

Hunnar was seated across the table from them, on the inside and several seats down the U. Ethan noticed that their little group was positioned well down the arm of the table, close to the Landgrave. A location of some honor, probably.

The richness of silks and furs was dazzling. Ethan saw neither fashion nor couture, only credit signs with lots of lovely
zeros trailing behind like newborn puppies. The attire of
Sofolds nobility offered every color. Gold, deep blue, and
scarlet predominated.

Great metal and polished wooden platters piled high with
smoking meat, baskets of breads and fruits, and cauldrons
of pungent soup filled the tables to overflowing. Light came
from huge, thigh-thick candles set on posts around the table.
He took notice of the controlled war that took the place of
plate-passing and reflected wryly that no one would put
candles *on* the table for risk of total conflagration over a
stuffed olive, or whatever those little green things were.

In addition, light came from baskets of oil burning in
wrought-iron cups set into the walls. And the great fireplace
sported a blaze that would have violated every fire regula-
tion a humanx hotel manager could envision.

His own plate was wide and formed of some coppery material. He also had a cloth napkin not quite as big as a two-
man tent and a knife more suitable for a cavalry charge than
a dinner.

In spite of some lingering hesitancy over the alien cuisine,
his mouth was beginning to water. At least, between his furs
and the fire, it wouldn't freeze.

Next to him, September was gnawing happily on a meat-
laden bone with all the delicacy and comportment of a famished hyena. He nudged Ethan in the ribs, gently this time.

"Dig in, young feller. By the Dying Dead Red, these people
know how to *cook*."

"Pardon me if I don't share your enthusiasm. It's my tender
unbringing and respectable charge account holding me back."
He turned to his other side.

Williams was nibbling absently on something that looked
like a cross between a carrot and a stick of emergency space
protein. Next to him, Walther seemed to be displaying about
the same amount of gusto in downing his meal.

Across the table, Hellespont du Kane was doing his best
with a pair of knives to slice some meat from a small bone

for both himself and Colette. The meat stayed off his clothes. Also off his plate.

Ethan looked around, then reached uptable for something that resembled corned beef but could just as easily have been the pickled liver of a pregnant krokim. Nonetheless, it looked inviting and smelled better. A knife came down and just missed his fingers. It was wielded by a rangy tran several seats up from them. The native gave him a good-natured closed-mouth grin and carved off a choice portion for himself.

Ethan gritted his teeth, half-closed his eyes, and made a long-range stab with his own knife. When in Rome-Vatican . . . Surprisingly, he came back with the rest of the roast, or whatever it was, and nobody's hand.

Two good-sized tankards sat in front of his plate. The meat, he discovered, had a flavor like roast pork, although it was more heavily seasoned than he'd expected. It certainly wasn't bland.

He tried the larger tankard and found that it contained a drink like thick hot chocolate with a faint hint of pepper.

He almost choked on it when September let out a whoop and clobbered him with a flying elbow. He thrust his own small tankard at Ethan and his eyes sparkled. "Now here, young feller-me-lad, is something worth fighting to preserve. Put some of this liquid starlight into your gullet. The thranx themselves never brewed half so good!" He turned and bellowed something to Hunnar.

Ethan stared at his own small tankard with a mixture of lust and terror, chewing slowly on some indefinable vegetable. He picked it up and peered inside. The contents were dark and had a startling silver color.

"Called Reedle," September informed him. "Reedle-de-deedle-de . . . " he sang as Ethan hesitantly put metal to lips.

It went easily down his throat and into his stomach. There it must have encountered something flammable, because it burst like a stretched bubble and spewed tiny fireballs all over the place. One of them crawled right back up his throat and burned itself to a miniscule cinder right between his eyes. He let out a long whoosh.

"Reed . . . raw . . . reedle, huh?" September didn't answer him. He was otherwise engaged, mentally. Shortly thereafter, Ethan was too.

A little while later he noticed a cloying sweetness in the air. It wasn't a by-product of his dinner. Instead he discovered it emanated from several of the rather provocatively clad ladies seated nearby. The tran used perfume, then. Interesting. By Terran standards it was pretty crude stuff. By thranx standards it was a total loss. Here was another opportunity for trade, olfactory desires being equal.

For the hundredth—or maybe it was the thousandth—time, he lamented the loss of his goods, out of reach on board the *Antares*. He took another gulp of reedle and turned his concentration to the more interesting types seated at the great table.

Eventually his eyes traveled to the far corner of the U and to Darmuka Brownoak. The prefect was well into his own meal. He appeared to be enjoying it without becoming over-exuberant or soused. Mostly he was smiling and nodding at the shouts and comments of those seated around him. A cool, sharp, dangerous customer, Ethan reflected.

His gaze continued around the table and was startled to encounter a pair of glowing yellow eyes staring back into his own. They belonged to a beautiful, overpowering, hirsute valkyrie named Elfa.

Great credit! He'd almost managed to wipe his distressing —well, awkward—encounter with the Landgrave's daughter from his mind. Hurriedly he averted his eyes and concentrated with full attention on dissecting a second chop—"vol," Hunnar had called it.

He was on his third helping and second tankard of reedle when Sir Hunnar rose abruptly and bounded onto his seat. Ethan poked September, who'd subsumed enough reedle to float an elephant, and whispered across to the du Kanes.

"Now's the time. Don't do anything or say anything even if provoked. Brownoak and his cronies will be looking for the slightest opening."

Hunnar put both paws in the air. Gradually the roar and howling subsided to a steady murmur, a grinding like surf on gravel. When it dropped further, to where a single voice could be heard easily, he began.

"So. Here you sit. The pride of Sofold. The wealth of its minds, the deciders of its fate, arbitrators of destiny. Pagh!" He spat. "You collective dung-heaps! Offsprings of vols! Hoppers. Gleaners of lavatories!"

Angry murmurings swelled around him. There were a few cries in Trannish of "Bring him down!"

"Oh, you claim to be otherwise, eh?" Hunnar continued. "While we sit gorging our fat selves, at this moment the Horde moves on its trail of slime and blood to visit our homes. Yes, the Horde comes. Like it or not, the Horde comes. Straight as the path of a thunder-eater grazing, the Horde comes . . . What will happen when it reaches us? Will you sit and laugh so heartily, merrily, then? When your purses are emptied and your daughters filled? What then?"

An old tran rose halfway out of his seat across the table.

"We will pay our assigned levy, as we always have, Sir Hunnar, take a few weeks of misery and burden, as we always have, and survive, as we always have!"

Hunnar whirled and faced the oldster. "He does not 'survive' who lives on the sufferance and humor of another. What if this time our offerings should not satisfy the Death, eh? What if ill humor should visit Sagyanak in the night and tell him to raze Wannome to the earth-ice? For pleasure, mayhap. Burn the fields and towns of Sofold, for amusement? What then of your 'survival,' old man?"

"My!" interrupted a familiar, penetrating voice from across the table. "Don't berate poor Nalhagen," continued Darmuka Brownoak easily. The prefect paused, took a tiny sip from his tankard of reedle. It was quiet enough in the great hall for Ethan to hear the container hit the table gently as the prefect set it down. Some things, Ethan reflected, were the same from planet to planet. On the surface this was a conflict of philosophy. In reality it came down to a battle of wills between young and old, between the rich and content and the talented and impatient. Everyone in the hall knew it. They waited to see what would develop.

"He only wants to live, like the rest of us. Most of us, anyway." Brownoak glanced around the table and there was a murmur of assent from the crowd. "Why," the prefect continued, "such a thing as you postulate has not happened in the hundreds of years of Sofoldian history. Why would Sagyanak have reason to do such a thing now?" His stare was one of profound amazement. "To destroy Wannome and Sofold would be to destroy forever the tribute the Horde receives from us at regular intervals. Would the Scourge cut out the bottom of their purse?"

"They have done this to other towns," Hunnar said.

"But never to Wannome."

"So we continue to dig our noses in the dirt, year upon year, to gratify this monster?" the knight snorted. "I say no longer. Fight, this time!" He opened his claws and made tearing motions at the other. "Fight once, and have done with ignominy and hardship forever!"

"I think I should agree with you in that," said Brownoak.

"What?" Hunnar was taken aback.

"If," the prefect continued, daintily wiping his mouth with one of the rag-napkins, "I did not dislike suicide. Indeed, we would 'have done with it.' You and I would be no more. Truly, death would end ignominy and hardship, but I am not anxious to employ such a solution yet. I'm as brave as the next man," and he glared sharply up at Hunnar, "but I am also a thoughtful being and a pragmatist. We would be outnumbered many times by a foe whose whole life is spent not in trading and growing, mailing and crafting, but in killing and fighting. We'd have as much chance of winning as a hopper caught in the path of a stampeding thunder-eater."

Hunnar countered instantly. "In spite of what *you* may think, prefect, I too am a thoughtful person, and I say we *would* win. The walls of Wannome have grown too high for the Horde to scale, too thick for the Horde to break, these past years. Nor could they breach the nets and the new chain that guards the harbor entrance."

"What of a siege?" asked Brownoak, sipping reedle.

"With a little preparation we could stand such far longer than they. No barbarian can sit on his haunches and stare placidly at his enemy. He is not mentally equipped for it. Sagyanak's own tribesmen would throw out any leader who ordered such. The Scourge knows that as well as you or I."

"You say all this," came a flat voice from uptable. A middle-aged tran with a short steel-wool beard looked up at Hunnar. "Yet you are but a cub compared to most of us, risen rapidly in the ranks of his elders. If you are the thoughtful one you claim, you can see my point. Why should we agree with you, a mere youngster? How much of your declaration is fueled by ambition and youthful impatience rather than careful reason?"

"Because I—" Hunnar began, but he was interrupted.

"I will have none of that, Hellort," rumbled an abyssal voice from down the table.

The tran who rose was stocky—no, even short—by tran standards, but so massively built that he was almost square. The powerful torso was bent and knotted with age. But the voice was like a scalpel in a field of butter knives. Tiny slit black pupils peered out of bony caves from beneath overhanging brows. The tran was all smashed and crumpled, almost deformed.

"I meant nothing insulting," apologized Hellort quietly. "I've no questioning with you, Balavere."

Ethan peered at the other more intently, not caring that he was staring. This, then, was the famous Balavere Longax, the most respected military man in Wannome. From Hunnar's brief description of him Ethan had expected a giant, not a blocky dwarf. But the tran general was clearly a giant in ways other than physical.

"Yes, you do, Hellort. Because, you see, I too have considered this question painfully. I find myself in agreement with the good Redbeard—his youth notwithstanding. He may appear impetuous. Do not perceive that as ambition. He has a sound military head on his shoulders, yes, and moves smoothly over difficult ice.

"Sofold is the strongest province in the area," he continued pridefully. "If any can make a decisive stand against the Horde, tis we. It *should* be Sofold. But we must do this thing on our own. No one—not Phulos-tervo of Ayhus nor Veg-Tuteva of Meckleven—will send a single soldier from his land to aid us, for fear of their being recognized and invoking the wrath of Sagyanak."

"Are you so confident of victory, then?" broke in Brownoak.

"Of course I am not confident of victory," the general replied softly. "I will not lie to you, sirs. A battle of such magnitude contains too many uncertainties. No intelligent soldier would venture a prediction on the outcome. But I say this," he continued, as the prefect seemed ready to add more, "I've seen Wannome rise and strengthen over these last few good years. Dangerously so, and Sagyanak should realize it. There is your reason for bringing us down, at least a little. But the Horde has grown fat and lazy on tribute. They've not fought a real battle in some time."

"And we also will have the aid of the strangers from the stars," added Hunnar, "for who can believe their coming at this crucial time to be accidental?"

A hundred pairs of slitted cat-eyes looked straight at Ethan. They all seemed to be focused on a point just below his hair. He wanted to reach up and scratch the place but didn't dare. He squirmed a little, though. The crowd wavered.

"Strange in form, perhaps," said the imperturbable, thrice-damned Brownoak, "but not in ability. Perhaps less so, in fact. And ability is what we need, not cries of star-sent omens."

"Ha!" said September. Ethan looked at him in surprise, as did many others. Which was the idea.

The big man put one foot on the table, stepped up, and walked across. He just missed a meat pie here, a tankard of reedle there. When he hopped down on the other side, every eye in the hall, human and tran, was focused on him.

Bending, he gripped the rear legs of Hunnar's chair. With a single, flowing motion, he lifted both knight and chair chest-high off the floor. There was a gasp of surprise from the crowd. It was followed by a few cheers and a babble of excited conversation.

September put Hunnar down, recrossed the table, and resumed his seat.

"Quite an exhibition," Ethan complimented.

"You could probably have managed it yourself, young feller-me-lad. I thought it worth doing. But Hunnar and I didn't have a chance to practice that in private. I'm glad the execution matched the theory. Would have looked awfully funny out there if I'd gone and tipped him over." He took a long draught of reedle and smacked his lips. "Though he went up a lot easier than some folk I've hoisted. Now, if I'd dropped him . . . "

Ethan didn't mention that he thought September probably could have made the lift even if the tran knight weighed as much as a human of similar size. Someone up by the Landgrave was waving for attention. It was Eer-Meesach.

"I can say," intoned the wizard in strong voice, "that among these strangers is also a being of great knowledge. A wizard equal to . . . well, nearly equal to . . . my own person in powers of intellect." He pointed dramatically down the table.

"Stand up, Williams, dammit," September mumbled around the lip of his tankard. The schoolmaster rose quickly and stood staring at the table, looking for all the world like a kid caught snitching at the cookie jar. He sat down almost instantly.

"And there are others among them of abilities even more astounding," continued Hunnar excitedly, "all pledged to assist us in this holy endeavor!"

"What's he talking about?" asked du Kane from across the table. "I've picked up a bit of the language, but not enough to translate what he's raving on about."

"He's telling everyone how terrific we are," said Ethan absently, trying to concentrate on Hunnar's speech.

"Oh," said the industrialist. He leaned back, looking satisfied. Ethan decided the tran could interpret that as overwhelming confidence.

"I am not so convinced," began Darmuka Brownoak, but Hunnar talked him down.

"A loosing, a loosing, then!" The cry was picked up, carried around the table like sherbet.

"Yes . . . now time . . . fight . . . but if we should lose? . . . weapons? . . . how much time? . . . family . . . a loosing!"

Eventually the Landgrave stood. There was immediate and respectful silence in the great hall.

"A proposal of grave consequence has been put to this gathering. Councilmen and knights of Sofold, the call has

been made for a loosing. Whatever else can be said, it is
sure there is enough interest for such. I so call it."

"Is this loosing like taking a vote?" Ethan queried September.

"That's it, me lad. You pledge your booze, is what." He
grinned. "That's serious. My kind of folk."

The Landgrave picked up his chalice. He held it at arm's
length, ramrod straight away from his body. Everyone stood
and did likewise, including the ladies, Ethan noted. The little
band of humans was tardy in copying the gesture, but no one
seemed to mind.

"We have no vote in this, of course," September told them,
"but we can participate. It looks better that way."

Into the silence the Landgrave said, "So that each may
know of his neighbor . . . "

At that, September and a large number of the assembled
dignitaries inverted their tankards, spilling magnificent reedle
over table, food, floor, boots, and selves. The other humans
did likewise a second later.

A herald had wheeled a high chair to the right of the Landgrave. Now he began a slow count, but Hunnar had started
ahead of him. Before the herald could finish, the knight roared
with joy and threw his tankard clear to the beams of the
vaulted ceiling.

"WE FIGHT!" he bellowed.

The cry was picked up by dozens of throats. "We fight, we
fight!" Hunnar ran and embraced old Balavere. Then everything degenerated into a confusing, heaving mass of hairy
bodies, sharp questions, and endless toasts. The musicians
added to the erumpent revelry with a sprightly semi-martial
tune. A few tran moved into the U and began dancing. Others
seemed intent on flattening their companions with crippling
slams to the shoulders.

In the noise and confusion, Brownoak rose and said something to the Landgrave. A frozen smile on his face, he retired.
Those tran who had been seated close to him accompanied
the prefect in exit. In the explosion of congratulations and
excitement hardly anyone noticed their withdrawal.

Ethan finally succeeded in drawing Hunnar's attention. He
pointed out the prefect's abrupt departure.

"You're going to have trouble with that guy," he warned. But the knight was too overcome at the final realization of his hopes to take cognizance of Ethan's warning.

"The vote in Council is against him," he said absently. "What can he do now? Nothing! He is more helpless than a cub, and embarrassed besides. Forget him. Do you not understand? We're going to *fight!*"

Ethan turned away and noticed General Balavere standing in a circle of older tran. Solemnly there was a gentle touch on the shoulders, quiet conversation with first one, then another. Closer inspection revealed another interesting anthropological fact about their hosts, which was that they did actually cry. Ethan turned away.

Meanwhile, the Landgrave had been attempting almost desperately to restore some semblance of order since the prefect had left. He pounded his staff on the floor and enlisted the vocal services of the herald. Then, apparently deciding it was hopeless, he signaled something to the musicians in the balcony.

A wild, strongly rhythmic tune replaced the pseudo-march. With a yell, the councilmen and knights separated the two long arms of the great table, turning it into a wide "V" shape. Instantly the funneled dance floor was occupied by swirling, flying couples.

It was interesting to note that the dancing, while highly energetic, did not last long at all by terran standards. No matter how husky-looking, many of the dancers seemed to get quickly out of breath. Apparently, with the wind to move them, the tran had not developed their lung-power overmuch. By the same token, the acrobatics of the lighter-than-they-looked dancers verged on the appalling. Their sense of timing and balance, logically enough, was inhuman. He'd keep that in mind if he ever found it necessary to dodge the local police. It had happened before.

On the ice, they would run circles around him.

Laughter and handclapping added to the feeling of merriment. Right now everyone was in the best of spirits. Later, when the enormity of their decision had sunk in, there would be time for quiet contemplation and thought.

Ethan was thoroughly enjoying the scene when there was

a tap on his shoulder. He turned and was confronted with the copious bosom of Elfa Kurdagh-Vlata. He hurriedly elevated his gaze, finding no relaxation in the return stare at the top.

"As thou can see, good Sir Ethan," she purred, "I have not yet been asked to dance." This was not entirely true, as several young tran with bruised shins could attest.

"Perhaps Sir Hunnar? . . " Ethan suggested desperately.

"Foo! He's too busy accepting congratulations for the way in which he outmaneuvered the prefect. Anyhow, I want to dance with you." She lowered her voice. "I have not forgotten your mastery at . . . hand-to-hand combat. Are you equally adept at dancing, mayhap?"

"Oh no," he said, shrinking back and finding the table blocking his retreat. "I know nothing of your local dances. I've got two left feet. And I'm naturally clumsy besides."

"That, for sure, I cannot believe," she said smokily. She reached out and grabbed his arm with a paw that might have been lighter than his own, but was backed by muscles of iron. Rather than be yanked from the chair, he got up peacefully.

"Come then, and we will disport ourselves with the others."

Before he could protest he found himself in the middle of the floor, trapped in a whirlpool of fur and giant shoulders. The music was alien but not impossibly exotic. The steps of Sofoldian dance were fairly simple. After a bit he was actually enjoying himself. Never mind that he was flirting with disaster.

A strange sort of rescue was provided by Sir Hunnar. The knight stepped up behind him, put a paw on his shoulder, and said in the cheeriest voice imaginable, "Sir Ethan, I challenge you."

"Beg pardon?" Ethan responded, stumbling over his own feet.

"A challenge! Yea, a challenge!" came the cry from the crowd. Almost as soon as he caught his balance, it seemed, the floor had been cleared around them. Everyone was staring expectantly at him and Hunnar.

Meanwhile, the knight was removing his cloak, decorations, and dress jacket.

"Wait a minute," began Ethan confusedly. "I was just

starting to get the hang of the dance. What's this challenge business?"

"In truth, tis really nothing, friend Ethan," replied Hunnar, flexing his massive arms and stretching his wings. "Just a simple custom. Tis good manners for guests and hosts to fight. I was reminded that this pleasantry had not yet occurred. Tis an opportune time as any to perform such."

"I disagree," countered Ethan cautiously. "Anyhow," he continued, backing up a couple of steps, "why pick on me? Why not exchange blessings of good fellowship with Sir September?"

"I would have," the knight grinned. "But look."

Ethan turned. September reclined full-length across the table. His flowing white hair lay half-in and half-out of a bowl of cold soup. A tankard was gripped limply in one massive hand. He was snoring with the melodious buzz of a broken bearing.

"I'll waken the good knight," Ethan stalled. "Really, Sir Hunnar, I'm not cut out for this sort of thing. Now, if you'd like to have a go on the links . . . would there be a course about?"

"Ah, your modesty is truly worthy of you, Sir Ethan," said Hunnar admiringly. He was now naked to the waist. The resulting pectoral panorama would give any barber pause.

"Let us to combat!" He came barrelling across the room, arms forming a great hairy crescent.

Well, at least it wasn't supposed to be a lethal conflict, Ethan rationalized. It was the least he could do in the interests of good fellowship, wasn't it? Besides, he'd seen the ease with which September had hoisted the knight, chair and all.

He tried to ignore the roar of the crowd—they sounded just like a bunch of inebriated conventioneers, he decided—and duck the roundhouse blow Hunnar threw at him. He stepped in and tried to get a grip on the knight's waist. What he got instead was a solid buffet on the side of the head. His vision was momentarily restricted to sights galactic—black spaces and colored stars.

He sat up and refocused his eyes. Sir Hunnar was standing several meters away, panting and grinning down at him. Obviously more subtle tactics were required. Cries of "Well struck!" and "Good blow!" came from the appreciative crowd. His opponent might not weigh in as heavy as he, but he could still knock your head off while you were looking up the proportionate discrepancies, Ethan reflected.

All right, he would try something else—if he could remember that far back.

Sir Hunnar came on again. He feinted with his left paw and swung the right. Ethan stepped to one side, blocked the blow with his left arm, and hit the other gently in the ribs, just behind the wing membrane, and then in the jaw. He spun and hit him in the lower back with his heel, almost falling down in the process.

His own weight and the blow combined to send the knight sprawling. For an awful moment Ethan thought he'd broken something. The tran were tougher than that, however. Hunnar rolled over and grunted.

"How did you do that, Sir Ethan?"

"Come on and find out," invited Ethan, breathing heavily.

Hunnar climbed to his feet and advanced again, more cautiously this time. Ethan let him grab his right shoulder. Then he spun into the other's charge, driving an elbow up and into the broad chest. Hunnar let out a whoosh, surprised. Ethan bent and grabbed a bladed foot by the ankle, yanked and straightened up, putting the knight on his back. Ethan turned and drove the heel of his foot into the other's midriff —gently. He walked away while Hunnar was trying to catch his breath.

The crowd was deafening. On Terra his movements would have seemed slow and clumsy. But here their alienness seemed to verge on the magical.

Sir Hunnar sat up, holding his middle. He smiled. "I could see that one, I think. Will you teach me that last trick, Sir Ethan?"

"Sure. Here, you start like this . . ." But he didn't have a chance to continue, because a moment later massive palms were literally pounding congratulations into him. If it continued he'd be asking for mercy from their admiring assault.

Even worse, he noticed that Elfa was staring across at him with gleaming, almost worshipful eyes.

Someone in the crowd pressed a tankard of reedle into his hand. His left leg hurt where he'd pulled something. He drained several swallows. He did not notice Colette du Kane, who was staring at him with a most peculiar expression.

VII

He woke in the middle of the night, and it wasn't from cold. The icy night air was sharp enough to keep him from falling asleep again, though. After several futile attempts, he put his hands under his head and stared up at the canopy which covered the bed. His suit crinkled under him and he edged up against the bulk of his survival parka.

Something was going to have to be done about the attentions of the Landgrave's daughter before a fatal misunderstanding occurred.

He knew next to nothing of local custom in such matters. But if someone should develop the wrong idea or walk in on them at another moment like that first one, it could be very awkward indeed. They'd be reminded very quickly of their alienness. Even Hunnar's friendship might evaporate with surprising speed.

Finally he rolled over and felt under the blankets for the parka. It was difficult to put it on in the light from the single remaining candle. The thermometer had plunged to regions where no human should have stirred from bed. But with his mind thinking furiously on other matters, he hardly noticed.

Once he'd donned the parka, he unbolted the door and slipped out into the hall. He had a fair idea of the location of the Landgrave's rooms. Tracing the proper steps and turns in the sub-freezing, windswept hallways was something else again. Only a few candles and oil lamps lit the way.

At night, with the wind moaning through the corridors and everyone but a few uncommunicative guards asleep, the castle seemed as forlorn and empty-cold as the mountains of the moon.

The whole thing was ridiculous. What was he going to do, rouse the Landgrave in the middle of the night? On the other hand, it might be the best time. In secret, without nosy courtiers around. An unguarded, unwatched discussion. It might also help minimize his embarrassment. And it was something that ought to be dealt with soonest.

Ah, the Landgrave's quarters were just around that turn, there. He would tell the guards . . .

He looked down the hall, peered harder. The flickering, uncertain light made it hard to be sure, but there didn't seem to be any guards. That was odd. He slowed as he approached the door to the inner chambers.

The guards were there, it turned out. Both of them. Immaculately clad in inlaid armor and leather. One was pinned neatly to the wall by a pair of long pikes. His expression was frozen in shock and surprise. The other's head lolled on the floor at an unnatural angle. His blood flowed over the smooth stones.

Several possibilities suggested themselves right away. None of them made any sense. In the shock of the moment he didn't stop to consider that where two competent armed guards had been neatly dispatched, he might prove singularly uneffective. He stuck his head inside the open door and looked into the room.

The tableau that greeted his eyes might have been drawn from an ancient Terrussian opera. It was crowded enough.

In the great canopied carved bed, the Landgrave lay pinned to the blankets by two husky tran wearing simple masks. A third stood over him with a standard ship-issue survival knife poised to strike. Hellespont and Colette du Kane sat to one side, securely gagged. They were tied to a couple of chairs much too big for them. A fourth tran, wielding a bloody saber, watched them.

Ethan turned, reached down, and hefted the pike of the fallen guard. Two courses of action suggested themselves. He could charge in and dispatch the four assassins, free the du Kanes, and earn the eternal admiration of all. Or he could turn and run down the hall screaming like a broker whose credit had submarined until he'd roused enough help to be effective.

Logic, plus the fact that he could handle a garden hoe more readily than a pike, inclined him toward the latter course. Not as glorious, but more practical. He turned and took several steps down the hall.

"Alarm, murder most foul, assassins, cutthroats! Rouse yourselves! Help, help, the Landgrave is being murdered! Guards, knights, priests, depression, devaluation, competition!"

Confused murmurs sprang up throughout the castle as the cold walls bounced Ethan's cries up corridors, around turns, down iceways. The pile of stone started to stir like a beehive poked with a stick.

Replies also came from within the room in the form of a string of curses. One of the assassins, a huge burly fellow with a sword slash on one arm and fur knotted like an old rug, came out with weapon at the ready. He looked to his left. This was a fatal mistake, since Ethan was waiting on his right.

It took little skill to skewer the killer through the middle.

The tran screamed like a girl, which added a satisfying note to the growing pandemonium. At one end of the hall, figures could be seen running toward them. Ethan started for them.

And tripped over the prone guard in the half-dark.

He rolled over on his back, stunned. Above him a tall, shadow-garbed figure raised a red saber over its head. Fangs glowed in the oil-light. The saber descended. He could hear the air it cut. The wielder grunted questioningly and Ethan heard the steel hit the stone floor at his side, so close that it cut his shirt and struck sparks from the rock. Something blunt hit him in the stomach.

It was the feathered end of the arrow that was buried in the other's gut. Another millisecond and he was buried in an avalanche of blood and fur.

It might be lighter than it should, but it was dead weight. In a minute, though, there were hands to help him. He stared into the gloom. Hunnar was among the crowd. Feet ran past him. Shouts rang like bells from the hallway walls.

"Very close, Sir Ethan," said the knight, giving him a muscular arm up. "Our thanks."

"Mine to you," he replied breathlessly. He fingered his middle where the back of the arrow had struck before snapping in half.

"Not to me." Hunnar pointed to another figure standing in the twilight beside them.

Suaxus-dal-Jagger was holding a bow half again as tall as himself, an arrow notched in the gut-string. He nodded curtly, turned, and started down the hall.

Hunnar knelt and rolled the body of the saber-holder over. He examined the silent face while Ethan tried to wipe some of the blood from his parka.

"Do you recognize him?" he asked curiously.

"No, but that is not surprising strange. Such men take care of their anonymity. What happened?"

Without replying, Ethan turned and led him into the room he'd seen so briefly. At least twenty armed tran were now clustered inside. Their faces were not pleasing to look upon. Right now they were giving the room a thorough search, even hunting for hollow places in the walls.

The du Kanes had been released. Colette was rubbing her wrists. In the freezing air Ethan could imagine how painful the ropes must have been. When she saw Ethan, she took a step in his direction, caught herself, and stared at the floor.

Crazy twit, he thought uneasily.

"You happened along at a propitious time, sir," said du Kane. "Those blackguards rudely assaulted us in the midst of a sound sleep. Before we knew it we were trussed tighter than a good copyright. We—"

The Landgrave stepped roughly between them. He put a paw on each of Ethan's shoulders, gently but firmly.

"This I do now promise you, Sir Ethan. We are bound to this fight that approaches and there is no help for it. But should Wannome triumph, I swear to you on my ancestor's honor that all our abilities and wealth shall be bent to the task of taking you to wherever you should wish, be it halfway around the world. I owe you my life. Few in Sofold carry such a valuable curam." He turned to greet his daughter, who had just arrived. She ran into his arms, her face twisted into an unreadable alien expression.

Ethan turned away. That ought to do as a lever for trade concessions, he thought, trying to push the sentimental scene from his mind.

"I'm not sure I understand, Sir Ethan," said Hunnar, rubbing his own arm. Maybe he'd literally fallen out of bed. Ethan became aware for the first time that the knight was naked except for his sword. "Why did they take your two friends?"

"It's obvious enough," explained Ethan tiredly. "They were going to murder the Landgrave and make it appear as though the du Kanes had done it. Not only would that have finished your plans to fight this Horde, but it would put *us* in a pretty fix, wouldn't it? C'mon, Hunnar, you know as well as I who's behind this."

Hunnar hesitated, then looked shocked.

"The prefect? But he wouldn't dare!"

"Someone did. Why not him?"

"For one thing, my friend, you are mistaken in your thoughts. Should the Landgrave die it would have no effect on our decision to fight the Horde. The Landgrave's daughter would inherit the throne and a new Landgrave would be chosen to serve beside her. Having been duly determined, the Council's declaration would stand."

"I see," said Ethan reflectively. "Tell me. Does Elfa get to choose her own Landgrave?"

"Certainly not! Should the Landgrave leave naught but female offspring, then the eldest receives a suitor selected by the Council. Someone to perpetuate a strong line."

"Really." Ethan was thinking furiously. "And who would the Council be likely to pick as a good match?"

"I had not given the matter any thought," replied Hunnar. "I doubt anyone has. The Landgrave has many years before him yet. In such a case I might hope it could be myself." He averted his gaze. "But twould probably not be."

His head came up and his eyes widened. He looked thoughtful. "I understand you now, Sir Ethan. Yes, for the sake of seeing himself on the throne, or his children, he could do that."

They stood quietly for a few moments. A soldier appeared at the doorway, his armor askew from the speed at which he'd donned it.

"Nothing is found of the other Unmentionables, sir," he gasped out. "Tis feared they have eluded pursuit and left the castle."

"Keep at it," replied Hunnar angrily. "They may be hidden

in a box somewhere, or in the kitchens. Search every corner, even the catacombs. Find them!" He turned back to Ethan.

"Did you see their faces?"

"Sorry. I'm afraid I didn't see much of anything after sticking this one." The thought of what he'd just done suddenly hit him. "I . . . sorry, Hunnar, I feel a little sick."

"I did . . . see one," said Colette. Ethan turned surprised eyes on her.

"I thought you didn't understand the language."

She looked at him pityingly. "Did you think I'd waste my time studying patterns in my quilts? I've been studying the language with our servants. So has father. His mind . . . wanders, sometimes. But when its all present, it's a shockingly competent one. He has a photographic memory, I might add . . . I think I understand what this Hunnar said. He wanted to know if you could identify those who got away, didn't he?"

"Yes. And you think you could?"

She nodded.

"What does the She say?" asked Hunnar interestedly.

"She believes she can recognize your two assassins if she sees them again."

"That would be excellent!" The knight's eyes sparkled. He showed his teeth. "'Tis something, at least."

"Look, why not pick up the prefect for questioning? It's certainly the best lead you've got."

"Lead? Oh, I see. Arrest the prefect?" Hunnar looked shocked. "On only personal supposition? It cannot be done! . . . No, not even the Landgrave would consent to it, though no love is lost between him and Brownoak."

"Don't you have protective custody?" Ethan asked.

"What?"

"Never mind. Well, that sticks it, then," he said disgustedly.

"I am sorry, friend Ethan. I do not understand."

"Forget it, Hunnar." He patted the knight on one massive, hairy arm. "I hope you find your assassins. Would-be assassins." On Terra, he mused, he'd be a prime suspect.

His reason for paying a nocturnal visit to the Landgrave was completely forgotten. Anyhow, this wasn't the proper time to discuss it.

He looked around at a sound from the doorway. September

was standing there, swaying slightly and looking a little bemused. Ethan didn't find the big man's drunkenness a bit funny just now.

"Now, what's all the racket here?"

"The du Kanes were kidnapped by a bunch of local nasties. They intended to kill the Landgrave and frame the du Kanes for it." He eyed September intently. "I broke it up."

"Bravo, young feller-me-lad, bravo!" He belched loudly. "Wonder what they do for hangovers here. This damned racket's given me a devil of a one—practically shook me out of bed."

"Then why don't you go back to it?" Ethan spun away in disgust.

September stared at him sharply for a moment, then sagged. "Yerse, young feller, I believe that's exactly what I'm going to do." He turned and stumbled off down the hall.

It was much, much too soon when the servant woke Ethan politely and brought in his breakfast. A carton of their own emergency rations, thank Rama! Not that the local food last night hadn't been edible. Even tasty in spots, but it was good to smell real terran food again, even if fast frozen.

He searched through the case and came up with a can of self-cooking bacon and eggs, a smaller cylinder of coffee, and a flat, two-sided slab that when keyed down the middle broke into two hot slices of buttered toast.

He wolfed it all down, rearranging the more persistent itches within the parka. Preparing to don his shoes, he found a pair of fur-lined boots next to them. They were a little large, but then the royal tailor no doubt had a hell of a time with their foot shapes. Not to mention the odd task, as the tran didn't wear footgear.

Probably September had slipped him instructions and a rough sketch or two. So they were ill-fitting and awkwardly stitched, but they were warm and that was all that counted. The soles were even studded with tiny metal shards, to give them some grip on the slick ice.

Unfortunately, he was still stuck with the too-large survival suit. He might do better with a native coat like September's.

The castle that morning was a carnival of conversation and gossip. It centered around the attempted assassination and the role played by the visitors from the sky. September went off somewhere with Balavere and Hunnar to inspect the city and harbor defenses and make pertinent suggestions. Ethan wondered about the big man's profession for the nth time and finally gave it up. An admitted criminal . . .

No, he cautioned himself. Being wanted on several worlds did not automatically con ict him. Church and Commonwealth notwithstanding, the legal tenets of planets varied hugely from system to system. They had to. Monolithic law would make the gigantic humanx Commonwealth unworkable.

So the same act that might condemn a man to death on one world could make him hero on another.

A servant told Ethan that on awakening Williams had been visited by no less a personage than the great wizard himself. So those two were off again somewhere trading anecdotes and information.

The du Kanes were keeping to their room. As for Walther, he was allowed out under guard for exercise only.

That left him alone to explore the town and the castle.

Several days of comparative freedom from official dinners and such gave him time to examine Wannome in more depth. In many ways it resembled a host of small ancient terran walled towns. Especially those few that had been preserved as historical monuments. Ethan knew a little of them from school and the traveldees.

Personally, he'd never been able to afford a trip to the home world. Nor had the company found it fit or necessary to send him. Someday, perhaps . . .

But there were endless differences.

For example, there were none of the fountains that decorated so many human and thranx towns. Naturally not. Not when it would require constant heating to keep the water flowing.

Alternatively, many of the houses sported fantastic roof decorations carved in ice, often by very young cubs. The inhabitants were gruff, but friendly. By the second day they'd gotten over their fear/uncertainty and had grown positively effusive. Clearly the word had been passed that the humans were not only guests but special favorites of the Landgrave. And he who favors one favored by the Landgrave favors himself—a universal tenet, if differently expressed, he reflected.

The cubs were a total and unexpected delight, rolling, bouncing, chivaning balls of fur that surrounded him wherever he went and threatened to get all tangled up in his clumsy legs. The blatantly displayed fact that he possessed neither chiv nor dan both astounded and delighted them. No doubt they looked on him as a new variety of friendly freak, a silly goblin called up just to please and delight them.

He visualized them lying in the street, running blood, impaled on pikes, and decided that if he'd been in Hunnar's place he would have fought for this chance to resist as soon as he'd grown old enough to articulate his position.

Or would you, my good salesman? Sure you wouldn't have found it more expedient to buy another two or three years of safety, of good business? Eh? So certain of your conscience?

The thought bothered him and he shook it off without resolving it. Of course it was tough to get out of the habit of buying peace. But it could grow too comforting, too degrading. A dedicated pacifist, he found himself shocked at what a few days on this backward world had done to his comfortable picture of the universe. Weren't the commercial practices of some of the great companies just as bloodthirsty and ruthless, if more discreet? Didn't Sagyanak have his counterparts in polished boardrooms and his spirit back of major stock manipulations?

By the end of the first week he'd already grown a little bored with Wannome. Even the harbor, with its ever-shifting panorama of rafts and cargoes, was growing stale. Heart and soul he was a big-city boy. While he could trade, and trade well, on the most primitive worlds, it was the thought of mechanized comfort and sybaritic civilization awaiting his return that pushed him along. His was most definitely not the soul of an outdoorsman.

None of the captains he talked with, nor any of their

crewmembers, had ever heard of Arsudun Island or Brass Monkey. Nor had they visited The-Place-Where-The-Earth's-Blood-Burns.

It was a fine, sunny day—meaning that the temperature was within cozy distance of freezing and some tran were going without coats. And you didn't have to lean into the wind to stay in one place. He met Colette in the hall. When she finally confessed to boredom exceeding his, he proposed that they explore some more of the island.

Hunnar took a few minutes away from his frantic preparations to provide them with instructions on how to get around. Certain sections of the island would be easier for them to see than for a tran, while others would be just the reverse.

A set of rations from their store of food, and they were off.

It was steep climbing to the saddle between the mountain tops. But from there the view, as Colette described it in one of the few complimentary adjectives Ethan had heard her use, was "magnificent."

From here one could look up to the sharp crags on either side that formed the high points of Sofold Island. To the east you could look down across the tightly packed, steep-gabled roofs of the city, then out over the busy harbor, with its ever-moving commerce and dozens of flashing painted sails, to the great harbor walls and the endless ice beyond.

This they'd anticipated. What surprised and pleased them was the view in the other direction.

Coming eternally from the west, the wind hit them hard when they topped the last rise. Below them, a long, broad plain spread out, dotted here and there with farms and clusters of little stone buildings. Herds of vol and monkey-like hoppers were visible in distant fields. Squares of crimson laisval, the local substitute for wheat, were patches of billowing flame in the bright sunlight.

Beyond, he could make out a field of green extending as far as he could see in a great fan shape toward the horizon like the tail of some monstrous bird-of-paradise. Off to the left, kilometers across the ice, he thought he could detect another patch.

Their guide, a sprightly adolescent named Kierlo, explained

what it was. "There, noble sir and madame, grows the great pika-pedan, in a field greater than several Sofolds. There the thunder-eater comes to browse."

"I've heard so much about this thunder-eater," said Ethan as they strolled along the broad path that ran along the crest, "that I'd like very much to see one close up."

The youngster laughed. "No one goes to look at the thunder-eater close up, noble sir."

"It's vicious, then?"

"No sir. Not vicious. But it can be very irritable, like some k'nith."

Ethan knew the k'nith. A small animal like a hairy rat. He found it repulsive, but it was apparently a favored pet among the cubs of Wannome. They seemed affectionate, despite their fearsome appearance, and tended to explode into frenzied squalling at the tiniest upset. The cubs found such outbursts amusing.

Clearly they were more tolerant of their pets than a human child, who would have grown disgusted with a k'nith in a day or two. The climate even made for hardier pets, he mused.

"I'd like to see the foundry," he said suddenly. It dawned on him that they must be quite close to this major source of Wannome's wealth and power.

"Yes, lord." The youth turned down a narrow path that Ethan would have walked right past. Once around a bend in the rock, he could see smoke from the mountaintops once again.

The foundry itself occupied a little valley. It was small to the eye, even tiny, at first. But once they drew nearer, he could see that much of it was cut into the naked rock and built into caverns to take advantage of the heat rising from deep within the planet's crust.

From this area of the crest he could see that several of the crags were old volcanic cones. Most were dead or dormant, but a few puffed black smoke skyward. All of the craters sloped to the west and had been invisible from the city side.

Wannomian smelting and metal-working turned out to be an odd mixture of primitive technology and some surprisingly advanced techniques. The drawing and tempering of sword blades, for example, and of spear points.

The foundry head was in Wannome conferring with the military councilors. They were met by Jaes Mulvakken, the assistant chief.

"We are most honored, noble sir and lady, that you have found time to inspect our poor—"

"Skip the flattery and formal self-deprecation," smiled Ethan. He'd almost perfected the technique of smiling without revealing his teeth. "We just want to have a casual look around."

Mulvakken was all business when it came to explaining the operation of the foundry. He even managed to get Colette interested. Ethan was impressed by the tran's efficiency and knowledge. He'd make a fine district supervisor for a major mine.

While he preferred talking about finished products, he had to admit the foundry was fascinating.

In order to get close to the heat vents and geysers within the mountain, tran workers were first doused with ice water. Moving their arms and legs to keep the joints free, they soon wore jackets of transparent armor on torsos, arms, and legs. It gave Ethan the shivers just to watch it.

It was strange to see someone donning special outfits to retain the cold. Everything backwards.

"Where are your mines?" he asked Mulvakken.

"At the west end of the island, sir. Some of our shafts and tunnelings extend out even under the ice."

"Don't you have trouble digging into this super-permafrost?"

"Oh no, sir. The deeper we go, the softer it gets. And the miners are out of the wind. But the pika-pina is rooted in that end of the island. Cutting through the roots is worse than trying to cut through rock. Usually we just remove the dirt and work around the roots themselves. The ice is easily melted and the water removed . . . Sometimes we can cut through an old or weakened root here, a dying linkage there. But it is so entwined and grown upon itself that tis near impossible to separate one bit from another.

"Nor would we want to kill it. The pika-pina gives us food, while the metal gives us wealth."

"An attack on that end of the island by an enemy would capture the mines, then," said Ethan unnecessarily.

"Oh yes! But a lump of iron ore is a poor weapon, noble sir. Even were an enemy so inclined, and knowledgeable enough to work the mines, he could not with us continually harassing him. We're well protected here in the mountains, sir, even better than the city folk."

"Oh, I don't know. This western slope doesn't look so bad."

"Perhaps not for you, sir. But I have heard you are built differently from us and that climbing uphill without wind aid does not give you as much difficulty."

That was probably true, Ethan reflected.

He was examining the huge windmills that powered lathes and grindstones and brought air to the forges when he felt Colette's hand on his arm.

"Oh look. There's professor Williams." She'd taken to calling him "professor" Williams now, though they didn't know exactly what level of upper school he taught. He'd not volunteered the information. Sometime Ethan would have to ask.

The schoolmaster was seated at a table along with the ever-attending Eer-Meesach. Both were so engrossed in a pile of diagrams that they didn't notice the arrivals until Ethan and Colette had stood behind them for several minutes.

"I'll leave you, noble sir and lady, to the company of the wizards. I have much work to do. Tis sure no one knows how to put a decent edge on a sword these days." Mulvakken gave them a bloodthirsty grin and bowed politely.

In other words, Ethan reflected wryly, I've wasted enough time showing you alien V.I.P.s around and it's time I got back to some serious work. He waddled off in the direction of smoke, heat, and ringing noises.

"Well, Milliken. Eer-Meesach."

"Greetings, sir and madame," the wizard said with sprightly enthusiasm. His eyes were shining. "Your friend has been showing me many things. Great things. I haven't been so excited since I was a famulus!"

"What have you been up to, Milliken?"

"Malmeevyn has been helping me with mechanical equivalents and local terminology. I'm not much of a fighter and thought I might be able to help some other way."

"Nor am I," said Ethan sincerely.

"Oh, but we all saw the way you handled Sir Hunnar that night." He couldn't keep the admiration out of his voice. "Even Mr. du Kane is a better fighter than I . . . But I did think I might be able to aid in other ways. I've read quite extensively, you know. I've been trying to help out the Wannomian armorers with an idea or two gleaned from terran and centaurian history. My first idea involved catapults, but both sides already understand and utilize the principle. Very powerful devices they have, too."

"They'd have to be," Ethan commented, "to do much in this wind."

"Yes. Also swords, pikes, axes, lances, halberds—all kinds of things for cutting and stabbing. Spears and bows for throwing. But I've been working closely with Malmeevyn and the metal workers and I believe we've managed to come up with a couple of beneficial developments."

He reached under the table and brought out an object the like of which Ethan had never seen.

It had a long, straight body of wood, with a short bow set on one end. There was also an obvious trigger and some sort of pulley and crank mechanism at the other end.

"Very interesting," said Ethan, conscious of his historical cretinism. "What is it?"

"An ancient terran weapon. It's called an arbalest, or crossbow."

"A marvelous invention!" shouted the wizard, unable to contain himself. "I showed it to Leuva Sukonin's son, a knight of archers. When I outdistanced his best bowman he fell on the icepath and nearly slid all the way into town!" The wizard chuckled at the memory.

"It can throw twenty to forty zuvits further than the finest archer," Williams said, "and it's more accurate and powerful besides. It cannot be loaded as fast, it's true. But it will penetrate the thickest of leather-bronze shields at close range. I made the bows extremely tough. I think this version is more powerful than anything ever used on old Terra. These tran have truly awesome arm and shoulder muscles . . . from holding their dan against the wind, I suspect."

Ethan hefted the weapon uncertainly. He tried the crank but could hardly budge it. "It's impressive, all right. I don't suppose you've succeeded in coming up with maybe a pocket laser or a nice portable thermonuclear device, hmmm? It would make things a lot simpler."

"I'm afraid not." Williams smiled slightly. "But we are still working on other developments. I hope one or two will be ready in time to do some good."

"That's right," muttered Ethan, "—time."

"No one's said anything to me about time either," protested Colette. "When is this Horde or monster or whatever due to arrive?"

"No one knows, Colette. It could be several malets yet. Or they might be sighted tomorrow morning. Hunnar says they might even decide to pass Sofold completely for another year. I can't tell whether that possibility pleases or disappoints him. Now let's have another look at that chap who does the interesting marketable scrollwork on the sword-hilts . . . "

In the weeks that followed Ethan got to know the people of Wannome as well as those of New Paris, Drallar, or Samstead. Preparations for battle continued apace, but the flow of commerce in the harbor never slackened. There was still no word of the Horde.

One evening he wondered if the whole story of the Horde mightn't be a gigantic fraud—a cleverly concocted story designed to keep these useful and interesting strangers from the sky in Sofold. He quickly discarded that as a thought not only unworthy of people like Hunnar and Balavere and Malmeevyn, but also illogical. Although he wouldn't put it past the Landgrave.

No, there'd been too much obvious passion displayed that night, when the inhabitants of Sofold had determined to fight their tormentors instead of groveling to them—too spontaneous, too genuine, even in its alien setting, to be a mere dumb show created for such ignoble purpose.

He, Hunnar, and September were seated at a table in the general castle dining hall, down near the scullery. This was where most of the castle folk took their meals. Hunnar then suggested a walk along the sky balcony and the two humans agreed.

The sky balcony was the highest open pathway in Wannome Castle, excepting only the High Tower. From its wind-lashed parapet one could stare down a sheer drop to solid ice below, and far out across the great frozen sea to the south.

Their sojourn was interrupted by the breathless arrival of one of the apprentice-squires. He scraped to a halt, gulping freezing air, and almost forgot to bow to Hunnar. His face was wild.

"N . . . noble s . . . sirs . . . !"

"Take it easy, cub," Hunnar admonished him, "and catch your breath. Your words ride the wind too far ahead of you."

"Not thirty or forty kijat to the southwest, noble sirs—the thunder-eater comes!"

"How many?" asked Hunnar sharply.

"On . . . only one, sir A Great Old One! A caravan . . . three ships . . . blundered into it, hoping to find some shelter in the pika-pedan and then ride the wind-edge in. Only one escaped. Its master sits even now in audience with his Lordship!"

"Come," Hunnar said curtly to the two men. He started for the stairs without even bothering to see if they followed.

"So one of these 'thunder-eaters' finally shows up," said September. "Excellent! I've been listing slowly to starboard sitting on my butt here. At least now we'll have a chance to see one of these things, what?"

"I don't know," Ethan commented carefully. "From Sir Hunnar's attitude, I don't think they run out day excursion rafts. And that apprentice did mention something about two ships being lost."

"Ah, that could have been from the storm," countered September. "Say, Hunnar!" They hurried to keep up with the knight. Hunnar was being polite in not making use of the downward ice-paths. If he had, they'd have lost him in seconds. "Will we have a chance to see this thing?"

For Hunnar, the reply was unusually curt.

"You must understand that this is not a frivolous matter, my friends. In its own unthinking way, the stavanzer can be as dangerous as the Horde."

"Oh, come on now," September replied in disbelief. "It can't be that big. No land animal on a Terra-type planet can. There's not even any water to buoy it up. A really big animal couldn't walk."

Hunnar halted so abruptly that Ethan bumped into him, bounced off the iron-hard back beneath the furs.

"You have not seen a thunder-eater, stranger from the sky," he said quietly. It was the first time since their initial meeting he hadn't used their names. "Do not judge til then." He started off again as suddenly as he'd stopped. Ethan followed, surprised. The knight was really worried.

"A stavanzer," Hunnar continued as they descended yet another stairwell, "could destroy the great harbor more completely than any Horde and would do so without thought or compassion for life. A barbarian wishes to conserve in order to enrich himself. The thunder-eater has no such thoughts."

"I see," said September, abashed. "Look, I apologize, Hunnar. I shot off my big mouth without having ammunition. Moratorium until I see the thing, okay?"

"You do not know so naturally you cannot imagine," said Hunnar, mollified. "There is no need to apologize for such." He didn't say anything about September's shooting off his mouth. "There will be no chance to 'look'—only the Hunt."

"You mean you're going to try and kill this thing?" asked Ethan. "After making it sound nothing short of invincible?"

"I did not say twas invincible, friend Ethan. Only very big. But no one kills a stavanzer. Not in recent memory, anyway. We must try to drive it off. Were it a herd I should not worry so much."

"Why not? I'd imagine a herd would be a hundred times worse," Ethan commented.

"No. A herd would move only for its grazing grounds—the great pika-pedan fields to the south. They migrate on a north-south polar axis, mostly in the empty regions to the west. As a group they have little curiosity. But a lone one, and a Great

Old One at that, might investigate Sofold from sheer perversity. It takes something extraordinary to excite a herd. Somehow, we must turn him."

"You say you can't kill it, but you speak of turning it," said September. "How? With pikes?" There was nothing mocking in his voice.

"No. There is one way to fight the thunder-eater. If your souls are sound, you may have a chance to try it. Many who do claim it is the supreme moment of their lives. For some tis also the last. Yet it must be tried," he concluded as they topped a rise in the passageway.

"Just how big *is* this boojum, anyway," Ethan finally asked, exasperated.

"The thunder-eater has been granted but two teeth. Do you know the Landgrave's throne?"

"Yes." Ethan recalled the chair, inlaid with stones and polished metal set into a tower of pseudo-ivory. It would fetch a fine price from a certain decorator on . . .

"The back of the throne itself, the white pillar . . . what did you think it was?"

"Some kind of stone," Ethan replied. Then he paused. "You aren't trying to tell me that . . . ?"

He held onto the thought as they left the castle, barely aware that other knights and men-at-arms had joined them. They passed the du Kanes. September barely had time to shout, "We're a-going a-hunting!" to them. Colette yelled something in return but Ethan didn't hear it.

Down at the harborfront, kettledrums were droning like fat beetles. A knot of moving, businesslike tran had collected around the Hunnar-nucleus. Ethan caught occasional glimpses of solemn-faced townsfolk.

As they continued downhill, he couldn't help noticing that the soldiers and knights carefully avoided the ice-paths out of deference to their crippled visitors.

He wondered if anyone else would be able to see what was going to take place. The wizard had a telescope in his rooms, but it might not be able to scan the area they were heading for. But Milliken would be there, and maybe also the Landgrave.

All this fuss over one animal. And it wasn't even a meat-eater, like the Droom.

They reached the harbor. The crowd parted to reveal three of the oddest craft he'd seen since their landing.

Three small rafts with large sails sat ready by the docks. Their sails and bodies were painted pure white. Arrow-narrow and long, they were clearly designed to stay hidden against the ice.

To the rear of each was tied a second, even stranger craft. Each consisted of a single tree-trunk, averaging about twenty meters in length and one or two in diameter. A single small sail was mounted on each. The front end was cut and shaped down to a needle-sharp point.

The bottom cross-spar of the sail ended on each side in a tiny wooden ship or large skate, depending on how one chose to view them. Each was equipped with an even smaller runner to its outside, making each into a stubby, one-tran outrigger. The cross-spar was connected to each skate-boat by a single pole.

There were two wooden runners under the tree itself, a single solid one near the bow, and a third skate-boat at the rear.

The sails on each of these massive lances—for such they clearly were—were furled. Three wind-powered spears suitable for battling a goliath.

Ethan had a thousand questions. Hunnar was already on board the first raft, giving directions and inspecting lashings. Ethan followed September on board. Almost immediately the strange little convoy started toward the harbor gate. All other ships gave them respectful clearance and some of their sailors came to the rail to watch quietly.

A moment later they were through the great gate towers. As they rode out of the lee of Wannome and its sheltering mountains they picked up speed. The sails crackled and the helmsman set course slightly into the wind, to the southwest.

"We must circle well behind the beast," Hunnar explained, "to allow the lightnings to build up speed. When they have, the towing raft casts free and moves clear."

"Those spears are maneuverable, then?" asked September over the howl of the wind. Sailors fought the rigging.

"Only a little," Hunnar replied grimly. "Once set on course, they can be turned only to right or left, and only with the wind. There is no turning about."

"What happens," asked September finally, "when you make contact with the creature?"

"Here Jaipor, take over!" Another tran hurried over to take a rope from the knight. Satisfied, he led them toward the stern of the fast-moving raft. Ethan could feel the tension building among the crew. They stood behind the helmsman and Hunnar pointed to the following raft.

"A strong but simple latch ties the lightning to the three skate-boats. Each is a tiny raft in itself, but without sails. See the high, padded back? That is to protect the rider and to catch a little of the wind."

"They look like big wooden shoes," commented Ethan. He recalled Ta-hoding mentioning that wooden skates wouldn't hold much of an edge on the ice. But then, these weren't intended for long journeys.

"Momentum should carry the three steersmen clear of the thunder-eater," Hunnar continued, "and to safety." Ethan peered closely at the tiny boats.

"Once you've released from the main lance, how do you steer the things?"

"With your body weight. The skates are well balanced. The release should take place in plenty of time to give the rider ample opportunity to veer wide of the target."

"Of course, the closer you get before giving up control," said September, "the more accurate the strike."

"Of course," agreed Hunnar.

"Then if you've no objection, I'd like to be one of your sparmen."

"I would be honored, Sir September." They exchanged shoulder clasps.

"Oh, well," said Ethan, "I suppose I'll have to take the other, then."

"Now young feller, this is no game, what? If you don't really want—"

"Oh, shut up, Skua. I'll take the opposite spar." He felt like a fool, but he'd be damned if he'd back away when September had volunteered.

"'Tis settled then." Hunnar turned and pointed toward their companion rafts skimming alongside. "Sir Stafaed will command the first bolt and Sir Lujnor the second. We will have the last."

"Does this thing have a weak spot?" asked September over the roar of the wind.

"It may. If so, none have found it. There is no hide protecting the eyes and they are nerve-centers if naught else. 'Tis best to strike there. They are small and set low. If we could blind him, that would be better than turning him from the city."

"If he has good vision it means he'll see us coming," added September thoughtfully.

They continued to swing in a wide curve, until Ethan realized all at once that they were now running with the wind. He looked over the sharp prow of the raft. Somewhere far ahead was a wavering green blur, the huge field of pika-pedan. They'd come a long way fast.

The sailors brought in the sail. Sharpened ice-anchors of dark iron stabbed ice. The three rafts with their trailing death slowly skidded to a halt, shaking and straining in the wind.

"Now we ride the lightning," said Hunnar solemnly. He scrambled over the side of the raft.

According to the surviving merchantman's report, the stavanzer was moving northeast. They would try to turn him southward again.

"You take the port side, lad, and I'll have at the starboard," September shouted to him.

"What?"

"The left side, the left! And don't let loose your latch-piece til Sir Hunnar gives the sign."

"Think I'll freeze at the wrong moment and let go early?" Ethan stared up at that buttressed visage. The eyes twinkled.

"No man can deny the possibility, young feller."

"Well . . . I might," he replied, almost defiantly. "But it won't be from fear. It'll be from this delightful climate."

The wind was blowing harder than usual for midday. That meant he had to grab twice at the wooden rail of the raft to keep from being blown away like an empty sack. It was bitterly cold out here, divorced from the castle's sheltering walls.

He was relieved just to scramble into the comparative shelter of the skate-boat.

The broad wooden back of the skate was thickly padded. It vibrated steadily in the perpetual gale, but the worst winds howled harmlessly past. Leaning forward slightly, he could see just over the central trunk. September waved and he waved back.

He leaned out, sticking his face into the wind again, and waved back at Hunnar. The knight would steer while he and September managed the sail.

The latch-piece that held the skate-boat to the lower cross-spar was a simple wooden pull. It was set into a pole which was based in the floor of the skate and the bottom of the spar. He noticed with satisfaction that it had been well greased. There would be no last-minute frantic tugging. The sail was harder to work, with only the single rope to keep it steady.

Two sailors from the big raft were on the tree-lance itself. They raised the lightning's own sail in unison with the sail on the raft. Both began moving together. Somehow the two sailors kept their balance in the wind until the pure white lance-sail was up. They moved carefully to the sharpened end of the log, jumped free, and chivaned up to the raft where ready hands pulled them in. Since both raft and tow-raft were now moving at appreciable speeds, it was a delicate bit of work.

The sailors and soldiers on the raft carried pikes and bows, more for their psychological value than out of any expectation of usefulness. It wouldn't do for a tran to go into battle weaponless. Not even if his only task was to watch and pray.

On the other hand, Ethan didn't feel the need for even a very small dagger. Despite Hunnar's expositions, he had only the vaguest idea what to expect. They were going to strike the stavanzer broadside. Hunnar would aim for the head. At his signal, a loud, sharp whistle, they would each release their skate-boats and shear off, to be picked up by the trailing, waiting rafts.

That was the theory.

Despite the obvious danger, Ethan couldn't contain a certain perverse curiosity. He wanted very much to see what sort of land animal could take the wind-driven impact of a twenty-meter sharpened tree that weighed maybe half a ton without being killed outright. There was a certain wealthy collector of rare animals on Plutarch who might conceivably . . .

But, he reminded himself, they would break off long before that. His only glimpse of the thing would probably be brief and distant.

Still, stavanzers did die, Hunnar had informed them. Of what? Old age? How long did the virtually indestructable thunder-eaters live?

There was a jerk and he looked up. The raft had cast them loose and was already swinging south to get out of their path. The other two lances had cast off seconds earlier and were speeding down the unyielding sea ahead of them. He squinted through his goggles, isolated in a world of ice, wind, and wood.

Ahead, a green blur gradually took form and substance, grew larger. Their speed continued to increase as they ran wildly before the wind. Now he could make out the size of the pika-pedan compared to its pygmy cousin. His breath froze in his throat then. It wasn't from the cold.

There was something moving on the outer edge of the green. Then he saw the thunder-eater, and was afraid.

The Great Old One was over a hundred meters long—a gigantic slate-gray mountain that heaved and pulsed like a great slug on the clean ice. Its back and sides were studded with grotesque ridges and spines, a bizzarre living topography.

There were no legs, no arms, no visible limbs of any sort. The belly of that awesome bulk was a horny pad thicker than the skin of a starship, as tough, and worn smooth as glass. A mouth as wide as a driveship dock inhaled air which was expelled through two lifeboat-sized valves near the tail, moving it like a squid.

It moved slowly now. But Hunnar had told them tales of stampedes, like steel-gray storms. A herd would strike a small island and leave nothing but a greenish-brown stain against the ice.

He shrank. He was a dog—no, an ant—attacking a whale. Only this was bigger than the biggest whale that ever was. It expanded in all directions, all dimensions, like a tridee projection.

From the side of the biblical behemoth projected a tiny splinter of wood. It leaked crimson. One of the lightnings had struck home, then.

He couldn't find any sign of the other and assumed it had missed. He was wrong. Later, a searching raft found part of the mast. That was all they ever found of raft and crew.

Somewhere, distantly, there was a shout, a whistle. Then a blackness grew ahead of him. Something dark as space at the Rim, gaping like a cave. A monstrous ebony cavern, two colossal stalactites of white hanging from the roof. Tons of vegetable matter vanished into that yawning abyss every day.

It was turning toward them, to the north. The wrong way. And they would miss.

Another, more distant, whistle sounded. The eager wind bit at it, tore it away. The latch rested tightly in both hands, sail forgotten now. Hunnar and September had cast free. But if he waited just a little longer, put a little more weight on the outside of the skate . . .

He stood. Bracing against the wind and the side of the skate, he leaned out over the ice, to his left. The huge lance began to shift, slowly, agonizingly, centimeters at a time, to port. Ethan leaned hard into the side, straining for just another millimeter of drift. Protesting wood shifted from its original course.

The black chasm grew until it blotted out ice, pika-pedan, sky. A dark hole swallowing the universe. It was opening and closing with a mechanical, slow-motion intensity, a ponderous cyclopean bellows. Above the wind came a dull roaring, like a dying stardrive. Eating air and excreting thunder, the stavanzer was moving.

Crosslatch . . . pull . . . whistle . . . get round . . . left . . . left . . . no, port-left . . . left-port? . . . !

The blood on his lower lip was beginning to freeze. Suddenly something or someone—he wasn't sure it was he—jerked convulsively at the latch. The tiny skate-boat heeled far over on its side, almost touching the ice. He had to scramble to keep from falling out. Almost calmly he saw that he'd delayed too long. He would not clear the creature.

He would not clear the mouth.

It would be open when he reached it, he knew instinctively. A prayer would have been appropriate but what he mumbled instead was, "Move over, Jonah. Here I come."

Then, startlingly, he missed, was past. He glimpsed an eye bigger than the whole skate-boat shooting past at blinding speed, black pupil like an onyx mirror reflecting his numbed stare. He was speeding past endless acres of roiling, heaving gray flesh.

The stavanzer's mouth was enormous. The throat itself was not. Moving at nearly two hundred kph, the half-ton lance struck the back of that gaping maw. Several seconds passed while the impact traveled down miles of neurons. A shudder passed through the gargantuan bulk. The thunder-eater heaved the upper half of its body off the ice, an Everest of dimly felt agony. It dropped with a force that snapped Ethan's speeding skate-boat off the ice like a coin on a taut blanket.

He sailed past an alien gray landscape, a vast confusion of ice and cold sky. Night came hard.

VIII

He remembered vanilla wafers. Then he opened his eyes and saw a familiar fur-framed face with a unique nose. September was staring at him anxiously. Other memories flooded in and he sighed. Likely there wasn't a vanilla wafer within half a dozen parsecs of where he lay.

Where he lay was in his bed in his room in Wannome Castle. He tried to sit up and was made aware of a fascinating phenomenon. Every square centimeter of his body was putting in an impolite claim for attention.

"I," he announced slowly, falling back onto the fur blanket someone had bunched beneath his head, "hurt. All over."

"Not surprising, young feller-me-lad," said September, the concern vanishing from his face. "But other than that, how are you feeling?"

Ethan chuckled. It was mentally satisfying, but it also compelled certain sections of self to protest violently. He followed the ensuing silence with a question of characteristic wit, scintillating brilliance.

"What happened?"

"Why didn't you let go your latch when Hunnar gave the signal?" the big man asked instead of answering.

Ethan thought, remembered. "We would have missed. It was turning the wrong way and we would have missed. Shot right past . . . " He tried to rise again. September put a hand on his chest and gently forced him back.

"That particular beastie is no longer a problem. Lord, what a sight! I've seen a lot of big and biggests, lad, but that hunk of ugly meat tops them all. Couldn't believe how fast something that big can move."

"Hunnar told me, before."

"I thought we'd seen the last of you for sure when you

didn't let loose with the rest of us," September continued. "Gone forever down that unholy gullet. Oh, by the way, you turned it fair and proper. Took off southward with a roar you wouldn't believe. Near to shake a man's skin off, what? Though how it could even move with that log down its pipe I don't know. Tough? Oh my, yes!"

"I don't mean what happened to it. What about *me?*"

"Oh, you? Well, I didn't see much myself, being a-scooting fast in the opposite direction. But there was a well-positioned lookout in the front-running raft. Said when the thing rose off the ice . . . unheard of thing to do . . . and whacked down, it tossed you into the air like a ballooning spider.

"You came down on the other side of the beast in the high pedan. That and the padding in the boat probably saved you. After contact, though, it was every chip and splinter for itself. If you'd landed on bare ice I expect we'd still be scraping up pieces of you. As it developed, you should have seen how much wood they pulled out of your skin. Good thing those survival parkas are tough. How you got out without busting anything, let alone *every*thing, I'll wonder over til my last days. You took a powerful sock in the head."

"I feel tolerable now," he lied. "How long have I been out?"

September grinned. "Off and on, about a week."

"A wee—!"

"Twas a near thing, I don't mind telling you, lad," he said solemnly. Then, more cheerfully, "Sure didn't hurt our standing with these folk, though. I expect they consider you the greatest thing to come along since warm." He scratched at his pants. "But it's just as well you're up . . . if not exactly about. It seems it's time."

If they'd just take the anvil off his head he'd feel almost decent.

"Time? What time?"

September slapped his head with a blow that would have taken an ordinary man's head off.

"Idiot! Forgot you couldn't understand anything while you were mumbling. Mumbled some weird things, too, you did. The Horde's coming, of course. Captain from someplace called Yermi-yin pulled into the harbor yesterday on his way to somewhere unpronounceable. Stayed just long enough to give the Landgrave the word before skimming out again. Poor fella was as white as the ice. He headed due south and didn't seem inclined to change course even when we told him he might run into a mad stavanzer. Alien or no, anyone could see he was plenty scared."

Ethan determinedly heaved himself up on his elbows and found that without warning the room had gone triplicate . . . just like everything at the home office.

"Then I've got . . . to get ready. We're going to fight, too . . ."

Again September eased him down into the mattress.

"You just lie there . . . alone, I'm afraid . . . and take it easy, young feller. They're at least a week's fast sail away. So there's no need to run around screeching and squawking like a plucked poonu. Hunnar and Balavere are organizing the militia. The populace is storing grain, pika-pina, vol, and suchlike like crazy, for a siege. Everyone is doing what they're supposed to. You're supposed to rest."

"Can they really stand a siege, Skua?"

September looked thoughtful. "Hunnar seems to think so. Says the enemy's sure to crack mentally before the Sofoldians run out of anything vital. The general agrees with him, though he's not as vocal about it. Crafty old bird . . . They're even stockpiling firewood . . . although with those natural fur coats they've got, they can do without it. Yes, when you start stockpiling luxuries I'd say that indicates a certain modicum of confidence . . . No, I don't think there'll be much of a siege. Just one double-helluva fight."

"Hunnar seemed sure he could beat them."

"According to that captain," September mused, "they cover the ice from one end of the horizon to the other. I've been talking tactics with the general staff. I think I've made a few points. Frankly, any change in normal procedure ought to confuse that bunch. If this Sagyanak's as stubborn as some of Sofold's best, then we shouldn't expect much new from the Horde . . . But it's a new situation for the Sofoldians. They're willing to try new ideas. Just takes a little subtle convincing, a bit of reasonable explanation. Also, Balavere threatened to crack a few heads . . . If I were in the spot they're in, I'd be willing to experiment too. Wouldn't you, me lad?"

"We *are* in their place," replied Ethan quietly. September grunted.

The battle armor was clumsy and too large, but Hunnar had insisted Ethan wear it. The leather leggings jolted and pulled at each step and the bronze breastplate was an unrelenting drag at his chest.

He'd absolutely refused one of the flaring, ornate helmets, though. Even a child's size wouldn't have fit well. His head would ring around inside like a clapper in a bell. While it wasn't designed for fighting, the parka at least wasn't a burden.

The wind whistled around him. He walked back over to where Hunnar and September stood together at the edge of the High Tower. September was pointing into the distance.

They might have had a better and clearer view from the wizard's telescope. But then they would see only one thing at a time. Besides, the learned miasma of the wizard's chambers palled after a while, along with the very real one from aromatic chemicals and half-vivisected animals.

According to their long-since-departed informant, the Horde would appear out of the northeast. But for now there was only the invisible thread that divided cold-ice land from ice-cold sky.

"No sign of them, Hunnar?"

The knight paused in conversation with the big man and looked down at Ethan. "Your eyesight tis good as my own, Sir Ethan. Yet I do detect naught of the assembled swine."

"Could they be circling to take you from the rear?" asked September. He scratched at a persistent itch with the edge of a big double-bladed sword.

Hunnar dropped a deprecating hand.

"No. They might try such a maneuver later, to annoy us if for naught else. But Sagyanak is unlike many barbarians. Nothing will be done without purpose . . . or so we are told. Still, any nomad is unpredictable."

"Like you," suggested Ethan.

"Perhaps, like me," the knight replied, not upset by the comparison. "As I said, all it would accomplish would be to anger us—hardly a sound motive. No, they'll parade up to the gates and make a fine show of themselves. They've no reason to think we'd be so foolish as to offer resistance." He grinned wolfishly.

"What a surprise the Death is going to get! Perhaps the Scourge will rave and rant enough to burst a skull-side blood vessel. That would spare us the necessity of a formal execution."

"Ah, there," said September. "Isn't that a sail? Or have I been dipping too deep into the reedle again?"

No, certainly that was a spot of blue far, far out on the ice. It grew, was joined by others of different size and shape and color. Every imaginable shade was represented in the concatenation of sails. Soon the far ice was a rainbow of barbaric coloring: magenta, umber, jet, crimson—there was a lot of crimson and other reds—azure, carnelian, sard . . .

Some of the sails were dyed in swatches of random color. Others boasted intricately designed motifs and mosaics. Some were woven, others painted—all of a bloodcurdling nature.

A few sported railings decorated with dull white trannish skulls.

They didn't cover the ice as the captain had warned. But they filled a disconcerting portion of it.

"Must be nearly a thousand rafts out there," murmured September. But the big man's nonchalance fooled no one. Even he was a little awed.

"More than we expected," Hunnar admitted. "Yet it only makes me gladder, for there will be more of the vermin to dispose of."

Beating into the wind, the nomad fleet moved closer. One by one they took up position along four-deep lines. One by one the sails came down and ice anchors went out.

"Settling in for a relaxing stay," September said.

Even at this distance, Ethan thought he could detect some rafts that were crowded with livestock, others with crates and supplies. It was a mobile city.

Soon all the sails were furled but one, which belonged to a small, rakishly set little raft. It lay alongside a huge ship with a double-storied, garishly painted central cabin. The small raft broke off and skimmed slowly for the harbor gate.

Ethan could make out toy figures straining at the mechanism that raised the obstructing nets and the Great Chain barrier.

"Parley raft," said Hunnar with satisfaction. "The Landgrave and members of the Council should be preparing to receive it. Let's go."

They followed him down the winding stairs into the castle proper.

"This will be something to tell one's grandcubs," he said back over a shoulder.

They were not part of the official greeting committee. Also, it had been decided that it would be better if the Horde did not have a look at the humans until it could upset them the most. Let them think then, as some of the Sofoldians still did, that the aliens were gods or daemons, not just skinny tran with severe haircuts.

The musicians' balcony was deserted and gave them an excellent view of the Great Hall. Down below, the Landgrave waited on his throne. This time he was dressed not in comfortable silks but in bronze and leather armor, steel helmet and breastplate. He was an impressive sight, but Ethan had to concede that Balavere or Hunnar or even Brownoak would have carried the royal armor with a good deal more effect.

Elfa, he noticed, was resplendent in armor of her own. No decolletage this time.

Grouped around the throne were the members of the Council, town representatives, and the more senior knights and their squires. Sunlight gave the assembled helmets and pikes and axes the aspect of the inside of a jewel. Migrating circlets of light were cast onto the bare stone walls and vaulted ceiling as they turned and shifted. They were an impressive group.

Curious, Ethan gave the huge, curving white column that formed the back of the Landgrave's throne another look. Rather puny, after all.

His eyes dropped and roved over the crowd as they waited. The du Kanes, of course, weren't present. Nor did they intend to participate in any actual combat. Hellespont begged off on his age, and Colette because it wasn't ladylike. He wished she could have a good look at Elfa Kurdagh-Vlata. But Setember had managed to convince them to don armor, at least.

Walther was safely locked away in his gilded cubicle, where he couldn't do anything foolish to himself or anyone else. And Williams was off with Eer-Meesach somewhere, seeing to some kind of mysterious alchemy of their own. Having seen the crossbow in action, Ethan awaited their next revelation with anticipation and not a little leeriness.

There was a commotion at the entrance to the Hall. All eyes turned in that direction. At the same time, it occurred to Ethan what had been bothering him about the assembly. He turned to Hunnar.

"Shouldn't the prefect of Wannome be present for this?"

The knight spoke without turning. "The prefect has expressed his manifest displeasure at the entire proceeding. He has confined himself to his manor until an unspecified time. I, for one, don't miss him."

Something was nagging still. It was shoved aside by a rhythmic booming of drums from outside the Hall. A herald's voice rang out.

"Here approach those representing Sagyanak the Death, Scourge of Vragan . . . "

" . . . All-powerful Destroyer of Ra-Yilogas," finished a powerful voice. It rolled and rumbled off the walls. "And Ruler of the World!"

A group of three tran came into view, striding down the central carpet. The leader of the triumvirate was the biggest native Ethan had yet seen, a towering figure resplendent in flame-colored cloak and coat. Under his left arm, snug into the dan, he held a helmet in the shape of the gutorrbyn, the flying dragon. His armor was nearly as red as the cloak itself, a burnished bronze crossed by polished vol-leather strappings and gold-silver buckles. A long, broad sword was fastened securely to his left leg. As he swung his arms Ethan could see that designs in gold dust had been glued to his tough wing-membranes.

His stride was long and hurried, as though he came on distasteful business best concluded quickly. Impatient to get on with the looting, no doubt, and upset at the delay.

His two companions trailed slightly behind, one to either side. They were nearly as brilliantly clad, one in blues, the other in yellow and black. Neither had the physical presence of their superior, however.

Ethan leaned over and whispered to Hunnar.

"Is that Sagyanak?"

Hunnar gave him an odd look. "Of course not, Sir Ethan. What a strange question!"

"Why . . . ?" he began, but September shushed him. The lead nomad was speaking.

"I am Olox, right hand and first servant of the Destroyer. It has been far too long since we last visited our gracious friends in Wannome. Far too long. And when we finally rectify this unfortunate oversight, are we greeted properly?" He expressed outrage and bafflement; his companions wore woeful expressions.

"No!" He looked up at the Landgrave. "We are not. What do we find instead? Armed men on the walls! Many armed men. Nets and chain bar our free entrance, passage to an open harbor.

"The Destroyer chooses to graciously assume, though, that this is done in error, perhaps through our own fault at not identifying ourselves sufficiently. Or perhaps," and here his tone changed to one of brutal coldness, "our friends in Wannome are subject to a peculiar forgetfulness. The Scourge has helpful ways aplenty to jog a loose memory here, a slipped remembrance there."

"Yet surely tis all a mistake, tis all unintentional!" he said cheerfully. "And now that we are truly made known to you, the Death expects prompt payment of the standard tribute . . . with mayhap a few thousand additional foss by way of compensating for embarrassment and upset nerves at your unkind greeting."

The Landgrave leaned forward into the silence that followed and shook an old fist at the three.

"Now listen well to me, butcher Olox. Yes, we know you. Those armed men on the wall who upset your nerves will do more, if you wish. Chain and net return as soon as your putrid self has taken leave of us. Then I can order this Hall cleaned thoroughly to remove the stench that will linger. Go back and tell your bug-master that the people of Sofold and the city of Wannome pay tribute no longer, lest you seek to collect a fortune in the edges of axe-blades and the points of spears!"

The one called Olox had stiffened at the first word. Ethan felt he could count every hair on the ambassador's head. But, surprisingly, he said nothing and waited until the Landgrave had concluded his speech.

"I have considered," said Olox slowly when the Landgrave had leaned back, "and answer that I relish your every word, every syllable."

"I am glad," grinned Kurdagh-Vlata. "Would you like to hear them again?"

"Twill not be necessary," replied Olox the Butcher, "for each and every word has been forever set down in my mind. They will be repeated to the Death with every inflection, all timing, intact and exact."

"Good," said the Landgrave. "Should you require any aid, do but send for it. I shall forward any lapses of memory in writing, with whatever suitable embellishments my courtiers can concoct."

"Then, Torsk Kurdagh-Vlata, Landgrave of Sofold, ruler of Wannome, I end thusly: put firm paw to sword and have an eye to your womenfolk, for when I next see you I will not find you so talkative, I think."

Cloak flying, the nomad general turned and strode from the Hall. His two servitors were hard pressed to match his stride without breaking into a run.

No one moved. Then, from the far side of the silent hall, General Balavere's voice shook them all.

"Well, will you sit there contemplating your fat bellies til doomsday? Get to your posts! See to your men!"

The hall dissolved in a flurry of sudden activity and excited conversation.

"Not quite as anticlimactic as I expected," Ethan commented. "Was it, Hunnar? Hunnar?" He and September turned together, but the knight had already slipped quietly away.

The big man rubbed his face. "Gone to his own post, I suspect. Probably wanted to use the ice-paths to move fast, take up position. He's in charge of the southeast third of the harbor wall, from the gate-tower to the castle. Didn't want to wait for us. We'd slow him to a walk and there are more important things on his mind now than courtesy."

Ethan turned, almost tripping over the sword strapped to his right leg. "I guess we should join him."

"Might as well."

The two humans passed small squads of troops running through the hallways or chivaning at seemingly reckless speeds down the stairway ice-paths. Most of the soldiers and militia were already on the wall.

As they left the inner keep and walked along the outer battlements of the great castle, they could peer down into the courtyards. Gradually these filled with clumps of well-dressed civilians and many women and cubs.

These were the wealthier country folk, evacuated from their impossible-to-defend homes about the island. They would spend the coming troubles in the relative comfort and safety of the castle itself. The great majority of country refugees would have to make do with the facilities available in the town.

Those would be badly overcrowded, but while food and heat held out there would be no problem. And according to Hunnar, Wannome had little to fear in those respects. Everyone would be uncomfortable, but they'd manage.

They passed through another long, dark hallway, rounded a bend, and nearly collided with a troop of archers who were moving to higher positions within the castle. Another turn and they were out in the brilliant sunlight and familiar, constant wind.

They jogged easily along the broad top of the wall that sheltered the harbor, protected the city. There seemed to be an archer or pikeman at every slot in the stone. At regular intervals there was a war-tower, through which they ran. Puffing cold clouds, Ethan could see one and sometimes two crossbowmen perched atop each tower. They seemed woefully few.

They were approaching the great gate now. The Great Chain was in place, enmeshed in a spider's nightmare of antipersonnel netting. Hunnar should be commanding this section.

Halfway down the wall September had grunted with satisfaction and tapped Ethan on the shoulder.

"Have a look, lad, to our left."

Ethan peered over the wall and saw nothing for a moment but the harbor itself. Then he spotted what the big man was referring to.

Halfway off the ice on the far side of the harbor lay the crumpled hulk of their lifeboat.

"How . . . ?" began Ethan.

September smiled. "Balavere *said* he'd see to it. Told him it would be a sensible precaution if they expected to hold on to it, so he ordered out a dozen merchant rafts to drag it in. They must have had a helluva time getting it free. Once it was moving I expect it slid along okay. Thank the No-Spaces for this ice! If they'd had to pull it over any kind of rough country they couldn't have moved it half a kilometer."

"I wonder," mused Ethan as he dodged a long pole designed for pushing off scaling ladders, "if Sagyanak even knows about it."

"Well, it wouldn't startle me," September replied. "You'd think the Sofoldians would have tried to camouflage it from the eyes of that envoy. I suppose they figure it doesn't matter in the long run."

"You think Olox saw it, then?"

"Don't let appearances fool you, lad. That character might have been constructed like a senile grizzly, but he had weasel eyes. I watched him close. While the Landgrave was feeding him insults he was taking in the armor and attitude of every knight and noble in that hall. Probably had time to count the percentage of metal weapons, too. That's one advantage the Sofoldians do have, a decent supply of bronze and iron weapons. If we get through this . . . " He paused. "I hear you had a look-see through their foundry."

Ethan nodded. He was getting winded from the long run. September didn't seem fazed. The younger man felt an unreasoning discomfort at this and tried to seem fresher.

"Then you know they've got plenty of heat available. A lot more than I guessed. Good access to volcanic chimneys, and those windmills, too. I think I might be able to rig an electrodyne forge, by Contusion! Scrap a few parts from the boat . . . Yes, if we survive this we might leave the Sofoldians a way to work that duralloy after all. Ah, there he is."

They slowed to a walk. Hunnar was resting at a pikeman's slot, staring out across the ice. They carefully crossed the ice-path that ran down the center of the wall-top. He turned at their approach.

"Well my friends, before very long we shall discover things."

"Don't look so moody. What are they about?" September asked.

Hunnar turned away. "Have a look for yourselves." He moved over and the two humans were treated to an uninterrupted view of the icefield.

Between the barbarian rafts little white could be seen. The ice was covered with shifting, sparkling, multi-colored furry bodies. Swords, shields, bucklers, and helmets flashed like night sky in the heavy sunlight. The Horde was leaving the rafts.

"There's a slight crosswind up from the south," Hunnar informed them, glancing at the sky. "I expect the main body will come from that direction. They'll slant due west and then up at us. The brunt of the attack will fall on this line."

Sure enough, clumps of nomad troops began to detach themselves from the main mass and tacking against the wind to gain distance to the west.

Ethan saw that they stood nearly at the end of the wall. The Great Gate Tower was to their immediate left, another battle tower to their right. He looked back the way they'd come. All along the wall, curving back to the castle like a gray snake, there was motion. Knights strove to adjust their men in accordance with the enemy's movements, made last minute changes, hopeful preparations.

"Will they attack only this section of wall?" asked Ethan a little apprehensively.

"That would be foolish. As they outnumber us by so many, they will assault the entire length of the harbor in strength, hoping to find a point we have vacated or weakened. Otherwise we could concentrate our strength here alone and have a

better chance of beating them off. But they can spread themselves thin and still outmatch us four and five to one at every
kijat. Tis merely that from this side they will have slightly better wind, therefore better speed and maneuverability . . .
Also, we must keep troops to guard the mountain passes.
They may try a thrust there, though I doubt it. Still, some of
our strength must stay there, though Sagyanak has no reason
to resort to subtlety. They will come to us with great confidence."

He paused and looked at September. "Friend Skua, you
have no weapon."

"Why bless my soul, so I don't! Forgot the damn sword."
He turned and hurried to the battle tower on their right.

"I see you carry a sword, friend Ethan. Can you use it?"

"I guess I'm going to learn in a hurry. I'd feel a lot better
with a nice new wide-aperture laser."

"I should feel better if you had one of your magical weapons, too," the knight replied, managing a slight grin. He
stared out across the ice. The raft-head was growing huge
horns to south- and northwest. Half to himself, he muttered,
"There will be archery fire to cover, despite the wind. Will
they try to move in close and shoot linear, or stay above us
and fire downwind? Distance or accuracy?" He shook his helmeted, red-maned head uncertainly.

September reappeared, carrying the biggest battle-ax Ethan
had ever seen. Of course, he didn't have a working knowledge
of such devices, but it looked godawful big to *him*. It was
double-bladed and made of black iron. September swung it
back and forth and over his head and behind his shoulders,
mimicking an action of a long-vanished terran sport.

A number of the men-at-arms gave a cheer when they saw
the ease with which their alien ally handled the monstrous
cleaver.

"You throw that axe around like a cub's toy, friend September," said Hunnar admiringly.

"Well," said September, taking a friendly swipe with it at
Ethan and nearly giving the salesman heart failure, "I'm not
much on thrusting, but I appreciate finesse. So I tried to select
something suitable to my delicate sensibilities."

Hunnar stared at him uncomprehendingly for a moment, then let out a jerking trannish laugh.

"I see. You joke. You will tell it in more direct fashion to our verminous friends when they come over the wall."

"I'll be as entertaining as possible," September promised. He took a deep breath. "When are they going to get on about it? Or do we wait until after lunch?"

The answer came several minutes later in the form of a low basso rumbling from across the ice. It sounded like distant thunder. Ethan thought he could detect an odd swirl of motion near the big raft, but it was too far off to make out details.

A weird sound was that deep drone. It reached right down inside a man and caressed the bones.

"The Margyudan," explained Hunnar quietly. "That means no quarter and no prisoners. Well, we expected no less."

Hunnar's men stood frozen at their stations along the wall. Ethan could understand their feelings. Death made its own music.

Surprisingly, it was September and not the memory-stuffed Ethan who was able to identify the sound.

"I've heard something like this on Terra and a few other worlds," he said, "only on a much smaller scale. On Terra they call it a bull-roarer. The natives of the northern continent on G'Dim call it a Rane. But this version must be much, much bigger to carry this far against the wind. Come to think of it, the device itself might be wind-powered."

Abruptly, the sound ceased. Ethan could hear himself breathing. Only the wind moved. Only the wind talked. Ethan drew his sword, the rasp of metal against scabbard gratingly loud.

The peace was split asunder by a monstrous howling from all sides. Ethan had never heard the like before. It came from everywhere, had no one source. And the enemy was barely in sight, since they were moving far west to gain wind.

"Working themselves up good and proper, what?" September whispered. "I expect when they've huffed and puffed themselves into a really fine old-fashioned frenzy, they'll come at us."

The howling and moaning continued for ten minutes, and

seemed more like an hour. Then there was a single great simultaneous bellow that shook the stones of the wall. A living gray blanket, the limitless mass began to move toward them. They came in a wide, easy curve up from the southwest, slanting up into the wind.

Soon he could pick out individual figures within the Horde. No two sets of armor looked the same, contrasting with the formal uniforms of the Sofoldian soldiery. The more garish the better, it seemed. Many of those in the forefront carried scaling ladders. Others held long knotted ropes with bone or metal grapnels on the end.

"Down!" roared Hunnar unexpectedly. Along the wall the defenders hugged themselves to the stone, trying to bury themselves in their armor. A hail of arrows, like the flight of a billion bees, came sailing over to clatter against the stones. There were a few screams from somewhere down the wall.

One arrow came whizzing through the slot a few centimeters in front of Ethan's scrunched-up face. It shot across the stone to hit the far side of the parapet, ricocheted back to die against the heel of his boot and lie peacefully next to the leather. The bone tip was shattered.

Another angry swarm hummed overhead. It occurred to him that despite four years of university, another year of advanced sales training, and on-the-job experience, he was utterly helpless in the face of a bunch of hysterical primitives.

There was very little time for thought. Hunnar yelled, "Up now!" and Ethan stood, turned.

He was confronted almost immediately by a snarling face framed in metal and leather and a pair of slitted yellow eyes that stared hypnotically into his own. He stood frozen in shock, unable to move, the sword dangling limply from one hand. The nomad raised a heavy mace in seeming slow motion over his head while Ethan watched, unmoving.

A long pike thrust out of nowhere and skewered the other through the chest. It gurgled, coughing blood, and dropped from view. That broke the ennui that had coated Ethan. Another minute and he was swinging his own sword rhythmically, jabbing and slashing and cutting at anything that showed itself above the clean gray stone. He never did have a chance to thank the pikeman who'd saved his life.

The yelling and shrieking, crying and bellowing drowned any coherent speech. In one harried moment he got a glimpse of September. Roaring like a pride-leader, the white-haired old giant was swinging the monstrous ax in great arcs, lopping off hands, arms, and heads like a thresher taking up wheat.

Hunnar seemed to be everywhere, dropping alongside for a quick thrust with his own sword, stepping back and running down the wall to rearrange a line of spearmen, offering encouragement to the fighting and solace to the wounded, always appearing where the fighting was heaviest, red beard bobbing in and out of the morass of blood and fur, receiving information from down the wall and offering some of his own.

All along the harbor wall lights were blinking demandingly as both Sofoldian and nomad flashers threw silent tirades of anger and agony at each other. Carnage was reported by peaceful sunlight.

Ethan thrust forward again, felt something hard and cold along his right side. September saw him falter and was at his side in a minute. He caught Ethan as the younger man staggered, dazed.

"Where you hit, young feller?" he asked anxiously. He had to shout to make himself understood over the noise.

"I . . . I don't know." Really, he didn't. He'd felt something strike, but he wasn't weak or faint. He looked down at himself, felt his body. Nothing. September had him turn slowly and examined his back. Ethan heard, "Bless my soul!" for the second time that day.

"Don't keep me in suspense," said Ethan tightly. "What is it?"

He felt a tugging at his back. September grunted once. Then he was grinning and showing Ethan a long barbarian arrow. "This was sticking out the back of your tunic, three-quarters through. Must have gone right down your sleeve. Sonuvabitch."

Ethan wanted to say something appropriately clever, but didn't get the chance. In the next minute it seemed that a solid wall of screeching, howling nomads were swarming over the top of the wall. In places some of the enemy had actually attained the top and were fighting inside. But reinforcements, using the ice-paths to move quickly along the wall, chivaned up and down to repair such cracks in the line.

Then, abruptly, the screams and bellows of defiance turned to howls of frustration. The great mass of enemy troops was moving backwards and down, retreating across the ice. Yells of derision accompanied them, along with arrows and crossbow bolts.

September walked over to Ethan, pulled his helmet off, and slung it across the wall. It bounced off the stone with a metallic clunk. His face was red and running with sweat. A tiny trickle of blood ran down one cheek, dribbled lazily off his chin. The huge ax was stained crimson.

"You're bleeding," said Ethan.

"Eh?" September paused, put a hand to his face, brought it away. "So I am. Well, just a scratch, it is. Right now, young feller-me-lad, I'm too tired to care." He let out a long, exhausted breath.

"I had a dozen brand-new pocket medikits in my baggage," began Ethan, but September waved him off and frowned.

"I've had enough of listening to you talk about the marvelous trade goods we haven't got, young feller."

"Sorry," said Ethan contritely.

"Getting too old for this sort of thing . . . what?" the big man mumbled.

All down the wall and across the harbor, the Sofoldian soldiers and militia were singing and celebrating their victory with a fervor that matched their fighting intensity. As word spread, a similar tintinnabulation arose from the town itself, as the townsfolk and their country visitors slowly received the news.

Hunnar joined them. The knight's eyes were glowing and his once-immaculate uniform was stained with dark splotches. "By the Running Plague of Deimhorst, we beat them! We beat them!"

"They'll be back, y'know," wheezed September.

Hunnar glanced down at him. "Yes, I know. But consider for a moment what has happened here. Ah no, you cannot. You cannot feel the same. For hundreds of years no one has dared to challenge the might of the Horde or any of their bloodsucking ilk. Whatever happens now, even should Wannome be razed to the ice, the word will be spread. Whether from us or from a garrulous drunkard among the enemy. It will be known that the barbarians can be beaten!"

"It wasn't exactly an overwhelming victory, you know," added September drily. "That last charge almost rolled us over."

Hunnar took a long, slow breath of his own. "I know, friend September. It was a near thing." He looked around, walked over to the body of one of the enemy. "If it had not been for this, I fear we would indeed have broken. Look."

He stuck a foot under the corpse and shoved. It rolled over onto its back. Ethan could see the stubby hilt of one of Williams' crossbow bolts protruding from the soldier's chest. It had gone right through the thin layer of bronze and the double leather backing.

"Twas not so much the greater range of your wizard's weapon, though that was important, but the fact that it carries so much striking power. Even, yea, into the wind!"

"You've lost that surprise now, though," September commented pointedly. "Next time they'll know what to expect."

"All the anticipation in the world will not slow one of these," the knight observed. He prodded the hilt of the bolt. A little blood oozed out as he moved it around in the dead tran's chest.

"And Mulvakken and his craftsmen are turning out new bows and many dozens of bolts constantly. Though we still have four trained men for every crossbow that is finished. That is our greatest weakness."

"Will they attack again today?" asked Ethan curiously.

Hunnar glanced at the sun, then looked down at him. "No, friend Ethan, I think not. The Horde," he explained with relish, "are not used to retreating. It will take their leaders some time to absorb what has happened to them. Tis completely foreign to their experience. For the first time they will have to ponder a real strategy. I cannot guess what that may be, except that it will *not* be another open frontal attack!" He smiled ferociously. "The ice is sick with their bodies."

"Well, I'm glad to hear we can rest awhile," said Ethan, "because I am completely and totally finished. Out of it.

Tired." His right hand was resting in a pool of ice water. He raised it and patted a little gently under his eyes, wiped it free with the back of a gloved hand before it could . . . wait a minute. Ice water? At this temperature?

He looked down. His hand had been resting in a large pool of rich red blood, which was just now beginning to congeal and thicken in the sub-freezing air. His survival glove and jacket sleeve had been soaked to a point halfway up his forearm. It looked like a scrap from a slaughterhouse.

"Darn! Now I'll have to find a fire and melt this out." Then he fell over in a dead faint.

IX

The following morning dawned clear and lovely—and windy. It was so beautiful that it was almost impossible to imagine the horror of the previous day. It was not necessary to call on the mind, however. All one had to do was glance over the harbor wall. The ice was littered for hundreds of meters in all directions with tiny clumps of fur and wide frozen ponds of dark red.

Warriors on this world, he reflected, were spared at least one of the great horrors of war. Since every engagement took place in a perpetual deep-freeze, there would be no lingering stink of moldering corpses.

"How do you feel, young feller?" asked September. "You keeled over so quick-like yesterday you had me worried a second."

"I'm sorry about that," Ethan replied.

"No need to apologize . . . " began September, but Ethan halted him.

"No, I've seen men killed before. And these aren't even humans or thranx. I thought I'd seen quite a bit, but this . . . " He indicated the ghastly litter on the ice before them.

September put a great hand on his shoulder. "In the universe, my young friend, it's always the familiar sights that shock the most. We're always expecting the unfamiliar."

Hunnar joined them, but his eyes were on the ice. Come to think of it, so were those of most of the men-at-arms stationed along the wall.

"What will they try today?" asked Ethan, aware that he was missing something.

"Don't you hear it?" the knight replied.

"Hear what?"

"It has been sounding for several minutes now. Listen."

Ethan waited, straining to hear something from across the ice. As usual, there was only the eternal infernal wind. Then there seemed to be something more.

"I hear it," growled September. "Sounds like singing."

"Yes," Hunnar agreed. "Singing . . . Ah." He pointed. "There."

Far out across the solid sea, a strange object of truly monstrous proportions was moving toward them. Four long lines of nomad warriors were harnessed to four thick cables of woven pika-pina. Ethan could make out individual words now. The singing was accompanied by a deep-throated thrumming from smaller versions of the great Margyudan.

"Hayeh, chuff . . . hayeh, chuff!" intoned the straining barbarians. "Haryen abet hayeh chuff . . . hoo, hoo, chuff! . . . "

They swayed in rhythm to the song, pulling first to the left, then the right, left, then right. After they'd moved another dozen meters closer, the design of the engine they were dragging became clear even to Ethan's untrained eye.

Hunnar said quietly, "That's the biggest moydra . . . catapult . . . I've ever seen."

Both singing and machine halted a few minutes later. The long lines of warriors rolled up their green cables. A crew of busy nomads began working about the base of the great war engine.

"Throwing out ice anchors," said September, staring into the distance, "and blocking down the skates. I don't wonder. The recoil on that thing must be terrific."

The singing resumed, on a much smaller scale this time. Ethan could see the huge cyclopean arm gradually sinking toward its base. It was hard to get a true sense of scale at this distance, but the crossbeam of the catapult was many times the height of a man.

There seemed to be a lapse in the activity. "What are they doing now?" he asked anxiously.

Hunnar yelled, "Get down!"

The cry was echoed by dozens of other voices along the wall. Ethan dropped as he had yesterday. Nothing happened. He raised his head slightly. There was a loud whistle in the sky and it wasn't arrows, and it wasn't the wind. Something went crunch in the distance, behind them.

Without waiting for an "all clear" he was on his feet, across the ice-path, and looking into the harbor. He almost stumbled on the ice.

Across the harbor, near the second tower down from the harbor gate, a section of wall at least five meters wide and three deep had been knocked from the back section of stone as though by the bite of a giant shovel.

Several twisted tran-shapes sprawled on the ice among the broken stone. From both walls troops were converging on the spot. A few started to scramble down the open break onto the ice.

There was a line in the harbor ice formed by three successive gouges, each about twenty meters apart. They lay in line from the broken section of wall. Twenty meters beyond the last gouge lay an enormous chunk of solid basalt. It sat placid and innocent in a slight depression of its own making.

Hunnar uttered something vicious that Ethan couldn't translate and started running toward the castle. From several towers, Sofoldian catapults began to twang in response. Their smaller stones fell far short of the huge barbarian war engine.

A broad crescent of nomads had assembled next to the catapult. When it became clear that their own machine was impregnable they set up a great cheering and screaming that didn't stop until the next stone was released.

This one landed short of the wall, took one bounce, and slammed into the masonry not ten meters down from where Ethan was standing. The concussion threw everyone stationed on that section off his feet.

Immediately, Ethan was standing and leaning over the side to inspect the damage.

A respectable portion of rock had been smashed free. Now it lay scattered on the ice like so many pebbles, the boulder a colossus among them.

"It's a damn good thing it takes them so long to wind that thing up," said September. "Just the same, Hunnar's going to have to do something about that toy—and fast. Otherwise, near as I can figure, Sagyanak can sit out there and enjoy the party while that one piece of oversized artillery slowly turns these walls into gravel."

The flickering candles illuminated the map spread before them, but did nothing to lighten their spirits. Balavere, Hunnar, Ethan, and September sat at the table. They were joined by the Landgrave and several other of Sofold's most important nobles, the latter forming Balavere's general staff.

One of the nobles was using a long stick of polished wood to indicate crosses and circles on the map, gesturing here and there at the line representing the harbor wall.

"The wall has been nearly breached—here, here, and here. Severe damage to battlements has occurred here, here, here, and here. Wherever you see a sting sign there is minor damage of varying degree. This is not to mention our personnel casualties, nor the damage to the spirit of the men. There is some talk of surrender and throwing the city on the mercy of Sagyanak. It is small as yet, but will surely grow unless something is done."

"Better to throw oneself on the sword," said Balavere. "But I understand their talk. Tis intolerable to sit helplessly and watch one's comrades flattened, unable to fight back." He shook his great maned head.

"We cannot endure more than another two or perhaps three days of this bombardment before they will have weakened us at so many points that it will become impossible for us to keep them from the harbor. Then it will be all up."

"So we must keep them out . . . somehow," responded Hunnar tightly. "We could never survive an open battle on ice with them. We killed thousands today, but they still outnumber us badly. Do any think otherwise?" he concluded half hopefully.

No one saw fit to dispute this depressing bit of truth.

Finally Balavere gave a sigh and looked up. "Tis a poor leader who does not solicit advice when he himself has naught to offer. Gentlemen?"

One of the nobles spoke up immediately.

"Surely our technology is greater than that of these barbarian primitives! Can we not build ourselves a weapon of equal, if not greater power?"

"In a few malvet, most surely we could, Kellivar," replied Balavere. "But we need one in two days."

"Could we not," proposed one of the older nobles, "establish several of our own smaller moydra within range of their own? From there we could throw animal skins of burning oil onto it."

"Have you seen how they surround it?" said Hunnar tiredly. "We could not disguise such a plan from them. We could never muster a protective force of sufficient strength to stave off an attack on such an advanced position."

"Even if it were protected," the noble added, "by all our new crossbowmen, who would have only a single small bit of ice to defend?"

"Well . . . " hesitated Hunnar. He looked questioningly at Balavere.

"The idea has merit, Tinyak," the general replied. "Yet, should we fail to fire the barbarians' engine quickly, even the crossbows would not be enough to prevent an encirclement. I cannot take the risk of losing them in such an enterprise. They were the difference on the walls yesterday."

"By the Krokim's tail, is it not understood that in a few days there will *be* no walls!" shouted one of the nobles.

"The way I see it," said September calmly, "is pretty simple, if I might have leave to say a few words, noble sirs?"

"You proved yourself the equal or better of any at this table," said the Landgrave, speaking for the first time. "We will give close attention to whatever you counsel."

"All right then." September leaned back in his chair, propped one foot on the table and began rocking back and forth. "Near as I can tell, there's only one thing to do. That's put on your warm woolies, friends, sneak out the dog-door, and set fire to that gimcrack by hand, yourselves, tonight."

"Fighting at night is unmanly," said one of the nobles disdainfully.

"So's getting terminated by a fat slab of street paving," September countered.

"Tis not worthy of a gentleman!" the other grumbled, less certainly this time. "At night."

Ethan glanced around the table, saw the same indecision mirrored in the faces of others.

"Look," said September, taking his foot off the table and leaning forward intently. "I've been amply supplied with the details of what this Sagyanak is going to do if and when the Horde gets in among your women and kids. You won't have to worry about the fact that such atrocities will be conducted in an unmanly and ungentlemanly fashion, because none of you will be around to condemn it. That's if you're lucky . . . Now, you can try this long shot with me, because I intend to try it whether any of you come along or not. Or you can get around this question of etiquette by sending along some of your wives or mistresses in your place. I don't think moral considerations will trouble them."

"Everything we hold dear and true is at stake," interrupted the Landgrave suddenly, "and there are still some among you who would sit at leisure and debate fine points of obscure protocol . . . Damn and hell!" He stood up, old and shaky all of a sudden. "Sir September and Sir Hunnar will take charge of an expedition to move against the enemy this very night. However, I will force no one to take part in this who would feel his honor forever impugned. Should the expedition be successful," and here he looked hard at Hunnar, "and it *must* be successful . . . there will be no question as to the honor of those who *went* . . .

"General Balavere," he continued, looking over at that stocky individual, "you will see to all necessary details. I must retire."

They all stood. Staff in hand, the Landgrave walked off into the dark, trailing a pair of bodyguards. The others sat down, muttering. Gradually they all came to look expectantly across at the alien being who sat as equal in their council.

"How many?" inquired Hunnar firmly. "How many will you need, Sir Skua? Tis certainly a bold undertaking for only the finest of knights."

"I think no more than twenty," replied September thoughtfully. "Ten to pull the oil raft and ten to act as escort. Also, see that everyone is outfitted in armor and outer dress taken from captured material. At night, even a superficial disguise can make all the difference. As for myself, well, we'll have to figure out something else."

"And for me," added Ethan with finality.

"Get me a helmet with a low front," the big man concluded. He turned to Ethan as the table dissolved in a buzz of conversation.

"Listen, young feller-me-lad. There's no need for you to take part in this. It's going to be the middle of the night out there. The temperature will be down in the Pit's own level and cold enough to sear the skin off your face if your heater breaks down. If someone got blown away on a night like that we'd never find him again."

Ethan considered. The last night-expedition he'd been on had been in the company of a delightful young lady on the colony world of Gestalt. She'd spent a balmy moonlit night introducing him to certain exquisite variants on Church theologies. Her conversion of him was short, but ecstatic.

Now there was the bare clean surface of a different sort of world. A man would freeze to death in seconds without special defenses. The cold bit into your teeth like an old dentist's probe.

"I'm going."

"On your own head be it, young feller."

"I'm going, too," came a voice from the back of the hall. Everyone turned quietly. Ethan stood to see over the wide shoulders of one of the nobles.

Darmuka Brownoak, prefect of Wannome, walked slowly toward them, patiently buckling on his silver-inlaid armor.

At night the open icefield seemed more than ever like a white desert. They'd gone over the mountain pass and arrived at a deserted little icefront town on the south side of Sofold. Hopefully, no enemy sentry had seen them depart from the single tiny pier.

Ethan lay on his stomach, the odd-shaped armor digging uncomfortably into his ribs, and dug his gloved fingers into the rough wood of the sled. The splendid barbarian helmet jounced awkwardly on his head, held there by facemask and straps. Goggles protected his eyeballs from freezing.

Ten Sofoldian soldiers pulled the sled, set in waist harness five on either side. The wind was almost directly behind them and they'd shot off at a speed that literally pulled the breath from Ethan's lungs. Even the wind seemed stronger than usual

tonight. At least the flared helmet gave him some protection.
Now if it would only stop chafing.

Laboriously he turned his head, the fur-lined metal scraping against the wood, and managed a glimpse of the lights
shining within the magical castle of Wannome. It rode the
sheer south cliff of the island like a dream.

But they were running for other lights, a thousand times
as many lights, scattered among the barbarians' unending
expanse of camp. It made an endless gleaming parade to
south and east.

"Now remember, lad," September had explained to him,
"if anyone speaks to you, play like you're deaf and dumb. Let
Hunnar and his two knights do all the talking." Ethan had
barely managed a half-frozen nod.

If they were intercepted, their story was to be that they'd
been one of the small patrols which had been raiding the
deserted towns and villages in hope of uncovering some forgotten cache of foodstuffs, utensils, or anything else worth
carrying off. They'd broken into an underground warehouse
half full of supplies—barrels of vol oil, for example—and had
spent too much time guzzling the small stock of good liquor
they'd found. Before they knew it, the ice-that-ate-the-sun
had performed its ugly act. Now they were trying to sneak
back to camp before captain-killer Slattunved could discover
their absence.

As the official surveyor of shifty stories, Ethan had picked
over the plot and pronounced it at least plausible. He knew a
decent sales pitch when he heard one.

Still, one wrong gesture, one word out of place, and they'd
go down under ten thousand aroused nomads.

"There, I think I can see it, young feller."

Ethan looked up, squinted through his goggles. Sure enough,
a black silhouette loomed against the speckled sky. There was
no mistaking the outline of the great catapult. All of a sudden,
then, they began to slow.

One of the unharnessed knights dropped his right wing a
little, skated close to the sled.

"Careful now. A patrol comes."

Below the howl of the wind—at least 60 kph, he thought,

shivering—he could make out Hunnar and the other knights scraping ice as they strove to brake to a halt. He lowered the helmet over his facemask, pulled his arms tight up against his sides, and tucked his hands under his chest, flattening himself to the cold wood.

Up ahead he could hear Hunnar speaking in gruff tones to someone unseen, explaining the provisioning party's strange luck in turning up a great supply of oil for the Scourge's tent, but no food to speak of.

Then he heard one of the barbarians ask, in a strange dialect, "What about those two?"

He could imagine the feet coming closer, a hand lifting off the helmet. Then a cry of shocked surprise at the sight of his alien face . . . and surely their presence was known to the enemy after yesterday's battle on the wall. A sudden swift descent of the sharp blade, cries, spurting blood . . .

"Oh, them?" countered Hunnar smoothly. "Well, the dwarf there is so ashamed of his small size that he tried to down twice the reedle of any of us. Even dipping him in fresh melt had no effect. The other one had just enough to make him think he was a gutorrbyn. He tried to fly off the roof of some dirtgrubber's barn. He flew all right—straight down."

There was a tense pause. Then the patrol leader let loose a hoarse series of jerking laughs.

Eventually he managed to contain himself. "'Tis best you get them back to camp, then," he finally snorted, "before your captain does find them, or he'll skin them alive. If Death-Treader should breach the walls of the Insane Ones, we will attack tomorrow."

"Truly," replied Hunnar, "they would be forever sorrowful should they miss the Sack."

There was another short exchange of pleasantries, too low for Ethan to hear. Then they were moving forward once more, though much slower this time. He raised his head just slightly, saw that they were alone on the ice again. The patrol had evidently continued on its way westward, tacking into the wind.

"Everything linear?" whispered September so sharply that Ethan nearly lost his grip on the sled. He'd completely forgotten about his big companion. September had lain like a dead man throughout the entire exchange.

"You wouldn't think to have any trouble talking," he replied, "but my stomach's halfway up into my throat." September chuckled. "For a minute there, when he asked about 'those two,' I saw myself spread across the ice like bread-dough."

"You're lucky," replied September, "I was so busy organizing things before we pushed off that I forgot to go to the john."

The meeting with the patrol must have been an omen, for they didn't encounter another soul the rest of the way. An attack by night was apparently as unthinkable to the nomads as it had been to the cultured coterie of knights back in the castle.

All but one of the guards at the great siege-engine were enjoying a deep sleep in the several tents at its base. These were pegged into the ice and benefited from the windbreak the catapult provided.

The one duty guard observed their approach and chivaned over, completely unsuspecting. He was probably curious as to what a group of his fellows were doing out on the ice so late at night with a raft full of barrels and two unmoving bodies.

Hunnar met him. He offered him the same explanation he'd given the patrol leader, explaining their partly successful raid. Then he presented the other with a "stolen" sweet-stick. The guard accepted it with thanks.

"Death-Treader did well today," Hunnar said conversationally. "Would that I had been closer, to better see the fear on the faces of those stupid towndwellers." The last word Hunnar uttered in the contemptuous tone the barbarians held for anyone fool enough to live in one place instead of moving free with the wind.

"The crew had some difficulty ranging him today," admitted the guard, "but all will be perfected for tomorrow. We will surely breach the walls, perhaps in several places. Some say it will not even be necessary to attack. With their walls down, the fools may finally realize their impossible position and surrender. That will be even better." He grinned horribly. "There will be more prisoners to play with."

"True," Hunnar agreed. "But I hear the strain on Death-Treader was great today." He pointed upward. "Is that not a crack in the bindings I see? There, on the Arm. After not having worked for so long, it may have rotted."

The guard turned to look. "I see no crack. But wait, Death-Treader was used only four kuvits ago, in practice for the usual care." He started to whirl, his voice rising. "Who—?"

Hunnar's dirk went right through his throat, ripping up into the larynx. The guard choked on the blood, staggered, and sank to the ice without a cry. Hunnar wiped the blade on his leggings.

"That's it, young feller!" said September, scrambling to his feet and slapping Ethan on the shoulder. "Let's go!"

"If you don't mind, I'd just as soon skip this part. I'll stay here."

"Oh." September looked at him understandingly in the dark. "I know, my lad. No problem."

Ethan and four others began unloading the raft. Hunnar, September, and the other knights and soldiers entered the tents on the far side of the catapult and silently set about the bloody job of disposing of the sleeping guards. By the time they'd finished their grisly work, Ethan and his companions were already scrambling up into the wood and fiber framework.

"Pass it up!" he yelled down, holding tight to the super-structure with both legs. The wind tore and battered at him, angrily trying to sweep him off his perch.

"Quickly now!" sounded Hunnar's voice. They were very close to the main body of the nomad camp.

Thick, syrupy vol oil was ladled over the wood, bracings, and bindings until the oleaginous mess became dangerous to walk on. The aromatic stink seemed sufficient to wake the dead. Fortunately, the wind carried most of it away.

There was a shout in the distance. Two of the knights stopped passing oil upward and ran toward the source. They returned a few moments later.

"Two," one of the knights told Hunnar and September. "Officers. Apparently they were just returning to their tents.

I don't know if they could tell who we were, but they must know there aren't supposed to be people climbing on the moydra at night. They ran before we could reach them."

A few minutes later this was confirmed by yells, queries, and concerned shouts from within the nomad encampment. The noise multiplied rapidly.

"Off, off, get off!" ordered September frantically. Slipping and sliding on the greasy wood, Ethan and the other soldiers scrambled down to the ice.

A dozen torches were readied. They'd been well soaked in oil and the wind wouldn't quench them. They were thrust in a circle at September, who paused momentarily.

"It's not the highest product of our technology, nor the one I'd like to have right now, but I'm glad we've got it." He held out Hellespont du Kane's expensive, filagreed, iridium-plated lighter.

One torch and then another blazed, stark shadows exploding onto the ice. The shouts behind them grew louder. One of the non-torch-bearing knights had moved toward the encampment. Now he turned to shout back at them.

"Hurry! Someone comes."

"Scatter them well, mind," ordered September. Twelve arms spun, released in unison. Only two of the blazing brands were blown out. With the wind behind them, the others carried well up into the superstructure.

They seemed to flicker there, tiny spots of isolated flame. For a horrible moment Ethan feared they wouldn't catch and the whole risk had been taken for nothing. Then, almost together, they went up.

With a roar that briefly drowned the wind and the rising shouts from the camp, the great wooden frame virtually exploded into orange flame so brilliant that the little knot of watching humans and tran were forced to shield their eyes.

"Onto the sled now, young feller!" bellowed September, giving Ethan a shove and not trying to keep his voice down. The tran took up their harnesses and in a moment they were speeding northward and west in a wide curve that should bring them back to Wannome and in through the main gate. If they didn't make the curve, Ethan reflected, they'd plow full bore into the far side of the enemy encampment.

Now it didn't matter if every sentry in the camp was alerted. The howls and shrieks of rudely awakened nomad soldiers sounded loud in their ears as they raced before the wind, building speed. Cautiously, keeping a tight grip on the raft, Ethan turned on his side to look behind them.

A tower of flavescent orange, crackling and splitting, clawed at the black sky like a mad thing, while the wind tore away ragged shreds of its head and swept them westward.

He could make out small dark shapes silhouetted against the base of the pyre.

"Look at it burn, look at it burn!" he yelled to September almost boyishly.

"No need to shout, young feller. I'm right here." He too was on his side, looking rearward. "Poor chaps don't seem to know what hit 'em, what?"

Something whizzed overhead.

"Whup! I withdraw any sympathy. Seems they do." A second arrow thunked into the base of the raft. "Damn!" the big man muttered. "Wish I'd thought to bring one crossbow." He turned and hollered to Hunnar who was chivaning alongside.

"Leave us if you have to, Hunnar! This thing slows you."

"Not a chance, my friend."

September looked ahead, then back into the night. "You'll never make it with us."

"'Tis as good a time and place to die as any," the knight replied easily. Then, ignoring September's curses, he let himself fall slightly behind the raft.

Ethan put his hand on his sword hilt. He peered desperately into the darkness, but couldn't determine how many were following them. There seemed to be more than twenty, in any case.

Something struck September on the side of the head and dropped him as though poleaxed.

Ethan turned, alarmed. "Skua! Are you hurt bad?"

"Relax, young feller." The big man propped himself up on one elbow, felt his head. "That smarts. Good thing they made these helmets tough. Goddamn arrows." Ethan peered closer, saw the dent in the metal just above the forehead. If September had been a tran he'd have lost an ear.

Their pursuers were close enough now for Ethan to make out individuals. There was something surreal in watching them move closer and closer with painful slowness, as they made up distance lost on the clumsy sled.

A couple of other soldiers had dropped back to form a rear guard. Now they were flailing behind themselves with swords and axes, trying to run and fight at once.

One of the pursuers shoved a long pike forward, caught a Sofoldian soldier in a wing. The barbarian jerked and the soldier, pulled off balance, fell to the ice. He vanished beneath the enemy and the night as they sped on.

One of the nomads had gained the end of the raft. He grabbed hold of the wood, thrust forward with a spear. September brought his sword down—he'd left the heavy ax behind in the castle. The thick wood of the spear shaft shattered. The other cursed, swung the wood hilt first. September parried it, slashed, and opened an ugly cut on the barbarian's arm. He dropped away from the raft, clutching at the bleeding limb.

It was growing crowded around the sled. One of the harnessed soldiers was down, a dead weight dragging them back. The others were too pressed to cut him loose. It was becoming impossible to keep speed and fight at the same time.

They were circling in toward the harbor gate now. Ethan did some quick figuring. They'd never make it. They'd be overpowered before they got close. Perhaps the du Kanes and Williams might eventually make it safely to the settlement.

One nomad chivaned in from the west and fairly flew onto the raft. Ethan swung clumsily with his sword but it only glanced off the other's armor. The broad muscular body hit September, knife at the ready, and the two grappled on the pitching, swaying sled. The other was trying to pull the big man off the raft onto the ice.

Desperately Ethan reached over. He caught September's leg just in time to prevent that fatal roll. Out of the sweat-distorted corner of an eye he saw another of the enemy move in close to the stern of the sled, spear held ready.

He was trying to decide whether to let September go to parry the spear or hope that his armor would ward off the first thrust, when something hit the barbarian with such force that he was almost cut in half. In a microsecond the confusion surrounding them had multiplied tenfold.

September had managed to break free of his persistent assailant and had shoved him from the sled. He gave Ethan an exhausted smile.

"What's going on?" asked Ethan bewilderedly.

"That fella was tough!" gasped the big man. "They must be sortieing from the city!"

Yes, now Ethan could recognize the armor of the Sofoldian troops as they swept and battered away the sled's pursuers. Minutes later they dashed under the gate chain and nets and were inside the cold womb of the harbor. The wind shrank to a bearable gale. Utterly winded himself, Ethan collapsed on the sled, not caring if he fell off. He tugged off the uncomfortable barbarian helmet and slung it far out onto the ice.

He lay there as they moved slowly toward the Landgrave's pier and the cheering nocturnal crowd. While the hysterical populace screamed and sang, he stared up at the strange stars and tried to guess which one was home.

When they finally tied up to the dock and were greeted by the Landgrave himself, not even September could explain why Ethan was crying.

"They're not going to be throwing even dogfood with that thing for a long time," September commented. The big man had had his cuts and bruises attended to and now, several days after their desperate sally, looked good as new.

There had been no sign of activity on the part of the nomads after their great moydra had been destroyed. It looked as though, contrary to Hunnar's expectations, they were settling in for a siege.

It had been nearly a week now, though, and Ethan was as bored as any Sofoldian sentry after days of sitting on the wall and staring out over the ice.

He'd taken to learning sele, a local kind of chess. Elfa was serving as instructress, on strict warning from him that sele was the *only* thing she would try and teach him.

Surprisingly, Colette kept interrupting their sessions with requests for a walk, or correction on a point of translation—she was getting good at the language—or some other trivial excuse. Once she'd even made a couple of attempts to learn the rudiments of the game herself. Standing behind him and leaning close over his shoulder, she gave the board her undivided attention.

However, she'd refused to have a dress made of the local materials; her shipboard outfit was by now ragged and thin, and whenever she leaned over him Ethan was subjected to several distractions of a nonverbal nature. Although he'd been the distracted one, it was Elfa who had quit in disgust and stalked off in a royal huff.

Frankly, it would have been pleasant to say that he was completely unaware of what was going on. But he'd worked too many fine cities and operated among plenty of sophisticated folk. He didn't like the way things were developing, but there wasn't much he could do about it. And darned if he wasn't a little flattered.

Today, however, September had had to come for him in the local library, a fascinating place despite the maddening lack of pictures in the books. But he'd gone quick and quiet when he saw the look on the other's face. They headed for a section of the castle Ethan rarely visited.

"What's up, Skua? And why the sour expression?"

"Hunnar once said that he couldn't picture our nemesis sitting on their backsides for very long without coming down with a severe case of the fidgets. Well, he was right. They haven't been sitting. In fact, it appears they've been working 'round the clock."

"Small area. On what?" They turned a corner and started up a ramp. "Another catapult?"

"Uh-uh. Hunnar says it would take months for them to rebuild something like that. After having seen it, I can believe him. No, it looks like this Sagyanak has come up with another surprise, and it's a damn good thing we found out about it when we did. Though I don't see what we can do about it in any case."

Ethan was badly upset by the big man's pessimism. Throughout the battle he'd never been so dour—an island of confidence in oceanic chaos. He sounded more discouraged than Ethan had ever heard him.

"How do we know about this 'surprise'?" he asked finally.

"Wizard's telescope," came the curt reply. As they turned another corner Ethan saw that they were indeed heading for the old magician-scholar's apartment.

It hadn't changed from the one time he'd visited it, and it still stank. It wouldn't have been very diplomatic to point it out, but the expressions on his face should have been sufficiently eloquent.

Hunnar was waiting for them, wearing a face that matched September's own. So was Williams.

Ethan had seen very little of the schoolmaster since the fighting had begun. They'd passed in hallways and occasionally joined for a meal. But as their familiarity with the language and people of Wannome grew, the need for the humans to stay together at all times had diminished. Ethan assumed that the teacher had been up in the foundry, helping the tran craftsmen in the vital business of turning out a steady stream of crossbows and bolts. He was a little surprised to see him here.

"It appears they are nearly finished, friend Skua," said Hunnar in a worried tone. He looked resigned. "Have a look, Sir Ethan."

Ethan seated himself behind the crude, baroquely decorated telescope and applied his right eye to the eyepiece.

"The little knob at the right side is the focus, lad," offered September helpfully.

"Thanks." Ethan twisted the knob slightly and the image snapped suddenly into sharp relief. It was still fuzzy, but that was due to the crudely ground lenses and not his own eyesight. Considering what the Wannomian lens-makers had to use for sand, the telescope was a remarkable achievement.

Far back amidst the solidly anchored barbarian fleet, a great open space had been cleared. Considerable activity was occurring around a single huge, low raft. Many big logs, like those used in the stavanzer-fighting lightnings, had been tied together with heavy crossbeams. The resultant raft was one huge, crude, open deck mounted on gigantic stone skates.

"We found out about this only this morning," September told him.

Eer-Meesach spoke from the background. "Tis fortunate indeed that I detected the vermin, else we should have no warning at all."

"What's it for?" asked Ethan, without removing his eye from the scope.

"I think it's pretty obvious, young feller," replied September. "Look off to the left, at that big pile of rocks they've assembled. You might have to move the scope a bit."

Ethan did. Yes, to the left a swarm of nomads was unloading great stones from heavily laden rafts, arranging them neatly on the ice. Sometimes two rafts were linked together to transport an especially huge rock.

"I see them," he said.

"They're building a helluva big raft, there," the big man continued. "Bigger than anything Hunnar or anyone here has seen. Its size and the construction that makes such size possible render it practically unmaneuverable, but that won't matter." His mouth tightened, the protruding chin cut air.

"They'll load it to the breaking point with rocks and boulders, tons worth, put a couple of monstrous sails on the thing, haul it upwind and let it go. With the wind behind it and a good start, it'll build up a pretty speed, what? It's an obscenely big ram, is what it is."

"Can it breach the wall?" Ethan asked quietly.

"I fear such is the case, friend Ethan," answered Hunnar. "There is enough stone assembled now, and still they bring more. I think twould penetrate the wall like vol butter."

Ethan took his face from the telescope.

"Can't you be ready to block the hole with nets and chain once the ram's gone through?"

"There is no other chain like the Great Chain that guards the harbor gate," replied Hunnar ruefully. "They will come close behind this monster. We will try the nets, of course, but it will be very difficult. We will not know the size of the hole, nor will it be easy to bridge such a gap and secure the nets before the Horde is upon us. And still we must be ready to defend all sections of the wall, lest they swarm over us at some too-weakened point. Once they break into the harbor, we are done. They will attack the town and we will be forced to abandon the perimeter to them." The knight looked terribly depressed. Ethan didn't feel too good right then, either.

Williams spoke to the ensuing silence. "I think we'd better tell them now."

"But we have done it only on such a small scale," the wizard replied. "Still, I must agree with you. It may help."

"What are you two babbling about?" asked Hunnar sharply.

"The great wizard Williams has shown me many things," said Eer-Meesach, ignoring Hunnar's lack of respect. "The crossbow of which your archers are so enamored, youngster, is the result of but one such thought. We have something else which may be of some use."

"But I'm not sure how to apply it!" said Williams almost pleadingly. "We don't have the proper facilities, or time, or anything!"

"Oh well," sighed September, "let's have a look at it, anyway. You never know."

X

Many of the people in the city had been working double and triple shifts, day and night, but there was even more activity than normal in Wannome that night. If Sagyanak's spies had been able to see inside the walls of the harbor, they surely would have been puzzled at the activity that filled the shoreline and enclosed ice. Vol-oil lamps and torches shed a cautious light on the scene.

They would have been even more puzzled at the strange activities taking place in certain crannies of the mountains, sections of dark abandoned countryside and old-town, and at the huge bonfires that shocked the main square with light.

In a room far up in the great castle keep, the war council of Sofold was meeting in heated discussion.

"I say tis far too dangerous!" one of the nobles exclaimed. He slammed a fist onto the thick table. "Tis too new, too alien. Tis not of us."

"Nonsense!" countered Malmeevyn Eer-Meesach from his chair near the Landgrave.

"The crossbows are equally new and alien," Hunnar riposted.

"They are not. They are but variations on our familiar longbow. But this . . . this is the work of the Dark One!"

"I'm not at all that dark," said Eer-Meesach.

"Do not be flippant, old man," snorted the noble. "I, for one, am not overwhelmed by your learned nonsense."

"You'll be overwhelmed, good sir," admonished Hunnar, "if we fail to prepare for when that ram bursts into the harbor tomorrow!"

"Can it truly breach the great wall?" asked one of the knights disbelievingly.

"You have not seen it, Suletja," said General Balavere

solemnly. "It will breach the wall. Unless it should hit at too acute an angle, and I think there is little chance of that. Though," and he paused thoughtfully, "once the ram is moving, it would take a thousand men to correct or change its course."

"If this new thing of yours does not work as you describe," said the old mayor of one of the larger country towns, "we shall all fall into the center of the earth."

"I keep telling you," September began, but he halted, spreading his hands helplessly—they'd been through this very question twice a dozen times already. "Sofold is as solid as the Landgrave's throne, and more so."

"All this may be true," replied the old mayor, scratching the back of his neck, "but we have only *your* word for it. You ask us to believe a great deal."

"I know, I know," September said. "If we had more time . . . and this is the only chance I see."

"Yet you say this will not stop the ram from breaching the walls."

"No. There's no way we can stop that thing. I don't think they'd let another night expedition within a satch of the ram. But this may save us all, afterwards."

"And if it should fail?"

"Then you're welcome to whatever Sagyanak leaves of my corpse," the big man finished.

"Fine compensation, fine satisfaction!" laughed the other hollowly.

"General?" The Landgrave looked over at his principal military adviser, thrusting the problem squarely onto his shoulders.

"This is the most difficult decision I have ever had to make," the old soldier began. "More so even than the first decision to fight. Tis because there are questions here that go above mere military matters. I must go against everything I was taught about the world as a cub. And yet . . . yet . . . our strange friends have been right about so *many* things. And there *is* always the outside chance that they will align the ram improperly, or that the wind will shift on them and it will strike the wall at an angle and not breach, mayhap even miss completely."

"Do not avoid me, Bal," chided the Landgrave gently.

The two old tran looked at each other carefully. Then Balavere smiled slightly. "I wouldn't do that, Tor. I recommend Sir September's plan. I should like to see this thing he promises . . . even if we do all fall into the center of the world."

"Let it be so, then," pronounced the Landgrave.

All rose.

"By your Patience, gentlemen," said September, "the wizard Williams and I must get down to the landings. We've a great deal to do ere the ice disgorges the sun." He turned to Ethan. "Young feller, you'll see to the assembly of the material?"

"Right away. Oh, du Kane wants to help, too."

"Not really?" said September. "Well, take him with you, then. I can't have the old bastard underfoot, but it's encouraging to see him recognizing the real world, at last."

But as he started off down the hall, Ethan found himself sympathizing with du Kane and not September. He knew the financier wasn't useless, only a victim of culture shock and belief in his own omnipotence. He'd felt more than enough of similar emotions ever since they'd smashed into that first little island.

The wind from the west the next day was powerful and steady—perfect for the nomads' needs. Ethan hugged the castle wall against the gale.

The great ram had been completed some time during the night and moved out of range of even the wizard's telescope.

"Shifting it far enough to the west to get room for building speed," Hunnar explained. "It will take that monster a dozen kijat just to build to raft speed."

"I don't know why they bother," said Spetember. "Even half that should be enough to knock down the wall."

"With all respect, friend September, I suspect they desire not merely to knock down a section of wall, but to make a clean breach large enough to drive a good-sized raft through."

"You don't think they'll try to come in on rafts, do you?" September asked. "Not that we could change things now anyway."

"No. That would require skillful handling indeed. Even a few good-sized rocks could catch a raft, tumble it, and block the breach. As we might try to do. But individual warriors could get through despite such obstacles, and before we could bring up anything to block the gap."

"Think not encountering something like that will make 'em suspicious?" continued the big man.

"Sagyanak, or Olox, or one like those might be taken by such thoughts. But I do not think those murderers so brave that they will be in the front line of attackers. The simple warrior will see naught but open ice between himself and the defenseless city. For animals like these, that is an irresistible temptation."

"Let's try that flasher once again," suggested September.

"Very well."

There were two of the brightly polished devices at their observation position high up on the castle's south parapet, in case one should fail or break. September gave orders to the two operators.

"Tell Williams there's still no sign."

Immediately the skilled communicators had the flashers in operation. Side mirrors brought the sun into the central reflector. An answer was blinking at them from down in the harbor almost before they'd finished.

"They acknowledge 'very good and waiting,' Sir."

"Fine. Thanks," replied the big man.

They had another hour to wait before the ram was sighted. The nomad soldiers were drawn up in their familiar crescent parallel to the harbor wall. As it had been days ago, the line was solid and unbroken. There was no indication of where the ram would come from. The concentration was, as always, heavier on the south side. No one expected the ram to come from the north or the east, into the wind. There would be no feint to this attack.

Despite the toll they'd taken among their tormentors on that first terrible day, the Sofoldian defenders were still badly outnumbered. But there were heartening signs in the barbarian line. It was still unbroken, but it no longer seemed to stretch to infinity as it had that first time.

As usual, it was Hunnar who made the first sighting.

"There! Over their heads by that dark spot on the ice."

Ethan leaned over the wall, squinting. Almost immediately the enemy began to move away, split. A huge gap opened in the lines.

The ram was a tiny dot at first, but it grew rapidly larger. Soon it seemed as big as a stavanzer, though it was not nearly so. Still, it was plenty big, bigger than the biggest raft Ethan had yet seen. It sparkled oddly in the sun-glare.

"What's that reflection from? Not the stone, surely."

"It is and it isn't, friend Ethan," replied Hunnar evenly. "They've taken meltwater and poured it over the stones. Letting it freeze has turned the load into a solid, unbroken mass."

There was silence among the Wannomian watchers, human and tran alike. The ram moved closer and closer with the deliberateness of an eclipse. No sound came from the distance, no pounding engines, no flaming rockets. The juggernaut moved mute.

Without turning, September spoke to the flasher operators. "Signal 'standby' to the wizards."

The ram grew larger, seemed to leap into sharp focus. It passed through the waiting gap in the nomad ranks. Rocking with sheer speed, it came hurtling on at close to 200 kph. With a roar, the barbarian crescent started forward in its wake.

"Brace All!" sounded the cry from several places along the castle battlements.

The ram struck.

The concussion climbed the walls and threw men within the castle to the ground. Ethan could hear masonry falling in the inner rooms, an occasional tinkle of breaking glass. A section of wall two towers west from the main gate erupted in a shower of stone shards. The sound of damned stone crawled inside the head and battered ears from both sides.

A rain of rock and wood splinters descended and everyone covered as best they could. Large chunks were thrown all the way across the harbor into the far wall, taking pieces out of the interior side.

The ram slid two-thirds of the way across the harbor toward that interior wall on its five remaining runners, trailing two broken masts and a sea of shredded pika-pina sailcloth. Boulders and raped wood formed ugly blemishes on the clean ice.

A clear gap showed in the wall, broad enough for tran to chivan through twenty abreast. A close-packed mob of screaming, ax-waving barbarians, thousands strong, had followed close behind the ram. They reached the walls and the breach.

Dozens of grappling hooks and scaling ladders assailed the walls, ropes were snugged tight. Howling bloodthirsty cries, others swarmed into the gap, ready to overwhelm any attempt to close it.

Those at the walls climbed up, and over. They found only empty spear-slots, deserted battle-towers. Deafening cheers rose from the entire perimeter. The interiors of the great gate towers were gained. The Great Chain was melted into place, but the antipersonnel netting was cut loose and a fresh stream of angry warriors poured in via the main gate.

Ethan saw a gaudily armored officer gain the open gap, hesitate, and look about him uncertainly, clearly puzzled at the absence of the defenders. Ethan's hand tensed on the castle parapet. But the cautious officer was swept away and into the harbor by the tight-packed river of attacking nomads.

Some of the barbarians began to run along the tops of the walls toward the castle and the city. They ran because the ice-paths had been melted and hacked into uselessness. They reached a point where the wall entered the castle itself—and were halted by a solid barrier of stone and a hail of arrows from above. A few began to batter ineffectually against the walled-up entrances.

Some tried to climb the raw stone itself. They were easily picked off by the archers above. Most turned and, spreading their wings, dropped in a semi-glide to the uncontested ice below.

The harbor was rapidly filling with screaming, thrashing warriors all milling about and looking for someone to fight. Confusion and uncertainty was beginning to take hold. The mass vacillated, shifted. Then, as one, they rushed on toward the undefended city with a horrible cry.

The entire remaining strength of the Sofoldian army met them at the shoreline.

Camouflaged barriers of rock and lines of sharpened stakes appeared, tied together by cables of barbed pika-pina rope. The tough, nearly unbreakable cord had been laboriously studded with sharpened bits of glass, wood, and metal. September and not Williams had been the one who had shown the locals how to make a fair imitation of concertina wire. A hail of crossbow bolts and arrows and spears felled hundreds of the surprised enemy in that first startling counterattack.

But it was only a last-ditch defense, screamed the nomad officers to their men! One more effort and the soft city-folk must surely collapse! The great wave swept forward again— to lose more hundreds to a barely covered deep ditch filled with sharpened stakes, tipped with vol dung and other poisons. The concealed moat was quickly filled with moaning, twisting bodies.

Yes again, urged the garishly garbed captains, the resplendent field officers! A last charge to sweep away the fatally weakened defenders! Yet a third time the nomad mass trundled forward, slammed into the Sofoldian line. Hand-to-hand combat sprang up at isolated points along the shore, the barbarian Horde gaining a centimeter at a time, the length of every spear and sword bitterly contested.

From high on the castle battlements, September calmly said, "Ready now" to his communicators. An acknowledging series of flashes came from a tiny house now perilously close to the front line.

Meanwhile more of the enemy poured into the harbor, slowed as they ran into their fellows. There must have been ten thousand pressing inexorably against the thin Sofoldian defenses, with more arriving each second, every tran a pillar of hatred and fury.

"Now," said September quietly. The message was flashed to the waiting receivers. The flasher operators had guts. They didn't drop and kiss stone until they were certain the command had been received.

There was a pause.

For one terrifying moment, nothing happened. Ethan raised his head slightly and peered through an arrow slot.

The ice convulsed.

Concussion lifted him from the ground and slammed him back into unyielding rock. He felt wet stickiness on his cheek, but he'd only scraped himself. A microsecond later he tried to metamorphose into a tiny ball. Down came a bitter squall of ruptured ice, mixed with pieces of barbarian armor and pieces of barbarian.

Far out on the southwest icefield, Borda-tane-Anst, knight of Sofold, felt the ice-earth shake under him, saw the huge column of flame and smoke erupt in the harbor of his home. His mind rejoiced because the magic of the alien magician had worked. But deep inside he was frightened near to death.

The earth did not open beneath them. Pulling at the pure white cloak that he'd been lying under all morning, he rose and waved his sword to right and left. Then he and six hundred picked Sofoldian troops spread their dan and started grimly for the rear of the nomad encampment. All carried torches in addition to swords and spears.

The Dantesque scene in the harbor was revealed as the smoke was borne away by the wind. There was no dust, but stinging, blinding particles of ice still hung in the air, and Ethan was grateful for the goggles.

Below, an awful cacophony had begun, not of defiance this time, but of pain and fear and terror. The two humans watched, completely oblivious to the antics of Hunnar. Usually dignified to the point of coldness, the solemn young knight had shed his reserve and was leaping about like a cub, hugging every man-at-arms within reach and whooping with joy.

Uncountable multitudes of barbarian soldiers, who had stood within the harbor a moment ago, now lay dead or dying from terrible wounds. The ice sheet had cracked from the hundreds of charges but had not broken through to the freezing depths below. Eer-Meesach and Williams' estimates had been proven correct. The ice was much too thick here to be affected by such ancient explosives.

Not as sound was the harbor wall, which had been subjected to another violent shaking. Several sections looked dangerously near collapse. The schoolmaster's fuse and firing mechanism, cannibalized from the wrecked lifeboat, had done its task efficiently. The hundreds of charges had gone off within seconds of one another.

During the night, funnel-shaped holes had been melted in the ice, then filled with glass, metal, bone, and wooden fragments, and a year's accumulation of bronze, iron, and steel filings originally destined for re-melting in the volcanic forges. Filled with anything that could cut or rend or tear.

Water had been poured over the pockets of crude shrapnel and allowed to refreeze during the early morning. The barbarians had been cut down like grass.

Now the battered, weakened army of Sofold came boiling out from behind its barriers and temporary ramparts, howling and shouting as barbarically as their supposedly less civilized tormentors. Axes, swords, and spears fell indiscriminantly among healthy and wounded alike.

Ethan stood shakily and turned away from the sickening slaughter.

Many of those who'd survived were in shock. They were completely incapable of putting up effective resistance to the ready, prepared Sofoldians. It must have seemed like a hundred lighting bolts had landed among them.

Now archers and crossbowmen broke from the castle and the stone barrier at the other end of the wall, began retaking their positions atop the ancient masonry. Only now they were firing *into* the harbor, picking off those still fighting and any trying to retreat.

The still considerable body of enemy warriors surged dazedly back and forth, with dozens dropping every minute.

Ethan stared out over the now cleared ice. Then he turned and got September away from his survey of the massacre.

The enemy raft fleet was burning. Some were raising sail and struggling to escape even as they went up in flames. Fanned by the uncaring, indiscriminate wind, the blaze spread rapidly from one raft to its neighbor, thence to three or four others. Ethan saw one sail rigged, only to be struck

by a ball of flame blown from a burning storage craft. Pika-
pina and mast went up like match and paper in the thirsting
wind.

Distant screams drifted over the ice to Ethan and chills
raced up his spine. He put his hands over his face and sank
in stunned silence to the ground. September put a gentle hand
on his head and tried to comfort him.

"I know what you're thinking, young feller-me-lad," he
muttered softly. "But you've got to consider what these folk
have suffered. The only difference between them and their
traditional enemies out there is a little book learning and
another philosophy of life. Underneath, they're very much
the same animal . . . just like most humans are, when we're
pushed. To them the nomad women and cubs are as dangerous
as the menfolk. Not because of what they can do, but because
of what they represent. Do you understand that?"

Ethan sat still as the stones. He looked up.

"No."

September grunted and walked away. To the end of his
days, Ethan would hear the far-away shrieking.

Confronted with a murderous, unstunned enemy in front
of them and fire behind, the once proud, invincible Horde
of the Death dropped helmets, weapons and armor, broke, and
fled toward their flaming homes. September was trying to get
Hunnar's attention. The knight finally calmed down enough
to listen.

"Your tane-Anst did his job well, what? Will he have
enough sense to watch for those who escape? They're scared
and many are weaponless, but hysterical humans, and probably tran, have little regard for their own lives. Makes for
difficult fighting."

"Tane-Anst is a good soldier," said Hunnar thoughtfully.
"He'll take care to keep his men together."

Finally Ethan stood and had a look at the retreating mob
of surviving nomads. "This tane-Anst only took about six
hundred men with him, Skua. Won't they be badly outnumbered by these?"

"No group of well-organized, disciplined soldiers is ever
outnumbered by a mob, Ethan. Remember that."

Ethan turned and looked down into the harbor again. The

ice was literally blotted out by a vast array of twisted, broken furry forms and a small lake of rapidly freezing blood. Hunnar came up to him. The knight was trembling now and Ethan thought he saw a little of what September had meant reflected in Hunnar's face. After hundreds of years of helpless genuflection, reaction to what he and his people had done today was beginning to sink in.

"The Landgrave watches from his rooms and can see well for himself what has been wrought this hour," said the knight, his voice slightly shaky. "I go to give him official word of his troops . . . and to remind him of his promise to you, my friends. Will you come?"

"No, this is your moment, Hunnar," said September.

The knight exchanged breath and shoulder clasps with both of them, then departed at a run into the castle. September strolled to the edge of the parapet and looked down into the harbor. The fighting had degenerated into a bloodcurdling mopping-up operation, with Sofoldian soldiers and militia examining each corpse and methodically slitting the throat of any who lived.

"It may not be a gesture of the morally highest," he began, "but for better or worse, by introducing gunpowder here we've brought a whole new kind of warfare to this decidedly bellicose people. And you know?" He turned and glanced at Ethan. "Try as I might, I can't convince myself we've done a bad thing."

"Bad or not," replied Ethan drily, dabbing at his cut cheek, "it's always one of humanity's first gifts, isn't it?"

There was a ball to end all balls in the great castle that evening. It served to cover the fact that many of Sofold's finest young men had passed to the Warm Regions that day. Sadly, the brave and methodical tane-Anst had been among them, felled as he personally led a squad in pursuit of just one more fleeing raft.

At least three quarters of the barbarian fleet had been burnt or captured, together with a province's ransom in armor, weapons, and treasure. And those ships which had escaped had not departed overcrowded.

To everyone's intense disappointment, Sagyanak had been among the successful escapees.

The Scourge's power, however, was forever broken. From a near god, the Death had been reduced to simply another annoying pirate, whose strength had been scattered with the wind.

By way of partial compensation, the head of Olox the Butcher was prominently on display atop a jeweled pike at the dinner table. It was joined by the crania of assorted companion warriors.

The little knot of humans sat in an honored position, far up the table near the Landgrave himself. But they'd seen too much blood to fully enter into the merriment of the night. Only September, sitting next to him, seemed able to throw himself into the spirit of the occasion with honest gusto.

Ethan stared curiously across the table at Hellespont du Kane. One of the wealthiest men in the Arm. Yet he still wore the same expression Ethan had observed back on the *Antares*, the day they'd had their private destinies inextricably altered by a pair of indecisive kidnappers. Nor was his appetite affected. He downed a delicately carved slice of roast with the same precision he doubtless employed in the finest restaurants of Terra or Hivehom.

Ethan felt an urge to put a fist in that robotic face. For a wild moment he thought du Kane might really be a clever robot, and that the flesh-and-blood du Kane was somewhere else, perfectly comfortable except for a mild upset at the loss of one valuable piece of machinery. It would explain several of the odder things about the industrialist.

But no. He may have been robot-like in some respects, but he was definitely human. Like his daughter. He was just a nice, slightly dotty, schizophrenic old man with several hundred million credits and a daughter as cool-headed as he probably was—once.

Ethan was discovering the interesting side effects which the steady consumption of reedle could produce in the human system when Hunnar came over. Standing between the two humans, the tran put a paw on each man's shoulder and leaned close.

"It is necessary that I see you both in private," he whispered.

"Aw, don't be a party-pooper," September huffed. "Sit yourself down with us and—" He broke off in mid-sentence when he saw the look on the knight's face. It was solemn—and something more.

They left the grand hall, the masquerading torchlight, the flashing, jeweled cloaks and blouses; left the polished dress armor of the nobles and knights and the gowns of their ladies; left them to follow Hunnar down quiet cold hallways and mocking stairs.

"Isn't this the way to our rooms?" said Ethan unquestioningly.

"That is so," Hunnar replied, but Ethan's probe failed to elicit any more information.

From distant chambers Ethan could hear shouts and laughter. The other inhabitants of the castle were celebrating the victory in their own fashion. Once, when they passed a chill open balcony, he had a glimpse down into the town itself. Bonfires blazed in open squares, and every torch and lamp and candle in Wannome was burning. The city wore a necklace of light.

Celebrating would continue for days, General Balavere had told him. Or until everyone was too drunk to lift another tankard or mug.

He wondered where Williams had gone. The schoolmaster hadn't been seen since he'd been introduced as a co-guest of honor. When the Landgrave had presented him and proceeded to make a flowery speech full of lavish praise and sugary compliment, the little professor had fidgeted and squirmed like a five-year-old posing for his first pre-school soloid.

On the other hand, old Eer-Meesach had expanded in the light of praise like a fat sunflower.

"Sulfur from the volcanic vents and springs," Williams had nervously explained to the rapt audience of chromatically clad nobles and ladies, "saltpeter from dry old vents, and charcoal from the townspeople burning cut wood and even furniture."

"But not any of the beds!" a voice had bellowed from downtable. Williams's voice was drowned in raucous laughter and he'd slipped away quietly.

Only to reappear behind Ethan and whisper, "Later perhaps . . . something rem . . . show you th . . . big . . . okay? . . . "

Ethan had mumbled a clever reply, something along the lines of "Yeah, sure," and ignored the schoolmaster. Williams and Eer-Meesach had then left the room. Maybe to resume the trannish wizard's lessons in galactic astronomy or to do new work on the big telescope Williams had promised to help him design.

They turned down a hall that in the past weeks had become as familiar to Ethan as his home apartment on Moth. They passed his room, then September's, then the du Kanes', and continued on down a slight ramp, around a corner . . .

A little knot of soldiers was clustered just ahead. The passage here was brightly lit. A heavy door to an apartment Ethan had never entered stood wide open.

The group parted when one of its members spotted Hunnar and the two humans. Parting revealed a single soldier crumpled on the floor. He lay on an uneven frame of dark scarlet. It centered at a spot on his back and the small but fatal stiletto imbedded therein.

"We've looked all over the castle for him," Hunnar explained awkwardly. "We've no idea of where he has gone to, nor how, or why. He may have slipped out some time during the fighting and caught an arrow, tumbled over the cliffs. Tis little point in searching fully til morning."

"You think Walther killed this one, then?" asked Ethan.

"I did not say that . . . but we would like to find him," Hunnar added unnecessarily.

"Did any of the nomads penetrate this far into the castle?" September queried.

"We do not believe so. But there were those of the vermin who tried to gain the interior. One or two might have been bold and daring enough to crawl along the stone to the side and thence slip through a window."

"I wonder if Walther could handle a small raft by himself?" mused Ethan aloud.

"Think he might have made off in the confusion and hopes to make Brass Monkey ahead of us, eh, young feller-me-lad? Beat us to his friends and maybe salvage their whole original plan . . . must have tempted him," the big man said thoughtfully. "I know I wouldn't try it. A few thousand kilometers of virgin ice to cross, scrapping with Droom and gutorrbyn and windstorm and pirates and who knows what else all the way. Crazy little punk might have tried it, though. If so, I expect he's saved us some trouble. He knew the best he could expect if we got back was at least partial mindwipe. Man'll do superhuman things for intangibles like memories."

"I don't see how he could have escaped the nomads," commented Ethan, shaking his head.

"Nor do I," agreed Hunnar. "However, that knife," and he gestured at the protruding hilt, "is no barbarian device. Twas made in our own foundry."

"What should we do, Skua?" asked Ethan.

"Do? Well, me, I'm going back to that hall and slobber reedle until I float . . . physically or otherwise." He turned on a heel and called back over his shoulder. "And I heartily suggest, young feller-me-lad, you come ahead and do likewise!"

Ethan glanced down again at the stone-still body. A gust of icy atmosphere sucked at his body heat and he shivered. Torchlight rippled like chiffon dolls' skirts.

Then he shrugged, said a bad word, and turned to follow September.

Ethan crossed his arms and flailed opposite shoulders. It didn't make him any warmer. As a method of raising his body temperature it proved effectively nil. But it did better psychologically. Excellent! He would freeze to death nice and sane. This self-flagellation is making you warmer, he repeated unconvincingly, it's making you warmer.

His skin fought the supposition tooth and nail.

It was a fairly cool day—minus ten or so outside. While it was perhaps thirty degrees warmer in the castle, it was still a long way from tropic. Modified to fit his human frame, his new hessavar-fur coat gave him considerable protection. They'd even managed to persuade the royal tailor to sew on real sleeves and leggings. At least now they could worry a little less about the dangers of frostbite.

Frost-nibble, however, was driving him crazy.

And he'd been wearing the coat for weeks now. Every so often an uncomfortable feeling crawled up his back as if the long-dead fur was beginning to take root to his chafed, abused body.

If it weren't for their occasional jaunts to the foundry for a really hot bath, the encrusted dirt and sweat could have doubled as a heat-sealing coating in itself. They hadn't fallen that far—yet.

It had been nearly two weeks, for certain, since the epic defeat of Sagyanak and the memorable battle in which the Sofoldians had shattered the power of the great Horde forever. In other words, the local population was just about sobered up.

Now he was making his way up to the vile-smelling rooms that Eer-Meesach called home. He passed an open balcony and spared a glance for the scene below.

Once again rafts were moving across the ice of the great harbor. Most of the frozen blood from the thousands of corpses had been chipped and melted away, the rough spots on the surface smoothed over. Hundreds of Wannomian stonemasons, carpenters, and other craftsmen were at work repairing the extensive damage to the harbor wall. Even the huge gap where the monstrous ram had broken through was beginning to be filled as loose stone was gathered off the ice and fresh rock brought from quarries in the mountains.

He turned from the balcony down a short hall, began to ascend a spiral ramp. He vaguely recalled that at the start of the victory celebration Williams had mumbled something about another surprise. Well, it couldn't be more of a shock than the introduction of gunpowder had been to their hosts. Heaven help the social system of this feudal ice-world if the little schoolmaster's subsequent revelations were half as overpowering!

The multitude of traveling rafts in the harbor would take the news of the Sofoldians' unprecedented defeat of one of the great nomadic Hordes back to their own towns and distant cities. They would also carry samples of gunpowder and formula for same so they could resist the bands which plagued their home provinces.

The elimination of those utterly ruthless, bloodthirsty groups would probably be a good thing for the body politic, not to mention individual political bodies. At least, it would until Tran-ky-ky ran out of barbarians. Then the various barons, landgraves, and dukes would be stuck with their new toys and no one to look at except each other.

Unless, of course, the barbarians managed to get hold of some gunpowder for themselves, in which case . . .

He gave it up. It was too complicated. Nor was he especially inclined toward sociological speculation. All he wanted to speculate on was getting over to Brass Monkey in one piece. Then, hopefully, to pick up his sample cases, dispose of a few thousand credits worth, and acquire a few decent orders. Smiling, he'd be off for the next world, definitely one with a generous sun and nothing more disturbing meteorologically than an occasional sensuous zephyr. Not a continual hurricane screaming eternally eastward.

He gained the top of the spiral, walked a few paces down the hall, and entered the wizard's apartments. He considered this time that there were no guards at the door. It hadn't impressed him until after the attempt on the Landgrave's life. All the nobles had guards also. Not Eer-Meesach. The inhabitants of Sofold were a thinking, practical people, but still sufficiently superstitious to hold a healthy respect for demons, elves, and wizards like Eer-Meesach. It would take a gutsy cutpurse indeed who would try for a few pieces of gold or some such when the wizard had threatened to turn any thief he caught into a swart worm.

The wizard was one of a little group gathered around a stumpy, weatherbeaten table. And on this world, "weatherbeaten" identified something shaky or ancient indeed. The antiquing on this archaic desk hadn't been put there by the local equivalent of terran or thranx professionals. Such contrivances are only practiced by advanced races.

Present along with the wizard were Williams and September. Monumental hooked nose, jutting chin, gold earring— the big man took up half the available space in his billowing hessavar fur. He looked up when Ethan entered.

"Hello, young feller-me-lad." He was radiating obvious enthusiasm over something. "Come have a peek at what our two intellectuals have been up to, what?"

Ethan rubbed his gloved hands together—that seemed to help a little—and edged in between September and the schoolmaster.

A sheet of vellum was tacked to the smooth tabletop. The drawing on it was not too complex, but it was sufficiently alien in nature for Ethan to have to scan it twice before he could guess what it might be.

"Looks like a raft," he said finally. "Of sorts."

"Of sorts indeed, cub," commented Eer-Meesach excitedly. "Twas your friend Williams who conceived the basic idea that lies gloriously before us. I merely executed it."

"I'm afraid I'm not much of an artist," Williams apologized.

Ethan had another look at the sketch. "It certainly *looks* different."

"My principal area of study was early Terran history," Williams confessed, squirming embarrassedly. "That's how I happened to know that old formula for gunpowder." He pointed at the drawing. "I've been thinking about this ever since we were picked up by Sir Hunnar and his men. As you know, three-quarters of Terra is covered with water."

"I've seen pictures," said Ethan, nodding.

"Well," the schoolteacher continued, "this particular kind of ship was developed and raised to almost poetic heights by a young Terran named Donald McKay, who lived and worked on the east coast of the North American continent. They were called clipper ships."

"Funny name," said Ethan. "Why?"

"I don't know." Williams shrugged. "The derivation has been lost. As you can see, I've modified the original design so that instead of having a curved bottom, as in an ocean-going boat, we will have a raft with a flat base. It will run on five runners—two fore, two aft, and one slightly further aft for steering purposes."

"It may not be quite as maneuverable as some of the local craft," put in September, "but it's going to be a damn sight faster than any kind of surface transportation this icebox world's ever seen before."

"Not an unreasonable expectation," agreed Williams cautiously. "It will require a considerable amount of wood compared to local rafts. Several large trees will have to be banded together to make the masts, and a great deal of sailcloth is needed."

"I'm no engineer," said Ethan bluntly, "but it just looks to me as if in a good blow, with all that sail, she'd turn over."

"The base will be carefully counterbalanced with just such a possibility in mind," the teacher replied. "But I think the double runners will give it a good deal of stability."

"And who's going to pay for it?" Ethan was on familiar ground now.

September grinned. "Despite all those glory holy-hosannas the Landgrave ladled on us, lad, he hemmed and hawed like a penniless beggar when we put an estimate to him. Went on and on about how repairs to the fortifications in the harbor and reparations to debilitated families were leaving the treasury empty as the inside of his promises. You'd have thought we were going to take his gold-inlaid shirt, too.

"Hunnar and Balavere were there. They listened quietly to the whole thing, real dignified and proper. When his majesty was finished they gave him a tongue-lashing that must have flayed his ancestors forty generations back! Then I pointed out to him that the moment we were delivered safe, healthy, and relatively unfrozen to Arsudun Island, the ship would become property of the Sofoldian navy. He'd managed to neglect that little item in his tale of woe.

"The raft's captain-to-be, Ta-hoding . . . you remember him?" Ethan nodded. "Ta-hoding enumerated the tremendous commercial advantages such a vessel would have over all competitors, especially with the forever sharp duralloy runners, and—"

"Wait a minute," Ethan interrupted. "I thought they couldn't work the metal."

"They couldn't," replied the big man with a trace of pride. "All last week I've been puttering around with Vlad-Vollingstad, the foundry boss. Ripped out the whole board on the lifeboat, emergency repair supplies, controls—everything. An electrodyne forge isn't too complicated. With the unlimited heat supply they have, I think I can get one going. I'm afraid they won't be turning out any suspension housing, but they'll be able to cut and bend until the lifeboat's completely reworked. We need a lot less than that for a few big runners. Might even be able to get away with just slicing off a few sections of hull and sharpening them.

"The biggest problem is one for pure sweat. Since we can't bring the heat to the metal, we'll have to bring the metal to the heat. That means hauling the whole wreck up into the mountains to the foundry. Surprisingly, the Landgrave didn't object to the cost of that one, even though it may take every vol on the island. I don't think he wants all that nice indestructable metal sitting in the harbor where a few imaginative visiting captains could tow it away."

"They wouldn't get very far," said Ethan. "Not pulling that mass across the ice."

"Probably not," the big man conceded, "but try and convince the Landgrave of that. So as soon as we can round up the men and animals, that gets first priority after starting the forge."

Ethan ran a finger over part of the drawing. "You *really* think this thing will stay upright in a high wind?"

"Not until we try it out in one, we won't be." Williams nodded agreement.

"The base weight should keep it steady," said the schoolmaster. "Also, note the airfoils front and rear. Something McKay did not have to worry about. With so much sail area on a raft that size, I'm more worried about the possibility of her becoming airborne than tipping over. These"—and he tapped the two foils on the sketch—"should eliminate any chance of that."

Ethan stared at the hybrid of nineteenth-century terran and modern tran technology and shook his head admiringly. "Congratulations, Milliken. It's quite a project." He extended a hand and the schoolmaster shook it shyly. "I only hope the damn thing works."

"What an enterprise!" Eer-Meesach began. "Nothing like it has ere been seen in Sofold or her neighbors. We shall call it *'Slanderscree'* after the dark flight of dawn-birds which precede the souls of the departed!"

"Encouraging appellation," commented Ethan drily.

The wizard didn't understand him. "Bards will sing of its sailing for a hundred times a hundred years. We will be all in song and verse immortalized, sirs. The greatness of our quest shall . . . " September gave Ethan a gentle nudge.

"I think you've heard everything you have to, lad."

"I think so, too, Skua."

They excused themselves. Malmeevyn was so engrossed in enumerating the magnificence of his anticipated immortality that he barely noticed them depart.

Out in the cool quiet of the hallway, Ethan couldn't resist a last question.

"Assuming this monstrosity actually gets built, Skua—"

"It will, lad."

"Yes, well, I'll believe it when the first sail fills. And when it isn't torn to splinters in the first honest breeze. Assuming that—can we make it? Can we get to the settlement? And how long will it take?"

"I've got confidence in the boat, lad. Williams may be a bit of a secret romantic, deep down, but the design is sound. We've got compasses. Now that we know we've got a landmark close by the island, this volcano . . . what do they call it?"

"The Place-Where-The-Earth's-Blood-Burns," reminded Ethan helpfully.

"Yeah . . . from there it should be easy enough to find the town. Let's see . . . given the speed that thing should be able to make, allowing time for the locals to get used to the different rigging, plus the fact that we'll be moving against the wind at times . . . I'd guess we should be able to do it inside of a couple of months. Depending on the weather, of course."

"What do you think of our captain? He didn't awe me the first time we traveled with him."

September grinned. "Ta-hoding? Looks and sounds like a fat whiner, doesn't he? Probably because he *is* a fat whiner. But he also impressed me as a being who knows his seamanship . . . icemanship, rather. I'd prefer to have him at the helm and wide awake as opposed to some smooth-talking arrogant braggart who can't tell a snow squall from a dust cloud. Give me a captain who's concerned first for his own precious skin above a gallant idiot any time.

"I'm going to be tied up with that forge and shaping the raft runners. Williams will be busy with Eer-Meesach grinding out crude blueprints and plans. But someone has to oversee the actual construction. By the Black Hole in Cygnus, you know who volunteered when he found out about it?"

"Do tell," said Ethan.

"Old du Kane, that's who! Actually asked if he could. Said something to the effect that he wasn't especially adept at decapitating belligerent obstructionists or getting drunk in comradely fashion with the local soldiery, but that he could manage large groups of people and materials. He's learned enough of the local lingo to get by, so I told him to go ahead."

Ethan didn't share the big man's confidence in the financier. "You think he'll handle things properly? He's not the most diplomatic type in the Arm."

"Don't confuse performance with personality," admonished September, scratching at a fur-hidden ear. "I'm not fanatically in love with the old pirate myself, nor any of his ilk. But we're not in the position of choosing from an unlimited workforce. Besides, I can guess how much credit every day he spends out of contact with his empire is costing him. He'll get that raft built as fast as possible, all right."

"I suppose so," Ethan conceded uncertainly. "I can't keep from wondering what happened to Walther."

September grunted at the mention of the vanished kidnapper.

"Probably a frozen smear on the ice by now, what? Or resting comfortably in the belly of a Droom or some other charming member of the local fauna."

"I suppose so."

Ethan broke away to make for his own room and a roaring fire.

XI

The building of the *Slanderscree* proceeded as rapidly as anyone dared hope, despite Landgrave Torsk Kurdagh-Vlata's royal howls of agony over the unending list of expenses. His moaning ran the unceasing wind a good vocal second.

September singed an arm when the first jumpspark was fired from the makeshift forge. After an hour's steady work and cursing, however, the recalcitrant hunk of machinery worked perfectly. Overawed, no doubt, at recognizing an elemental force greater than itself.

With the big man sweating at the foundry, Williams and Eer-Meesach running from mountain to harbor to village with drawings and corrections in the dozens, and du Kane supervising the actual construction, Ethan was left with the thankless job of handling the thousands of minute, attendant details.

He couldn't believe that building a primitive, crude raft could involve so many little decisions and questions, all made and answered on the spot. Surely an interstellar freighter could be no more complicated.

Brown-green sailcloth was matched to design specifications. Meters of pika-pina cable were measured and trimmed. New crates of fresh-forged bolts and fittings had to be shepherded down to the ice-dock.

Put together with equal parts sweat and invective, the *Slanderscree* began to take shape.

Something else was taking shape, too, and Ethan liked it a lot less than the a-building raft. This was Elfa's continuing attempt to become something other than a casual acquaintance.

One day, despite the offense it might cause the Landgrave and the damage it could do to their cause, he erupted at her.

To his surprise, she took it rather calmly—almost as though she'd been waiting for it. After that she didn't bother him again. He was puzzled but decided not to press for the facts. He was ahead on points. Better leave it that way.

Despite delays and the inevitable confusion arising from problems in translation, despite a temporary failure of the electrodyne forge, despite endless hours of frustrating explanation from Williams on how the complex rigging was to be installed, there came a day and hour when the *Slanderscree* was finished, stocked, and ready to depart—though Ethan had a hard time convincing himself that it would ever move.

It sat there at the end of the Landgrave's dock, dwarfing the commercial rafts that skimmed its flanks like waterbugs. Nearly two hundred meters long, with three towering masts, bowsprit, and dozens of tightly furled sails, it radiated enormous power held in check. The tran arrowhead design had been slimmed down to needle-like porportions. Only the two big airfoils marred the raft's rakish lines.

There was nothing unusual about the morning set for their departure. A typical trannish day—sunny, windy, freezing to the core. Last-minute supplies and spare parts were being taken on. A considerable crowd had taken time from the unending drudgery of making a living to see them off—or preside at an entertaining crack-up. They lined the shore and spilled out onto the ice. Cubs ignored mothers and darted in and out around the great duralloy runners.

Sir Hunnar came on board as nominal commander of their military compliment. But General Balavere was making the journey, too. When he was a cub he'd experienced a rain of ash and hot stone from the Place-Where-The-Earth's-Blood-Burns. It had darkened the sky over Wannome for four days. Surely it was a holy place—and the general had reached an age when such things took on increasing importance. He was going to see that legendary mountain.

Old Eer-Meesach, of course, couldn't have been kept away by a herd of famished krokim.

The raft had nothing like the carefully arranged chain of responsibility that existed on board a spatial liner. Nor did Williams' arcane knowledge yield any counterpart for the ancient terran clippers, beyond the rank of captain. So Hunnar's squires, Suaxus and Budjir, came along as his seconds. Ta-hoding retained much of his own raft crew and worked through them.

Another side of Hunnar was reflected in his choice of squires. Neither was a type Ethan would choose: Suaxus always dour and suspicious, Budjir laconic to the point of apparent idiocy. However, both were almost severely competent.

The crew and passengers trooped on board to the accompaniment of tremendous cheers and shouts of encouragement, a few good-naturedly obscene, from the assembled townsfolk. Some had come from as far away as Ritsfasen at the far western tip of Sofold Isle for the departure.

The Landgrave stood at the dock surrounded by his important nobles and knights. When all were on the raft and the boarding plank had been pulled back, he raised his staff. A respectful silence settled on the crowd.

"You have come from a strange place and you go to a strange place," he intoned solemnly. "In the short time between you have done deeds that will be remembered forever by the people of Sofold and myself. You have also said that the universe is a vast place, vaster than we could ever imagine, with thousands of being as different from us as we are different from you living in it.

"Should these worlds and beings extend to infinity and you were to go among each and every one, you will always find a home and fire for you and your children's children here, in Wannome.

"Go now, and go with the wind."

"WITH THE WIND," echoed the crowd somberly. Then someone made a rude noise and they broke into wild yelling and cheering.

"A predictable sentiment," commented Hellespont du Kane flatly.

"Yes? They might be cheering for us, or because their exalted ruler kept his speech admirably short," September theorized, turning away. But had that been a hint of moisture at the corner of the big man's eyes? Or was it only distortion from the scratched and battered snow goggles.

"All right, Ta-hoding!" he bellowed aft. "Let's see if this firetrap will make it out of the harbor!"

The strange new commands were issued in modified Trannish sailing terminology, relayed across the deck and up into the rigging to the sailors stationed aloft.

Just watching the huge natives scramble up the rigging into the shrouds in the continual gale gave Ethan the jitters. And it would be much worse once they left the sheltering bulk of the island. But those powerful muscles and clawed hands and feet held them steady as, one by one, the rust-green sails began to drop and dig wind.

Slowly, smoothly, the *Slanderscree* began to slide away from the dock, while the shouts from on shore grew louder and louder. Eyes on the sailors above, September walked over and gave Ethan a sly pat on the back.

"By-the-by, young feller-me-lad, did you ever manage to get that business of the Landgrave's offspring straightened out?"

"It was never out of line," Ethan riposted. "I thought I did, but she wasn't exactly in the forefront of the crowd, waving tearfully as we departed. Perhaps not."

"I didn't see her either. Though I notice you've warmed up to du Kane's daughter." The lady in question had vanished belowdecks the moment she'd come on board in order to get out of the wind. Raft or boat or castle, that was next to impossible on this world.

"Glassfeathers," Ethan countered, leaning over the rail to watch the ice slide past. "She's human, too. She just had to have someone to talk to, finally. I don't wonder that she doesn't chat much with her father. Certainly you and Williams aren't exactly the most charming conversationalists around."

"Sorry, young feller, but when I see her it's without that fur and survival suit, figuratively speaking. That kind of crimps my inclination to easy banter." He patted Ethan again in fatherly fashion and sauntered off forward, whistling.

The *Slanderscree* was moving out of the lee of the mountains. She picked up speed rapidly as the quickly maturing crew put on more and more sail. Even the moonraker was

out by the time they reached the main gate—completely
repaired once again. By then they were moving at a respectable 30 kph. But they'd be lucky to hold that, moving to
the westward. Moving east, with the wind, however, the
Slanderscree's speed was limited only by the strength of her
sails and masts and her ability to keep from becoming airborne.

The last cheers they heard came from the guards at the
gate and the operators of the Great Chain as they shot between the towers. Once free of the harbor's confining walls,
Ta-hoding, praying all the while, swung her in a wide curve
designed to bring her back to the southwest and on course.

Ethan held his breath as the raft came around. No one
could predict how the radical new mast-and-sail configuration
would respond on a craft and world far different from long-
dead Donald McKay's wildest imaginings.

The sails cracked like Williams' crude gunpowder, the
masts creaked, but the raft came about neatly. Everything
held together as they slammed across the wind. They'd follow a zig-zag course, plodding for thousands of kilometers.
Even so, the *Slanderscree* would make good time whenever
she turned southward, building up to a nice 60 kph or so
before she'd have to turn west into the wind.

He turned and scanned the deck in search of September
but failed to locate him. The big man had probably gone
below to get out of the wind himself for a while. Ethan saw
no reason why he shouldn't do likewise.

He'd reached the hatch when the sounds of yelling and
hooting reached him. It was several seconds before he thought
to look skyward.

There, perched outside of the wicker observation cage at
the top of the mainmast, was Skua September, gripping the
top of the windswept pole with his legs, waving his arms
and braying like a hairy jackass.

Ethan remained rooted to the deck until the big man
finally tired and climbed down. He held his breath all the
way, expecting at any minute to see the big man slip or lose
his grip and be torn away by the clawing hurricane like the
last leaf of autumn.

But he reached the deck easily enough. He walked over to Ethan, tiny particles of ice coating his snow goggles. A gloved hand brushed absently at them. He was panting heavily.

"Quite a view, lad, quite a view! A blood-racing experience, what? How about giving it a go?"

"As you should know by now, I'm not the reckless explorer type, Skua."

"All right, lad, all right," the other sighed. "You're the feckless metropolitan type. Shame. It's an exalting experience."

"I don't doubt it, but I'm quite cold enough right here without having to add fatal exposure and bodily danger to it. I prefer the deck. I'll prefer my cabin even more." He turned and opened the sliding hatch door.

To find a familiar and totally unexpected figure blocking his way.

"Good morrow, Sir Ethan," said Elfa Kurdagh-Vlata coquettishly. "It *is* less cold belowdecks."

"Elfa," he said haltingly, "I don't find this a bit funny. How did you talk your father into letting you on board ship?"

She walked out of the hatch, stood on deck. "I didn't ask him. I hid on board til I thought it was too late for you to turn. It is too late for you to turn, isn't it?"

"You didn't ask him? How the hell did you sneak on?"

"I hid in an empty crate and the sailors brought me on with the other stores. Only it wasn't empty." She smiled prettily. "It was full of me."

Hunnar had joined them as soon as he'd recognized Elfa. If anything, he was more stunned than Ethan.

"Elfa!"

"Really, the powers of observation of this expedition's leaders amaze me. You are the second person, Sir Hunnar, to identify me right away."

"What," continued Ethan doggedly, ignoring the sarcasm, "is the Landgrave going to say when he finds out you're missing?"

She looked thoughtful. "I expect he'll be furious. He'll rave and curse and threaten and break things and turn Wannome upside down. Eventually he'll find my note—"

"Note?"

"—and know I've gone with you. Then he'll *really* get mad."

Ethan turned to September. "What are we going to do with her, Skua?"

"Well, we could turn back," he considered, admiring the fur-clad Elfa openly. "With the wind behind us it wouldn't take that long. But I hate like hell to give up the time and distance we've already made just to return this hot adolescent to her daddy, what? And there'd be all sorts of awkward recriminations and explanations and such . . . more time gone. No, tell the steward there'll be another for supper and let's keep on our merry way, hey? We can always find a place for her . . . eh, Hunnar?"

"What?" replied the startled knight. He looked at the big man unsurely.

They were a thousand kilometers out of Wannome. Even as they breathed, another few meters of ice slid beneath the duralloy runners and vanished astern. Now they were gliding over strange ice that none of Hunnar's men or Ta-hoding's sailors had ever traversed before.

They'd passed few islands during the last hundred kilometers, none of them inhabited. The sense of desolation touched everyone.

"An empty land," Hunnar commented quietly, subdued.

"Yes," agreed Ta-hoding. "'Tis plain to see there'll be no trading here. Yet, some of the land we passed looked hospitable."

"The volcano might have something to do with it," said September. "I shouldn't wonder that at this distance these islands might receive periodic rains of hot ash and pumice."

"Even so," mused Ethan idly, "the possibility of establishing a few trading centers with an eye towards expanding intersurface commerce might—" He paused at a cry from the mainmast that froze both tran as thoroughly as a hundred below.

"Gutorrbyn! Nor'east!" Hunnar, Ta-hoding, and dozens of sailors and soldiers rushed for the rail.

"What's happening?" yelled Colette from a hatchway. Hunnar beat Ethan to the answer.

"Get thee below, lady du Kane!" It was uttered as an order, not a suggestion. Colette bristled.

"Now, wait a minute—" she began hotly.

September's tone was menacing and devoid of humor. "Do just as he says, Miss du Kane."

She hesitated, looked at him uncertainly. Still muttering, she disappeared belowdecks.

"I see 'em," the big man mumbled, shielding his eyes with a hand.

"So do I," concurred Ethan.

Far off to the northeast, a small cloud of tiny brown specks had come into view. The cloud of gnats grew to fly-size, changed into a mass of dark T-shapes.

"Can we outrun them?" asked September. Hunnar's reply was terse.

"No, my friend. Perhaps with the wind behind us . . . but they would still have the angle. Tis certain they've seen us. We may have to fight, though there is always the chance they will not be interested in us."

There was a querulous bellow from across deck. Ethan recognized the voice of General Balavere.

"Dragons, sir!" Hunnar called back.

"How close?" barked the general, buckling on his sword.

"Five, maybe six kijat, and closing on us."

Balavere cursed, strode to the forehatch, and absently yelled into it. Almost immediately, soldiers came gushing out of the hole as though it was a disturbed anthill. Meanwhile, the general hurried to join them astern.

"We'll never keep them out with this rigging," observed Hunnar, staring worriedly aloft. "We'll put the archers in the center in a group, and spearmen along the rails."

Ethan watched the flock grow larger. "How smart are these things?"

"Less so than a k'nith," Hunnar replied. "They hunt by vision, sound, and smell, not their brains."

"Here's a thought," began September. "We might try this . . . "

No one moved on board the *Slanderscree*. Everyone tried to dig himself into the rail or one of the makeshift barrel-and-crate barricades. Not even the bravest of the ship's pilots could be persuaded to stand at the wheel while the dragons attacked and neither Hunnar nor Balavere would force anyone. So steering was being handled from belowdecks with a crude tug-and-pull system of ropes.

The flock came on, gaining steadily on the big ship.

"Must be close to a hundred of 'em," whispered September conversationally. "Ugly looking devils, aren't they, young feller?"

There was the twang of a bow and Balavere's voice reached them from up near the bow.

"Hold your fire, there! Make those arrows count, idiot!"

The gutorrbyn did not attack. The leader veered off at the last moment and began to circle the raft. The *Slanderscree* continued to plow wind, her decks devoid of motion, while a halo of squealing, squawking monstrosities danced round her masts.

Broad and bat-like, the leathery wings were attached to furry, streamlined bodies which ended in long, forked tails. There were claws halfway up each wing and great taloned feet coiled like springs under soft bellies. Each head was a nightmare cross between crocodile and wolf, with a long, wrinkled snout stuffed with double rows of razor-sharp triangular teeth. Huge tarsier-like eyes glared down with blank, mindless malevolence.

"Watch the leaders," warned Balavere. "If they come it'll be in a curve."

There was no point in holding your breath. Might freeze if you didn't keep it moving. The ship moved on, quiet, with the rustle of a hundred pairs of wings drumming against the wind and the creak of spars and sail.

A hatch opened. Colette du Kane walked halfway out.

"When is something going to hap—?" She happened to look skyward, saw the mass of circling demons. One hysterical scream.

"Trinska!" cursed Hunnar. "They *might* have lost interest!"

Colette screamed again.

September suddenly shouted, "Ware zenith!" in Terranglo, hurriedly translated it into Trannish as a single line of gutorrbyn folded their wings, dipped to their right, and dove for the isolated frozen figure on deck.

"Loose, loose!" screamed Hunnar at the archers. Bows began to sputter.

Nearly as big as a man and twice as powerful, one of the monsters crumpled to the deck not a meter from Ethan. He thought he heard the neck snap when the creature hit the planking. It had three arrows imbedded in its chest.

Colette had apparently recovered her senses. Ethan heard the hatch cover slam shut. He didn't see it because teeth flashed suddenly in front of his face and there was a clack like a beartrap. He slashed half-blindly with his sword, felt it bite something soft. There was a hoarse giant-rat scream and a sticky substance covered his bare wrist. A foul, fetid odor assailed his nostrils. Then it was gone and his sword was free.

It was hard to tell the screams of tran from dragon. He swam through an alien nightmare of blood and teeth. He saw one dragon skimming low over the ice, the limp corpse of a sailor firmly caught in its talons. Once the toothed maw dipped low, slashed almost indifferently at the lolling head.

Dead gutorrbyn bodies matted the clean wood. Small bunches of spearmen kept the attackers away while protected archers took a terrible toll among them.

A wounded dragon flashed by, screaming, and smashed into the ice below. It was feathered with arrows. Ethan spun, cut at a spinning, snapping horror that dove at his back. He ducked, and another pair of claws missed his head by centimeters, their owner shrieking in frustration. It backed air, started to pull up for a turn over the deck.

Something slammed it violently sideways and it crashed into a mast. Ethan now could see that a fair proportion of the mounting pile of dragon-corpses on deck were studded with short, thick darts. He spared a glance upward.

Wicker cages were bound at the top of each towering mast to protect lookouts from the wind. Now they served a pair of crossbowmen in each. They'd kept still until the fight was joined. Now they were beginning to make their presence felt, picking off the gutorrbyn below and those crawling in the rigging. In the confusion, none of the dragons looked to find where the stubby, deadly bolts were coming from. They dropped in pairs and threes, now.

Ethan thrust his sword forward again, but by now there was little to strike at. Screeching defiance, the remnant of the fatally mauled flock abruptly lifted with the wind and shot away to the westward.

Panting heavily, he walked over to where Hunnar was trying to bind up the arm of a badly gashed spearman.

"Well, we beat them off, Sir. How are our casualties?"

"There might be more, but we seem to have lost only one man and have few enough wounded. Again the wizard's magic has served well."

"That, and perhaps another," said Ta-hoding. Their captain had spent the battle huddled alongside Hunnar, jabbing occasionally with his sword while expending most of his energy in imprecating his ancestors for getting him into this trouble. As a result, only his ego was scratched.

Now he was standing at the rail, staring at the northern horizon. "Tis long til night, yet darkness comes. Have you noticed, sirs?" Ethan hadn't. Frankly, he couldn't see much difference in the light even now.

But Hunnar apparently saw, as had Ta-hoding. "You are right, captain."

September came over. "What's all this about, now? Another attack? Good thing those beasties aren't very bright. They could have picked us off neatly with a little thought."

"I don't know, Skua," Ethan confessed. "Ta-hoding and Hunnar seem concerned about something in the light."

"Not the light, noble sirs," said Ta-hoding. "Look there, to the west a little more." The two humans did so. "There, the Rifs!"

Now Ethan saw. A great dark cloud was just barely beginning to crawl over the stark horizon. Its front sparkled and flashed like the visible pulse of some huge animal. And the sky did seem to dim slightly.

"It comes early," intoned Hunnar. "I wondered at seeing gutorrbyn come out of the north. Usually they move with the wind or into it. Clearly our flock was driven south."

"Meaning we didn't beat them off, then?" asked September.

"No, Sir Skua. I suspect they fought as long as they did only out of strong hunger. They've probably been running before *that* for some time. Now they are forced to try and cross to the west before the Rifs reaches them."

Above, sails snapped and buffeted the masts, flailed uncertainly against spars in the unfamiliar cross-winds.

"We'll have to turn further south and run before it as much as we can," said Hunnar. "If we can stay well enough west it might even be a help . . . if everything holds together."

"Good sir," began Ta-hoding nervously, "I would recommend instead—"

"And we'll reef in as much sail as you deem wise, good captain . . ."

Ta-hoding relaxed slightly.

". . . less ten percent additional which I will order on, for I suspect you may value your hide above the swiftest completion of our journey."

"You do me a terrible disrespect, noble sir, for in truth I would gladly sacrifice my poor self to insure that the honored and glorious friends of—"

"Enough, enough!" said Hunnar disgustedly, but without malice. "See to your sails and not platitudes, captain, and quickly!"

Ethan looked back at the cloud. It had doubled in size and was rapidly dominating the entire horizon, swallowing light and blue sky at a furious rate. He started forward.

"Going below, young feller-me-lad?"

"No!" Ethan was shocked at the vehemence of his response. But the big man's words had been just a mite patronizing. Maybe he wasn't ready for dancing atop the mainmast, but by Rothschild, he could damn well stay topside and take a little storm!

Hellespont du Kane surveyed the deck, left the hatchway, and strolled over. Ethan didn't much feel like talking to the financier, but courtesy was part of his character. Besides, he might have a chance to make use of his famous acquaintance one day—if he ever thawed out.

Du Kane nudged one of the dragon-corpses that hadn't yet been reached by the clean-up crew. Probably estimating its potential price per kilo on the interstellar marketplace, thought Ethan drily.

"Is it over, then, Mr. Fortune?"

"That much of it is," Ethan replied, trying hard not to be brusque. "However, it appears that we are in for a mild blow. I suggest you go below and tie down anything you don't want banged about."

"Only my daughter, and she can take care of herself." Was that line for real, or was du Kane playing straight? The perpetual poker face gave no clue. "The Rifs, then."

"You know about them?" said Ethan, a little surprised.

"Oh yes, I shall remain on deck to absorb the experience. If you've no objection?"

"I? Object?" He'd enjoy seeing this stuffed shirt scramble for safety when the first strong gust struck. "Be glad of your company."

Hellespont du Kane looked at him squarely. "There is no need to play irony, Mr. Fortune. I know what you think of me."

"Just a second, now, du Kane," said Ethan, turning from the rail. He'd been caught badly off-balance. "What makes you think—"

"Never mind, never mind." The financier waved a hand negligently. "It does not matter. Some of us, Mr. Fortune, are not born to the comradely, easygoing, instant-intimate manner. I have friends, but they are relationships based on mutual respect and, in some cases, mutual fear. I should like to be more . . . more . . . "

"Human?" supplied Ethan, and instantly regretted it. Du Kane looked his age, then. The glance he gave Ethan was almost—almost but not quite—pitiable.

"I would not venture to express it quite so strongly, Mr. Fortune, but we cannot help the way we are, can we?"

"I don't know, Hellespont." He clutched a strand of the rigging to steady himself in the rising wind. Sailors were beginning to string safety lines across the deck. "Is that a question or a declaration?"

Ethan stood at the stern. Ta-hoding manned one side of the huge wheel and his helmsman the other. "It will take two of us to manage her—for the first hour, at least," he'd explained. All but a few of the top sails had been taken in. The raft skimmed smoothly toward the northwest. Ta-hoding was trying to make as much distance that way before the front struck and forced him to swing south with the wind.

By now the stygian nimbus blotted out most of the northern sky. Lightning crackled like a mad composer's composition on three sides of the ship.

"Soon," moaned Ta-hoding. "Soon. I can smell it coming."

"Hold fast, friends," warned Hunnar. "The first moments are the worst. Tis a live thing." He moved off forward to double-check the safety lines.

"According to the captain," said September, having to shout to make himself heard over the wind, "it's kind of like an atmospheric tidal bore. You know what a tidal bore is?"

No one did. Before the big man had a chance to explain, the Rifs struck.

Ethan was prepared for anything, and that's exactly what happened. He was knocked free of the rail and blown several meters across the deck before he rolled up against the feet of a sailor. The tran iceman was hugging one of the safety lines like a mistress. Somehow he maintained his hold, reached down a massive hairy paw, and grabbed Ethan by the scruff of his jacket. Ethan practically climbed his leg until he could get a grip of his own on the line.

The concussion from that first hammer-like gust had gifted him with a bruised cheek and a cut lip—worse than he'd suffered in the gutorrbyn assault. Slowly, carefully, he dragged his way back toward the rail.

Somehow, Ta-hoding and his helmsman were holding the ship on course. Hunnar had suggested lashing the wheel, and it had been a surprise when the captain refused.

"A rope has no brains, noble sir, and the Rifs is an angry great cub. You cannot trust it with a lashed wheel." But he'd agreed to have the two alien airfoils locked in position.

The *Slanderscree* suddenly tilted and Ethan made a dive for the rail. Up and over the wind heeled the flying raft, until she was hurtling along on her port runners alone. Then Ta-hoding slammed the wheel over; she turned south, and crunched back to the horizontal with a violent crash. But she continued to run easily and nothing appeared to have broken or buckled.

September pulled himself up to where Ethan clung. "Held her heading a little long, there. Got plenty of guts, our fat captain. You okay?"

Ethan carefully extended a gloved hand and moved another step closer. "One of these days I'm going to tell you I'm dying, just for the hell of it," he shouted back.

The wind flailed at them, intent on smashing the unyielding raft to kindling. Now that they were in the storm proper and moving with it, the raft ran easier. Fury pushed them but the initial insantiy was gone south.

"How fast do you reckon we're going, young feller?" Ethan didn't have the damndest idea, but a barely audible voice from behind him apparently did.

"I should estimate the initial front at well over 150 kph. Now I perceive we are riding a wind of slightly more than a hundred. Invigorating, is it not?"

Moving hand over hand on the safety lines, Hellespont du Kane pulled himself to where Ta-hoding and his helmsman fought with the wheel.

"Old man or not," began September, blatantly disregarding the fact that he was no swaddling babe himself, "I'm going to put a fist in that smug puss one of these days."

"I don't think it's smugness so much," replied Ethan, wondering that the aged industrialist was still on deck at all. "It's just that whether it's a million credits or the proper setting of silver at the table that's in question, du Kane is very matter-of-fact about things."

"Probably react to a fist in the snoot that way, too," the big man grunted.

Ethan blinked beneath his goggles. The ice was gray under the streaking storm clouds, which raced the ship like an endless herd of galloping hippos. Lightning threw geysers of ice-chips when it struck the ice.

Several times the iron rods at the tips of the three masts drew million-volt white scimitars, but without damage to the raft. If you ignored the pain in your arms from gripping the rail, or the way your goggles dug circles around your eyes, why then, Ethan admitted, it had a wild and wonderful kind of beauty.

In fact, it was magnificent.

"I'm going below for something warm. Coming, young feller?"

"I'll . . . I'll be along in a minute," Ethan murmured. Lightning jumped in a gargantuan triple arc from one tiny island to another. "You go on."

September grunted, then paused, swaying in the gale. "Did you ever hear of the Analava System?"

A part of Ethan's mind managed to drag itself away from the meteorological asylum. "Sure, vaguely. Weren't those the two planets in the Vandy sector that went to war despite intervention of a Commonwealth peace team and a Church edict . . . oh, some twenty years ago?"

"Twenty-two. I told you I was wanted. Well, you want to know what I'm wanted for? I think, young feller-me-lad, I may just tell you."

That drew Ethan's attention away from the howling weather. September faced him broadside, clinging to the railing with one hand and a safety line with another, fighting the wind.

"Hundred twenty million people died in that war. Lasted a whole week. There are one or two people who think I'm responsible for it. That's why they want me." Then he turned, put both hands on the safety line, and started to make his way to the nearest hatch.

Ethan was too shocked to try and keep him from going, too stunned to frame any questions. The Analava War was one of the great horrors of modern times, a blot on the history of the Commonwealth, a running sore on the record of mature homo sapiens, and a throwback to the Dark Ages. His personal recollections of it were of the faintest—he'd been only eight or nine at the time. Details he'd learned later, in maturation. But the shock and terror it had on the adults around him were memories he retained from childhood.

September was crazy, of course. No one man could possibly be held responsible for the deaths of 120 million human beings.

Lightning cut and ripped at the gray ice. He looked out and saw none of it.

A giant hand picked him up and threw him out of his bunk. He didn't think the joke was a bit funny and said so at length as he flailed angrily at his blankets in the dark room. Sleep evaporated from his curtained brain as he untangled himself and absorbed several facts at once.

First, while he was sure he was sitting up straight, he seemed to be leaning at an angle. He was sure the fault was with the universe and not him. As his eyes grew used to the darkness he was positive of it. He fumbled a bit, lit an oil lamp. Yes, the deck was canted to the left at an unnatural angle.

A respectable rumble of trannish curses drifted in to him from the main hold. Terranglo related semantic species came from September's cabin, next to his. Cries of uncertainty and anxious questioning were already beginning to supplant the first howls of outrage. He opened his door.

Someone had already lit the lamp in the hall and lights were beginning to go on down in the main hold. If there was a sailor or soldier who hadn't been dumped from his bunk, Ethan didn't see him.

Fighting with his jacket and survival suit every centimeter of the way, he walked to the end of the hall. Tran were struggling to their feet, trying to straighten bunks and sort bedding, repeating the same inane, unanswerable questions to each other over and over. A single moan of pain came from somewhere far forward, but otherwise everyone seemed more shaken mentally than physically. He walked back and rapped on the door of the cabin across from his own.

A concerned Sir Hunnar confronted him almost immediately. The bedraggled knight was trying to banish the sleep from his own eyes and buckle on his sword at the same time.

"We're stopped!" Ethan blurted.

Hunnar shook his great red mane. "Tis assured you can find the sum of some things, Sir Ethan. Most definitely, we are."

Ethan glanced past the massive torso and saw General Balavere struggling with his own garb. September joined him a moment later and the three started up the passageway.

They nearly collided with Ta-hoding. The expression on the plump captain's face was not reassuring.

Hellespont du Kane stuck his head out of the door of his cabin and shouted across to them, "What has happened, gentlemen?"

"We're going to find out, du Kane," Ethan yelled back at him. "Soon as we do, I'll let you know." The financier nodded and vanished back into his rooms.

Ta-hoding led them up the steps, grumbling over his shoulder. "It seems we may have run aground. That in itself is no insignificant worry, noble sirs, but I am more concerned about the damage. Tis almost a certainty one or more of our runners has collapsed. By the angle the raft lies at, I should guess one. I only hope tis the bolting to the hull and not the runner itself."

"That's duralloy we're riding on, captain," reminded September. "Reworked or not, it won't crumple. I think you're probably right about the bolts."

Ta-hoding shoved at the hatchdoor. As always, the two humans braced themselves for the expected blast of groping, heat-sucking air.

The Rifs had degenerated into a mere gale. By morning the storm would pass them completely. Carefully shielded from the wind, lanterns threw dancing tendrils of light onto the deck. Ta-hoding was met by the waiting night-duty helmsman. Then another sailor came over, breathing unevenly, to stammer out a long string of information.

Hunnar and September walked to the railing while the conference continued. Ethan listened briefly, then joined them.

"We're aground, all right," suggested September.

"Can we pull free?" Ethan asked.

Hunnar pondered the question. "This southeast wind will die by first light. Then we'll have the normal westwind in our faces. That should enable us to pull off with little trouble."

Ta-hoding rejoined them. "Well, noble sirs, it seems I was woefully wrong. We have not run aground. Not exactly, anyway."

"I don't follow you," said Ethan, squinting ahead into the darkness. "Certainly looks like an island up forward."

"It does," the captain agreed. "Again the world lies. Come."

They followed him toward the bow. As they approached the sharp prow of the ship, Ethan noticed something shining in the moonlight off to the right. A big, cream-colored pillar. It looked oddly familiar.

They had to step carefully to avoid the fallen rigging and shattered spars that had been knocked down. The upper half of the foremast had snapped in the middle and the huge log had crashed to the deck, bringing rigging and furled sail down with it. Only a stub of the bowsprit was visible, and the left railing near the bow was crumpled, though the hull seemed sound.

To their left, sailors with lanterns threw rope ladders over the side and started down to the ice.

The stavanzer was quite dead. Extending into the dark to port and starboard, the uneven crusted back loomed over the prow. By terran standards it was a colossus. Compared to the only other member of its species Ethan had seen, this one was small, even tiny.

Ta-hoding scrambled awkwardly over a broken topspar, reached the bow and leaned forward.

"A young one, very young indeed. I wonder how it happens to be here alone."

"Probably it was separated from its herd in the storm," Hunnar guessed. "And sought the shelter of an island." He stared at the wide, arching back, at the two flaccid air jets. "It must have been very weak and perhaps also asleep when we struck. I think it must have died instantly. See? We've hit just behind the head.'

Indeed, the sharp prow of the fast-moving raft had impacted just behind the huge closed eye. The long, tapered bowsprit had plunged mortally deep into the great animal, wreaking havoc with that endless nervous system.

"We're damn fortunate it's not an adult," September observed.

"Fortunate indeed," agreed Hunnar.

"Here, captain!" The cry came from their left, up from the ice. They followed Ta-hoding over.

Budjir had been on night-watch. Now he reached for the paws that dipped to help him back over the shattered rail.

"We struck the thunder-eater at an angle, sirs. The front port runner has broken completely loose from its mounting and now lies alone on the ice. The fore starboard runner is bent sharply, but the bolting held."

"Vunier!" muttered Hunnar. "Well, we have spare fastenings. The mast will be no trouble, but the other . . . " He sighed. "We will have to make the repairs. Another delay, my friends."

"Don't fret," said Ethan cheerily. "It won't make any difference."

At least the weather proved predictable. The receding storm held a little longer than the tran had expected, but by mid-morning the same familiar westwind gale had regained sway.

Ethan chatted with Budjir as the squire helped raise a fresh case of crude nails from the hold.

"Quite a storm we had, wasn't it? How often does it get that bad?"

"Oh, that was a very light storm, sir," the squire replied, his open peasant face devoid of duplicity. "Tis but bad luck we were caught out on the ice. Soon the *real* storms will begin." He walked forward with the case, leaving Ethan thinking cold thoughts.

With the prow of the raft buried in the dead stavanzer and the rear runners holding firm, the *Slanderscree* was high enough off the ice at the bow for men to work underneath. Nevertheless, timbers and blocks were cut and placed to further reinforce the bow and assure that it would not collapse on the men working below at a sudden shift in the wind. Soon sounds of hammering and sawing, pounding and scraping rose above the gale.

Ta-hoding leaned over the side and grunted his pleasure. "At this rate we may be on our way before another day has passed. That is wondrous metal that your strange skyboat was made of, Sir Ethan. Even steel would have broken and twisted on that impact."

"There are ways you might obtain more of it, you know," said Ethan thoughtfully, beginning to enjoy himself. Shop talk! "Also ways to make it into things you need, easily and quickly. You have some things of manufacture that might do well in trade . . . nothing extraordinary of course . . . among my people. Your fine woodwork, for example. And such as this coat of hessavar. And other things."

He looked over to where a group of crewmen were removing—excavating would be a better term—the enormous tusks of the dead stavanzer.

"Those teeth, for another example. What are they used for, anyway? Surely not for defense."

"Eh?" Ta-hoding had been dividing his attention between Ethan and the repairs. "Oh, naturally not. The stavanzer has no enemies. The avaer are used for digging up the ice to get at the roots and the rich grenloen of the pika-pedan."

That was simple enough. He had more questions, but they were interrupted by a shout from the mainmast lookout.

"Sail on the horizon!" Then, seconds later, "Many sails!"

"Convoy?" bellowed the captain loud enough to make Ethan wince. There was silence above. Other eyes turned from their work to stare at the basket atop the mast. Below, repairs slowed as the word was passed.

"Too far!" came the eventual answering shout. "But tis too many! And the pattern is not right!"

September was just coming on deck. Ethan met him halfway to the stern.

"Company, lad?"

"Looks like it, Skua. Ta-hoding thinks it might be a merchant fleet. The lookout isn't so sure. I guess you could meet anyone out here."

The repairs continued, but the metalworkers, carpenters, and supervisors kept throwing uneasy glances at the northeast horizon. They worked a little faster.

Word came up that the starboard runner had been straightened and the bent bolts replaced. The new foremast was already in place and other tran were retying the rigging and setting in new sail. Work was proceeding apace on the broken port runner. Then came a cry from the lookout that stopped everything.

"The Gods mock us! Tis the Horde, the Horde that comes!"

Hunnar uttered a violent oath and launched a vicious kick at the rail. Extended in anger, his chiv cut triple gashes in the wood. He whirled and stalked off to inform Balavere. September was shaking his head.

"Now if that isn't just the loveliest thing," he groaned.

"How could they have known to follow us?" cried Ethan. "How?"

"Ah, I'm not at all sure this meeting is by design, young feller. They've probably been running, running. Just our bad luck they ran this way. They may think we're just another big merchant ship . . . They'll recognize us when they get close enough, all right."

"We could take down the banner," Ethan suggested, "and let Ta-hoding and some of the crew try to bluff it out."

"Bluff what out? Young feller, you don't understand. If this were only a two-man raft bound with cargo of firewood for the ol' homestead, or twice as big as us and loaded with silks and precious metals, they'd still swarm all over it. It may make a difference to Sagyanak that we are who we are, but it won't to us. Result'll be the same as if we'd never met them before. We're still prey. Damnation!"

Soldiers were swarming into the rigging, crossbowmen taking up their posts in the three lookout baskets. Archers stationed themselves along the rail. Tarps were removed from the three small catapults that were useless against gutorrbyn. The complement of the *Slanderscree* now bent all energy toward preparing an unfriendly welcome for their unwanted visitors.

All except the repair crew, who worked faster than ever.

Hunnar stared across the stern. The rafts were now close enough to count, and he was doing just that.

"Too many. A shred, a short tailing of their former selves, but too many for a single ship, even this one." He muttered another few choice curses. "If they could fix that venier runner we could outrun them easily!" He noticed Ethan's inquiring gaze. "No, Sir Ethan. We will never be ready in time. The men will work until they are discovered by *those*, but they cannot make repairs while under attack. Perhaps . . . " his voice dropped to a mumble as he glared at the oncoming rafts, "we may even finish her this time, at least."

Something sounded wrong to Ethan. He found it.

"Her?"

Hunnar looked down at him in surprise. "Why, yes. Did you not know? The Scourge is a woman."

On board her tattered, shaken grand raft, a shadow of its former magnificence, Sagyanak the Death received the word of her lookouts. Yes, the runners of the oddly formed stalled vessel were truly made of metal the color and sheen of the demons' sky-boat. And the Sofoldian banner flew from her masthead.

She smiled a half-toothless, ferocious smile.

The young warrior on her right stiffened as she turned to him. "Norsvik, I want as many taken alive as possible, do you hear? Even should it cost a few more of the People. These should be kept as healthy and undamaged as is manageable— so that they may last long."

"It shall be as you say, Great One." The warrior bowed and left the room.

Sagyanak placed wrinkled, clawed fingers together and began to stroke the arm of her throne. It was built of the bones of those she had vanquished. Soon she would add another set to the elaborately enscrolled frame. Perhaps even some demon-bones.

She wondered with interest if they would scream as did a normal man. That was a good question for the Mad One.

"They're leaving the rafts," said Hunnar, protecting his eyes from the high sun with a paw.

"I'm kind of surprised they don't try to board us from their own rafts," admitted Ethan.

"Well, young feller, I'm sure they've got their reasons. For one thing," and he squinted as the wind shoved at his goggles, "none of those rafts look to be in good shape. In addition to what Hunnar's folk did to 'em, that storm couldn't have done 'em any good, either . . . And remember what Hunnar told us about these folk being able to move better on chiv than most rafts."

The Horde poured onto the ice. They didn't cover it with their numbers this time, and when, finally, they began to move forward, their yelling and chanting did not deafen. Or maybe they knew who rode the strange craft before them and their relative quiet was indicative not of lack of spirit but of terrible purpose.

They charged without pause. A hail of grappling hooks and scaling ladders hit the sides of the stalled raft. Soon Ethan was swinging his sword with the same lack of expertise but determination he had displayed on the walls of Wannome.

September ran one warrior through the chest, pulled his ax free, and yelled instructions to the tran at the miniature catapults. There was a simultaneous release of celluloid tension. Four small smoking bundles arched out over the ice. A shower of glass and iron shrapnel and blinding powder exploded in the middle ranks of the attackers.

Bleeding and torn, they fell to the ice. But their companions didn't falter. Again the catapults fired and more nomads were knocked unmoving or moaning to the frozen sea.

"It doesn't frighten them anymore!" Ethan shouted over the confusion.

Several times it seemed certain the barbarians would swarm onto the deck and overwhelm them. Several times the archers and spearmen were forced back from the rail or cut down. Only the constant rain of crossbow bolts from the tran in the masts closed off the breakthroughs, sealed the temporary gaps.

The battle continued all day, the tran and men on the ship fighting off wave after wave of attackers. Only when the ice had begun to devour the sun did they at last give up and retreat.

Not caring who noticed, Ethan sank exhausted to the deck. His sword clattered beside him.

Hunnar headed forward, no doubt to confer with Balavere and compare losses. The general had taken a bad arrow wound in the shoulder but had remained on deck throughout the fight.

September looked subdued and worried as he wiped his broadax.

"No miracles impending here, lad. Unless Williams can turn these sails into posigrav repellers. Shame I don't believe in magic. To have come this far, have worked this hard . . . only to end up hamburger in the hands of a bunch of washed-up primitive alien bandits like these . . ." He shook his head, the great nose dipping and bobbing, and surveyed the corpse-laden deck. "Looks like we've lost at least half our complement. I think we'll have to press a sword on du Kane, and his daughter, too."

"How badly did we hurt *them?*" asked Ethan tiredly.

"Bad, young feller, bad. But not nearly bad enough. To-morrow they'll be all over us. If they should decide to break down that unrepaired runner or to fire the ship . . ."

"I'd have thought they'd have tried that already. Wonder why they haven't?"

"Why, lad, this raft's the fastest thing short of an air-car on this planet. I'd think she'd want it in one piece, this Sagyanak, if she can get it." He paused, staring into the distance. "Ah, take a look."

Ethan scrambled painfully to his feet. A ring of nomads, half of the surviving force, were drawn up in a broad circle around the *Slanderscree*. The rest were returning to the rafts. Archers at the ready rested near the bow, just out of range of crossbow.

"They've seen the busted runner," said September. "And they're not about to let us fix it, not by the Horse's Head, what? Any work party we put over the side will get cut to pieces. Somehow we're going to have to get that thing fixed so's we can make a break tomorrow. No way we can stand off another all-day assault. We're almost out of our pacific school-master's bombs, too."

It was a grim group that gathered in the captain's cabin that night.

"There it stands, sirs," concluded Hunnar. He'd just repeated, with embellishments, what he'd told Ethan earlier. "As is apparent, our chances of repulsing the vermin's next attack is, realistically speaking, very low. We have few thunder-packages left, few crossbow bolts, and far too few men. When the bombs and bolts run out, they will have us. We *must* try to break away. Yet we cannot get a crew safely outside to repair the runner."

"The starboard runner is completely repaired and repositioned," added Suaxus-dal-Jagger. "I would say that the other would collapse the moment any pressure is put on it. Truly, we cannot move unless it is fixed."

The raft's plan was laid out on the table in front of them. Now Ta-hoding, who'd been listening quietly while studying the schematic, spoke up.

"There is one thing that might be tried, sirs."

"At this point all suggestions are welcome ones, captain," said Balavere, holding his shoulder.

Ta-hoding leaned forward and ran a finger over the diagram. "We might chop through the flooring around the central runner brace here, and here. Our craftsmen could then work safely from *within* the raft. Possibly even part way outside, for the enemy will surely be looking only for men trying to slip over the side."

"Can the runner be fixed from inside?" asked Ethan.

He was disappointed at Ta-hoding's negative gesture. The captain continued. "Not very well, nor permanently, no. There is no way to perform the necessary final metalwork. But a temporary hold might be fastened through the bolt-holes with double-thick cable, which could then be lashed and tightened around the interior bracing."

"Sounds not firm," mused Balavere. "Would it hold at all?"

Ta-hoding made the tran equivalent of a shrug with his eyes.

"There is no way to predict, noble sir. Such an arrangement could hold fast for days. Or it could snap, as the squire says, the moment pressure is put to it."

"I'm placing this in your hands, captain. Do *you* think it will hold?"

Ta-hoding hedged, obviously not fond of being put on the spot. Finally, "I would think for a morning, certainly. The cable should be strong enough to handle that much friction, if it is made very tight and does not work loose too quickly. Yes,

I would stake my life it will hold for a morning-time. I *will* stake my life to it."

"A safe wager, captain," said Hunnar. "If you are wrong there will be none of us about to collect. Can this be made ready by morning?"

"Not if we sit here jabbering all night," broke in Balavere excitedly. "Captain, see to your men and to your repairs. And mind they proceed quietly. We have no wish to arouse the animals' curiosity."

Ta-hoding nodded and departed at as close to a run as Ethan had ever seen him use, the schematic of the ship held tightly in his paws.

"Then sirs, if that is all there is to be decided upon . . . "

"Your pardon, General, but that is not all," said September. "Let's say we make the repair secretly and in time. Let's say further that this jury-rigged setup of the captain's actually holds together. We pull free of that meat-mountain and start running into the wind. I assume we can make better time into the wind than they?"

"No question of it," said Balavere.

"All right then, we show them our fundament and laugh ourselves silly as they disappear astern. What's to prevent them from following doggedly in our tracks . . . this thing does leave tracks . . . and catching up with us as soon as that temporary hitch *does* fail?"

Balavere thought, hesitated. "We must take that chance. Likely we can lose them. Or, not knowing the precariousness of our situation, they may believe we are beyond overtaking."

"And they may not," September countered. He looked around the table. This awkward thought which the big man had raised refused to run away and hide. It demanded an answer, and no one had any.

"I beg your pardon, noble sirs," said Eer-Meesach from the quiet end of the table. "I am not often involved in matters military, I know, and would prefer to shun this one. But I have had a thought. We may have other allies in this."

"Don't talk in riddles, wise one," admonished Balavere. "I am too tired for games, and my shoulder hurts."

"Very well. Tis a risk, and a considerable one. But as seems certain, our lives are balanced on the blade of fate as this ship is on those runners. One more risk should not drive us onto it any deeper . . . "

XII

One thing, Ethan reflected moodily the next morning, was that the wind wakes you quickly on this world. There's no dawdling in bed. Right now he'd happily sign away a year of his life for a modest comfortese bed, which he would immediately set at roasting level before freezing the controls.

He turned and eyed the bow warily. The sailors had withdrawn to the rear half of the ship. Everyone huddled behind something solid in the pre-dawn chill.

There was a violent explosion. A fountain of raw meat and flesh vomited into the clear air. The westwind caught most of it and carried it off at right angles to the ship proper. He stood and stared out across the ice as the enemy encirclement, barely visible in the growing light, scrambled awake at the sound of the explosion. What were the demons up to now?

At least they'd had the pleasure of rudely waking the entire enemy camp. He took a deep breath, but cut it in the middle. Now that the gigantic carcass was laid open to the air, the smell of internal decay slowly permeated the entire ship despite the untiring efforts of the wind to sweep it away.

There was a cry from the lookout and then everyone was running for the stern.

A small cluster of four . . . no, five barbarians had broken from the circle and were chivaning slowly toward the motionless *Slanderscree*, moving in single file. They appeared to be unarmed.

"Parley party," Hunnar explained laconically. "I do not believe we have anything to discuss with them."

"I beg to differ, friend Hunnar," said September. "We've as much to say to them as we possibly can think of, and for as long as we can say it without becoming obvious. We can gain time for that work crew. They still may not finish in time, but

251

every minute we can stave off the final attack . . . " He left
the rest unsaid.

One of the nomads was helped—none too gently—over the
railing. Balavere and the others clustered around him.

The envoy's once-magnificent helmet had a bad dent on
one side. His leather frontispiece was cut and stained. But he
seemed neither tired nor disenchanted, as Ethan had hoped.
He spoke directly to Balavere without formal by-play.

"The Scourge would hold converse with those among you
who lead. I am Haldur the Talker. I and my three lieutenants
will remain here as hostages in bond for those you send." As
he spoke, three more of the nomad party were being helped
on deck.

"We agree to the terms," said Balavere, after a quick conference with Hunnar.

"Suaxus, make one of the noan ready." The squire moved
to do so.

The *Slanderscree* carried two of the little rafts, or noan, to
serve as lifeboats or scout vessels as occasion demanded. Now
one was being lowered over the side to serve as transportation for them all—but mainly for the human members of the
parley party, who would only slide and slow the others on the
ice. Three of the *Slanderscree*'s crew came along to handle
the sail and steering.

Hunnar, Ethan, Skua, and Suaxus comprised the exchange
group. Once aboard, the noan raised sail. The nomad who'd
remained behind on the ice guided them through a gap in the
barbarian encirclement. A low murmur came from that ugly
gathering as they passed through. Many of the nomad warriors wore bandages and splints in addition to badly battered
armor. They were in a murderous mood and Ethan hoped
Hunnar knew what he was doing in agreeing to this exchange.

They passed squads of nomads chivaning toward the ring.
Preparing for the final effort, no doubt.

September was thinking along similar lines. "Getting ready
to attack again."

"Was there any doubt of it?" declared Hunnar. "I am twice
surprised at this parley request. Does she think us fools
enough to surrender?"

"Whatever the reason, be thankful for it," September replied. "It buys time."

"Listen," put in Ethan, "are you sure we can get back to the raft? This charming lady's character doesn't impress me. How honorable is she?"

"As honorable as the lowliest slime that seeps from the garbage tailings," spat the knight. "Yet there will be no question in this matter. All respect the person of an envoy. Without such concord it would make surrender awkward. Such as these prefer not to fight if it can be arranged. Remember when I said they have grown fat."

Ethan watched another pack of taut, tightly armored tran chivan past. "I don't see any who look especially corpulent."

"No longer, since the defeat, friend Ethan. Had this happened two or three hundred years ago, when the Horde was still new in our land, I do not believe that even with your wizard's crossbows and thunder-making we could have defeated them as we did."

They were nearing the anchored nomad fleet—or rather, the pitiful remnant thereof. Their guide directed them among the rafts until they drew alongside what once must have been a veritable palace on runners.

Now the bloodcurdling motifs and designs carved into the rails and central pavilion were scarred by fire. The golden leafing on the central structure had been seared and melted.

Waiting hands helped them onto the deck, holding firmly. To see how much meat was left on him, no doubt, Ethan reflected. He tried to imagine some get-togethers he'd attended where the company had been worse, but the private jest brought no hidden smiles. It was hard to be flip when at any moment some unpredictable primitive might try to make steak out of you.

They entered the pavilion and passed through several rooms. The interior of the big cabin was still rich-looking, still comfortable. Eventually they reached a room larger than all the others. Several well-built specimens of trannish manhood stood along the walls, armed with huge double-edged swords.

At the far end of the room was an incredible throne made

from tran bones and skulls and inlaid with precious metals and gems. The thing that sat on the throne was, even to alien human eyes accustomed to a different meterstick of beauty, outstandingly repulsive.

Instead of the huge, glowering warrior Ethan had first envisioned, Sagyanak was a shrunken, wrinkled old crone. An ugly sack of bones and bile, made the more hideous by childish attempts at facial and body makeup.

This ancient construct of weak ligaments and venomous eyes leaned forward and stared at them, a finger rubbing lower lip like a pallid bristled worm.

"So, there you stand, as the Mad One said you would." They did not question or reply. "That you have even come to this parley says you are not so strong as I thought. Better and best, better and best."

"That we come to this parley," replied Hunnar evenly, "means we are proper in respecting the rules of conflict . . . something you have never bothered to do."

"There are no rules to war," the crone answered indifferently. "There is but victor and defeated. Methodology is irrelevant. But you have come."

"Already established," Hunnar replied impatiently, despite September's anxious glance. "What is it you want? You've interrupted my morning meal."

"So you have plenty of supplies, too. Excellent. Additional stores are always welcome."

"If you can catch it before the wind does, you may follow and be welcome to our garbage."

She leaned forward slowly, showing broken yellow teeth.

"When I have taken you, you will not long be fit to serve even as garbage." With an effort, she sat back and tried to essay a pleasant smile. The result was horrible. "But there is no need for this unpleasantness. I do not need you to justify my actions in battle, good knight. Leave that for another visit. Now, I have been known never to break my word. To do so would dishonor me before the Gods and the Dark One. Know you this to be true?"

"'Tis so," admitted Hunnar.

"Then I say this to you." The head leaned against the throne-back and the slit eyes narrowed. "Give up to me the

great raft the demons have built for you. Yea, you may even
keep your weapons, including the magic bows-which-are-not-
drawn. I covet them, but you may retain them. Also the thunder and lightning your catapults throw. Keep these and go
freely wherever you wish. I swear this."

Hunnar must have been startled at the seemingly generous
offer, but he did an admirable job of not showing it.

"We cannot do that. We are too far from Sofold to safely
chivan back over open ice."

"I will give you rafts enough for all your people, including
your wounded, and enough supplies to return. I swear this
also. And you will have the wind with you." There was a
predatory gleam in her eyes. "What say you?"

Hunnar appeared to consider, then turned away. While
Suaxus remained at attention, the others discussed the proposal in whispers.

"She can't be trusted, can she?" asked Ethan.

"It is strange she offers us our lives. Yes, if she so swears,
she can be."

"I don't share your confidence," put in September. "If we
make it back we'd have to start building another boat from
scratch. I don't know if that toy forge could manage it. This
thing smells worse than that great stinking carcass in front of
the ship. That crazy Eer-Meesach!"

"I concur with you, friend Skua. We face very probable
death if we do not agree," Hunnar explained. "We might not
live out this day. The offer will not be made again."

"We still have a chance to break and run for it."

"The moment we put on sail, friend Skua, they will attack.
With irons and fire. If they cannot have the ship they will
surely not allow us to escape."

"There's still the wizard's idea," said Ethan.

"Of which nothing has come," September countered. The
debate was interrupted by a new voice. Recognition escaped
Ethan for several seconds.

"Come on, gentlemen, you've been stalling long enough.
You may as well accept. It's all you can do and you know it."

They turned. Ethan hadn't thought to hear that voice
again.

Walther walked through the screened door to the right of

the throne, took a seat at its base, and smiled at them. No one offered greeting.

"Well, don't look so stunned," he admonished them in fluent Trannish. It was the first time Ethan had heard him speak the native language, though he'd admitted to knowing it before. "I confess I was in tight for a while there. Afraid one of these hairy berserkers would run a spear through me before I could explain who I was and what I had to offer. Once I got through to a perceptive captain-type, he had me brought to the boss-lady here. We had a nice chat.

"Of course, it was too late for me to do anything about the battle she'd already lost, but I had a few other suggestions. I managed a private looksee at the shrimp's plans for a big raft. Wasn't hard to figure out what you intended to do with it. The main remainder of the Horde slunk off for a little subsistence raiding and thieving, but small rafts made up to look like merchant ships were always shuttling back and forth between us and the harbor.

"We knew when each mast was set in place, when every box of stores was taken on board. As soon as you shoved off and got a little out of sight, we followed. Not only do I know where you're headed as well as you do, but that big raft cuts a helluva gash in the ice. Easy to follow.

"Only thing I hadn't figured on was the speed that thing makes. If you hadn't had the decency to run into that big grass-eater, we'd still be chasing you. Everything will work out nicely now, though."

"Yes, I can see it, too," said Ethan, surprising himself again by breaking in. "You'll take a picked group of these murderers and sail on to Arsudun. Not knowing you from normal humanfolk, the humanx authorities will ignore you. Then you find your associates. If they don't fry you out of hand for bungling the whole enterprise, you'll explain the situation to them, fly back here in an air-car, pick up the du Kanes, and with only a little time lost, continue your original plan to hold them up for ransom. Neat. And us?"

"Believe me," said Walther sincerely, "I wish I'd never set eyes on either of you. Or that teacher, either. Yes, that's a fair scenario. You can make your own way into Brass Monkey. By the time you can get another boat built, make it to

Wannome from here, and then to Arsudun, we should have received our credits and scattered to the far corners of the Arm."

September pointed at the listening Sagyanak. "One other little item. What does she get for providing you with transportation and protection, um?"

"Oh, in return for her help, Her Majesty will retain the lovely big raft you've built."

"That all?"

"Well, I *did* sort of promise her a few crates of modern arms and maybe a small cannon or two once we've been paid off."

"Leaving aside the fact," September continued, "that that's a violation of every rule for contact with Class Four-B worlds, just what do you imagine this she-scorpion will do with 'em?"

"Why, I expect that Her Majesty," he said, glancing over at her, "will sail pronto back to our frigid foster icebox and reduce the place to rubble. After which, without killing off too many of the populace, she'll resume her former status as protector of commerce in the territory. As for 'laws,' " he continued contemptuously, "through sabotage of an interstellar liner and kidnapping of you all, I've already made myself a candidate for mindwipe. I'm not in the least concerned with what the locals intend to do with any new toys I might choose to give them."

"I should have broken your neck when I had the opportunity," observed September calmly.

"Yes, you should have. But you've missed your chance. Agree, and you can at least get out of here with your hide. Refuse and we'll take the boat from you anyway. Fight and you'll be overrun. Try to run away and we'll cut that broken skate free and fire the sails. You are good and well stuck, friends."

"Even if we do agree, what if the tran don't go along with us?" asked Ethan. Walther shrugged.

"That's your problem. I think you'd better convince them. Oh yes, one other thing. I'd like you to leave the brat . . . what's her name? . . . Colette . . . with me, as a guarantee you won't try and follow us into Brass Monkey on the rafts we leave you. It wouldn't do for you to sail in a couple of days after me and let the peaceforcers in on our little secret, would it?"

Something very like a cackle came from the throne. This request, demon-origin or not, she could understand.

"Maybe you'd like me to cut off my right arm, as a further gesture of insurance?" asked September sarcastically.

"Naw, keep it. I'm feeling generous today." He grinned, a small mind in a sudden position of power and enjoying every minute of it.

"We will return to our ship and inform you of our decision," said Hunnar, unable to listen to any more of this without going for certain throats.

"You've got half an hour by the sun," replied Walther easily. "You can spend the time counting houris for all I care. If you agree to the terms, take in the banner at your stern. If not, well," he shrugged, "I've done my best for you."

"I don't wonder that she calls you the Mad One," guessed Ethan.

Walther started and lost a little of his composure.

"Watch your mouth, bright-eyes. This is no sales convention."

"And you're certainly no door prize," he said as they left the throne room.

Ethan tried to affect a nonchalant attitude as they slid back over the ice. But he didn't really relax until they had passed through the encirclement. Now there were plenty of women and cubs in the group, who looked every bit as ragged and vicious as the menfolk. Obviously Sagyanak was leaving nothing to chance. This was to be a supreme effort on her part.

And why not, with such a prize? With modern weapons she could rule as much of the planet as she chose without far-off humanx authorities ever finding out about them.

"Of course we can't agree to this," he said to no one in particular.

"Of course not," September said. "But it did kill some time. Maybe enough. In any case we must try to get away now. The thought of even a single decent pistol in the hands of that horror makes my stomach crawl."

"You'd know about that, wouldn't you?" said Ethan suddenly, giving him an odd look. September chose not to reply. He turned instead to talk to Hunnar.

"We'll have to hold them off and pick the best opening, then break for it."

Balavere and Ta-hoding were waiting with anxious expressions when they reboarded the raft. It felt good to be back on the high deck, even if it was destined to become a baroque coffin within the hour. The barbarian hostages scrambled with poor grace to get over the side. Hunnar watched them speed for the safety of the encampment with obvious disdain.

Something unseen hit Ethan, planted a freezing kiss on one cheek and vanished down a forward hatch. Ethan caught only a glimpse of flying fur and a hint of a pink face.

"What was that?" he mumbled, rather stupidly.

"Why, that was Colette du Kane, young feller." September grinned. "Wonder why it is that impending destruction always gives women the hots?"

"Deity, Skua! Sometimes your crudity exceeds all standards!"

"Please, no compliments before battle," he replied.

They explained to the others the results of their one-sided "parley." Ta-hoding was rapidly being reduced to a quivering wreck. Balavere just listened quietly, nodding now and again at something Hunnar said, questioning September, until they'd both finished.

"Twould be unthinkable to give them the ship under any circumstances," said the General finally. "I would rather raze it to the ice than let the Evil One near it."

Ethan sniffed the air and gagged. The miasma from the rotting colossus seemed powerful enough to stand off an attack by itself. In fact, after a look over the rail he noticed that the section of the encirclement directly to the east of them had actually grown thinner. It might really be of some aid. When they made their break, they would have a weakened section to try for. But Hunnar and Ta-hoding wanted to run the other way. Ethan sighed and looked at the thinned line of enemy troops with regret. The tran were probably right. And the nomad rafts were drawn up to the east, forming a second barrier there.

Extra weapons were passed to all, along with the solemn

word that there would be no quarter, no let-up in this next attack. Once again preparations were made for steering from below deck. Not because of impending storm, but in case the helmsman topside should be cut down when the raft tried to break the enclosing circle.

The wounded took swords or spears. So did Elfa and Colette and even Hellespont du Kane, who at least could wield one like a cane. The crossbowmen scrambled aloft, settling themselves in their baskets and stacking bolts nearby. Archers and pikemen moved to positions at the railing.

Waiting.

Ethan surveyed the poised Sofoldians, a pitifully reduced group, then the hundreds of tensed nomads. There were no reserves this time to take up an empty place on the rail if a man fell. He was beginning to lament all the sales, commissions, deals, promises, and women he'd failed to make. It must have taken more than a half hour.

It could have been his imagination. Or maybe Sagyanak and Walther had decided to give them a little extra time in the hopes that the increasing tension would weaken the resolve of those on the *Slanderscree*. Another precious few minutes for the furious repair crew.

They finally broke, howling and screaming, chivaning toward the raft from all sides. No disciplined assault this, but a shrieking, angry, uncontrolled mob.

Arrows began to thunk into the deck, the masts, the railing. A man went down a few meters to his left. Meanwhile their crossbowmen and archers were returning the fire from superior height. Dozens of barbarians dropped, hundreds came on. Again the uninvited grappling hooks and ladders sprouted. One hook narrowly missed pinning Ethan to the rail.

A helmeted head appeared over the side. September swung at it—he had the great axe in his hands again. Ethan hacked and flailed at the knotted rope attached to the hook.

One voice drifted down through all the noise and confusion. Ethan hardly recognized it. It was the voice of the mainmast lookout, posted aloft with the crossbowmen. He was using a megaphone—another, simpler invention by Williams. His message was brief.

"THEY COME!"

Ta-hoding, who'd been shaking every time an arrow whizzed within half a dozen meters of him, heard it also. Suddenly he was moving his fat bulk about the deck at an insane pace, bodily pulling sailors from their positions and all but booting them into the rigging. Ethan prayed that the captain wouldn't run into a mast and knock himself flat.

Dropping swords and pikes and spears, they scrambled into the shrouds. Sails began to drop, grew convex with wind. The wheel creaked, a ghostly turning as the below-deck system struggled to move the half-frozen fifth runner. The soldiers fought all the harder to compensate for the manpower loss.

Gradually, a strange lull seemed to settle over the combatants on both sides.

"Hear it, young feller?" murmured September.

"Yes . . . yes, I do," he whispered back, unaware that he'd done so.

The sound was faint, distant. A carefully controlled tsunami. Continuous rumble welling out of the ice itself.

Their attackers heard it too. Questioning looks assaulted the eastern horizon. As the susuration grew louder it began to assume a definite rhythm, rolling and booming like heavy surf.

A nomad hesitated in mid-cut with his sword, another thrust his spear with less authority, yet a third drew his bow and let the bowstring sag limp.

The *Slanderscree* began to back free of the dead mountain. Ethan was sure he could hear a slight metallic groan from forward and belowdecks. He ignored it. Maybe it would go away. Whatever it was, the roped-together runner did not buckle.

Fires erupted in the encirclement on all sides of the raft as stockpiled wood was ignited. Rafts of dried wood soaked in oil were made ready to be pushed against the ponderous, slowly-moving great raft. Here and there torchbearers began to move toward the ship.

But at the same time, other nomads were beginning to slip back down their boarding ropes, stumble off the ladders. They fought against those pressing forward.

The torchbearers got halfway to the turning raft, now dripping warriors from its sides.

"There, I see them!" Ethan yelled. September turned too, and then Hunnar, and then the few of the enemy who still fought.

Far off in the distance eastward, a tiny clump of steel-gray bumps hove into view, like a herd of great whales. Except that the slightest of these was greater than the greatest whale that had ever swum Terra's seas.

Adamantine sunlight encountered thin paired strips of white and flashed. The sound of thunder floated ominously over the glass-earth.

Ta-hoding ignored the occasional arrows which still flew over the deck and scrambled for the wheel. Another sailor joined him. Now there were four sets of powerful arms pulling at the fifth runner, two above and two below deck. Ethan watched the captain's suety face swell as he strained to get the ship clear of the corpse.

They would only need seconds to pick up wind and start southward. There was no question of running into the wind now. Against it they could outrun the Horde, but not the herd. They might get out of their path. They *had* to get out of their path.

Utter confusion extended invisible claws, gripped the barbarian ranks as the word was passed. Spears and axes and torches were dropped as the remaining nomads spread their dan and chivaned for their lives. A few of the barbarian rafts were struggling with reduced crews to pull out their ice-anchors and get under sail as well. It was impossible to tell at that distance, but Ethan supposed many of those anchors were being cut free.

The majority of the nomads seemed determined to gain the distance to the rafts, the only homes they'd ever known. A few, less concerned, scattered in all directions, though it was hard going against the wind, or north, or south. A few milled about aimlessly. Others were trampled under chiv by their hysterical fellows.

Hunnar was growling low in his throat, glancing from the sails to the straining captain, then astern.

"Get her nose around, Ta! Get her nose around!"

Now the herd was close enough for Ethan to discern individuals. Close enough to see the long, gargantuan tusks curved partway back into the cavernous mouths. Even battling windnoise, their thunder dominated as they inhaled cubic liters of air, forced it out of the fleshy jets near their rear.

The tran of the *Slanderscree* fought like demons to put on every centimeter of sail. There was a crackling and snapping. The still shattered bowsprit turned with agonizing patience to the south. Nearly free now of the attentions of the Horde, she began to move.

She passed the half-putrid corpse with nail-biting slowness —the corpse whose rotting stink had drawn the furious, bellowing herd from feeding grounds far over the horizon to gather and mourn over one of their dead.

Just as Eer-Meesach had said it would.

Ethan found himself pounding the rail with a fist.

"Move, ship, move! Please move!" Rippling wave-thunder drowned out all sounds now, hammered relentlessly against his eardrums. Prayers went unheard.

A few, a very few, of the barbarian rafts had put on sail. The rest were trying.

The herd moved in slow motion upon the rafts. With them. Among them.

Through them.

There were no more rafts.

The *Slanderscree* was pulling away as her sails ate wind. The bad runner held for a minute, then a second, and another, until it was forgotten in other concerns. Ethan stood frozen to the rail as the herd approached at an incredible pace. They were moving at least 100 kph—into the wind!

What remained of the once omnipotent Horde of the Scourge vanished beneath several million kilos of gray flesh, became a red-brown smear on the shining ice.

The herd drew closer. For a second time Ethan gazed down the throat of Leviathan.

It paused, froze in space.

Began to recede.

"They're stopping at the body," murmured Hunnar finally,

long after they were safely away southward. He had to clear his throat once before the words came out. "Thank all the Gods!"

"It didn't look like many of *them* managed to escape," said Ethan.

"No," agreed Hunnar, curiously unemotional. "Not many."

"Cubs, too," continued Ethan, his voice dropping to a barely audible mutter.

September showed no such concern. He was rubbing both hands together and chatting with sailors and soldiers, as happy as if a freshly baked cake had exited the oven without falling. Hunnar was leaning over the stern, straining to pick out shapes among the rapidly receding forms.

"I didn't see Sagyanak's raft in those final seconds. Could the devil-bitch have escaped again?"

"Sorry to kill all the bad dreams you half-hoped to have, friend Hunnar," said September. He grabbed at his hood as a sudden gust of wind threatened to tear it off. "I did."

"What do they do with the dead young one, the stavanzers? Now that they've found it?" asked Ethan.

"If the wizard's information is accurate, and it has been thus far," the knight replied, "then the thunder-eaters will remain with the dead for several days. I have never seen such a thing myself. Supposedly they prod the body with their tusks, nudge it every so often in the apparent hope that they may stir it to life once again . . . Eventually, some inner desire satisfied, they will move off, never to return to that spot again. Or perhaps they merely grow hungry. None know for certain. Among my people, at least, the observation of the thunder-eater's habits from close range tis not over-popular. And thunder-eaters do not die often."

"I don't wonder at your caution." Ethan noticed that Ta-hoding was only a short breath from total collapse, now that the *Slanderscree* was out of danger. A sweaty heap of fur and flesh, the captain had sunk to the deck next to the big wheel. He stared into nothingness. All his efforts seemed directed to following each breath with another.

"Noble animals," Ethan mumbled.

"What?" September came over. "Those supra-nourished grotesque herbivores? Get a hold on your self, lad!"

Ethan sighed. "Skua, sometimes I think you have no poetry in your soul."

"Now as to that, young feller-me-lad, firstly you'd have to establish the existence of the latter. And you're one to talk!" He sniffed with exaggerated force. The resultant supercilious pose was so comical that Ethan couldn't keep from laughing. "You kindly explain to me, lad, the poetry in volume buying or discount pricing."

Ethan started to do just that, but had to pause in the middle of the first sentence.

Why did someone have to keep reminding him of where he wasn't?

XIII

There was little new to look at as the raft continued to devour the kilometers. The journey rapidly became a dull cycle of rising, pacing the too-familiar deck, talking, eating, and returning to sleep. The humans, in one respect, were fortunate. They had the added extra task of fighting to stay that one step ahead of frostbite.

They'd entered a new region, filled with innumerable small islands. Many rose nearly perpendicular from the ice—dark, black stone, the stumps and cores of long-eroded volcanos. They served to break the monotony of flat horizon, but just barely, since the next was much like its predecessor.

A few of the islands were inhabited. Tiny villages clung precariously to the cliffs.

Occasionally a small raft or party of wandering hunters would parallel the *Slanderscree* for a few dozen meters. The dialect here differed from that of Sofold. Ta-hoding, a good merchant, was able to converse with them like a neighbor. After the first few encounters, even Ethan and the other humans could make themselves understood, though they lacked the captain's fluency.

The Trannish language had a universal planetary base, then. Local variations did not preclude adequate communication between widely scattered groups. Another plus as far as trade and commerce were concerned.

No matter how skilled or strong, the locals rapidly dropped behind, unable to match the big raft's speed.

Things grew so dull that Ethan found himself wishing for another storm—but not a Rifs. That bored he wasn't.

He got it.

After the third consecutive day of freezing wind and even a little razor-sharp sleet, he was damning himself for a romantic idiot and praying for a return to the clear sameness of days before. Anything for a reprise of calm weather!

Constant maneuvering in the high wind had finally cracked several of the top cross-spars and weakened the repaired foremast. Ta-hoding also wanted to fix the still-amputated bowsprit, and there was no telling what the storm had done to the awkwardly repaired runner. They still had a long way to go and you couldn't tell when you'd need every square centimeter of sail and solid, dependable runners.

The little informal council met once again—on a much less anxious note than the last time. Suggestions were easily made, as easily rejected. It was finally agreed that they would take the time to put in at the first town or village which offered the raft protection from the westwind, a decent harbor.

Ethan was on deck the next morning when the lookout gave the cry, so he was one of the first to see the monastery of Evonin-ta-ban. He joined Ta-hoding as the refuge came into full view, shining dark in the light of the fast-rising sun.

"Odd-looking sort of place," said Ethan. "What is it? We haven't passed anything like it before. Surely it's not a hunting or farming community."

"I do not know what it is, noble sir," the captain replied uneasily. "Truly, I have ne'er seen the likes of it before. But Dagstev, the lookout, was right about the harbor. It looks to be sufficient . . . at this distance, anyhow. There do not appear to be any ships within, so it cannot be a trading community. Very, very strange. Perhaps . . . perhaps we'd best not land here, noble sir."

"Glassfeathers. You've got to learn to face the cosmos with a more open mind, Ta-hoding. One of these days you may even skippership between the stars."

The captain's reply was direct and left no room for semantic nitpicking.

"Not if all the devils that ever were got behind me and pushed, Sir Ethan!"

"Why not, captain? Your own ancestors probably had the power of flight."

"And had the good sense to give it up, too," Ta-hoding countered religiously. "Give me a good ship with sharp runners, smooth ice beneath her keel, and a strong wind astern and I'll be quite satisfied. I leave the skies to those who wish them. And say nothing about their sanity, however questionable." He concluded on a note of finality and commenced barking landing orders to the crew. The *Slanderscree* was angling for the harbor entrance and Ethan decided to leave the captain alone.

One by one the wide sails were reefed in. He went below, roused September from his lingering breakfast and informed Hunnar, the du Kanes, and several others of their incipient landfall.

Hunnar joined him and they ascended to the bow. Together they stared over the broken bowsprit.

"Ta-hoding said he'd never seen anything like it, Hunnar."

"Nor have I, friend Ethan, nor have I. But I find its aspect only unusual, not threatening. Though whoever built it surely had an eye to its defense. It seems impregnable. A strange place indeed."

Such as it was, the harbor was simply a natural gap in the crust of the island. Fingers of dark, worn rock extended on two sides to embrace the slowing *Slanderscree*.

Except for some flat land to the right of the harbor, the entire island consisted of several sheer, jagged peaks that shot straight out of the ice to a height of four and five hundred meters.

Low vegetation struggled in the shelter of the shadowy cliff-face. A band of the ever-present pika-pina was just visible as they entered the harbor, extending from the west side of the mountains into the wind. The flat area to their right appeared to be under intensive cultivation.

Three-quarters of the way up the vertical basalt, cradled in a notch between the two highest peaks, sat an odd jumble of multi-tiered structures which seemed to grow from the naked stone. The architecture was elaborate, far more so than anything Ethan had observed to date.

Turrets and battlements he knew from Wannome, but these buildings also boasted spires, minarets, and even true domes —the first he'd seen on the planet. What looked to be a long, surprisingly spacious series of ramps and stairs began near the base of the cliff and ascended via a number of switchbacks to the lowest of the precariously situated structures.

The single dock gave every indication of being carefully kept and maintained, if not often used. There were no ships tied up to it and none in the harbor. But the preservation and nearby cultivated fields were signs that the place was inhabited. At least they'd have a place to tie up and could forgo the trouble of utilizing the bulky ice-anchors. In the lee of the skytickling crags there was hardly a hint of wind. It was almost calm.

September joined them silently, staring upwards until he risked a neck-crick.

"Whoever put that pile of vertiginous masonry together, friend Hunnar, spent more than spare time at it. Without the aid of lifters and impellers, and in this climate, I'll not hesitate in calling it a tremendous piece of raw engineering. Going to be a respectable hike to the front door."

"You think we'll be going today?" asked Ethan.

"I could not venture a prediction," put in Hunnar hastily, before the big man could verbally commit them to another arduous enterprise. "But if you will lower your eyes you will see that our arrival has not gone unobserved."

A figure was coming toward the dock from the base of the stairway. Apparently male, the tran's stride was purposeful but not hurried. Open greeting, or forewarned is forearmed, mused Ethan. They watched the native with interest.

He seemed in no way unusual. While his beard was longer than Hunnar's and whiter than Balavere's, the welcoming committee of one showed no other signs of advanced age. He was of average trannish height and built slimmer than most of the tran on board the raft.

He wore only a long white fur, done up in a sort of toga arrangement, instead of the now familiar tran outer garment that snapped closed at the shoulders. It and its wearer were devoid of personal ornamentation—unless you counted the body-length staff in his right paw.

At first Ethan thought it was wood, but as the native came closer he saw that it had been carved from some porous green stone. More importantly, the tran didn't seem the least bit afraid of them. That suggested once again either honest friendliness or the presence of ten thousand spearmen hidden in the rocks. As it developed, the more reasonable guess was correct.

The landing ramp was put across. Hunnar, Ethan, and September debarked while the sailors and soldiers on deck and in the rigging continued their tasks. Each kept a curious eye on their oddly-clad host's approach.

Ethan was thinking it would be a good idea to have Tahoding present to handle any language difficulties. As it developed, the captain's linguistic abilities weren't needed.

"I am Fahdig, gentlesirs," he said. "And this is the monastery of Evonin-ta-ban. You are welcome here."

"Our thanks," replied Hunnar. "I hight Sir Hunnar Redbeard, and these," he indicated the two humans, "are visitors from a far place, noblemen of another land: Sir September and Sir Fortune. We ask to remain within your protecting harbor for a few days to effect needed repairs. If there is a harbor fee we can pay . . . "

The other gestured with the stone staff.

"There is no fee. The facilities of the monastery are open to any reasoning man. Few have ever been turned away wanting. But it is for the Brotherhood to decide and not I."

"I didn't know you had religious orders," whispered Ethan to Hunnar. The staff-bearer overheard.

"Know I not what you mean, strange knight. The Brotherhood is an association of free spirits and minds, gathered in this place to preserve the knowledge and histories of the universe against the onslaughts of the Dark One. We are scholars, sir, not sychophants."

"Starseeds," mumbled Ethan. "Wait til Williams and Eer-Meesach find out we've stumbled onto a local society of researchers."

September's comment was blunt. "Frankly, I couldn't give a damn about how they built rafts or grew pika-pina on this ice cube a couple of thousand years ago. That's the sort of thing you're likely to find in these old storehouses of 'knowledge.' Useless trivia. Religious nuts, all right!" All of which, of course, was declaimed carefully in Terranglo. "They just worship something other than a supernatural being, is all. Doesn't change their style from religious fanaticism to enlightened guardianship."

"Well, they don't seem very fanatical to me," Ethan countered in Terranglo, as Hunnar continued to exchange pleasantries and information with their host.

"Maybe it's not obvious, but . . . " September grunted. He looked heavenward to where windswept towers and steeples had been hewn into the naked rock. "Anyhow I'd like a look-see inside their cubby. I admire good workmanship no matter what the source."

September didn't have to translate his request. Unbidden, Fahdig had invited them to accompany him to the monastery for the Brotherhood's ruling.

"I hope they keep the haggling to a minimum," September grumbled undiplomatically in Trannish. "I, at least, am still in a hurry."

"The decision-making should take but a heartbeat of time, gentlesir," replied Fahdig. "Only long enough for the Prior to satisfy himself as to your reason. Until then you are guests. The harbor is yours."

"Before we start unpacking," pressed September, "how long before the Brotherhood and your Prior can take action on our request?"

"Do but follow me and it shall be seen to as soon as we arrive."

"Well, that's fine! Just fine." The big man turned, cupped hands to mouth.

"Hey, du Kane! Hellespont du Kane!"

The slim figure of the financier appeared at the railing of the raft.

"Yes, Mr. September?"

The big man switched to Terranglo again. "The lad, Hunnar, and I are going for a hike with his beardship, here! Seems we've run across a bunch of hermetic scholars! Harmless enough. We've got temporary permission to park here and make repairs, but we've got to make the walk-up to satisfy the local high mucky-muck we're reasonable . . . whatever that means. Tell Ta-hoding to get cracking on his work and

to keep an eye on the monastery . . . that's what they call
it. If he doesn't see my coat waving in the next hour he can
go ahead and work full speed. Got that?"

"I rarely misconstrue any information consigned to my
care, Mr. September. Rest assured that I shall convey the message to the captain with the utmost precision. What if you
should be detected gesticulating with your garments?"

"Then he's to raise sail and get the hell out of here!"
September snorted and turned to their guide, speaking in
Trannish.

"All right, friend Fahdig, let's go meet your Brotherhood."

Ethan was quite sure that heights held no terror for him.
He'd sipped cocktails on transparent balconies ninety stories
above steaming swampland.

However, he'd been completely enclosed in a comfortable
tower suite at the time. It was rather different mounting hundreds of steps with a sheer drop of hundreds of meters on
your right, then on your left. Almost unconsciously he edged
away until he was walking with a decided preference for the
section of stairway nearest the mountainside.

The stairs themselves had been cut from the bare rock, an
agonizing task that probably took more years than he cared
to speculate at. At least it was broad enough for several men
or tran to walk side by side. So he didn't feel cramped. There
was also a wide, if low, stone railing on the cliffside.

But as the raft, which now seemed to sit directly below
them, and the harbor grew smaller and smaller, so did his
stomach.

Halfway up he found himself beginning to pant. September
still looked fresh, but Sir Hunnar was gritting his teeth at the
pain shooting through his thighs and calves. The tran were not
constructed for steady climbing. Fahdig, on the other hand,
was clearly inured to the pain.

There was no guard at the simple, solemn archway which
framed the entrance to the monastery. The door was of un-
adorned wood, through which Fahdig led them.

Ethan spared a last glance over the side of the stairway.
They were now nearly five hundred meters above the harbor.
The raft was a child's toy resting on a plate of waxen crystal.

Then he was through the door and standing in a darkish, tomb-like hallway. Lamps glowed along the walls even though it was bright day outside.

"Kind of a gloomy atmosphere you fellas take to," said September as they strolled down the hall.

"We are in the lower levels of the monastery," their guide informed them. "As we go higher it will become lighter. Windows here are neither necessary nor would they be structurally sound."

Fahdig was as good as his word. They soon found themselves walking through well-lit, high-beamed rooms and halls. Occasionally they encountered another of the Brotherhood, some older, some younger than their guide. A few were mere cubs. They reacted to the presence of the humans with a lot more open surprise than had Fahdig. A few stopped to stare after them long after they'd passed by.

"I didn't see an ice-path outside," September said to Hunnar. "On the stairway."

"I am not surprised, friend Skua. There are limits to any tran's skill with dan and chiv. Coupled with a tricky breeze and sharp turns, such a steep descent would tax the skill of the most accomplished soldier. Nay, even of a Dancer."

"I thought so. But there could be other reasons why they've dispensed with it. Aesthetic, maybe, or ascetic."

"That is possible," the knight agreed. "It may be considered virtuous among them to move only on foot."

They hadn't been walking too long before Fahdig bade them wait outside an iron-banded door. He disappeared within, reappeared several moments later.

"The Prior will see you now." They followed him in.

Ethan didn't know what to expect—another throne room, perhaps, like Kurdagh-Vlata's. But the room they entered was plainly furnished, without being spartan. Only the wide, richly carved and polished table hinted at wealth of any kind. A few chairs completed the alcove's furnishings.

They were obviously in one of the upper levels of the monastery now. Light poured in through windows set in the eastern and southern walls. But most of the illumination came from the skylight, another first for Tran-ky-ky.

The startling feature, however, was the walls. From floor to ceiling on all sides, save the one they'd entered from, the walls were solid with shelves, crammed row upon row with meticulously kept, neatly aligned books.

He'd encountered tough, long-wearing paper of pika-pina fiber in Wannome, but very little. The Sofoldians seemed to prefer vellum and parchment for writing, since the fibrous paper was difficult to write on without constant blotting.

Obviously the Brotherhood had solved that problem. Or else it had been solved for them, because the open books on the table were filled with neither parchment nor vellum.

He whispered to September. "We'd better reconsider before bringing Williams or Eer-Meesach up here. We might never drag them away."

"Huh!" September gave the shelves a quick survey. "Wonder if they just collect and store them, or if they really bother to read any."

The Prior himself turned out to be a placid-looking old tran. He sported a beard much longer than Hunnar's. His mane was pure white and his manner pleasant and relaxed. If he was shocked by Ethan and September's appearance he was too courteous to show it.

He also retained one of the ubiquitous staves. It rested against the table.

"You'll forgive my not rising to greet you, gentlesirs. I am not in the best of health today."

"We sorrow for you and wish your Priorship to recover vibrant as the winter wind," Hunnar said smoothly.

The oldster smiled a little. "Fahdig has told me of your magnificent ship and your request to remain with us for a few days. And of your haste."

"Especially our haste," put in September. "Now, about this vote or whatever . . ." The Prior waved him down.

"It will not be necessary to consult the Brotherhood, to draw them from their daily labors on so simple a matter. You may remain as long as you wish. Our fare here at Evonin-ta-ban is simple but nourishing. Do us the honor of taking evening meal with us and enjoying our hospitality for a night!"

Hunnar nodded before either of the humans could speak, so Ethan assumed the knight anticipated the food's being edible, if not up to the level of the royal chefs.

"Retire now, gentlesirs, and leave me to rest. We will talk more tonight, of your plans and needs and journey."

They walked out.

"Thanks, Fahdig," said Ethan sincerely, "for your help in speeding things through for us."

"Your thanks are welcome but ill-directed, gentlesir. No one 'speeds' anything past the Prior. I merely repeated to him what you told me. He decided in your favor by himself."

"You'd already agreed to let us stay the day," declared September. "What if he'd overriden that decision and told us to leave immediately?"

Fahdig looked shocked. "He would not do that! Not even the Prior will counter a decision previously reached by a Brother. We live by reason and logic here. This trust in one another's rationality is an integral part of the Brotherhood."

"Yeah, sure. But let's say he had . . . differed severely with your evaluation of the situation."

"Why then," said Fahdig, obviously struggling with an unfamiliar concept, "it would be good manners for me to withdraw my recommendation."

"The Prior keeps a very impressive library," put in Ethan to change the subject.

"Oh, that was not the Prior's library." Their guide seemed amused. "Twas merely the room in which he is studying today. There are a great many similar rooms in the monastery. All are filled with histories, studies, and scientific papers accumulated over thousands of years."

"I see," Ethan murmured. "There are two men with us of identical sentiment with the Brotherhood. One of your kind and one of mine."

"Their profession makes them thrice welcome, then," said Fahdig.

"Yes. What I want to know is, would it be possible for them to have a look through your libraries? They'd both be forever grateful."

"'Tis not often done with outsiders, but then few express the desire to share of our knowledge. Peasants! Most who stop at the monastery are of lower lifes, merchants and dealers with goods to barter."

"I understand perfectly," replied Ethan with a straight face.

Fahdig continued more cheerfully. "But if these companions of yours are true scholars, I am sure the Brotherhood would be pleased to have them enjoy the results of many years' labor. Yes, consider it agreed!"

"Thank you, Fahdig. I'm sure they'll be demonstrably grateful."

"If knowledge is spread," intoned their guide a bit pompously, "then that is thanks enough, for it holds back the encroachment of the Dark One!"

"Oh, absolutely," agreed Ethan.

Fahdig accompanied them to the bottom of the switchbacks and said he would meet them there an hour before the sun disappeared behind the mountains.

Hunnar formally accepted the Prior's invitation and they started back to the raft.

Ta-hoding's anxious face conveyed more questions than a thousand words.

"Everything is fine, captain," said September. "This place is run by a crowd of desiccated old bookworms. Didn't see a spear or bow in the whole mausoleum. We've got permission to use the harbor for as long as we need. They won't give us any trouble . . . Oh, one other thing." He paused. "We've been invited to supper."

Ta-hoding raised his eyes meaningfully. "Up *there?*"

"Did you think it was going to be catered?"

"Then," the captain replied, "you will extend my regrets to our hosts for my absence. I must decline . . . until you return to us with another sky-boat. Your pardon." He shuffled off and began bawling out a crewman who'd mistied a knot.

Their report drew a mixed reaction from the others. Balavere in particular found their isolated hosts too polite for his liking. But Hunnar reminded the General that the small farming and hunting villages they'd passed had seemed equally open and unmilitary. Clearly this area was not visited by such as the Horde.

"We've also been extended the services of the monastery for this night, at least," he added. Ethan expressed his own pleasure at the chance to sleep in a real bed for a change. One that did not rock with the wind.

Hellespont du Kane professed indifference, but Colette was plainly as excited by the offer as Ethan. Even if it meant a five-hundred-meter ascent.

When they received the news about the libraries, of course, there was no holding the two wizards, just as Ethan had predicted. In fact, they insisted on leaving immediately and making their own way to the top.

Hunnar argued mildly that arriving early might be construed as a breach of local etiquette. But Ethan and September disagreed, citing the unfailing kindness and open helpfulness of the Prior and Fahdig. Without waiting for an official decision, both Eer-Meesach and Williams vanished up the nearest hatchway.

"That's the last we'll see of those two for a while," said Budjir gruffly. Ethan was surprised. Rarely did either of the squires offer an unsolicited comment.

"Why do you say that, Budjir?"

"I do not understand those two," he replied. "Their constant chatter hurts my head."

"Don't let it bother you, Budjir," said September jovially, clapping the huge tran on the shoulder. "Sometimes I find myself in complete agreement with you. Now a tall tankard of reedle and a shapely female, eh? . . ."

The squire grinned and the slitted pupils focused fondly on something in the far distance.

Ethan observed this comradely by-play and muttered, "Communication . . . it's wonderful," and turned to go to his own cabin to prepare himself for the overnight stay.

Work on the repairs proceeded steadily and at a relaxed pace. There was no need to rush the workmen. This time they could make a decent job of the foremast, too. And while the temporary repairs on the fore port runner had held up better than anyone had a right to expect, Ta-hoding was relieved at the chance to fix it properly.

Timbers and bracing had been set up beneath the bow and the metalworkers were already beginning to rebolt the recalcitrant skate to the raft hull.

That would be finished by the time it grew too dark to

work. The broken spars, foremast, and bowsprit could be fixed tomorrow. On the open ice in an average wind the work would have taken at least a week. In the protective shadow of the towering crags they could finish the same task in two days.

The humans were not alone in their desire to experience a soft, stable bed. Most of the crew would have gone along too. But Hunnar and Ethan remembered the Prior's comments about his "simple but nourishing fare." Despite the old scholar's obvious willingness to share all, there was no need to overdo their welcome.

So the overnight party consisted of the little band of humans, Hunnar and his two squires, and Elfa. The two wizards were already on their way up. Still suffering from his arrow wound, General Balavere elected to remain on board.

Fahdig awaited them at the cliff base. His clothing was the same white robe, but he carried a lamp in case, as he put it, "some among you should find the climb excessively strenuous and wish to turn back with some light."

As it turned out, everyone finished the ascent. Colette's fear of the black abyss to one side was openly evident. Ethan felt no shame in joining her in hugging the mountainside.

Much to everyone's distraction, Elfa insisted on running and skipping alongside the inadequate stone railing, not to mention leaning over the edge and pointing out this or that unusual feature in the depths below.

Once, laughing, she even climbed onto the rail itself. She walked along the narrow stone coping, teetering on the lip of the drop. Ethan couldn't watch her. It didn't go on for long, because Hunnar threatened to tie her wrists to her ankles and drag her the rest of the way up.

She grumbled, but climbed down—to everyone's immense relief.

Once they'd passed through the first dark hallway, Fahdig led them upwards via a different route than the one they'd first traversed. They passed a long, comfortable-looking room and he indicated the beds neatly lined against both walls inside.

"For tonight," he informed them unnecessarily.

There was no wall fireplace. Instead, a central pit was

sunk into the center of the floor and filled with logs and brush. Just above the pit a large wooden funnel lined with copper narrowed into a long black pipe that disappeared into the ceiling.

In one respect, then, these isolated scholars were ahead of the busy commercial port of Wannome. They'd developed a rudimentary form of real heating. It was more efficient than a fireplace—provided all the waste particles went up the funnel and not onto one's bed. Several windows in the east wall would let in the morning light. Lamps and torches were mounted on the walls. With the single door shut it would be very comfortable.

"Very pleasant-looking dormitory," complimented September. "Is this how you fellas live?"

"Oh no," Fahdig replied. "Each of the Brothers has his own small vestibule. This is a study room."

"With beds?"

"In a gesture of friendship, some among the Brotherhood have given up their beds for the night. They will sleep on pallets. Tis good for the body and the mind, now and then. Tables and chairs normally fill this room. They will return when you have departed."

"That's very considerate of you," said Ethan. "We're sorry to put you to so much trouble."

"Hospitality is never trouble," their imperturbable guide replied. "If you will come this way, please."

They continued down the hall and went up one more level, where Fahdig motioned them into another room. They seemed to be in one of the highest levels of the monastery. Evening light poured in from the huge skylight that occupied most of the ceiling.

Ethan wondered if the beautiful skylights had been developed and built by the scholars themselves or if they were a bit of art once known but long forgotten in Wannome. There was no way of telling, and it might not be good manners to ask.

The table was long and simple. So were the foods that other members of the Brotherhood were setting on it. The Prior sat at the head of the table with several other elderly tran. Williams and Eer-Meesach were there to greet them.

The little schoolmaster fairly exploded out of his seat when they entered. He walked straight to Ethan.

"My dear friend, you have no idea, no *idea* what a treasure-house this place is! Malmeevyn and I have been overwhelmed by one amazing volume after another. Some of the older books stored here go back literally thousands of years . . . or so Malmeevyn tells me. There's much I can't translate. The books themselves are astonishing. But the amount of pure information and data stored inside . . . it would take a hundred xenologists years with a good computer just to properly document and catalogue the material the Brotherhood holds."

"I don't want to dampen your enthusiasm," replied Ethan, gazing at the fresh vegetables set in front of him with similar excitement, "but we'll only be here another day. The repairs will be completed by then and we'll be on our way back to civilization. You remember civilization?"

"Not with overwhelming fondness, Ethan. You're right, of course. But the things we have discovered already . . . did you realize that at one time this world averaged a hundred-fifty degrees warmer? There was ice only at the poles. For some reason the climate changed suddenly. The seas froze and most of the land was pressed beneath the water. It was yesterday, geologically speaking."

"That's interesting," agreed Ethan absently, his stomach growling for attention. He took a seat.

"And besides that . . . " Williams stopped, his tone changing to one of admonishment. "You weren't even listening. You're like the others, only interested in liquor and money and women."

"Look, Milliken, I'm fascinated. But I'm also starving after those two climbs. Later, huh?" He fastened his gaze on the platter of steaming meat that magically appeared in front of him.

Williams ignored him and stalked away. He took his seat and seemed to forget the conversation entirely as he plunged into debate with Eer-Meesach. They might have been alone at the table.

They quieted, however, when the Prior raised a clawed old paw and gestured for silence. Ethan hadn't expected a pre-meal prayer. What he got was just that, and a curious something else.

"We eat of the product of resourcefulness and thought," said the Prior solemnly. "Our reason says that this is so. May the Brotherhood never falter in its purpose, nor its strength diminish, so that we may forever continue to hold back the ravages of the Dark One."

That was all. Then the other Brothers—not servants, but members of the society acting in that capacity tonight—began to pass around the plates of meat, vegetables, and baked foods.

Ethan tried several dishes, found them bland but filling.

Hunnar and the two squires fidgeted noticeably at this polite departure from normal table manners. They were not used to eating in a restrained manner. Here, the "he who gets there firstest gets the bestest" theorem did not apply. They managed to keep from attacking the table and allowed themselves to be served like all the others.

For a while, then, no one did anything but eat. The members of the Brotherhood seemed willing to permit matters to continue that way.

But gradually, as stomachs were filled, thoughts other than of consumption occupied the minds of those seated around the table and they began to ask questions.

With Hunnar doing most of the talking, they explained to their attentive hosts how they fought and defeated the Horde, how they came to build the great ice clipper, and their subsequent use of a herd of thunder-eaters to destroy the remainder of the Horde.

When it came to the origin of the humans, Ethan thought a few of the Brothers looked more than just casually interested. One was unabashedly fascinated by the bowdlerized version of their initial landing and first contacts with Hunnar's folk.

September chipped in with occasional comments and corrections. The du Kanes continued to eat and listen in silence. And the two wizards were off in their own private world, oblivious to human and tran alike.

"An amazing account," commented the Prior finally, with becoming control. "And one that should be set down for the records . . . even though some of it taxes the credulity. Alas, you maintain you have not the time."

"I'm afraid not," said September, not at all contrite. "We ought to and will be on our way again as soon as repairs on the raft are completed."

"What a shame," the Prior added. He sipped easily of a mild brew from his large earthen mug. "Twould make a fine subject for a poem, would it not, Brother Hodjay?"

"Truly it would," sighed Hodjay. "A pity existence is so brief. You are quite positive you cannot stay?" He looked at Ethan.

"I'm sorry, we really can't. We should take advantage of the good weather, too."

The Prior picked at something that looked like a baked pudding with his knife.

"How far have you still to travel?"

"Fifty or sixty satch," said Hunnar. He added conversationally, "But first we have to reach the Place-Where-The-Earth's-Blood-Burns."

There was a crash.

"I . . . my clumsiness shames me," said one of the Brothers. He pushed back his chair and knelt to help one of the servers gather up the shards of broken mug.

"Alas, Brother Podren's development has gone wholly to the brain," chuckled the Prior easily. The other Brothers made the tran laugh-equivalent. To Ethan it seemed a little forced.

The Prior continued as though nothing had happened.

"Do not be surprised at Brother Podren's reaction. Not many folk travel to the Place-Where-The-Earth's-Blood-Burns."

"Why not?" asked September a little sharply, and then Ethan knew he wasn't alone in detecting their hosts' reactions.

The Prior spread his arms, opened his paws. "Superstition. The common folk say strange things about the great smoking mountain."

"It *is* a volcano, then," muttered Ethan to himself. They'd assumed as much all along, but it was nice to have additional confirmation.

"Could you elaborate, Prior?" September pressed.

"Surely. Those who pass too close are said to have their

minds affected. Some report seeing odd visions, while others see nothing at all and remain untouched. Others, they say, are drawn toward the mountain as a starving being may be drawn to food. Again, their companions may experience nothing. There is no soil and little grows there. None would live there anyway."

"Superstition is all that keeps them away?" asked Ethan.

"That, and the fact that the mountain throws out melted earth and choking black dust very often."

"Oh."

"But you've been there," said September shrewdly.

The old tran nodded. "I have been close by the place," he conceded. "I did not set foot on the ground."

"Because of the superstitions?" September toyed with his pseudo-pudding.

"No. Because at the time it was throwing out melted stone in huge quantities and the heat was appalling. The danger was real and not imaginary. My spirit was quite safe, but there was a real danger to the body. So the ship I was on did not linger in the area. Hopefully, you will have better luck."

"We expect to," September replied.

"And now, tell me once more of your miraculous sky-boat and its unfathomable mechanisms. I did not understand the first time and probably will not this time either, but there is merit in trying."

Dinner ended with a pleasant little liqueur. Conversation continued for another hour or so. Then Colette yawned widely, and Budjir confessed that he had to rise early on the morrow to help oversee the setting of the new bowsprit. So the Prior declared the gathering at an end.

The group of visiting humans and tran were guided back to their communal sleeping room. Ethan walked next to September.

"What do you think of our hosts?" said the big man.

"Hmmm? Oh, I guess they're okay. A little dry and self-centered maybe, but okay. For a second there, when Hunnar mentioned our destination and what's-his-name dropped his mug . . . "

"Podren."

"Yes, Podren. I thought there was something very unfriendly in his expression. He covered it fast, though, and I'm sure no expert at interpreting alien facial expressions. On the other hand, it didn't seem to affect the Prior at all."

"He was probably right . . . our going to a place regarded as a home for devils and spirits and what-not, young feller. Leaking gases could explain the hallucinations and weird reactions among passing natives."

"I suppose so. In any case, we'll have the chance to find out for ourselves before long."

They reached the room. The central firepit was crackling and spitting merrily, throwing welcome heat to every corner of the room. It had apparently been burning during the meal, as a respectable pile of coals had accumulated in the bottom of the pit. These added to the pleasant heat.

Ethan made his goodnights to everyone else. There were no dividers between the beds. It wasn't a problem, however, since none of the humans had any intention of exposing their bare skin to the still-frigid air.

He climbed into bed. Hunnar and September split up and set about extinguishing the lamps that burned on the walls. Ethan would have helped, but they hung at tran height and and that was a bit too high for him.

There were fewer furs and blankets on the bed than he'd grown used to. Their hosts, of course, had no way of knowing that the hairless strangers were far more affected by the cold than Hunnar and the squires and Elfa. Then, too, this was not the castle of Wannome, nor were they the privileged passengers on a great raft.

Hunnar and the squires took the beds placed farthest from the firepit. Elfa insisted on doing likewise, as did old Eer-Meesach. That was fine with Ethan. He had no desire to play the Stoic Terran. A place near the dying blaze was worth any moral oversight.

He drifted almost immediately into a deep, dreamless sleep.

It seemed minutes later when he awoke, but it wasn't. He sat up in near total darkness to an uncomfortably familiar scream. The fire was gone, but there was enough light from the star-filled windows and the failing coals to make out shapes.

The room was filled with struggling, swearing, darting forms. The first scream wasn't repeated, but there were plenty of yells and bellows of outrage. He could recognize Hunnar's and September's among them.

The half of the room nearest the doorway was full of white-robed, bearded silhouettes. A pair of muscular paws grabbed at him as he sat in the bed and pulled him bodily out of it. He fought in the tight grasp and got to his knees.

Leaning backward, he pulled hard. His proportionately greater body weight obviously startled his attacker. The clutching paws went limp in surprise as their owner was suddenly tugged off balance.

Something struck him on the right shoulder and he turned and swung blindly. He felt a bearded face under his knuckles.

Still frantically trying to blink the sleep from his eyes, he was knocked roughly sideways into a huge figure. He pulled at it.

"It's me, young feller-me-lad, it's me!" September pressed a still-warm log into Ethan's hands and turned to swing at a dim shape.

They were shoved backwards by the sheer press of bodies pouring into the room. The Brothers also fought with clubs, but they seemed to be taking care not to kill anyone. However, that did not necessarily hint of compassion to come.

It did make things a bit more difficult for them, since no such compunction existed on the part of those they were fighting. But the tightly-packed crowd made it hard just to swing a club.

"This way!" came a cry from the back of the room. Ethan whirled, spotted Budjir leaning from the sill of one of the high east-side windows. He parried another blow, swung downward and felt the wood meet bone with a satisfying crunch.

Then he turned and ran. Hunnar was there to give him a boost up. The powerful arms of the big squire went under his. Another moment and he was through the window, standing underneath the impartial stars on a chill, pebble-topped roof.

Fortunately there was little wind. Dark, monolithic forms loomed to the west, the spires and steeples of the highest monastery. Elfa and Suaxus were already on the roof.

Another second and he was helping Eer-Meesach through.

Ethan braced himself against the wall and the old wizard came up easily. His breathing was ragged. Aged eyes blinked in the darkness.

The sounds of fighting below seemed far away, surreal. Hunnar himself fairly shot through the opening. September followed close behind. One of the Brothers was wrapped around the big man's left leg. It took several kicks from its powerful twin to dislodge the persistent scholar. Ethan was still in too much of a daze to ask questions. He glanced around and saw that their company was far from complete.

"Hey, where . . . where are the others? Milliken and . . . "

"Our pacific hosts got 'em," September growled back. "I don't think for the purposes of advancing the frontiers of beneficent research, either. They nearly got us all. Would have, if Hunnar hadn't gotten up to put some new wood on the damned fire. So he was awake when the first of them came sneaking in."

"I don't understand it," mused the knight, as stunned as Ethan. "There is no reason for this. They seemed so really decent and—"

"—schizoid," finished September. "We'll chat about their unfortunate aberrations later." He knelt and stuck his head a little ways into the room.

"They've gone. I expect they'll be out on the rooftops after us in a minute. Deity knows they're more familiar with them than us. Now, there's only one way down from this rockpile. And while our knowledgeable friends don't appear to be militarily inclined . . . witness their performance in that room . . . sooner or later some bright boy among them's going to realize that by blocking off the stairway they'll have us trapped up here."

The next minutes were a slow-motion dream-scheme of running, hurtling parapets, darting across rooftops, and dropping one level at a time. Hunnar and September assumed the lead. They all had to move fast and carefully. One wrong step in an unfamiliar place and they might step off the side of the mountain.

Ages later the two lead men returned to the group with a sign to keep silent.

"We're just above the gateway," September whispered.

"There's a single Brother on guard there and he doesn't look awkwardly tense about things." Ethan looked past the big man, saw no sign of Sir Hunnar.

A minute later there was a short, sharp whistle from below. They ran to the edge of the building. September didn't hesitate. He turned, grabbed the coping, and let go. Without thinking, or he might have hesitated, Ethan copied him.

The drop wasn't bad, and the big man and Hunnar were there to catch him. Suaxus came next, and immediately took up a position next to the closed door. Lanterns burned on either side of the entrance.

Crying mournfully, the slight breeze flowed over the peaks and down into the black abyss.

Carefully, old Eer-Meesach was lowered to the stairs, then Elfa. Budjir hung from the edge for a second and then they were all gathered below. They turned to descend.

Hunnar held back a moment. He picked up the green stone staff of the unconscious brother, stripped off the white robe. Carefully he lifted one of the lanterns from its holder.

Transferring it from the staff to one paw. He whirled it once in a circle, arced it against the wooden door. Flaming oil splattered on the grain, flickered unsteadily for a moment, then sprang up brightly.

"That ought to keep their reasoning minds busy for a while," he muttered grimly.

They ran as quickly as they dared in the darkness. Eer-Meesach had to be considered, too. The wizard was holding up well under the strain, but there would come a time when his body, no matter how strong his spirit, would fail him.

They made fair speed down the black stairs. Now fully awake, Ethan took a cautious look over the edge. The unending ice sheet shone unreal in the starlight, speckled here and there with ebon spires that were other, friendly islands.

A last glance behind showed a bright glow from the still-burning doorway.

By the time they reached the last stair, Ethan was puffing noticeably. Eer-Meesach, on the other hand, was near collapse. They moved the wizard into the shelter of some big boulders.

Budjir had gone on ahead to the ship. He returned and

between gasps told them he'd seen tran moving on board the *Slanderscree*—and too many of them had beards, wore long robes, and carried green staves.

Simultaneous curses passed among the little assembly. Languages differed but sentiments were identical.

"Not quite as naive as I thought," September murmured. "Could you see any of our people, Budjir?"

"Not a one of the crew. They must all be trapped below-decks."

"Couldn't have been too hard," the big man mused. "One man on watch, and him not expecting anything."

"They couldn't have overcome the whole crew," said Ethan in disbelief. "Not with clubs."

"Hah! I doubt if they even had to hit anybody, except maybe the watch. Quietly bolt all the hatches, what, and keep a look-see for anyone trying to break out elsewhere. Balavere and the rest probably still don't know what hit 'em. How many'd you spot, Budjir?"

"Eight . . . perhaps nine. There may be more I did not see."

"Not likely. That much know-how I don't credit them with." September looked thoughtful. "Ta-hoding and his bunch weren't expecting them. *They* won't be expecting us."

Durnad was the one who noticed the tiny band coming toward the dock. He started. Fully six of the infidels were in the group. They trooped along, heads downcast, with their hands/paws clasped behind their backs. A single Brother followed behind.

"Come here, Brother Tydin." Another white-robed figure joined Durnad at the head of the landing ramp.

"What, Durnad . . . oh!" He'd also spotted the approaching procession. "What means this?"

"Hail, Brother!" shouted Durnad. "What has happened at the Home? We saw a great light."

The Brother's reply was low, but intelligible.

"All fairs well. These are to be kept aboard their ship until the morrow."

"That is strange, Brother," said Tydin, clearly puzzled. The group marched up the ramp. "I had heard that all the infidels were to be dealt with in the great dome this very night. Why do you hide your face? Have you been hurt by these devils?" Tydin took an uncertain step backwards.

"There's been a change in plans, Brother," yelled September. He brought his clasped hands around and came down hard with the rock concealed in them. Tydin collapsed without a sound.

"Help, Brothers!" shouted Durnad. "We are tricked!"

As it developed there were nine of the Brotherhood guarding the *Slanderscree*—less Tydin. The odds were bearable.

The Brothers fought furiously, wielding their clubs and green staves like madmen. You'd have thought they were battling the devil himself. But they were not trained fighters. Without the advantages of surprise and overwhelming numbers, such as they'd possessed in the monastery, they were only a good exercise for the likes of Budjir, Suaxus, and Hunnar. Elfa swung a broken staff with as much skill as any of them.

Ethan used his surprising mass to bowl over a pair of opponents. It would be more even in an honest fight with a knowing tran, but this time the surprise was his. September had thrown one Brother halfway across the deck and was dismantling another like a pale chicken.

Ethan stooped and grabbed up a club dropped by one of the Brothers. His attacker pursued him and swung his staff again. Ethan ducked to one side, rammed the club blunt-end-first into the other's midsection.

The Brother whoofed and doubled over. Ethan brought the club down hard and whirled to face the next attacker.

There was no next attacker.

Suaxus stood to one side, panting heavily. "What shall we do with them, Sir?" The expression on the squire's face was typically noncommital. But if he were asked, Ethan didn't doubt he'd have a ready suggestion or two.

"Tie them up and dump them belowdecks," Hunnar ordered. He paused, startled. "Belowdecks!" A sharp turn and he was over the nearest hatchway.

A simple pin and loop arrangement sufficed to dog the hatch cover down. Hunnar pulled the pin, released the loop. Up came the cover.

The anxious face of captain Ta-hoding stared up at him, blinking in the torchlight.

"We heard sounds of struggle above," he grunted as he exited the hold. "We had hoped twould be you and our friends, Sir Hunnar."

Sailors and soldiers streamed out on deck. They set about binding the white-robed figures. A few of the Brothers were beginning to regain consciousness. The men who'd been locked in the dark hold all evening were not particularly careful in their handling of the bodies.

"We were embarrassedly surprised, but none were hurt," Ta-hoding informed them. "All is well now, then."

"All is *not* well," countered Hunnar as the two tran walked over to where Ethan and September stood. "Three of our friends are held still in the lair of these monsters."

Ta-hoding sputtered. "Counterwind! We must mount an expedition, then! Besiege the place and—"

September shook his head slowly. "No, my good captain. It cannot be done that way."

"Sir Skua is right, Ta," said Hunnar. "Those virians above will probably assume we've been taken by their minions here." Said minions were now being unceremoniously hauled below. "But even so, they will post guards upon the stairway. Not to do so would be an act of such cub intelligence that I cannot think they would fail to do it. A few could hold the entrance to the monastery against an army. Which," he continued, turning to September, "worries me greatly, friend Skua. How are we to rescue our companions?"

"Frankly, Hunnar, I'd been too busy the last hour to give it much thought. Let's see, now . . . "

"I suppose we'll have to find a way around them," said Ethan hesitantly.

"Sir Ethan," reminded Hunnar a bit impatiently, "there *is* no way around. There is but the single carefully watched entrance, with a sheer drop on one side and, I venture to say, equal precipitousness on the other."

"I agree," said September. "It will have to be a small group in any case. Too many people . . . too much noise and movement." He turned to Ta-hoding. "Captain, is there any climbing gear on board?"

Ta-hoding was obviously confused, and with reason. Mountaineering was not an art practiced by his folk.

"Climbing gear? Well . . . we have rope, of course, but I do not know what you mean by 'gear.' "

"I see. Another problem." September grunted. "My fault I should have guessed you wouldn't know a crampon from a creampuff. Glassfeathers!"

"Strange words," said Hunnar. "More of your odd devices, friend Skua?"

"In a sense." The big man stared thoughtfully at the deck for a moment, then back at the knight. "Do we carry any kind of solid, strong hooks on board?"

"Hooks?" The red-tinged mane shook. Then he brightened, "Why surely! We must have a number of fine boarding grapples, taken on the last attack. They would be in the armory."

"Those would be perfect."

"Suaxus!" snapped Hunnar. The squire nodded and disappeared down the hatchway.

"What do you think, young feller-me-lad?"

"Well, actually," replied Ethan, who'd listened to the progress of the conversation with the fascination of a bird watching the approach of a king snake, "I've always been kind of afraid of heights and—"

"Nonsense, lad, nonsense! All in your mind. Just don't look down . . . course, climbing at night'll be a little rough, but there's nothing to it, what?"

"Oh sure."

September looked at them all intently. "Now, we'll stop at the last bend in the stairway, just out of sight of the monastery entrance. If we're lucky they'll still be occupied with Hunnar's fire. They won't be looking for anyone to be dropping in on 'em from above. I'll plant the first grapple . . ."

XIV

The room wasn't very large, and the members of the Brotherhood filled it to capacity. Each pressed close upon the other for a better look at the minions of the Dark One. Real infidels were rarely available for purging and none among the Brotherhood wanted to miss the infrequent, interesting ceremonies.

Light from lamps and lanterns surrounding the curved circular room threw dancing shadows against the dome. High braziers were filled with burning oil and wood. The stars shone brightly through the round skylight.

Three bronze basins with sloping bottoms flashed green-gold on the paved floor. Each contained a single body with head set higher than feet. Hellespont du Kane was the tallest of the three and his head did not reach the top of the basin. Like the others he was tightly bound with his hands fixed to his sides.

Milliken Williams occupied the basin to his right, with Colette to his left. She'd managed to break the bonds on her feet early and leave a number of very sore Brothers in her wake, but to no avail.

The Brothers had slowly been filling the basins with water, a bucket at a time, brought in from the melting room.

Since the room was not heated, the cold night air of Tranky-ky was gradually freezing each successive dose of water. The captives were now encased up to the shoulders in a jacket of diamond-clear ice.

Colette continued to rain verbal destruction on the gathering in several languages, none of which the Brothers understood. A small chorus of same continued to moan the same unmelodic drone they'd sung since the water-pouring had begun. Only their superb survival suits had kept the captives from serious frostbite thus far—and these wouldn't help when the ice rose over their heads.

Colette looked from her father, motionless in both ice and trance, and then up at the watching Brothers.

"We've done nothing to you. Why are you doing this thing?"

The kindly Prior stared amusedly down at her. "Tch! That a servant of the Dark One should have the audacity to ask for mercy."

"Listen," she sighed tiredly, giving a little shiver. The cold was beginning to exceed her suit's capacity to withstand it. "We don't even know what your damned Dark One *is!* If you're moronic enough to believe that we're the disciples of some local devil of yours, I feel sorry for you!"

"No, She, it is I who must be sorry for *you*," replied the Prior righteously. "Tis known to all that the Place-Where-The-Earth's-Blood-Burns is the home of the Dark One himself. From whatever homeland people come, all know that. Twas fortunate that you inadvertently revealed your destination to us, so that we could take proper steps. We are not ignorant peasants here!"

He looked skyward into the night. "And as you shall partake of the Cold that has held our beloved home, lo, these many centuries, so shall the Time of the Final Warming be brought closer!" He looked back at her. "That is our end and goal."

"Look here." Williams was feeling the cold more than any of them and now he was having trouble speaking. "If we're minions of this Dark One or not, freezing us isn't going to heat your world."

"Tis written in the Great Old Books that for every servant of the Dark One who is returned to the primeval cold, our world shall grow a little warmer, a little softer, a little greener. To this end is the Brotherhood pledged!"

"Listen," continued the schoolmaster desperately, "Tranky-ky *might* be made warm and green again. My people know a process called terraforming that could conceivably melt this ice and raise the planetary temperature. But you couldn't adapt if it were to happen in your lifetime. Besides, you'd all drown."

"You lie most intriguingly, Evil One, but think not to deceive us."

Two of the Brothers approached. They carried a large bronze kettle between them. Carefully, they distributed its load of water between the three basins. Colette tried to pull herself higher as they poured the ice water into hers, but it brought the water level up to her neck. The pair left for the melting room for another load.

Almost immediately a crust began to form on top of the water. Another few trips and the ice would be over her head. Or maybe the insulation on her suit would give out before that.

"We come openly, as guests, and you receive us with murder," she said, a little frightened now. Any kind of reasonable, logical argument she could fend aside and handle. But religious fanatics! . . . "We needed your help, dammit!"

"We *intend* to help you," soothed the Prior. He turned to the shifting, watching mob.

"Brothers! These poor, degenerate minds cry out to us for salvation! Let us pray for them, that their souls may meet in the next plane of existence uncontaminated by illogic and unreason."

"Let it be so!" hummed the assembled Brotherhood. They joined the uninspired choir in its steady, dissonant drone, the noise broken only by Colette's hysterical sobbing.

There was a sudden, violent crack from above. A deep voice moaned in terrifying, sepulchral tones . . .

"LET IT BE KNOWN THAT THE DARK ONE PROTECTS HIS OWN!" Rapidly, it added in Terranglo, "COVER YOUR EYES!"

Immediately all the trannish eyes in the room shot upward, while the trio of imprisoned humans bent their heads and squeezed theirs shut tight.

Explosion. Bodies flying. Those left standing made a concerted, panicked dash for the exit, trampling some of the wounded in an unbrotherly haste to escape. Above, the weird vox boomed.

"I AM THE POWER AND THE GLORY OF DARKNESS AND ALL WHO STAND AGAINST ME SHALL BE SLAIN!"

There was another explosion and more of the Brotherhood fell. A lesser crash sounded from above. It was followed by brilliantine tinkling as the skylight was shattered. A cable ladder snaked into the room. Before the bottom had unrolled, Skua September was already halfway down its swaying length. Ethan, Hunnar, and several soldiers followed.

The big man went immediately to the single doorway. He needed Hunnar's help to clear away the bodies.

"Thank Deity for small favors!" he breathed. "It bolts from the inside!" Hunnar threw the latch.

"'Tis not strong, Sir Skua. It will not stand against a determined rush."

Ethan and the soldiers all had torches strapped to their waists. They were intended to provide light if the Brothers blew out lamps. Now they were put to a different use. A quick thrust into a hanging lantern and they were lit. Then they began the slow, dangerous job of trying to melt the trapped prisoners free.

Ethan was working on one side of the copper basin that held Colette.

"Hurry, please!" she pleaded. "I . . . I can't feel my legs anymore."

"How much time?" September asked Hunnar.

"One cannot say." The knight stared at the bolted door. "These are not soldiers and do not react as such. Yet it will soon occur to the last of the escapees that we are far from supernatural in shape or form, and some might have recognized us."

It took four of them to lift each metal coffin. Two tilted the heavy container upward. One at a time, the three prisoners slid free, each still encased in a block of ice. Now the melting could proceed at a decent pace.

"'Tis a difficult decision for them," Hunnar continued. "If we are truly servitors of the Dark One, as our ability to throw thunder and lightning might suggest, then I would not expect them to attack again at all. But they might consider us to be only mortal servants of the Dark One, deluded mortals, in which case—"

"Shove the Dark One! How much time've we got?"

There was a thump as someone tried the door, then a

rattling of the latch. This was quickly followed by a series of heavy bumps, then silence.

"Well, that answers that," the big man growled. He turned back to the center of the room.

The melting was nearing completion and Williams, Colette, and the motionless senior du Kane were almost free.

"You know," said Ethan conversationally as he melted away the last of the clinging ice from her ankles, "you'd look absolutely awesome in a martini."

"I could use one about that size right now," she replied tightly. "Thank the Devices for these suits!" He started to rub her legs and she didn't protest.

"I'm okay," she said finally. "Help the teacher." Ethan looked over at the senior du Kane, who lay still and quiet on the stone floor.

"Your father . . . is he . . . ?"

"Watch." She bent over him and Ethan heard her whisper in his ear. "Free credit . . ."

A hand twitched, then a leg. Stillness, and then the old man sat up, blinking, and looked up at his daughter. She put a big arm under his left and helped him to his feet.

"Well my dear, are we safe or are we dead?"

"It's still a moot point, father, but we incline to the former."

He sighed. "Ah well. Pity." Click. "I was so wondering what kind of flowers they have in the next world."

"Only flower-souls, I've told you that, father. Come on now, move around a little. That's it." At Ethan's slack-jawed stare she replied, "Automatic protective trance. He goes into it whenever his system is overloaded. This isn't the first time it's saved his life."

There was a loud crash and the door shook violently.

"We've overstayed our welcome," suggested Ethan.

September stood facing the door, watching it silently. He held a small, tightly bound package of vol leather in one hand. It had a short, stubby fuse projecting from it and he nonchalantly tossed it from one palm to the other, back and forth, back and forth.

"Let's step lively there, folks, what?"

There was another crash and the door bulged inward alarmingly. Williams was being helped through the shattered skylight. Hellespont du Kane was halfway up the ladder and Ethan waited with Colette at the bottom.

"Let's go," he said finally.

She looked uncertainly at the swaying ladder. "I . . . I don't know. I'm not built for this kind of exercise."

"Would you rather be in that martini? Come on, go. I'll help you." She started up. He put a hand under her enormous rear—it felt like a cake of sherbet—and tried to give her weight a boost upwards. Then he mounted the ladder close behind. If she fell he didn't know what he could do. While she climbed and grunted, he climbed and prayed. Hunnar was right behind him.

September walked to the bottom of the ladder. The crackle of splintering wood filled the room and the door exploded inward. A mob of howling, robed scholars piled into the entrance. They pulled up short at the sight of September standing calmly under the ladder.

A few carried knives this time, probably appropriated from the monastery kitchens. The Brothers were fast losing their intellectual detachment. September reached out and touched the fuse to a nearby lamp. He looked at it for a moment, then gently tossed it.

It landed at the feet of the unmoving Brothers. September coutinued to watch it with interest. The fuse shrank. Then in one motion he turned, leaped, and was halfway up the ladder before someone in the mob unfroze and threw the first club.

Ethan was peering anxiously down through the broken glass. He extended a desperate hand and Hunnar another. Together they yanked hard and Ethan fell backwards. September came out of the opening, tumbled onto the roof, and was followed by a geyser of dust and pulverized stone.

"Quite a banger," he murmured, feeling his side where a thrown staff had grazed him. "Glad I saved that one for last."

For the second time that night Ethan found himself running blindly over rooftops, dodging pillars and buttresses, dropping from level to level toward the stairway. Apparently the Brothers were too disorganized, or demoralized, to offer ready pursuit. Or maybe that last bomb had eliminated the sanctimonious Prior and several of his deputies.

At any rate, they met no opposition in their hectic scramble downwards. They reached the last roof above the stairway without being challenged.

To their left a long black streak extended back into the monastery, a charred wound. The results of Hunnar's covering blaze set earlier that night. A large band of Brothers stood in front of the burnt entrance, armed with the usual clubs and staves.

They were expecting an attack from the front. Clearly no one had brought them the word about the return of the Dark One's other servants. Not very military. Hunnar's soldiers surprised them completely.

There was no pursuit as they started their second dash down the stairway.

"So much for rule by reason and logic," September grunted. He was breathing heavily. The run down from the monastery had finally tired even him. But now they were safe on board the *Slanderscree* and there weren't enough Brothers in the world to get them off it again. The big man was staring up at the monastery buildings, faint ghosts against the black crags.

"Well, it performed well enough—within their own tight little precepts," Ethan countered. Behind him, Ta-hoding was sending the crew aloft, yelling dire threats at imagined slackers.

The *Slanderscree* began to move out of the harbor. Astern, a quartet of soldiers were ungently dumping the Brothers who'd taken the raft earlier. It was more humane than similar actions that had been performed on Terra ages ago, for there was no water for the captives to drown in.

On the other hand, the ice wasn't especially soft.

The wind blew and the *Slanderscree* enslaved it, cutting west, then south, to take advantage of the slightest counterbreeze. Ta-hoding didn't miss many.

A week later they saw the first smoke. It blew steadily to the east, black and sooty and well up in the atmosphere. From there Ta-hoding was able to ignore the compass and follow the black line. They made even better time. It was another two days before they had their first glimpse of The Place-Where-The-Earth's-Blood-Burns, and another two before the base of the giant volcano came into view.

Mottled brown and black, splashed higher up with ice and snow—fourteen kilometers of vertical hell shrouded in polar ice and rock. It was magnificent, awesome, and a little bit frightening.

"Well, no hallucinations so far," Ethan mused.

"How," Colette snapped back, "could you tell the difference?"

Williams voice sounded behind them. "I'd very much like to land."

Ethan turned. Eer-Meesach was there, too. "Really, Milliken, in light of the past weeks, don't you think . . . "

A huge paw came down easily on his shoulder. "We did leave without properly fixing the bowsprit, friend Ethan," said Hunnar. "Nor did the crew receive their promised chance for a rest on shore."

"You're not afraid the spirits and goblins will object?"

The knight didn't smile. He gazed over the ice at the sky-rubbing cone.

"As a cub I might have been. As a younger man I'd have been uncertain. But the wizards have explained to me what it really is, a thing neither supernatural nor inherently inimical, and I am not afraid."

They followed the jagged shore southward, searching for a place to put in. Hundreds of meters of broken, tortured rock fell in undisciplined cataracts onto the clear ice. But nowhere did it level off.

Just as they rounded the southern tip of the island-mountain, hitting into the wind again, the plutonic crust abruptly gave way to a smooth, level stone beach. Ropy lines of pahoehoe marched gently into the frozen sea.

They tied up half into the wind, still protected by the sheltering bulk of the volcano. Ice-anchors were used this time, set with care and precision under Ta-hoding's experienced watch. Once again the repair crew set about their tasks—for the last time, one hoped.

Considering what they'd gone through the past weeks, though, there were none who blamed the craftsmen for an occasional over-the-shoulder glance. You couldn't be too sure that the ground would not still deliver up yet another fiendish surprise, hey? So the carpenters and sailweavers worked a little slower, a little more observantly.

Roiling blackness. Distant night-stars of plasmoid terror. Vast spaces unmeasureable. False concepts of life and death. The living dark came, a loathsomeness of long licorice tentacles and soul-draining fangs.

It groped for him in the emptiness, reaching, twisting. He ran faster and faster on a sea of gurgling tar, an oil-sky overhead. The ocean grabbed and tugged at him. Down he looked and saw in horror that it wasn't a sea at all. He was running on the back of an amorphous amoeba that humped and shook and laughed.

He tried to jump, but now fat greasy pseudopods held him firm. All about the nightmare, shapes flowed up and around. In the middle of each the faces of things not human chuckled and puckered at him.

Black fronds clutched tighter, enveloping, suffocating. He tried to scream and one of the inky ropes dove down his throat, choking him. They crawled over his eyes, under his ears, into his nostrils. Cilia brushed and tickled obscenely.

He couldn't breathe. He coughed, gagged. The thing in his throat was curling into his belly, swelling, filling him with gravid blackness.

The interior of the cabin was dark, too. But it was a comforting, familiar, prosaic dark—not sticky, not malevolent, not full of nightmare shapes. Despite the cold he was sweating profusely and heaving like he'd just finished marathon.

Shaking, he reached for the lamp, then caught himself. His hand paused in mid-air, drew away slowly. No . . . no. It was a bad dream. Nothing more. Happens to everyone.

He put both hands on the bed, palms flat against the blankets and furs, and lay down slowly, staring at the bare outline of the ceiling. With a conscious effort he closed his eyes and breathed out, long and low. Then he hunched slowly on his side and fluffed the blanket under his head.

His last thought before falling asleep was that he hadn't

had a nightmare since childhood. He wondered about it, for a second.

Morning light bit like a mosquito. The volcano did not shine or sparkle in the false alpenglow. If anything, the black volcanic rock absorbed the light. Only at upper elevations did ice and snow work to do eye-pleasing things with the rich light.

A dark, brooding ziggurat, the mountain gave no hint of the burning core that steamed in its depths. Even the cloud-scudding black smoke was a cold coal.

There was nothing so palpable as an air of menace about the mountain, but neither was it pleasant to be near. It needed companion mountains, a sibling range around its base, before mere humans could relate to it. Alone, it was as impersonal and alien as a lost moon.

Ethan leaned on the rail and gazed at the ropy beach. He'd almost have preferred to stay on board, but there was always the thin chance that something interesting might turn up. He only stumbled once as they made their way across the ice and onto the rock. Small cause for pride.

On the frozen lava the humans had an advantage over their tran companions. The natives had to pick their way carefully on unclad feet over the nastier sections of aa and scoria.

The two wizards could have gone by themselves. However, someone had to go along to tell the two learned beings when it was time to return to the *Slanderscree*. Left to themselves, they would wander about the island til dark, get lost, and then there'd be a broken leg or twisted ankle and the hard work of carrying them back to the ship in the dark.

The slopes of the gigantic cone seemed to soar up and up into the opalescent blue until they merged at the artist's vanishing point. You could tell there was a top only because of the black smoke that issued therefrom somewhere in the clouds.

Well, they could spend the morning picking around at the rocks in the shelter of the east slope, acquire a few specimens, and return to the ship. The rocks ought to keep Williams and Eer-Meesach occupied and out of trouble until they'd reached Arsudun.

Ethan didn't expect any surprises—even Williams had enough sense to forgo suggesting an ascent—but he hadn't counted on the cave.

It was well concealed by rock and low brush as he walked past the entrance. It looked no different from any other section of immolated stone. Only the early morning light shining straight into it gave any hint that it might be larger than the thousands of similar pockets which dotted the lava. He bent and peered inside.

It was large enough for a tran to walk upright in, so he called the others over.

"Fascinating," said the schoolmaster, staring inside. Before anyone could stop him, the teacher had stepped carefully over a chunk of aa and was standing on the smooth floor of the cave.

"Get out of there, Milliken," said September. "The whole business could come down on you any second."

"Pish-tosh! This is a structure built by nature, not mere man, Mr. September. Once a tube like this has been formed, it will remain so until a violent upheaval cracks the set rock. My dear Eer-Meesach, you must see this!"

"What is it?" The tran wizard had knelt slowly and was staring into the hole now.

Williams' voice floated back from some ways in. "The walls of the tube are lined with a luminescent lichen or fungi of some sort. I can see quite clearly even though I'm well away from the entrance." There was a pause. "It appears to extend into the mountain for some distance."

"Then by all means," replied Eer-Meesach, scrambling over the lip of the hole, "we must explore further."

Hunnar looked resignedly at September. "I'd as soon wait here, Sir Skua. But those two would surely lose themselves at the first pairing of passageways."

The big man dug into a coat pocket and pulled out one of the small compasses from the survival supplies.

"I expect you're right," he agreed. "Might as well go myself."

Hunnar hopped down into the tunnel, followed closely by Budjir and Suaxus. September went next, turned and looked back at Ethan.

"Coming, young feller-me-lad?"

He hesitated. The tunnel did not look especially inviting. But they could be watching from the ship. Colette had already confessed a fear of the dark; it was the only thing that seemed to faze her. Naturally he had to go in.

It was a good thing he had no time to work on the logic of his thinking or he wouldn't have been terribly happy with the resultant picture.

They walked at a leisurely pace, moving deeper and deeper into the mountain. The walls, ceiling, and floor had been scoured almost slippery smooth. There were places where the ceiling rose to two and three times the height of a tran. And here and there there were vents of green clay. Green clay in volcanic vents. Now, where had he seen that before? He puzzled over it.

The glowing plant life grew no more luxuriantly as they moved down the tunnel, but it didn't grow dimmer, either. And it supplied enough light to show occasional boulders and rocks that had fallen from the roof (green clay in volcanic vents?). The number was small, Ethan noted gratefully. He moved ahead to listen to the schoolmaster.

"Lava has gone through this passage fairly recently," Williams explained, "which accounts for the smooth sides."

"Now that's a comforting thought," grinned Ethan. He thought of the millions of tons of hot magma beneath their feet, whose outlet had once been the tube in which they now trod.

After an hour's hike Hunnar finally declared a halt. The wizards gave no sign of tiring and the tunnel no signs of ending.

"Scientific exploration is all very well and good," the knight said, crouching against the cold gray wall, "but we've brought no provisions with us. I do not believe further exploration of this hole, which could run clear through the mountain, is worth missing the midday meal."

This opinion was seconded immediately by September, Ethan, and both squires. Outvoted, the two scholars capitulated gracefully.

"I, too, confess to being somewhat wearied and hungered," admitted Eer-Meesach. "And we seem to have learned all that we might. Yet it would be interesting to know if this tube opens near the central vent itself."

"I'm cold," September quipped, "but not that cold." He sat down across from Hunnar and began flipping pebbles against the far wall.

Ethan took a few steps forward and prepared to rest also. He squinted hard down the tunnel.

"Hey . . . it does seem to get a little brighter ahead."

"Your eyes are tired from straining in this light, lad." The big man glanced down the tunnel without getting up. "Looks the same to me."

"No, really, it does," Ethan continued. He took another couple of steps forward. "It does." He started to walk down the tunnel.

"Don't go too far," September warned him. "Don't go out of voice range. I don't want you making a wrong turn into some endless maze. If you do, I'm not coming after you, what?"

"Don't worry, Skua. I'm not going to go far." The tunnel made a sharp turn to the right, just ahead. That would be far enough.

He turned and stepped into the chamber.

It was larger than the tunnel, perhaps three or four times as wide as the passageway and equally as high. There were no more phosphorescent plants here than behind him, but the light was blinding. Blinding, dazzling, overpowering—and green.

Now he remembered where he'd read of green clay in volcanic vents.

Ozmidine was mined in only two places in the known universe. One was on a tiny island in the middle of a lake on the thranx world of Drax IV. Drax IV was a hell world, a steaming, sweltering moldy ball of corruption that would drive a man insane if the Po'pione or Turabisi Delphius didn't get him first. The thranx could survive the heat and humidity, but the local flora and fauna made no species distinctions when it came to dinner.

But there was ozmidine there, so they stayed.

The other lode had been found on Mantis, one of the first worlds settled by humanity after the discovery of the KK-

drive. It had been discovered, not by lonely prospector, nor
by mining combine, nor by official survey. A driller pushing
a new subway tunnel through the heart of downtown Locust
had come on the first deposits. Now there was an ugly,
dark, smoky hole in the middle of the planet's capital city.
But the inhabitants didn't mind. It made them rich.

On the scale of comparative hardness for minerals, diamond is the hardest at 10. Or rather, it was until ozmidine
was found to have a hardness rating of about 14. And the
crystals of the raw mineral were of a deep green shading to
violet that made the finest emeralds look like soapstone.

Ozmidine was only found in igneous rocks, in vents of
greenish clay.

Ethan stumbled forward, his eyes adjusting to the light
thrown back at him from an endless hall of green hexagonal
crystal. Ozmidine hung from the ceiling like stalactites. It
grew outward from the walls like decorative swords, filled the
floor with spikes and crushed crystals from the ceiling.

He'd once seen a picture of the Green Nova. The Green
Nova was a piece of pure ozmidine from the Drax IV mine. It
was as big as a man's fist and had taken thirteen months to
cut and facet by the finest stonecutter on Terra, using laser and
ozmidine cutting tools. It had no price.

He stumbled, wincing at the pain in his toe. He'd tripped
over a chunk of clear ozmidine the size of a basketball.

This wasn't wealth—there was no way, no means of com-
paring this to normal human pursuits. The ownership of
whole worlds lay in this tunnel. Power to alter the structure
of governments, even enough to shake the Church itself.

"Hey, young fella! . . . " came September's voice. "It's
time to . . . "

Dimly, Ethan recognized the voice of September and the
others behind him. But he didn't turn. He knew what *they*
looked like.

Something shook underfoot. He felt it, ignored it.

"My dear Eer-Meesach, this is wonderful!" Williams whispered. "Such symmetry of form, such amazing variety . . . "
He frowned. "Was that a tremor?"

"EEYAHOO!" bellowed September. He grabbed Ethan and

danced in a circle while Ethan hung on for dear life, his feet centimeters off the floor. "Gods and Devils and broken hearts, and broken names, and all the lost promises down the trail of time!" He stopped, let Ethan down. Ethan felt himself to make sure no bones were broken.

He grinned up at the other. "My sentiments exactly."

September bent to pick up a flawless piece of crystal as big as his thumb. He landed on his rump.

The earth shook.

Shards of priceless gemstone, any one worth a king's life, pelted Ethan's unprotected face. When the shaking stopped, he felt himself gingerly. He'd received some very expensive scratches.

Below, a steady rumbling had begun. There were demons afoot in the mountain.

Williams was backing toward the tunnel proper, a little of his scientific detachment gone. He watched the walls warily.

"I . . . I do believe it would be best if we returned to the ship. I think something may happen."

His words penetrated the green haze surrounding Ethan. He was dimly aware that September was shaking him.

"Better do what he says, young feller. We can come back tomorrow . . . maybe. Time to leave."

"Leave . . . ?" Ethan stuttered. "Return . . . ?" He looked up at the big man, blinked. "Leave this . . . no, absolutely no!"

"Now young feller . . . " began September.

"No, I won't . . . I found it, dammit . . . I'm staying . . . you go!"

September chuckled. "All right, lad, have it your way." He turned and walked past Ethan . . . and clipped him neatly on the jaw as he passed. He knelt, scooped up the slumping body, and threw it over his shoulder.

"Let's go." He took a last glance over his shoulder, muttered so low no one could hear him, "Shana . . . forgive me," and started out of the tunnel.

The run back to the raft turned into a nightmare, with groanings and heavings and cyclopean creakings alternating with distant detonations. One was powerful enough to throw them off their feet. It bloodied September's nose. He uttered a few choice curses, hefted Ethan higher on his shoulder, and continued forward at a jog.

If anything, their emergence from the cavern into clean daylight inspired them to move faster. They were met at the shoreline by Balavere and a party from the ship.

"All be thanked!" said the old General, clasping Hunnar by the shoulders. "We thought the mountain had got you." Then he noticed the scrapes and bruises and Ethan's unmoving form. "What *did* happen in there?"

"I shall tell you later, honored General," replied Hunnar, "if I still believe in it myself, then."

There was an awesome roar behind them and they were nearly thrown again.

"But if that interesting talk is to take place, we must depart this accursed island now. Quickly!"

They hurried to the ice. Two of the soldiers carried Ethan between them. They moved much faster on the ice than September could have.

"Put your men aloft, captain!" Hunnar bellowed as they boarded the raft. But it wasn't needed. Ta-hoding had heard the explosions and was moving over the deck like a frightened k'nith, swearing tearfully that though he lived a thousand years he'd never see this befouled ship fully repaired.

The ice-anchors were brought in. Wind caught the sails and the *Slanderscree* moved.

Drawn by the noise, the du Kanes emerged on deck. Colette looked at the volcano and turned to question September. Then she saw Ethan's unconscious form.

"What happened to him?" she asked casually—a little too casually, September thought. He squinted down at her as another explosion—they were growing more frequent—drowned out all possibility of communication.

When it had died slightly, he shouted, "He . . . ah . . . bumped his head coming out of the tunnel." He shoved the limp form at her. "Why don't you take care of him?"

Colette backed away a step. "Me? I'm not a damned nurse. Let Williams or Eer-Meesach look after him."

"Oh, just watch him for a minute, hey?"

She considered, chewing her lower lip. "Oh, all right, give

him here." September bent and passed the dead weight to Colette. She handled it easily and sat down next to the mast with him, studying his face. September grunted appreciatively.

They'd rounded the last spur of black earth and were leaving the volcano astern. The smoke now billowing from the cone was tinged with crimson and seemed to have grown greatly in volume.

There was a tremendous ear-shattering explosion, coupled with a moaning, ripping sound. The *Slanderscree* was lifted off the ice and slammed down a dozen meters on. A few spars cracked. Somehow, the runners held.

Tran were picking themselves up off the deck, some of them very slowly. One had been thrown from the rigging and was now a grotesque tangle of arms and legs near one hatch.

"Bedamned!" sputtered September, shaking the wrist he'd fallen on as he pulled himself off the planking. Ethan had come around just in time to get thrown into Colette. He bounced off.

"Green clay," he mumbled, then looked confused. "There was something about green clay . . . but I've forgotten."

"What happened to me?"

"You hit your head coming out of the tunnel," supplied Colette. She gently but firmly moved him off her legs. "And I don't know anything about any green clay."

Ethan rubbed his jaw . . . funny place to fall on . . . and thought hard. He looked up at her and she was staring down at him strangely.

"Oh well . . . couldn't have been very important," he said.

"How would you like to be rich beyond your wildest dreams?"

"Huh?"

"Marry me."

"I beg your pardon, Miss du Kane?"

"Under the circumstances, you may call me Colette. Well?"

"Wait a minute, Wait a minute." He must still be dazed. "I didn't even think you *liked* me . . . let alone loved me."

Those startling green (green?) eyes stared down at him. "Who said anything about love? I'm asking you to marry me! You're reasonably attractive, reasonably intelligent—and kinder than most. The only people who ask me to marry *them* are money-hunters. I can read the contempt in their eyes. There's no contempt in yours. A little pity, but I'm used to that. Well?"

Ethan thought. "This is too fast and I'm still dazed. Let me . . . let me think it over. What would your father say?"

She gave him a twisted smile. "Father? Father's been intermittently insane for the past four years." She stood up and stared down at him from a great height. "Who do you think's been running du Kane Enterprises for the last four years, Ethan Fortune?"

"Look to the mountain!" yelled a voice. Those who could staggered to the rail.

A kilometer or so up the side of the volcano, a huge fissure dozens of meters wide had cleft the mountainside like an ax-blow. A broad river of fiery red and yellow spilled from the gaping fissure, overflowing the edges of the break.

The amber stream gained the ice. Immediately a jet of superheated steam roared skywards, obscuring much of the peak from view.

"Quite a sight," said September appreciatively. There was a loud yelp behind him.

Williams was absolutely terrified. He was flailing and gesturing as though he'd lost control of his arms.

"Easy, schoolmaster. What's the matter? Spirits?"

"We've got to put on more sail!" he piped frantically. "Tell the crew to blow into them, if we must! We've got to . . . to get *away* from here!"

"Why?" September glanced behind them. "We've got a little wind with us now. At this rate we'll be out of sight of the island before dark."

"Not . . . not good enough!" panted the out-of-breath Williams.

"Now look, surely we're in no danger from the lava. I'm no geologist, but . . . "

"Not the lava. Not the lava!" Williams was pleading. Tahoding had walked over and was now an interested listener. So was Hunnar.

"You don't understand! The lava will melt the ice. And that fissure may have cracked the whole island. If the cold sea

water beneath the ice reaches the core . . . the pressure
. . incalculable . . . " He subsided, out of breath.

"What does the small wizard mean?" asked Hunnar uncertainly. September rubbed the full crop of whiskers that now coated that jutting chin under his face shield.

"He says the mountain's going to blow up, I think."

"Blow-up?" Ta-hoding's fat face was comical. His anxiety was not. "Blow-up?" he repeated stupidly. Then he whirled and began rattling off hysterical orders and commands. The deck of the *Slanderscree* became a madhouse.

The crew strove to mount every square centimeter of sail left in the lockers. They were even stringing it from rigging to hatch covers. Green-brown pika-pina sailcloth went up everywhere, until the *Slanderscree* resembled a moving island.

Nothing happened all the rest of that day, nor all night. They were still running rapidly to the southwest the next morning when it happened. The volcano was far astern and long out of sight. But they heard the rumble. There was a crackling.

The whole sky northeast of them lit up in a titanic eruption of fire and flaming gases. Lightning smashed every section of unbruised sky. A pillar of red-black smoke and ash sown with lightning billowed into the stratosphere. This time it was September who grabbed the megaphone and roared for everyone to hug the deck. A second later he was imitating a termite.

Nothing happened. The eruptions continued. An ominous owing breeze swept over the ship, challenging the westwind. Then the full force of displaced air struck them as the giant volcano began to tear itself to pieces.

The maelstrom that came down on the raft made the Rifs seem like a spring zephyr. The *Slanderscree* exploded forward across the ice. But most of the super-tough sails held. Most of the rigging held. And the lashings on the great wheel held.

The borean monster fell to a simple cyclone. September crawled to the rail and raised his head into that skin-tearing gale. Then he rose to his full height, somehow keeping his balance in the gale.

"Sonuvabitch!" he howled, "what a ride!" Then his fe
were blown out from under him and he had to wrap h
arms around a shroud to keep from being swept off the dec

Pity the lad couldn't see this, he thought. Or mayhap bett
he doesn't. The ozmidine? Melted, or pulverized to gree
dust, perhaps. Immortality was short. He looked across th
planking. Colette was using her bulk to shield Ethan fro
some of the wind. On the other hand, he reflected, smilin
mining is work. A soft touch of a friend, now . . . that w
much more civilized!

The *Slanderscree* shot southwestward at close to thre
hundred kilometers an hour.

The prop-jet hummed smoothly on the two-man ice-skin
mer as it curved in its daily patrol out from the humar
settlement of Brass Monkey and headed up the frozen fjord

The two men inside had grown accustomed to the icelocke
world and its gruff, somber native populace. But they we
completely unprepared for the gigantic raft, dozens of sa
billowing, which rounded the entrance to the fjord and sh
past them before they could waken to challenge it.

"Mother, did you see that?" exclaimed the pilot.

"How could I miss it, Marcel," replied his copilot, "seei
as how it practically ran us down." He was doing things
dashboard controls. "Take over your stick before we p
into a cliffside, will you?"

Abashed, Marcel did so. "Thought I'd seen every size a
shape of ice-craft this backwater had to offer," he mumbled

"Moving like the proverbial bat out of hell," the copil
agreed admiringly. "Somebody did a helluva job on that baby
They swung the tiny skimmer around. The prop groaned
the strain.

"You'd better get on the comm, tell Docking and Receivi
to expect that thing or someone's liable to have a fit and ta
a shot at it. I want to meet the natives who built that."

Marcel goosed the engine to a high whine. "I'll *have* to ca
For sure we're not going to overhaul it." He leaned to k
the comm switch and chuckled.

"You know . . . it's funny, this glare and all . . . b
that damn thing went by so fast I thought I saw a set

broad's underwear flying astern in place of the usual native banner. Biggest pair I ever saw. Ain't that a kick?" He hit another button and the screen over the angled windshield began to brighten.

"Aw, you're batty."

"Sure . . . all in the mind," the pilot agreed.

The copilot looked thoughtful. "Then it's all in mine, too, because I could swear I saw the same damn thing."

The glance they exchanged was profound.